~~Eleanor~~ ~~Simmons~~

Dec. 1944

Miss Doris L. Solomon

HARD FACTS

Books by Howard Spring

Novels: FAME IS THE SPUR   MY SON, MY SON!

         SHABBY TIGER   RACHEL ROSING

Autobiography: HEAVEN LIES ABOUT US

Literary Criticism: BOOK PARADE

For Children: TUMBLEDOWN DICK

HARD FACTS

A NOVEL BY

Howard Spring

THE VIKING PRESS · NEW YORK

1944

This is a work of fiction. No character in it is founded
upon or intended to represent any person who is now
living or who has ever lived.

Chapter One

AT five o'clock on a Wednesday afternoon in March 1885 Theodore Chrystal was walking to his lodgings in Hardiman Street, in the Levenshulme district of Manchester. He was happy enough, though no physical reason for happiness was apparent. It was a vile day; the darkness had come down on the breath of a thin fog, and the street lamps had not yet been lit. Even had the full light of a summer's day fallen upon the scene, it would have been hideous. Theo knew this, although Manchester was a strange town to him, for there had been light enough when he set out to take tea with Mr. Burnside, the Vicar of St. Ninian's. He had seen then the little houses standing in rows, with their bare sooty patches of earth railed off from the streets as though they were precious; he had seen the sky low upon the grey slate roofs, an immense and everlasting frown that seemed to lie over the whole city; he had seen something of the pale artisan population, depressing and respectable, appearing now and then from behind doors whose front steps were yellowed with the daily rubbing of stone, or glancing through windows hung with lace curtains looped back to reveal ferns in pots of fantastic shapes. A swan with outspread wings was the most popular, he noted. The fern fitted neatly down on to the swan's back—an improbability alike in botany and ornithology.

He crossed the main road which runs from Manchester to Stockport, and was impressed by its granitic and uncompromising hideousness. A stony waste, a weary wilderness, an abomination of desolation: these were the sort of phrases that crossed his young mind—he was twenty-four—but he murmured them almost gaily. He was on life's threshold, and nothing had power to dismay him: not even the death of his mother, though that had been bitter to bear. But he had succeeded in tucking her away into the category of the saints, and Theo saw no reason to be sorry for the saints. He prayed daily that

1

he might in the fullness of time be worthy to be included in
their number.

Theo's life had been pleasant and uneventful. His father
had managed a bank in a charming Somersetshire township,
and had married the youngest daughter of a family not rich
but ancient, who had owned a little land thereabouts for centuries. Theo's father rented from his wife's people the small
Tudor house on the main street where the boy lived till he
went to Selwyn College, which had recently been opened at
Cambridge. That was after the father had died. Mrs. Chrystal
found herself with small means and one devoted and beloved
son, tall and fair, blue-eyed, good to look at. He was paler than
she would have liked, for he took to books more readily than
to games, and at the time of his father's death he was in a passionate adolescent phase of religious obsession. It was this
which decided Mrs. Chrystal to send him to the college so
lately built as a memorial to good Bishop Selwyn. Theo was
among the first students entered there. Its comparative cheap-
ness and its religious bias were both in its favour, and Theo,
reading under the willows or in a drone of dragon-flies with
his back down in a punt and his eyes on the pale blue of the
Cambridgeshire sky, dreamed many happy dreams of a country
parsonage, with his mother moving graciously between the
garden and the parlour, and himself in the study writing the
book which he felt was so much needed on the authorship of
the *Epistle to the Hebrews*. He would not marry, he decided.

These fair delusive dreams, which remained with him
throughout a pleasant year of diaconate in Sussex, seemed already to belong to fairyland as he walked through the stony
realism of Levenshulme after keeping his appointment with
Mr. Burnside who had engaged him as curate of St. Ninian's.

Mr. Burnside had engaged Theo on the strength of a recom-
mendation from an old Oxford friend. Vicar and curate had
not met. Mr. Burnside had written to say that he had taken
lodgings for Theo at Mrs. Hornabrook's house, No. 92 Hardiman Street, and when Theo arrived at London Road Station,
having travelled from London in the morning, he took a four-

wheeler cab and made the journey to Levenshulme in comfort. He had 150 pounds a year of his own, to supplement what
Mr. Burnside called his "stipend" of thirty shillings a week, so
he could afford a small luxury like a cab now and then. It was
three o'clock when he reached Mrs. Hornabrook's, whose house
was the replica of every other house in the street, and whose
street was not to be distinguished, save by the name upon it,
from most of the streets running off Stockport Road. The cabman dumped Theo's leather trunk on the yellow-stoned doorstep and drove off, leaving him with a feeling of being at last,
alone and unfriended, committed to the adventure of life.

Mrs. Hornabrook was a widow of sixty whose daughter
worked in the dress-making department of a great Manchester
shop. She was never without a lodger, and hoped, for the rest,
that the sixpence a week she was paying to an insurance company would somehow see her through when she "realized her
policy." If things were bad at 92 Hardiman Street, Mrs. Hornabrook would put all right with her Pisgah vision: "Don't worrit.
There'll be nothing to worrit about when I realize my policy."

When she appeared in answer to Theo's timid knock, she
looked the negation of all worriting. She was short and broad
and rosy, with a tendency to gasp and put her hand to her side.
She held out her hand and grasped his. "Tha'll be t'parson's
lad," she said. "Come in. Ah've got a fire for thee, an' tha looks
fair clemmed."

Theo left his trunk in the narrow oil-clothed passage, and
followed her down it to the back room. It was a dark little
room, for end-to-end with the short back-gardens of Hardiman
Street were the equally short back-gardens of Palmerston
Street whose houses shut out the day. But Theo, standing ir-
resolutely within the door, felt that this was a snug enough
place and that Mr. Burnside might have done worse for him.
In the black-leaded fireplace a fire was burning, and Mrs.
Hornabrook, kneeling to poke this unnecessarily, looked over
her shoulder to say: "Sit thee dahn, lad, and tak off thy coat."
She added with a smile: "Why, tha's nobbut a boy. Surely tha's
not goin' to preach t'Gospel?"

Slightly nettled by this, Theo made no answer, but dropped

his large ulster on to the back of a chair and himself sat in it. He looked about him and noted that on either side of the fireplace was a cupboard with shelves above it behind glass doors. The shelves were cluttered with crockery. When the right time came, he would ask Mrs. Hornabrook to remove all that, and he would put his books there. Happily, there were no pictures in the room save an enlarged photograph over the mantelpiece of a jovial man with a drooping moustache and a Masonic emblem in his tie. He would have that removed, too, and hang his print of *The Light of the World*. The table at which he sat, covered with ball-fringed green material of a velvet texture, a comfortable-looking chair by the fire, a rag mat in front of the fender: these made all the room's furniture. An oil lamp with an opaque white shade hung from the ceiling. Yes, he decided, Mr. Burnside might certainly have done worse for him.

At the thought of Mr. Burnside, he looked at the large gold watch that had belonged to his father. It was a quarter past three. "I have to be at Mr. Burnside's at four," he said. "Have I far to go?"

Mrs. Hornabrook had risen to her feet and was looking at him—with inner amusement, he feared in his sensitive youth— her hands on her buttocks. "Far or near," she said, "tha'll go to no Mr. Burnside's till tha's had a sup o' tea. T'kettle's boilin' in t'kitchen. Ah'll go an' mash."

She went briskly, leaving him no time to protest. He moved round the table and sat in the comfortable chair by the fire, holding out his long white hands to the flames and wondering what the verb "to mash" might mean. He had never been in the North before, and Mrs. Hornabrook's speech altogether had an uncouth and alien ring in his ears.

He sat facing the window, curtained with the same heavy green material that covered the table. On either side a brass band, gleaming in the firelight, clasped the curtain two-thirds of the way down and gave it a fashionable wasp-waist. Above this stricture it fanned out, the two sides nearly meeting, so that little light entered the room. Sitting there gazing through the meagre clear expanse of glass, he could see nothing but the

back bedroom windows of Palmerston Street and the grey drift of cloud above the ridge of slate roofs. He thought of the glowing mellow pantiles of his Somerset village, running with many a break and kink—a dormer, a mansard—with white fantail pigeons preening themselves; and of the window behind which he had worked, with no curtains at all and a clear view of his mother walking among chrysanthemums and Michaelmas daisies and dahlias in the faint luminosity of an autumn twilight. He thought of Cambridge and the honey-coloured stone of colleges and the weeds undulant as banners in clear river water and of the lean Sussex downs.

Mrs. Hornabrook came in, butting open the door with her plump knee, carrying a jingling tray. She whipped off the green table-cloth and covered half of the table with a white one. On this she set out an immense brown tea-pot, a plate of bread and butter, a ham at which a cut or two had already been made, and a cake of noble dimensions. "Ah've not prepared thee a proper meal," she said, "but sit thee down an' 'ave a stay-bit."

Theo's active mind catalogued the word, and when Mrs. Hornabrook was gone and he was champing ham with a young healthy appetite, he suddenly saw what it meant and laughed aloud. He looked at that food fit to take the edge off ten men's hunger and repeated: "Stay-bit! Stay-bit!" It was a rich expressive word, and a rich notion. He took a hearty swig of tea as deep brown as the pot that contained it, and felt that life could be much worse than it promised to be.

St. Ninian's was no more handsome than one would expect a church in Levenshulme to be. It stood on a corner made by the Stockport Road and a tributary side-street, and it was recognizable as a "sacred edifice" by its cruciform shape and squat tower surmounted on one corner by an inelegant spire, and by nothing else. It was built of millstone grit, that perdurable Derbyshire stone that will defy the years to add beauty to its face and will acquire—in Manchester—no patina save a uniform and well-nigh ineradicable black. A railing of iron spikes was about it, and inside the railing the mottled leaves of laurel and the mat green leaves of a common rhododendron

were indistinguishable beneath a corroding film of soot.

Within the gate was a notice-board, and Theo's heart leapt
up when, at the bottom of all the faded gilt lines, he saw one in
gilt that glistened like a new sovereign through the murk of the
darkening afternoon. *Curate: the Rev. Theodore Chrystal,
B.A., B.D.* Mr. Burnside had lost no time.

Mr. Burnside's house was in the side-street, the first house
beyond the end of the church. He was hospitably awaiting
Theo in his study, where a gas-globe was a centre of mellow
light and the shabby brown velvet curtains were already
drawn. The room altogether was shabby but comfortable, and
the same might be said of Mr. Burnside. The fire was lit, and
Mr. Burnside was in carpet slippers and a frayed black alpaca
jacket; and there was a common black cat dozing by the fender;
and on a low table tea-things were set. Theo said nothing about
the magnificent stay-bit he had eaten at Mrs. Hornabrook's.
He sniffed with appreciation at the smell of good tobacco that
was upon the air, heavy as incense in a church, and looked with
appreciation at the long rows of leather book-backs, familiar
and comfortable in the room's soft light.

He had bothered a good deal about this interview, wondering whether Mr. Burnside would try to trip him up on some
point of scholarship, or test him on doctrine and tenets, or pry
into his social standing. There might even be a chance, he had
thought, of bringing the conversation to the *Epistle to the
Hebrews*, and he would have liked very much to do that and
mention modestly the research he was making and the notes he
was putting down. But none of these matters arose. Mr. Burnside inquired about his journey, pushed him into a wicker
chair by the fireside, and pulled an old-fashioned bell-cord. "I
hope you like cake and ham at tea-time, Chrystal," he said.
"You'll have to get used to it in Lancashire. It's my housekeeper's one idea when I have a guest. When I'm alone I have
the cake only. I'm not married."

"We should have been more than thankful for it at college,
sir," said Theo. "We weren't overfed."

"I should be glad if you would call me Burnside—on this sort
of occasion, anyway."

The housekeeper brought in the tray, and its contents made so perfect a replica of the meal he had already eaten that Theo was hard pressed not to laugh. Mr. Burnside carved the ham and put everything on the low table between the wicker chairs. He awakened the sleeping cat by tickling its belly with stockinged toes that protruded like a tongue through the wide-open mouth at the end of one of his slippers, and he fed the animal daintily on pieces of ham. He ate heartily himself, and pressed Theo to do the same, and then he filled a large brier pipe. Theo was glad to be able to join him. Smoking was, he liked to say now that he had been at it for precisely a month, his one vice.

Mr. Burnside did not speak for some time, but leaned back in the chair, his skinny length relaxed, his toes waggling sensuously in the warmth of the fire. Theo watched him covertly. He would have put him down at sixty or thereabouts. The head was long and narrow, surmounted by thin grey hair, quite lustreless. The face was hollow, clean-shaven, deeply lined. Tired-looking, too, Theo thought. The dark eyes under black brows that jutted like eaves were damped down, but looked as if they could flame.

"I'm going to talk to you about the work here," Mr. Burnside said. "There's plenty of it. You've only got to step outside this house and walk for a quarter of a mile in any direction to realize that. And when I say the work, I don't mean preaching and singing, though you'll have that, too." Disconcertingly, he added, with a smile: "Do you like the sound of your own voice?"

Theo blushed and fumbled with his pipe. Then suddenly, and to his own surprise, he found himself saying: "Too much, I'm afraid."

Mr. Burnside did not ask him to elucidate this, but his silence seemed to suggest that Theo should go on.

"There was a chap at Cambridge named Brown, a retired actor. He used to take a few pupils in elocution, and three other Selwyn men and myself went to him. In the long holidays we went for a walking tour together, and Brown suggested that he should come with us. We wandered all over Devon and

Somerset, and one day in an empty country church one of the fellows began to intone, to see how his voice sounded. Then we all had a go. Brown said it was an excellent scheme and that we should all intone whenever we came to an empty church. He made a competition of it and said he would give a prize to the winner. One day a verger came out of a vestry and we felt awful fools. However, I won; and Brown gave me an engraving of Holman Hunt's *The Light of the World.*"

A moment ago Theo could not have imagined himself making this confession of an adventure which still, from time to time, made his ears privately burn. Mr. Burnside was looking at him with a kindly and understanding smile. *"The Light of the World!"* he said. "That didn't intone. It just shone."

Theo must have looked a trifle crestfallen, for he added: "I hope you intone well. I dislike a slovenly and slipshod service. But remember that the best part of the Church's service is done outside the church. This place is black with poverty, depression and despair. You've got to help me to find it out, wherever it is, and deal with it. It doesn't often come to us. It won't come to the church, I mean. Sometimes it comes here. For example, you needn't have knocked at the door today. You could have walked in. The door is on the latch always, day and night, and anyone can walk in who wants to. I never refuse to see a soul."

"But what about your private devotions, sir—er, Burnside—and your studies?"

Mr. Burnside did not directly answer. Leaning back with his eyes closed, he recited, marking the rise and fall of the verse with movements of his hands on the chair:

> *And so the Word had flesh and wrought*
> *With human hands the creed of creeds,*
> *In loveliness of perfect deeds,*
> *More strong than all poetic thought;*
>
> *That he may read who binds the sheaf,*
> *Or builds the house, or digs the grave,*
> *Or those wild eyes that watch the wave*
> *In roarings round the coral reef.*

Mr. Burnside did not open his eyes. The gaslight purred softly, ash dropped tinkling into the pan beneath the grate; the black cat arched its back, yawned with a great show of red tongue and white teeth, and settled down to rest again. In the silence Theo heard himself asking in a small voice: "Is that enough?"

Mr. Burnside got slowly to his feet, knocked out his pipe, and looked down at his young visitor. "Enough for me," he said. "Perhaps at my time of life a man gets lazy. Don't let me discourage you. Go on with your studies by all means. And don't let me put on you. If I'm asking you to do too much, tell me. There are more ways of living than mine. We must have another talk later. For the next few days just look about you. Get the feel and smell of the parish." Theo rose to go. "There's just one thing: make a call for me, there's a good fellow, on your way home. A man called Dunkerley. He's a printer—lives at No. 16 Palmerston Street. That's the next street to yours off the Stockport Road. Dunkerley's doing some handbills for me about a bazaar. They're overdue. Speed him up, will you?"

Theo promised to do so.

In the thickening fog of that March evening—an evening unlike any other Theo had known, for never before had he been in a great industrial city—the shops in the main thoroughfare were achieving a sickly yellowish luminosity as gaslights went on, and in the tripe saloon at the corner of Palmerston Street a bubble of blue flames warmed the dishes whose steam clouded the windows. The sky was quite gone now, and the lights on earth increased. They appeared behind fanlights, they threw the shadows of pot-plants on to the thin linen of window-blinds, they spouted suddenly out of the dark as a lamplighter clattered on his clogs along the street, applying his small dusky cresset to the lamp-posts.

One of these lighted lamps showed Theo the number 16, and as he pushed through the little iron gate a girl rushed past him, opened the door, and disappeared into the house. She was swathed from head to foot in a garment that seemed to be hood and cloak in one, and in her hand she carried a sopping

newspaper parcel which released on the heavy air a pungent
smell. Theo guessed she had returned from an errand at the
tripe shop on the corner. He followed her up the short tiled
path and was hesitating at the door which she had left flung
open, when he heard her voice saying within: "Auntie! Someone to see you!"

A moment later she reappeared clinging to the skirts of a
woman whom Theo guessed to be in her early thirties. The
child had now pushed the hood off her head, and in the light
of the passage lamp Theo thought she was a good-looking
little girl.

"I'm looking for Mr. Dunkerley," he explained. "Is he in?
Mr. Burnside asked me to call about some handbills that are
overdue."

The woman smiled. "I know," she said. "Everything's overdue this last fortnight. I don't know what's come over my husband. He didn't use to be like this. He'll have us all ruined."

She continued to smile, as though ruin were something she
was looking forward to with most pleasurable expectation.

"He's not in," she went on. "He's at the works in Stockport
Road. Grace has just brought his supper. I'm going to put it up
in a dish with some mashed potatoes. Grace isn't my little girl.
My little girl's in bed. Grace is my brother's little girl—aren't
you, Grace?"

Grace did not answer. She stared at Theo's cold classic profile, outlined against the blur of the street lamp, as though
she would take her fill of radiance while it lasted.

"My brother—George Satterfield—works with my husband.
You'll see the name up over the shop on the Stockport Road.
You can't miss it: Dunkerley and Satterfield. So I'm just send-
ing supper round to both of them. Aren't I, Grace?"

Theo was rather overwhelmed by the amount of information Mrs. Dunkerley conveyed, and to cut her short he said:
"Well, I'll just step round to the shop and see your husband
there."

"Oh, no!" Mrs. Dunkerley exclaimed. "You mustn't do
that! Daniel'd be furious. 'Don't send anyone round,' he said,
and he said: 'It'll be no good if you do. I'm locking the doors.

And expect me back when you see me.' But he can't do without supper, can he, Grace?"

"Well," Theo began, when a great voice roared from somewhere within the house: "Agnes, for God's sake shut t'door. This blasted fog's fillin' t'bloody 'ouse. If tha wants to wag thy chin come in an' do it by t'fire."

Mrs. Dunkerley giggled: "That's Daniel's father—a fair caution. Swears like a trooper and as innocent as a kitten. Isn't he, Grace?"

"Congestion o' t'bloody lungs'll be the least of it," Daniel's father continued; and Theo made another effort to get away. "Well," he said, "I'll look into the shop in the morning."

"That's right," Mrs. Dunkerley agreed. "In the morning— at ten o'clock. That's what Daniel said: 'All of you be there by ten o'clock, dressed in your best.' Didn't he, Grace?"

"Dressed in my bloody coffin, that's what I'll be," thundered the invisible chorus; and this time Theo really did go. Turning his eyes from the little lighted passage, carefully shutting the hideous iron gate, he found the darkness by contrast profound. There was some reason for the upbraiding of that invisible old man, for now the fog had ceased to be a gauze and had become a blanket. Through its almost tangible obstruction Theo slowly made his way back to his rooms in Hardiman Street. Mrs. Hornabrook had lighted the hanging lamp and kept the fire bright. "Now, settle down, lad," she said. "Tak off thi boots an' warm thi toes, an' Ah'll fetch thee a bit o' summat to ate. If tha wants owt to read, Ah've put t'Bible there for thee."

When she was gone out, he looked at the immense brass-bound book. An inscription on the fly-leaf showed it to be twenty years old, but it had an immaculate look. Nothing sullied its virginity but the brown paper-thin flattened petals of what he guessed, from their shape alone, to have once been pansies. He appreciated the kindness which had exhumed this venerable and monumental relic, but after supper he settled down by the fire with his handy little Greek Testament. He did not give another thought to the flattened pansy petals. He was not a young man of much imagination, and it did not

enter his mind that Mrs. Hornabrook had opened the pages, and looked at the petals, and remembered a day when she was younger than Theo was now, and in a hayfield at Marple her head lay in a lap that did not belong to the man with the Masonic tie-pin whose photograph was over the mantelpiece.

That photograph certainly must go, Theo thought several times, looking up from his book. Presently, he unhooked it and hung experimentally the engraving of *The Light of the World* that had been the reward of his beautiful voice. It looked well, and he decided to ask Mrs. Hornabrook in the morning to leave it there.

Chapter Two

AGNES DUNKERLEY, pottering about in the room in Palmerston Street that was both living-room and kitchen, did not at all believe that her husband would ruin her. She was only nineteen when she married Daniel, and he was then twenty. There had been no sort of engagement at all. She often laughed when she thought of it: she laughed at most things. There was a dance at the Athenæum Club, where her brother, George Satterfield, was a member, and George, who seemed to her then to be very grown up, for he was five years older than she, had taken her along. It was a stupendous occasion to young Agnes. Never before had she been to a dance in town, and she would not have gone then if poor George's wife had not just died, leaving him with the baby, Grace. All that winter George was like someone daft, she thought: dances and theatres and concerts, so that neighbours clicked their tongues and wagged their heads. *With her only just under the ground.* But young Agnes knew her brother's misery, and how, when he came home from his bright occasions, he would sit heavy-eyed and heavy-hearted, not answering when he was spoken to, and rigid in his chair long after she was a-bed.

He was rigid in the fusty old cab that he hired to take Agnes to the dance; a grim, four-square young man, dark-eyed and saturnine, with side-whiskers that made him look middle-aged, and a hand, she noticed, that trembled a little and kept clenching and unclenching on his knee. He seemed, she thought, as weary and dead-beat as the old horse that clip-clopped along the Stockport Road in the misty cold of that winter night and finally stopped, as though it had suddenly died upright, outside the doors of the Athenæum.

She hardly saw George again that night, but she did not miss him. The heat under the gaslights, the pulsing rhythm of the band, such a galaxy of young men, such shirt fronts and

whiskers and hair gleaming with bear's grease! She was happy
and excited and successful, and she had drunk much lemonade
and danced three times with the same young man who told
her that he was a designer at Hallcroft and Rigby's.

It was then, when for a moment she stood alone, her face
glowing, her lips parted in a smile, her breast heaving a little
with pleasurable excitement, that a boy—he seemed no more—
had stood before her, a smile on his lips, too, and an impudent
air of appraisal on his face. He was rather short, dark and
blunt-looking, with thick black hair, unruly and ungreased.
His eyes were of the deepest violet-blue, and the chin was
stuck on to his young face like a piece of rock. He was not
wearing evening clothes, but had fixed an incongruous-looking
white bow under that jutty chin.

Agnes was in the mood to smile at everybody that night,
and she smiled at this boy. He continued to look at her as
though she were a picture that pleased him mightily, and
then, saying nothing, he took the programme from her hand
and examined it. There was but one dance unbooked—a
waltz—and opposite that he wrote "Daniel Dunkerley" and
handed back the card. "In the year 1843," he said, "this club
was opened by the late Mr. Charles Dickens. He used the
words: 'High above the noise of loom and hammer, whisper-
ing encouragement in the ears of workers.' Bear that in mind.
That is what this place is for. I shall come back and expect to
have encouragement whispered into my ear."

The band was throbbing again, the floor clearing, and a
youth came to claim her. He bowed and said: "May I inter-
rupt? May I claim this lady?"

Daniel Dunkerley said: "You may have the loan of her.
Take good care of her. I shall be coming back for her
later."

She did not see him again till the time for their waltz came,
and then he appeared suddenly at her side. "We shall sit this
out," he announced, with a finality that he seemed to give to
many words.

Agnes was disappointed. "Oh, but I don't want to miss a
single dance," she cried. "And I love a waltz above all things."

"I don't dance," he told her simply, and showed her his card. It was blank save for the one name Agnes Satterfield.

"Why on earth do you come to dances if you don't dance?" she asked.

"Because sometimes I like to be with crowds," he said. "I like to watch 'em. I like to know what crowds are up to. Did it ever occur to you, Miss Satterfield, that there's a fortune in understanding what crowds are up to? But never mind that. Let us sit under the palms."

There were a few gilded spindle-shanked chairs in a nook over which palms nodded and potted cinerarias made a gay embankment of cerise, white, and indigo blue. They sat there together, listening to the music, not saying much, and Agnes felt that she didn't mind missing the waltz whose swoony rhythm was now filling the air. To be waltzing with this Daniel Dunkerley would be exciting; but he didn't waltz; and so—well—merely to sit with him was exciting, too. Now, he was not even talking, and strangest of all was to feel that it was exciting to be sitting here with him, dumb. She was not disturbed by the strangeness of his dress. He wore such a black suit as a man might wear on most occasions, supplemented by that extraordinary large white bow and white kid gloves with three black cotton lines worked into the back. She was aware of the strong fists beneath these gloves.

Presently he said: "I suppose you're George Satterfield's sister?" and she nodded. "Do you know George?"

"Only slightly. I live in Levenshulme, too. I know about his wife dying. I hate to tell you, but we must take him home at once. He's getting very tight."

Agnes's heart missed a beat. A flood of bitter knowledge rushed upon her mind. She had kept house for George since his wife had died and had looked after little Grace. Sometimes he had come in at night dull and owlish and had stumbled straight upstairs to his room. She had been baffled and puzzled. Now she knew. All the joy went out of this first great festive night of her young life. A horrible shadow dimmed the lights; the music was derisive; and she suddenly hated the young man who had so calmly reduced all to dust and ashes. She

rose, quivering. "You liar!" she cried, defensively, hopelessly, piteously.

Dunkerley was unperturbed. "He's all right at the moment," he said. "Now you must do as I tell you. Go and get your cloak."

She felt passionately rebellious. She stamped her foot. "Don't order me about!" she commanded him. "How can I go now? What about all these other dances?"

"They must look after themselves," he said. "Come along now."

She was wearing white kid gloves up to her elbows, and puffed silk sleeves. Between kid and silk there were a few inches of flesh. Dunkerley pulled off his gloves, stuffed them into his pocket, and laid his hand on this gleaming flesh. "Come," he said. "Don't be childish."

She felt her whole body thrill at the contact, and followed him meekly. "Get your cloak and meet me in the hall," he said.

She did as he told her, and he led her out into the street and called a four-wheeler. He put her into it, and said to the driver: "Wait just round that corner. I sha'n't be a moment."

She crouched miserably in a corner of the cold cab as the horse clattered a few paces on the hard setts and then came up with a jerk in a dark side-street. She had not long to wait before Dunkerley came, his hand under George's elbow. "Come on now," he said. "The dance is over. It's two o'clock." It was only half-past eleven.

Dunkerley did not speak to her during the journey. Folded in her cloak, she sat aloof on one seat; he, on the other, kept an arm round George who dozed and snored, his head sagging on his chest, and occasionally mumbled incoherent words. When they got home, Dunkerley paid the cabman, helped George out, and propped him against the door. "Don't worry," he said. "He'll be all right in the morning."

Then he walked away without so much as a good-night.

This was a Saturday night in 1873. The next morning, nothing was said between George Satterfield and Agnes con-

cerning the events of the night before. George complained of a slight headache and said he would take Grace out in the perambulator. Agnes went alone to morning service at St. Ninian's. When she was returning she saw Daniel Dunkerley on the other side of the road. He was wearing the black suit he had worn last night, but now lacked his remarkable tie and gloves. He wore a bowler hat. With him was an old man, tall and white-haired, thin and erect as a flagstaff. He wore moustaches of great length, but there was no droop in them. They stood out as though on an internal structure of wire, and the ends were twisted to needle-points. The old man looked something of a dandy. He wore a tall beaver hat, a frock-coat buttoned so tightly that he appeared to be compressed within a tube, and yellow gloves. His boots had shining toe-caps and lavender cloth uppers, and he carried a short Malacca cane. Moreover, unseasonable though it looked, there was a flower in his button-hole. But what struck Agnes most in that first glimpse was the rigidity of the old man's figure and that he wore no overcoat. The damps of last night were gone, but frost made the sunny air seem like a bright keen knife.

Agnes, with her hands in a muff of cheap fur, with a feather boa fluttering round her neck and a garden blooming on the structure of straw and wire that almost concealed her face, would have hurried by, for her heart had given a dangerous flutter; but Daniel Dunkerley, taking the old man by the arm, led him across the road and cut her off.

He raised his hat and said: "Good morning, Miss Satterfield. This is my father. Sim, this is the girl I'm going to marry."

She saw now that the old man's eyes were blue—not the dark violet of Daniel's, but the cold light blue of ice. His hand went to his hat in a military salute, and he said: "Don't be a bloody fool, Daniel."

Daniel laughed. "All right, Sim; you'll see," he said. And then, turning to Agnes: "I always trust my intuitions, Miss Satterfield. You and I are going to get married. Good-bye for the present."

Agnes had not opened her mouth. She was afraid to trust her voice. She felt her limbs trembling a little. And yet her

native inclination to laugh was powerful. She waited till she was round a corner and then exploded. "What a cheek! I never heard such a thing! He thinks he's somebody, that young feller."

Simon Dunkerley was not so old as he appeared to Agnes's young eyes. He was forty-five. When he was twenty-seven he had looked a fine and terrifying figure, his great height amplified by a bearskin. And then he had looked no sort of figure at all: a frost-bitten wreck of a man, lying in the snow, with his ribs stove in and his life flowing out. There wouldn't have been much chance for Sergeant-major Simon Dunkerley if it hadn't been for Florence Nightingale. "That bloody woman," he called her. "What did I go out to Crimea for? To empty piss-pots for that bloody woman. As soon as I could crawl. Emptying piss-pots and scrubbing wards."

He was lucky to be able to do that. He was clamped into a surgical jacket of steel and had worn it ever since. He never mentioned it. He preferred it to be thought that his strikingly upright carriage was due to soldierly deportment. It was only in the early days of his return from the Crimea that he would speak of what he had endured. He opened a small shop in Levenshulme, where he and his wife sold sweets, newspapers, and tobacco. He would stand about the shop in his rigid fashion for hours on end, and when his wife urged him to sit down—"Don't overtire your heart, Sim"—he would burst out: "Heart! How d'you know I've got a bloody heart? How d'you know what they cut out of me? Half of me was hanging out— heart an' liver an' lights an' God knows what all. How do I know they ever put it back? That bloody woman was capable of anything. Angel of mercy! My God—she was more like a sergeant of dragoons. Piss-pots! Me!" He couldn't get over it.

Mrs. Dunkerley died when Daniel was twelve years old. Old Sim, as everyone called him—he had returned white-haired from the Crimea and looked twenty years more than his age— kept house and did the cooking and Daniel delivered news-papers and looked after the shop. He had finished with school and Sim said it was time he began his education. "I don't want

a gormless bloody galoot about t'place," he casually explained. "Look at me. I could have been a shapeless wreck. I look a soldier." He smote his chest with a round ebony ruler and Daniel was fascinated by the metallic ring. "Very well, my lad. We can be what we want to be."

This was one of Sim's favourite remarks: we can be what we want to be.

He was remorseless with young Daniel. It was no wonder the boy never learned to dance. Sim was a great reader, and he made Daniel read too. And when the shop was shut and they sat together in the back room behind it, he would cross-question him about his reading. More than that, he insisted on a *précis* being written of every book the boy read. This began with a simple tale by G. A. Henty and went on to Carlyle's *French Revolution* and Ruskin's *Unto This Last*. Every morning Daniel was compelled to read the long leader in the *Manchester Guardian,* to summarize its arguments, and to do his best at night against old Sim, who would take the opposite point of view.

So the boy grew up to have a mind that was sceptical of any argument till he had examined and tested it, and to have a remarkable ability to assimilate information. When he was old enough, Sim chivvied him to the Mechanics' Institute where he studied mathematics, and by some means of his own old Dunkerley got hold of sheaves of company reports and balance sheets. Between them, they waded through the finances of widespread business ventures.

When Daniel was eighteen Sim apprenticed him to a printer. When he was twenty he began to earn a wage. Then Sim sold the corner shop and moved into the small house in Palmerston Street. All was now to be pleasant. His pension and what he had saved and what he got for the shop would keep him; and if it didn't, he saw no reason why Daniel should not help him. That children should keep parents was a commonplace among the poor. So, Daniel went to work daily, and Sim looked after the cooking and housekeeping. At forty-five, his habits and dress had become as rigid as his steel torso. The frock-coat, the yellow gloves, the Malacca cane, the flower in the button-hole:

these were part of a character and were rapidly becoming part of a tradition. He would never wear an overcoat. He had frozen in Russia and learned to do without the bloody thing, he said.

Sim and Daniel Dunkerley went side by side along the sunny pavement of the Stockport Road that frosty Sunday morning. They did not speak to one another for a while. Sim was aware of late that this Daniel of his, whom he loved with a secret devouring love that was never expressed, had ceased to be the amenable boy who could be driven, or even led. They were on the happiest terms. They had by some miracle avoided the formalism of relationship that was usual between Victorian parent and offspring. But Daniel—largely Sim's own creation—was now his own man, and no one else's.

"A girl, eh?" said old Sim at last.

"Ay."

"She looks all right."

"She looks champion."

"What'll you keep her on?"

"I'm going to buy the works."

It sounded grand. Daniel said it proudly. But it also sounded lunatic, and Sim stopped dead in his tracks.

"Buy the works? What with?"

Daniel stopped, too, and outside St. Ninian's faced his father with an impudent grin. "Borrowed capital," he said airily.

"Borrowing is sorrowing," old Sim declared, bringing his cane down with a thud on the pavement. "Where are you going to borrow it from?"

Daniel looked him hard in the eye. "From you."

"You're bloody well not."

"I damn well am."

He did. It was his first financial transaction. By the fireside at Palmerston Street that night he showed Sim his figures. When all was said and done, "the works," as he grandly called them, did not come to much. It was a very small printing-shop on the Stockport Road. Himself, one other, and a boy could run it. Sim's life savings and the sum that he had received for

the corner shop would help. "Then there's this house. I've inquired about a mortgage on it."

In the lamplight, Sim looked across at the cool young face and licked dry lips. "Anything else?" he asked, with what he hoped was a sufficient sarcasm.

"I shall only need another two hundred," he said.

"And where's that coming from?"

Again Daniel did not flinch. "I was thinking you could capitalize your pension."

At that Sim's patience gave way. "My God!" he cried. "I've bred a financier!"

"You'd never regret it," Daniel said. "I give you my word of honour, Sim: as long as I live you shall not want." He held out his hand. The old man hesitated for no more than a moment, then took it. "And I feel," said Daniel, "that I'm going to live for a long time."

That was how Daniel Dunkerley acquired the small printing-shop on the Stockport Road when he was twenty years old. Two months later, having seen but little of her in the meantime, he married Agnes Satterfield. A month after that, when the first whispers of spring were in the air, he went one Saturday night to the Cricketers' Arms and ordered half a pint of bitter. It lasted him till he saw George Satterfield's face through the clear glass of the swing door. He was at the door before George was through it; he hooked an arm into his brother-in-law's and drew him out into the street. George struggled feebly. "Let go," he said. "I want a drink."

"So do I. We'll have one together in Heaton Mersey. A walk'll do us good."

They set out to tramp the couple of miles of grim pavement: two young men of much the same height and build, one brown-eyed, one blue-eyed, one clean-shaven, one decorated with black side-whiskers; one joyous, with his hands full of happy life, one in the trough of misery and despair.

"What the hell can I do now?" George asked, when they had walked some time in silence. His eyes were fixed gloomily ahead on the long hard vista.

Daniel knew what he meant. George had been a chemist's dispenser in Manchester. He had made a mistake, one which fortunately had not been serious but had cost him his job.

"For one thing," said Daniel brightly, "you can swear off the drink."

Satterfield snorted impatiently. He came mulishly to a stop. "Look here," he said. "If you've brought me out to preach, you can damn well go home. Will swearing off the drink give me a job? Will it—bring *her* back?"

His voice trembled, and Dunkerley did not pity him. George, he thought in his young wisdom, had pity and to spare for himself. They faced one another on the pavement, looked into one another's eyes, and each knew that Daniel Dunkerley was the master.

"George," he said, "what are your hopes of getting another job as a dispenser?"

The other spread his hands in a gesture of helplessness. "Damn all," he said. "Old Chowne would never give me a reference. That sort of thing gets known." Reasonably he added: "Quite right, too. I asked for it."

"What other job can you do?"

"Nothing."

They walked on towards Heaton Mersey. Presently Dunkerley said: "George, I'm what they call a master-printer, and I could teach you to be one. Normally, you'd pay to learn. But I'll pay you enough to keep body and soul together. Are you on?"

Satterfield said: "Damn your charity."

"All right. Take it or leave it."

They reached Heaton Mersey, and Dunkerley said, pausing at a bar door: "Well, let's have a quick one. I want to get back to Agnes."

"Never mind a quick one. Let's go on walking," Satterfield answered; and they sloped down towards the banks of the murky Mersey River. It was now dark and cold; bright stars burned overhead, and they walked briskly. "This is good," Satterfield said. "I used to walk a lot, Dan. I must do more of it."

They came through Heaton Moor and back on to the lamp-lit vista of the Stockport Road, headed for home. Then Satter-field said: "Listen, Dan. Forget what I said just now. I don't want to be a printer. I'd never make a printer. But I'll tell you what. You want to extend that business. You don't want to sit there waiting for orders. You want someone out and about getting 'em for you. I could do that. It's work I'd like. And I'm not going to have charity, either. If I come in, I shall bring some capital with me, and it's going to be a two-man show. You'll put both names up on the board."

Daniel's ears pricked at the word "capital." It was a word destined to haunt him through life.

"Capital?" he said. "I didn't know you had any, George. I thought you had nothing beyond your wages."

"It was chiefly Louie's insurance," Satterfield explained, his voice shaking again. "She was insured for five hundred. And there's about a hundred I managed to save besides."

Daniel took his arm. "Come and have some supper with me and Agnes and Sim," he said. "What have you done with Grace?"

"She's all right. She'll be in bed by now. There's a neighbour in to look after her."

When Agnes Dunkerley, twelve years later, said to Theo Chrystal: "You'll see the name up over the shop on the Stock-port Road: Dunkerley and Satterfield," the firm had settled down to a modest prosperity. Daniel and Agnes, with old Sim and their two children, Laurence, who was ten, and Dinah, who was eight, still lived at 16 Palmerston Street, and No. 18 next door was occupied by George Satterfield and Grace, who was near her thirteenth birthday, and a woman who kept house.

Daniel blessed the day when George Satterfield had refused to be a printer and had elected to be a traveller instead. He had from the beginning brought in considerable orders for print-ing companies' note-paper and bill-heads and reports of meet-ings. All these things he obtained within Manchester in the course of the first couple of years; and Dunkerley was able to handle them with the help of Ernest Entwistle, who was a

good printer, and a young apprentice named Alec Dillworth. Satterfield said it was all a matter of the social touch, and this was the only side of the business that caused Daniel Dunkerley any anxiety. George's claims for "entertaining" were not light, and as time went on did not become lighter, but that could be put up with: the business he brought in was worth it. The trouble was that George himself shared all too fully in the entertainments and was impatient of any reproof. "Damn it, Dan, shut up. You're not my boss; you're my partner. I *like* drinking—see?—and if I'm not drinking while bringing work to the shop I'll be drinking while sitting on my backside. Have it which way you like."

Daniel sighed and let the matter drop. He liked George, and George in these days looked a credit to the firm. He had lost his grim and sullen air; he was gay and alert, liking his job, and he dressed in the conventional uniform of a successful business man: frock coat, grey trousers, silk hat.

When the firm was five years old George announced that he was going to "expand his orbit." His genial presence became known in Oldham, Bolton, Preston, Liverpool, Warrington. He justified this, too; the labels for jam-pots, the wrappers for a world-famous soap, the cardboard packets of a popular brand of cigarettes: all these things and others like them began to swell the work of the shop in the Stockport Road. It was necessary to extend by taking the shop next door when its lease fell in, and to engage two additional printers; and just before the time when Theo Chrystal went to be a curate at St. Ninian's, the firm of Dunkerley and Satterfield was doing so well that George announced to his brother-in-law that he was leaving the house in Palmerston Street.

Daniel was at this time thirty-two years old and George a few years older. George believed himself to be now the dominating partner. He did not see how Dunkerley and Satterfield could get on without his increasing "contacts"; yet at the same time, watching Daniel working at a form, or distributing type, or doing any of the odd jobs which he loved still to handle, he would be struck with a sudden uneasiness, a feeling that he'd never got to the bottom of Dan, that there was in the

younger man's quiet purposefulness a power which he himself had never known.

They were alone in the shop when he told Dan that he intended to leave Palmerston Street. It was a Saturday night in January of 1885, and everyone else had gone home. George, who had come in from a round of calls in Lancashire, looked about for somewhere clean to sit, dusted a chair with a newspaper, and for a moment contemplated Dunkerley, wearing overalls and setting a stick of type under an unguarded buzzing gas flame.

"Well, Dan," he said at last, "the time has come, as the Walrus said, to talk of many things."

"Talk away," Dan answered without looking round.

"*In primis,* as the scholars have it, re my residence."

"What's wrong with your residence, as you call it?"

"Everything. The house itself and the district it's in. I'm going to make a shift. I shall miss you and old Sim and all that, but Palmerston Street doesn't suit George any longer."

"Watching you set forth of a morning in that outfit, I've often thought the same," Dan said with a grin. "You look like Lord Muck."

"I don't know," George answered, slightly offended, "where this firm would be if I didn't look as I do and get around as I do."

Daniel put down his stick and turned to face his brother-in-law. He removed the green eye-shade he wore to protect his sight, and as he did so his thumb ran a smudge of ink up his cheek. He looked absurdly young, George thought, with his violet eyes and unbrushed hair, his ruddy, healthy, hairless cheeks: almost like an enthusiastic apprentice. But what was there to be enthusiastic about? That was the thing that always made George feel Daniel's inferior. The beggar had been at this printing game for twelve hard slogging years, and today he was as—as what?—as when he began. George couldn't define it —that gusto—that inescapable quality of the spirit. For himself, he was beginning to feel like an old mill-horse plodding his rounds. It was difficult to pick up new jokes to tell the chaps, and it was a long time since he had learned a new conjuring

trick. He relied on these things. It was this sense of staleness, as much as anything, that had made him decide to leave Palmerston Street. A new house . . . a new district . . .

"George, you're getting a bit tired," Daniel said.

George shuffled uneasily. "Query what is tired?" he asked. "I can go my rounds as well as ever."

"I know. You've done a lot for us all. I realize that. Now I want you to be patient for a bit. Don't shift yet. Stay on in Palmerston Street till you see how things jump."

George looked bewildered. "What are you talking about, Dan? How d'you mean—jump? Things don't have to jump. They can just go on. We're all on velvet, aren't we?"

"Look, George, with me things don't just go on. I've been thinking something over for the last few years——"

"Years! My God! And kept your mouth shut?"

Daniel nodded. "George, I'm going to ask you to have a lot of faith in me."

George sat up. "Query what is faith? D'you mean money? Are you going to try some stunts with the firm's capital?"

"I mean that you had the idea of leaving Palmerston Street for Greenhow Street, or some such pretty little place as that."

George nodded. "Well?"

"Well, don't. Not yet. When you move, you'll either move into something ten times the size of a Greenhow Street house or you'll move into the workhouse. Just hang on a bit."

George sprang from his chair, very excited. "Look here, Dan, what the hell *is* all this? Am I a partner in this firm or am I not?"

"There are three partners," said Daniel steadily. "Old Sim, because he gave me the money to start the show, you, and I. What I have been doing I have done on my own—not a word to a soul, except Alec Dillworth."

"This is getting funny," said Satterfield, with rising annoyance. "Two partners are in the dark, and the third is conspiring with a printer's apprentice."

"That is exactly the position," Dan answered. "Look at this."

He took up again the stick of type he had been setting, fitted

it into the bottom of a galley that was nearly full, and then slid the type out of the galley into a form. The form already contained three shortish columns of type. Now that the fourth was in, Dan locked the form, spread a blanket over it, took up a block of wood and a mallet and began to pound the typefaces flat. Then he rubbed an inky roller over and over the type faces and applied a sheet of newsprint to them. He got hold of another roller of heavy metal, and this rubbed the newsprint upon the inked type. He lifted the sheet off the form and handed it to George. "Now come into the office and I'll tell you things."

Chapter Three

ALEC DILLWORTH was eighteen years old. He was five feet high and he weighed eight stone. He was never any higher and he never weighed any more. When George Satterfield told himself that Dan had an enthusiast's face he was not quite right. Dan's face was lively and alert, betraying an unquenchable love of life and interest in all its manifestations. Dillworth's was the face of an enthusiast in the word's ancient and authentic meaning. It was almost a fanatic's face. The grey eyes under the tumble of lank careless flaxen hair, the thin cheeks, the sensuous lips, all had an extraordinary appearance of rapture. Sadness settled on the face in repose; any emotion, joy or anger or sorrow, would impart to it a sudden mobility that made it exceptional, at times startling.

It is safe to say that George Satterfield had never *seen* Dillworth. Dunkerley saw and appraised him from the moment the young apprentice set foot in the shop. Mr. Burnside had raised the money from goodness knows where to have the boy apprenticed. Dunkerley would never reprove Alec Dillworth or permit anyone else to do so, for fear the boy might go out and commit suicide. He had to step very delicately with Dillworth in order to find out something about his background, and he did not do this by questioning the boy himself. He discovered in ways of his own that Alec's father and mother were hopeless drunks who abused one another, threw pots and pans at one another, fought like tigers; and that a sister, a year younger than Alec, was a prostitute on the Manchester streets. Again, it was not from Alec that he learned the story of a black eye and a deeply cut lip that the boy brought one morning to the shop. It was from Mr. Burnside. Alec had met on the stairs his sister with a client. He had lost his temper and flamed suddenly into abuse of the man, who at once turned and fled from the house. "I can well believe it," said Mr. Burnside. "Alec must have looked like an avenging angel."

there, and presently said, speaking quietly and conversationally, so as not to alarm the boy: "Well, Alec."

But Dillworth was as startled as though a gun had been discharged at his ear. He leapt round and faced Daniel, panting
and glaring. Then, recovering himself a little, he turned and
shook the type from the stick haphazardly into the case.

"You'll have a job sorting that lot out, Alec," Dunkerley
said with a laugh. "You've made a proper pie."

"I'll put it right. You needn't worry," the boy said defensively. He reached out furtively, picked up some printed slips
and stuffed them into his pocket. One of them fluttered to the
ground, and he did not notice it.

"Well," Dunkerley said, "time you were in bed, Alec. I'll
lock up here."

Dillworth went to the washbowl, washed his hands, rolled
his shirtsleeves down over his skinny forearms, and pulled on
his coat. "Thank you, Mr. Dunkerley," he said shyly.

"That's all right. Get to bed. And, look here, I don't know
what you're doing, but you can go on doing it. Any night you
like. Understand?"

He hoped the boy might confide in him, but Dillworth
merely said again: "Thank you, Mr. Dunkerley," and slipped
away like a shadow.

Then Daniel picked up the printed slip from the floor.
There were some verses of poetry—a carryover from something
which had appeared on a previous page; then, towards the bottom, a new poem began, headed: "The Harlot." There was
only one verse:

> *Through dirty window-lace I lean*
> *Over the street so grey and mean*
> *To watch the sly night sidling in,*
> *Ambiguous cloak of filth and sin;*
> *And from my lips the white birds fly,*
> *The vespers of virginity.*

Dunkerley was strangely moved. "Well, I'm damned," he
said, glaring at the buzzing gas. "I'm damned. So that's how it
takes him. He's got that sister of his on the brain."

Dunkerley went back into the office, lit the fire and made himself a cup of tea. Then, with a pipe clenched in his teeth, he sat in the one comfortable chair and took a pad of paper on to his knee. He wrote:

DICKORY DOCK.
RANDOM.
PATCHWORK.
FACTS AND FANCIES.

He didn't much like any of these names; but what did the name matter, anyway? It was for the paper to establish the name, so that people everywhere would walk into the news-agents' shops, plank their pennies on the counter, and say almost automatically: "Random," "Patchwork," or whatever it might be.

He took from his pocket a few sheets of manuscript headed "Hard Facts" and began to read them through. Every hour so many millions of gallons of water pour over Niagara Falls. The smoke annually discharged into the atmosphere of Man-chester is the equivalent to so many tons of coal. The cab horses of London eat every week a quantity of hay equivalent to the crop of so many acres. If all the hair cut each year by Birming-ham barbers were stuffed into mattresses, beds could be pro-vided for so many people. He had gone to a lot of trouble to assemble these facts. It had taken him weeks. The devil of it would be, he told himself, to fill the page every week. Perhaps his readers would help him to do that. Give half-a-crown a week for the most interesting fact published. He smiled as this simple solution of his problem submitted itself to his mind, and made a note on his paper: "Let the readers do the work themselves."

He sat there thinking for a long time of many matters which he knew as well as anybody to be banal and childish, but he had become obsessed with the idea of setting this thing going, and go it should, for good or ill.

He put out the light, got into his overcoat, and was about to go, when he heard a key in the lock. He waited, expecting Alec Dillworth, and Alec came. As soon as the boy was in the

office Dunkerley lit the gas again and said: "Sit down, Alec. I want to have a talk with you. You've missed one of your sheets and come back for it, I suppose?"

Dillworth did not sit down. He stood glaring at Daniel like the fierce young animal the elder man sometimes imagined him to be. "You haven't *read* it, have you?" he demanded.

Daniel sat down and bent to poke the fire. "Yes," he said over his shoulder. Dillworth's voice reached him, tense and furious. "You dirty prying dog."

Dunkerley sat up slowly, weighing the poker in one hand. "Go on," said Dillworth. "Hit me with it. Kick me out."

Dunkerley sighed and laid the poker gently in the fender. He reached out an arm and pulled Dillworth down upon his knees. The boy sat there, suddenly stilled by this unexpected action. Daniel laid a hand on his disordered hair and said: "Alec! Alec!"

Then Dillworth fell upon his breast and sobbed, clutching him as a child would a father.

Presently Dunkerley got up and placed Alec in the chair, and said: "I'll make some fresh tea. There's biscuits in the tin."

When they sat down to the tea Dillworth's face was shining. "I feel grand," he suddenly shouted; and Dunkerley, who had so casually cast out the devils, patted his hand and said: "Good, Alec, good."

It was Alec himself who came back to the subject of the poems. Suddenly the whole story was pouring out of him. He was setting them all on the sly. There were enough to make a book, and when the sheets were ready he was going to pay someone to bind them. "Then out of the profits," he said grandly, "I'd pay you back for the paper I've pinched. Have a look at them." He began to pull pages out of his pockets, his thin face twitching with eagerness.

Dunkerley read some of them; then from his own pocket he took the sheets headed "Hard Facts" and handed them to Alec. "What do you think of those?" he asked.

Alec began to read and presently looked up with a puzzled face. "What's all this rubbish mean?" he asked.

Daniel was slightly hurt. It was rubbish—he knew that well enough—but all the same, he was slightly hurt.

"Alec," he said, "I'm going to take you into my confidence, and I know you'll respect it. Dunkerley and Satterfield are going to start a weekly paper, and this will make one page of it."

"Oh, one of *those* things," Alec said with contemptuous indifference. "What are you going to call it?"

"That's one thing I haven't decided."

"Well, if it's one of *those* things, there's the title staring you in the face." Alec pointed to the heading of the sheet he held: *Hard Facts.*

"But it won't be all facts."

"Very well. You can have in small type underneath: *With Some Fancies.*"

And so, when it came to the point, it was done, but the readers who began with their thousands and ended with their tens of thousands never asked for anything but *Hard Facts.*

Meanwhile, in the little office on the Stockport Road that night, Dunkerley proceeded to bind chains upon Pegasus.

It had seemed to Dunkerley from the first that Alec Dillworth might be important to the matter he had in hand, but he knew the boy well enough to be aware that his intolerance and arrogance would scarify the whole project. The way in which Dillworth said: "Oh, one of *those* things," confirmed what Dunkerley all along had feared. But as he sat there that night under the gaslight with Alec's proofs on the table before him, he knew how the boy's allegiance could be won, and he was unscrupulous in playing his hand. He replenished Alec's cup from the strong black brew in the teapot and said: "Alec, when you say 'One of *those* things,' you're not being quite fair. This paper is going to be a bit different from any other."

Alec sipped his tea noisily and laughed. "I suppose," he said, "any maggot is in some particular different from any other. Their father's eye might know them apart. To anyone else they're just maggots. These papers are silly drivelling rubbish, Mr. Dunkerley."

His very assurance infuriated Dunkerley. "I tell you this

paper is going to be *different*, Alec," he said hotly. "After all,
facts are important, aren't they?"

"Oh, facts," Alec answered wearily. "You should read De
Quincey, Mr. Dunkerley, on the difference between facts and
power."

Dunkerley felt that he could have hit him, but he remembered what Mr. Burnside had once said. "Alec is younger than
an unborn child and older than Pharaoh's mummy. When he
talks like the one, I remember that he is also the other, and so
we get on well enough."

"One difference, Alec," Dunkerley said now, congratulating
himself on his cunning, "is that, with your permission, I shall
print one of your poems in each issue."

The effect of these words astonished him. Alec Dillworth
swept the pages together and stuffed them into his pocket.
Then he leapt to his feet, with his nose pinched and white. "I'd
see you in hell first," he cried, trembling. "*My* poems in *your*
lousy paper? Don't you believe it!"

At that, Dunkerley felt that his patience must give way. "Oh,
get to hell out of it," he wanted to shout. But he fought down
the impulse. He rose and pulled on his overcoat. "See you on
Monday morning, Alec," he said. "Think it over. You'd be
paid for the poems, of course. And there'd be a salaried job for
you on the paper. You'd be able to run a small house for you
and your sister. Good night. Lock up, will you?"

He walked out into the black night, feeling incredibly small
and mean. He had failed with all other baits to lure this wild
creature, and so he had used what he knew about the shocking
situation in the Dillworth household. "A small house for you
and your sister." Alec stood by the door on the Stockport Road
watching Dunkerley till the darkness swallowed him up. His
face was contorted with hatred, because he knew that Dunker
ley had got him.

Chapter Four

ON his first night at Mrs. Hornabrook's, Theo Chrystal sat up late, reading his Greek Testament. He looked such a young Greek himself, with his blue eyes and pale chiselled face, that it would not have been inappropriate had he been reading from a parchment instead of from these printed pages that were a gift from Lady Pinson on his leaving Sussex. Theo's profile, captured by an excellent photographer, filled a silver frame that stood on the grand piano in Lady Pinson's drawing-room. It was in this drawing-room that Theo had given her her Greek lessons, and always, when the lessons were ended, there was tea, and then she would play to him. Theo had little ear for music and no great liking for it, but he understood the importance of Lady Pinson, whose brother was Bishop of Chanctonbury; and so he would sit with his head well back in the easy chair, his eyes closed, his delicate finger-tips touching, and a simulated rapture lighting his face. Hard work might get a man on in the Church, but he was aware that the Lady Pinsons of this earth were not without their weight.

She was thirty, and a childless widow, and very rich. She was an amateur of the arts, and a blue-stocking, with an intelligent but haphazard face. She dressed beautifully, and sometimes Theo wondered if she were in love with him. She was. He would have been shocked had he known of the horror and humiliation crowded into the two years of marriage that preceded her inheritance of Cotter's Court and the wealth of Sir Brian Pinson, seventh baronet. Looking under long lashes that veiled the eyes which were her most attractive feature at Theo's head lying back in the chair, she romantically compared this sleeping angel with the too wide-awake satyr whose remembered embraces could still cause her to shudder. She would never marry again—she was sure of that—but it was delightful to have someone so young and beautiful about the place, engaged in so charming and harmless an occupation as the teach-

ing of Greek. Brian had been twenty-five years her senior, and
a barbarian. Looking across the low sunny room, whose open
French window admitted the scent and drowse of summer, she
knew all too well that Theo was on the point of slumber, that
music rather bored him, and that, when she ceased playing, the
appreciation and applause to which he would be called by the
sudden silence would be but simulated and insincere. But she
liked to have him there, and could Theo but have read the
thoughts behind her rather low forehead, he would have seen
them racing ahead to a time when he would be writing to her
above a signature of mounting splendour, ending—who knew?
—with Theodore Ebor, or, not inconceivably, Theodore Can-
tuar. To keep him with her was a strong temptation; to send
him away was a matter both of prudence and wisdom, for
Adela Pinson was a wise woman after her fashion and she was
not unaware of the currents of her time. A sojourn in the industrial North, she was sure, was a necessary part of the working out of her dream. Theo himself hardly realized that it was
Lady Pinson who had sent him to Levenshulme.

Theo Chrystal was no sluggard. Though he had sat up late,
he rose early, as was his custom. There was no need for Mrs.
Hornabrook to call him. At six he was out of bed, aware of a
dark reluctant day through whose murk he saw, drawing the
curtains and looking towards Palmerston Street, squares of
wan light flower silently here and there upon the unseen backs
of the houses. For two hours he was at his reading and devotions in the cold bedroom, and at the end of that time the day
was no lighter than it had been when he rose. It was to be another day of fog. Mrs. Hornabrook, coming at eight with a can
of hot water, was surprised to find her lodger out of bed,
wrapped in a black woollen dressing-gown which he had had
specially made with a hood that cowled his head, open books
on the small bedside table, and an ebony crucifix, carrying a
sagging ivory Christ, yellow as an old tooth, on the wall. Mrs.
Hornabrook, as she herself would have put it, was not much of
a one for religion. When she went anywhere, it was to the
Wesleyan chapel where the singing was hearty, the heating

system efficient, and the sermon bright and brief. This crucifix upon her bedroom wall, this monkish garment that her pale young lodger was wearing, seemed to her Popish and dubious. She noted these phenomena as something to be discussed with her daughter Em, put the can of water on the washstand, and bustled off to prepare Theo's breakfast.

Theo came willingly enough from the austerity of his bedroom to the crude and cheerful comfort of his firelit sitting-room. He would not on any account remit one moment of those two hours which he gave each morning to solitary devotions; but he was sometimes perturbed by the joyous alacrity with which, when they were over, he plunged into warmer mundane matters: as, for example, this hearty breakfast of eggs and bacon which Mrs. Hornabrook carried in under an electroplate cover. She noted with satisfaction that he did not now look like a monk. She was not clear in her mind about monks, but was troubled by the thought that they were not all that they might be. She associated them with little but tortures and the stake, vaguely recollecting some early efforts to distort her mind which had gone by the name of her education. It was pleasing to see that Mr. Chrystal, wearing his neat dark suit, with collar back to front, looked reassuringly like nothing more forbidding than "t'parson's lad."

Theo commented on the continuance of the fog, and Mrs. Hornabrook, having placed the dish before him, stood for a moment contemplating him in a characteristic attitude, with her hands on her buttocks. "Ay, tha'll see plenty o'fog i' Manchester, lad," she said cheerfully. "When tha blows thi snout, tha'll find soot i' thi handkerchief. Ay, Manchester's a fair scream, Manchester is."

This diagnosis of the local climate seemed to afford her pleasure, and she went cheerfully out as though she herself were the creator and proprietor of this outrageous but unique weather.

Theo was a young man of good business method. Perhaps to the end of his life he would never realize that the foundation of his character lay in the habits of order and punctuality that he inherited from his father, the bank manager. Having looked

through the *Manchester Guardian,* which he had ordered to be delivered daily, he took out his diary, wherein he had carefully entered the only engagement for the day. He could have remembered it well enough, but an engagement should be entered in a diary, and so he had entered it. "10 A.M. Call on Dunkerley and Satterfield re handbills."

When breakfast was cleared away, he smoked a pipe as he wrote a letter to Lady Pinson, giving her a full account of his Manchester impressions, including thumbnail portraits of Mr. Burnside and Mrs. Hornabrook, and ending the whole with a passage in Greek. "P.S.," he added. "I shall take you at your word, dear Lady Pinson, and inflict my scattered and doubtless superficial impressions upon you at least once a week. Oftener, if I find things unbearable and must take my burden to one whose sympathy and understanding I remember as precious. T.C."

He slipped the letter into the pillar-box where Hardiman Street joins the Stockport Road, and then heard a voice ringing through the fog: "Bloody nonsense, dragging me out on a day like this! My lungs won't stand it, Agnes."

He remembered the voice he had heard issuing last night from the back room in Palmerston Street. This surely was the same. An apparitional group slowly clarified, and he saw a tall soldierly man, a boy and two girls, and a young smiling woman. Yes; the woman was the one he had talked to on the doorstep the night before, and he recognized one of the girls as that small Grace who had darted into the house, bearing a pungent parcel of tripe. He took off his hat as the group came level with him. "Good morning, Mrs. Dunkerley," he said.

They were moving in good order. The old soldierly chap came first, with the boy's hand in his own yellow-gloved one. Behind these two was the woman, holding a girl by each hand. The woman was as loquacious as she had been the night before. "Oh good morning, Mr. Chrystal," she cried. "And I expect he's wondering, isn't he Grace, how I know his name is Chrystal? Everybody knows everything in Levenshulme and everybody knows that Mr. Burnside's new curate is called Chrystal. Sim, this is Mr. Chrystal."

The old gentleman had gone ahead. He was almost obliterated by the fog. He made no reply to Mrs. Dunkerley's chatter,
but said to the boy with him: "Come on, Laurie."

"That's Laurie," Mrs. Dunkerley felt obliged to explain.
Theo smiled, falling into step. "Yes; and who are the
others?"

"Oh I'll never stop if I start explaining who we all are!
There's Dunkerley and Satterfield of course that's my husband
and my brother, Daniel and George by name, and Sim is
Daniel's father hence Laurie's grandfather because Laurie is
my own little boy ten if he doesn't look it. Grace isn't my own
little girl. You met her last night, didn't he Grace? She's my
brother's little girl a widower but Dinah here *is*—my own little
girl I mean though only eight so that I have the two of them
Dinah and Laurie and quite enough believe me Mr. Chrystal
but how I run on!"

They had by now come within sight of Messrs. Dunkerley
and Satterfield's printing-shop. Indeed, the old man and the
boy had disappeared through its door, and Theo noted with
interest and surprise that the ignoble façade was decorated
with bunting and swags of paper flowers and little glass pots
of various colours. In each pot a candle was lit, making the
effect of what was called optimistically at that time fairy lights,
and all these lights, Theo now saw, were so arranged as to
spell out *Hard Facts*. Dimly, but unmistakably, the words
shone upon the heavy greasy darkness of the morning. A crowd
of some three or four urchins, attracted by the lure of this ad-
vertisement, stood thumbs in mouths upon the pavement.

"I'm sure I don't know what it's all about nor so far as I
can see does anybody else, do they Grace?" Agnes Dunkerley
cried. "Just be there at ten in your best clothes was all Daniel
would say to me so here we are we can't do more than obey,
can we Grace?"

Theo followed Agnes and the children Grace and Dinah
into the shop. It was only when everything was over that he
remembered he had said nothing to Daniel Dunkerley about
the handbills. This Daniel, whom he had not till then met,
was the youngish-looking thickset man with remarkably deep

violet eyes. He was dressed like an artisan in his Sunday clothes, with a rose backed by maidenhair fern in his buttonhole. Sometimes, in later years, Theo Chrystal would be smitten by a doubt whether the first Baron Dunkerley of Dickons had ever been quite so plebeian and ingenuous. He had only to look at the photograph to assure himself that it was all too true; and this photograph was itself, he would reflect, an extraordinary document of English history. How he himself came to be in it was something he was never very clear about. He could remember how he had entered the shop and how the warm gaslit air had smitten his face and how he had blown his nose and seen that Mrs. Hornabrook was literally right. A deposit of soot smudged the white linen. Then Agnes Dunkerley had erupted into introductions, and several people shook his hand, though they appeared to have no more idea of why he was there than he had of what all this excitement portended. Excitement was the outstanding impression he carried away—a sense of a lot of people talking, though, in fact, there were not many, but the small over-heated room made it seem as though there were. Looking at the photograph, brown and faded, Theo Chrystal— so different a Theo Chrystal from the boy of that morning— saw that there were no more than these: Sim Dunkerley, his son Daniel, Daniel's wife Agnes and their children Laurence and Dinah, George Satterfield and his daughter Grace, he himself, Theodore Chrystal, Alec Dillworth, and three people who were to have no further connexion of any importance with the Dunkerley saga: three printers who remained printers. That made a dozen. The room must have been smaller than he remembered, for this dozen seemed to congest it. Soon they had burst its bonds and exploded into the flash rocket that still streamed across the English sky.

At one end of the room there was a table covered by a white linen cloth decorated with trails of smilax and vases of tulips, glasses, a few bottles of champagne, cakes and sandwiches. Daniel Dunkerley passed behind this table and knocked upon it with a bottle to command silence. Then he said: "My friends. In these dingy premises something has been brought to birth:

a paper called—thanks to Alec Dillworth's inspiration—*Hard Facts*. We don't know what the outcome of this will be. George there is convinced it will be bankruptcy; my father is non-committal, but on the whole inclined to think that I have bitten off more than I can chew; Alec believes that, whether the thing succeeds or fails, we should blush to be associated with it; and as for me—well, I think the sort of paper I have produced is the sort of paper people want to buy, and in that faith——"

Alec Dillworth interrupted: "Faith?"

Theo Chrystal, who thought this the strangest company he had ever been in, and the strangest ceremony at which he had ever assisted, looked towards the interrupter and was caught by what he saw. No gleam penetrated the shop from the grim day without, and the light of a gas-burner directly above his head fell yellow upon Alec's face, upon the untidy slant of his hair across his forehead, the bony ruts and ridges and hollows of his countenance. Theo thought it was one of the most impressive faces he had ever seen, lit now by a mocking, half-affectionate, half-ironic grin. "Faith?" Alec demanded; and the man with the side-whiskers and frock coat, whom Theo understood to be George Satterfield, murmured: "Query what *is* faith?"

For an imperceptible moment Daniel Dunkerley hesitated, his eye flicking in Alec Dillworth's direction; and then he emended: "In this confidence, and in this certain opinion, it is my intention to go on with this thing to success or disaster. Not that there is much reason to fear disaster. I have a feeling in my bones that this is an important moment in the lives of all of us here present, and I ask you to drink good luck to our venture."

"We'll need it," George Satterfield declared in the brief moment of silence that followed Daniel's words; and then George moved towards the table, as though he felt that, if talking was Dan Dunkerley's line, here was his. He untwisted wires, thumbed out corks, and deftly caught the frothing wine in glasses. Theo said to Mrs. Dunkerley, who was standing next to him: "I had no idea I was intruding into a ceremony of this

sort. I'd better go now and come back later. Though really," he added with a laugh, "I feel I ought to tell Mr. Burnside that Dunkerley and Satterfield are no longer interested in handbills."

"Oh, Mr. Chrystal, you can't go now!" Agnes cried. "Here do have a glass of champagne I'm sure I never indulge in such a thing from one year's end to another but on such an occasion. . . ."

George Satterfield, with glasses on a tray, and his handkerchief on his arm in facetious imitation of a waiter's napkin, was standing before them. "Well, Ag," he said with a grin, "don't bother with a one-horse affair like a victoria. Order a carriage and pair while you're about it."

Theo took a glass and held it till everybody had been served. Then Daniel shouted: "Well, you've all got your glasses, and I invite you to drink to *Hard Facts.*"

Alec Dillworth, whose lips were already to his glass, spluttered suddenly with laughter. Theo caught his eye and was given a wink in which all Alec's amusement and contempt of the occasion seemed to be summed up. It made Theo ask himself once more what on earth *he* was doing there; and setting down his glass on the table, he approached Daniel Dunkerley. "I'm afraid I'm here under false pretences, Mr. Dunkerley. I must be off. I wish your paper luck."

"Oh, don't go yet," said Daniel. "However you got here, you're here; and I think everyone who's here ought to be in the photo. The man's due any minute. So wait, if you can, Mr. Chrystal."

Theo turned away and found that Alec Dillworth's thin arm was linked into his and that he was being drawn towards a corner of the room. "Excuse me," said Alec, "but I heard Mr. Dunkerley call you Chrystal. You'll be Mr. Burnside's new curate?"

Theo nodded, and Alec went on: "Mr. Burnside is a friend of mine. He told me you'd be coming. Well, Mr. Chrystal, what do you think of all this?"

"Really," Theo answered, "I don't know what to think. You see, I just dropped in on a matter of business and found all this going on. I don't know anything about these people or

the paper they've produced, or what backing they've got, or anything else. No, I wouldn't care to express any opinion."

Alec Dillworth went to the table and held out his glass to George Satterfield, who refilled it. He rejoined Theo and took a gulp. The unaccustomed wine warmed him through, brought a slight glow into his sallow cheeks and a gleam into his eye. He took Theo familiarly by the lapel and looked up into his face. The young parson was a foot taller than he. "Well, let me give you *my* opinion, Mr. Chrystal," he said. "All these people" —he waved a thin yellowish hand—"are soon going to be rolling in it—yes, rolling. Do you see that chap there—the one who made the speech? You may think he's a suet pudding . . ."

"Oh, no," Theo protested mildly; and, George Satterfield passing at that moment with a bottle, Alec signalled and had his glass refilled. He gulped again, and then held up the glass to the gaslight. "You will observe, Mr. Chrystal," he said, "the beaded bubbles winking at the brim. Until this morning I never realized—except imaginertively," he amended, rocking a little, "what a perfect line that was. I have never drunk champagne before. Now I perceive the bubbles are bearded—excuse me—*beaded,* and they wink. If they were bearded and wunk they would be satyrs. But they are bubbles—mere beaded bubbles. Very well: I am in wine and I shall prophesy."

He went to the table, put down his glass with a vehemence that snapped the stem, and then returned to Theo. "Very well," he said. "Suet pudding. I say that man is not suet pudding. That man is Force. And that man George Satterfield is not the fool he looks."

Theo protested again and sought to move away, but Dillworth held to his lapel and kept his eyes earnestly on his face. "That man," he said, "is Restless Energy. He worked for this business till there was nothing more he could do. End of the tether. So now he looks a fool. But now between them they've started something: the damndest, silliest, cheapest, lousiest thing that was ever started on earth. And it will go on and on and on and on and on, because people are the damndest, silliest, cheapest, lousiest things." He rocked again, wrenching Theo's lapel. "I am *telling* you, Mr. Chrystal," he said, "because

I *know*. Things are revealed unto me. Despise not the day of small things, Mr. Chrystal. Behold and consider the infinite within the seed of the finite. For the tulips and smilax think of orchids; for these few people think of table after table lined with faces; for Mr. Dunkerley banging on that table with a bottle think of a toastmaster, and think of Mr. Dunkerley himself in a fine stiff white shirt. For Mr. Chrystal think of the Archbishop of Canterbury, sitting beside Mr. Dunkerley and blessing his ventures: not because they are less cheap and lousy but because now they are successful. For Levenshulme think of London. We are, Mr. Chrystal, on the eve, as they say, of great things: which is to say, being interpreted, that one more mob is off on a money-making ramp. I am tight, my dear Theodore, tight as a newt, but *in vino veritas*. Mine eyes have seen the glory of the coming of the lord. Lord Dunkerley."

He returned unsteadily to the table, picked up the foot and stem of his broken glass, and held them hopefully towards George Satterfield. George grinned and shook his head, and Alec, waving the fragments above his head, shouted in a thin cracked voice: "Ladies and gentlemen, I give you an egg on toast: Lord and Lady Dunkerley and all the honourable little Dunkerleys. Long may they rain cats and dogs."

Dan Dunkerley took him by the arm and sat him in a chair, and then the photographer arrived.

As the door swung open Theo was aware of the undiminished gloom of the morning. A vague iridescence from the fairy lights painted the street's opacity. A swirl of greenish-yellow fog came coldly into the room as the photographer bungled in the doorway with his camera in one hand and tripod in the other. There would be some picturesque matter, Theo reflected, in his next letter to Lady Pinson, and thinking of her and of Sussex in summertime, he was overcome suddenly with nausea in the heat of that congested room, with the unholy Stygian street without, and endlessly stretching away on all hands the great black mysterious city of which thus far he had seen nothing. He felt as though he were among a strange race, and he wanted to go back to the privacy of his room in

Hardiman Street to adjust, in quiet, his mind to sensations so perplexing. He moved once more towards the door, but the photographer, straddling out his tripod just within it, was barring his way, and Daniel Dunkerley took his arm, holding out a box of cigars.

Theo was able to recall clearly, whenever he looked at that old picture, his feeling of being a perfect fool. The photographer belonged to the symmetrical school of his art. It was he who had composed the picture, leaving nothing to chance. In the back row he stood five men. Sim was in the middle, the centre forward as it were, with Daniel and George playing right and left wing. Theo was the outside right, and Alec the outside left. Sitting on chairs in front of these were Agnes, with Grace and Dinah on either hand. Little Laurie stood at his mother's knee, half slumped across it, and squatting on the floor in front of this half-back line were the three printers, their legs precisely and identically crossed. Every one of these twelve people held a copy of the first issue of *Hard Facts*.

It took the photographer some time to achieve this grouping to his satisfaction. His head kept popping in and out of its little black tent, lined with red silk, his eyes peering through the lens as his hand motioned this person a shade to the right, that, an inch to the left. At length the masterpiece was as he wanted it. He emerged for the last time, slipped in the plate, and stood with one hand on the bulb, the other on the shutter, ready to remove it. "Now, look steadily into the camera, please." Off came the shutter, and at that moment Alec Dillworth lifted his copy of *Hard Facts* and held it before his face. The whole thing had to be done again; but somehow Alec obtained from the photographer some prints of the first plate. It was he who gave the copy to Theo. It was this copy that Theo always kept, showing little Alec, so short that he is standing beside George on a small box, and wearing instead of a face the cover of *Hard Facts*. The picture is inscribed in Alec's hand: "Obliteration of a Poet."

And now, thought Theo, I really must go. There was all the parish of St. Ninian's, as it seemed to him, claiming his atten-

tion, and he wasting his first morning. With no farewells, he slipped through the door into the murk of the Stockport Road. The public was unaware of the portent that had come to birth. Not a soul stood on the pavement outside the shop. Even the few scarecrow children who had been there, attracted by the fairy lights, when he went in, had disappeared into whatever habitations the surrounding night held for them. It was an unpropitious day for investigating the parish. Perhaps, he thought, he had better go back to Hardiman Street and re-assemble his disordered mind. A few drays with their lamps palely glowing ground slowly past him and an occasional pedestrian materialized suddenly, was seen, was gone, foundered in that silent all-enveloping sea.

A light patter of footsteps sounded on the pavement behind him. It was that birdlike creature Dillworth, with the tiny feet and hands, the starved body, and beautiful irregular face.

Dear Lady Pinson:—I have already written to you today, and you will no doubt think that I should now be out and about, learning something of this parish. But I can't find the parish: it has disappeared: it is sunk in the bottom of the sea: it is gone up into peculiarly murky clouds: it has banged a very dark and heavy door in my face and left me outside. In other words, over the whole place there is such a fog as you, in your blessed climate, cannot begin to imagine. Fortunately, my landlady understands the importance of a good fire. It, and the gaslight, at midday, are helping to dissipate the gloom, although the fire, no doubt, is also adding to it as its smoke belches from the chimney. Isn't it characteristic of human life that our remedies should aggravate our diseases?

Well, here I am, just back from a most remarkable adventure. I had to call this morning, on Mr. Burnside's behalf, at a printer's office near here, and when I arrived the whole place was festively decorated and the families of the printers were present in their Sunday clothes. It seems that I had arrived just at the moment when a new weekly journal, called *Hard Facts,* was to be launched on the world. I need not weary you with an account of the crude festivity that accompanied the launch.

A man named Daniel Dunkerley, thirtyish I should think, seems to be the leading spirit, but he looks to me the sort of fellow who would be well advised to stick to handbills and circulars. I have had a chance since getting back here to look at this journal he has produced, and it is really of an unbelievable crudity. What are we to do about our working-classes? Believe me, dear Lady Pinson, I would not bore you with all this if it hadn't its serious side. Here are all these people learning to read and to write. Their education, such as it is, costs the country something, and anybody like this man Dunkerley is then entitled to make use of the minds, prepared by public money, as blotting paper to be charged a penny a time for the privilege of absorbing his ink.

And such ink! Happily, this journal is so fantastically, almost farcically, bad that even the working-classes, I imagine, will reject it. Let me give you some idea of it. The first page is filled with "facts"—such facts! Information, which may or may not be accurate, about such idiotic matters as the speed with which one pair of herrings, if they had the Atlantic to themselves, would populate its waters! Another page is devoted to a short story—wisely unsigned. Then there is the first of a series of articles to be called "The Apparatus of Government," not, as one might have hoped, something to interest the people in the inwardness of the matter, but mere external detail. This first article, for example, is called "The Mace," and is filled up with all the old stuff about taking away the bauble, and so forth. There is another series of articles on "Famous British Regiments," historically worthless. "Great British Cities" is yet another. It begins with Manchester, and here I must confess I learned an interesting fact or two. But you can readily see that this is merely an attempt to spread the circulation of the sheet. Bradford is promised its photograph for next week, and Wolverhampton for the week after. I suppose a guinea a time paid to a hack in the local newspaper office is all that is required here. There is an article on "Great Writers and Their Hobbies" and the usual "helpful" articles: on the keeping of hens in the backyard, simple medical advice, and so forth.

You begin to see the sort of thing it is. What horrified me was that the readers are promised a weekly "sermon-talk," whatever that may mean, by one Phillip Strong, D.D., whom I imagine to be a myth. His name certainly is not in Crockford. Doctor Strong's discourse this week is on "The Message of the Flowers," and is a platitudinous piece of semi-nonsense.

Strangely enough, there is one excellent thing in the paper: a poem by a young man named Alec Dillworth. I met this youth at the affair this morning, and though the champagne went to his head I was inclined to like him. We walked home together, and he told me some facts about this new journal. The man Dunkerley is the general presiding genius, and his brother-in-law, named Satterfield, looks after the advertising side, and certainly, so far as advertisements go, this first issue has nothing to complain of. Dillworth himself is the editor, at a salary of four pounds a week, which seems to him to be wealth untold and also to be a traitor's pay, for he has a very just understanding of the rubbish which this paper is. At times he is very quiet, at others madly boastful. For example, he informed me quite seriously this morning that he is a better poet than Rossetti!

Poor fellow! He seems to have had a hard life with brutal drunken parents. I see clearly that it is the prospect of leaving them which has induced him to sink all he hoped to do and take this absurd editorship. He has rented a small house, and asked me to help him to carry some of his books there. The place we called at to get the books was indescribable, and rendered the more horrible by the fog. We went up an uncarpeted stairway between greasy walls to Dillworth's bedroom, and each of us took up a portmanteau stuffed with books. On the landing, Dillworth tapped at a door and muttered, "Come on, Else." A girl came out, and she, too, was carrying a portmanteau. She was rather an extraordinary creature, very tall and thin, with the reddest hair I have ever seen. Her face was white and her lips so red that, if such a thing were not incredible, I would swear they were painted. We all three went down the stairs together, somehow furtively, as though we were escaping. I carried the books to Dillworth's little house and

promised to go and have tea some day with him and his sister.
He lives not far from here.

Well, dear Lady Pinson, what a rigmarole! But I feel I've
done my duty, and that when this detestable fog clears I shall
be able to go forth and take my bearings without feeling that
I am neglecting you. I do not expect to have anything more to
tell you about *Hard Facts*—except, no doubt, in a few weeks'
time, that it has swallowed whatever capital Mr. Dunkerley
may have and left him penniless. In return for all this verbiage
from the heart of gloom, send me some tidings of dear Sussex,
and believe me to be your devoted friend,

Theodore Chrystal.

On one of the windowpanes at the printing-works a bill was
pasted: "*Hard Facts*. Editorial and Advertising Offices opposite." The premises thus indicated had been until recently a
small private house. On the door of the front room downstairs
was painted: "Mr. Alec Dillworth, Editor"; on the door of
the front room upstairs: "Mr. George Satterfield, Advertise-
ment Manager." Behind George Satterfield's room was one
labelled "Mr. Daniel Dunkerley, General Manager"; and behind Alec was "Mr. Simon Dunkerley," functions undefined.
In what had been the kitchen dwelt two boys wearing navy
blue uniforms, red-piped down the trouser-legs. They were
furnished with peaked caps, upon which, as well as upon their
upstanding coat-collars, were the words "Hard Facts." They
looked as though this were an accurate definition of themselves.
One or other of them answered with a shambling reluctance
whenever, from any room, downstairs or up, someone shouted
"Boy!"

It is immemorially established in newspaper practice that
editorial offices may look like dustbins but that the advertise-
ment departments must shine like prosperity's mirror with
polished mahogany and bevelled glass. It had not yet come to
this with *Hard Facts,* but at all events George Satterfield's room
was the only one in which some money had been spent on
furniture and decoration. It had a red and blue Indian rug on
the floor and a divan in front of the fire. The walls had been

stripped and painted white. George worked at a large mahogany desk in the window, and at a smaller mahogany desk he had, as he put it, "installed" a clerk.

Just inside the front door of this house a gadget was attached to the passage wall. The names of the four great men were painted on it and a slide obliterated the word "In" when they were out and the word "Out" when they were in. On this April day in 1885, when *Hard Facts* was four weeks old, the indicator said that Alec Dillworth, Editor, was "Out," and Alec was sitting in his editorial room with his feet on the trestle table. He was punctilious to indicate his absence whenever he was present and his presence whenever he was absent. "If people are such damn fools that they can't open a door and look," he said, "that's their affair." The room was in a fearful state of litter. Alec had been amazed to discover the tremendous literary ambition of Great Britain. Daniel Dunkerley had advised him that the "Hard Facts," that tricky first page which had been expected to give so much trouble, would solve its own difficulties once a small prize was offered. This was too true; but Alec had not expected the short stories three times as long as anything that could be used, the manuscript novels, the articles, the poems, that descended upon his little room. He dealt with the poems swiftly at sight by tearing them up and throwing them on the floor, where now for a month they had been deepening like snow in a hard winter. There was no humility about Alec Dillworth. He recognized but one poet in that office: all competitors were savagely disrupted and destroyed.

He had simplified his method in other directions. The regimental histories were being written, from handbooks and encyclopædias, by Sim Dunkerley. The town histories, as Theodore Chrystal had surmised, were produced by hacks in the newspaper offices of the places concerned. Other articles came in from people, more or less expert, who were commissioned to write them. Alec himself was both Phillip Strong, D.D., and Martha Merriman who knew all that was to be known about the innumerable problems that plague a working woman's life. So there was not much needed to fill the rest of the space.

His method was to open the envelopes of contributors till he found what he wanted, and then to throw everything else, unopened, on to the floor or the trestle table or the mantel-piece. He was beginning to be troubled by letters demanding the return of articles, novels, epic poems, or some statement as to their fate; but these, too, were summarily dealt with by a flight over his shoulder, to alight where they would.

He was not unhappy. His father had been arrested for burgling a cotton merchant's office, and as this was not the first offence there was hope that he would disappear for a useful stretch of time. Mrs. Dillworth, unable to keep up the house now that both Elsie and her husband were gone, had departed to join some relatives in Bacup. And so, for Alec, the sky at the moment seemed clear. There had been some diffi-culty about setting up the small house he had taken for himself and Elsie, but Daniel Dunkerley had lent him fifty pounds, to be repaid within a year by the deduction of a pound a week from his salary. The possession of this fifty pounds had gone to Alec's head. He had never before handled so much money, and it promised the possibility of all sorts of tricks. To begin with, the sight of the two errand boys in their labelled uniforms filled him with derisive delight. From the tailor who had made the suits he ordered one for himself, red piping down the trousers and all, and with the words "Editor, Hard Facts" on collar and cap. This opened a major crisis in the new offices. George Satterfield, who was in a state of nerves at what he still considered to be the reckless adventure into which Daniel Dunkerley had led them all, summoned Daniel and Sim to his room and demanded Alec's instant dismissal. The whole business, he said, was trembling on a pin-point. It was touch-and-go for the future of all of them. What was going to happen if some important advertiser called and saw Dillworth playing the ape and making everybody a laughing-stock? It was with difficulty that Daniel soothed him down. Daniel believed in Alec Dillworth, and fortunately Sim believed in Daniel. And thus Alec, who while the interview lasted, was happily at work below, his uniform on, his cap on his head, and the two office-boys grinning at him through a chink in the door, escaped the

swift disaster that would have overtaken him had Satterfield alone been concerned. Daniel said nothing to Alec, but he said a lot to Elsie Dillworth, knowing well who was the strongest influence in Alec's life. So now Alec wore the uniform as knockabout clothes in his own house; and in the office of *Hard Facts* he played the part of a real editor with an open-necked Byronic shirt that almost exposed his navel, flowing hair, and, for the streets, a flopping black sombrero and a plaid cape. He nearly collapsed with hidden glee when George Satterfield, meeting him thus arrayed on the office doorstep, said with approval: "That's better, Alec. Try to look the part."

Daniel Dunkerley had forgotten all about the young parson who had been present at the birth of *Hard Facts* till the day when he went to warn Elsie Dillworth that Alec's humours must be restrained. He was then a little surprised to find that Elsie was giving tea to the Rev. Theodore Chrystal. That was not the first time she had done so.

My dear Lady Pinson:—You see, I cannot help beginning that way. But if you must address me as your dear Theo and sign yourself my Adela, well, so much the happier I. But my sense of indebtedness to you, which is very real, puts you in my mind in a position which is different from any I could ever hope to hold in yours. And now my indebtedness deepens! What was my surprise last week to receive a letter from your brother! "Adrian Chanctonbury" is an august signature to present itself to the eyes of a curate! And over so friendly and encouraging a letter! Your brother is right, of course, about the importance of these great industrial parishes and sees. I suppose in this one town there are almost as many souls as once there were in the whole province of York: an exhilarating and yet somehow terrifying thought. You may depend—for I am sure your kindness is behind your brother's letter—that I shall use to the full the opportunities I have here.

I have not wasted the last three weeks. After the Stygian and sulphurous couple of days that greeted me, the weather has improved, though it is hardly weather at all as you would

understand the word in dear Sussex. But at least I have been able to see from one side of the street to the other, to walk without crashing into lampposts, and to gain some idea of the immensity of this town. Though I give the place my labour, I fear I shall never give it my love. Mr. Burnside has been very undemanding and has allowed me all the time there is for endless peregrinations. Well, I have dutifully trudged the heart of the place and all its tentacles and find it a stony wilderness without oases. I say this not as a complaint but as a fact. Who am I to complain? It is not for me to choose the corner of the vineyard, but to labour wherever the Lord's work calls me.

In my personal circumstances I am comfortable enough— perhaps too grossly comfortable. My landlady is alarmed by my Friday fast, and even Mr. Burnside is uninterested in it. I find him a good colleague, if his ways are hardly those I should wish to follow myself. His services are "low," and he is not much concerned about church attendance. I have done a great deal of visiting with him during the last three weeks, and I have not once heard him invite a person to a service. "In this parish," he says, "I am the Church—not that ugly building on the corner. If they come to me, that's all right. You know, my dear Chrystal, Jesus Christ never said 'Come unto Church.' He said 'Come unto Me.'" I'm not sure that I liked this comparison, but certainly plenty of them come to him. I have told you about Alec Dillworth, the youth who edits that atrocious paper *Hard Facts*. I am always finding Alec at Mr. Burnside's, and the other night, to my surprise, I found his sister there. She is the girl I told you about who keeps house for Alec. He is only eighteen, and she is a little younger. I told you how I helped them to shift some books and how Alec asked me to come in and have tea with them some day. I went, and I think the poor girl was unused even to so simple a social occasion. She had dressed herself up as if to entertain a bishop to dinner. Alec is frank, and confessed that he had borrowed fifty pounds in order to furnish his house and had given twenty of them to Elsie to buy clothes. If I am any judge, she had bought with an intelligent sense of her own appearance. She was wearing a long simple pale-green frock, which was just the

thing with her striking red hair and her eyes which really are green. One often hears of green eyes, but hers really *are*. She seemed very constrained and ill at ease, poor girl, but I am glad to see that she and Alec have a nice little home. Mr. Burnside hints that their lives have been tragically unhappy.

When I met Elsie Dillworth at Mr. Burnside's the other night, he was, of all things! teaching her to play the violin. She left when I arrived, and when I asked Mr. Burnside if she were a promising pupil he said: "I don't know, but perhaps it's her way to Heaven." That's the sort of man he is!

Well, dear Lady Pinson, your missioner to Ultima Thule must bring his present report to an end, there being nothing to add but that the fantastic *Hard Facts,* so Alec Dillworth assures me, has leapt to a circulation of nearly 100,000 copies and the printing has already been transferred from Mr. Dunkerley's flat-bed press to hired rotary machinery in town. The senselessness of the world! *Votre serviteur devoué,* Theodore Chrystal.

Chapter Five

AGNES DUNKERLEY didn't know whether she
wanted to laugh or cry. She would have to do one or the
other before she was fit for the ordeal before her. To
think that breakfast could be an ordeal! But it was to be such
a breakfast!

All my life I've been happy, Agnes thought. I've lived in
Levenshulme all my life, single and married. It's an appalling
place, but I've been happy there. She could not remember a
single day since she had married Daniel, except when she was
bearing the children, when she had not got up and cooked
Dan's breakfast. Eggs and bacon, or a bit of fish, fried potatoes,
Marmalade, bread-and-butter, good strong tea. She had liked
doing it. She had liked the way Dan had of coming into the
kitchen, his face fresh and rosy from shaving, his blue-black
eyes twinkling with morning good-humor. "Well, lass, what
is it today? 'Pon my soul, eggs and bacon!" She couldn't count
the hundreds of times he had said that, as though her tiny
morning repertory were constantly producing new and startling and satisfying effects. It had happened only yesterday
morning. For May, it was unusually warm. The kitchen in the
little Palmerston Street house was stuffy. Through the open
window she could see the black wall at the end of the garden
that was only a dozen yards long. She could see the elderberry
tree which had achieved its yearly miracle of green leaf, never
followed in that blighted atmosphere by flower or fruit; and
beyond the wall she could see the windows of the Hardiman
Street houses. A thousand times she had thought it inexpressibly harsh and chilling, and had longed for change, for space,
for sun, especially now that the children were growing up;
but that morning, with a milky blue sky stretched even over
the roofs of Levenshulme, it was all so dear and accustomed
that she could think of nothing but the pangs of parting and
of the happiness she had known in the little house. She remem-

bered the day when Laurie was born, and Daniel was waiting downstairs. No one had told him, and he had suddenly rushed into the bedroom shouting "Is that his voice?" Then he had kissed her, and she remembered nothing more except passing out to the tinny Hallelujah Chorus of St. Ninian's bells.

Things like that she was remembering when Daniel came in and said: " 'Pon my soul—eggs and bacon!" He took his place at the table, looked across at her with a grin, and said: "Aren't you tired of cooking 'em? Well, this is the last time."

She stood at the kitchen window, looking out, her back to him. And suddenly he was at her side, and had swung her round to face him. "I know," he said. "I know."

Then she cried a little in a sharp access of misery, and he said: "It's going to be all right, Ag. Don't worry. Everything's going to be all right. Thank you for all you've done here. You'll do just as well there. When I was a kid, Sim used to say: 'A man can be what he wants to be,' and so he can. And so can a woman. So can you." He patted her cheek and kissed her, and then she felt better and carried Sim's breakfast to his room upstairs. Laurie and Dinah were still asleep. She came down, and she and Dan ate their last breakfast in Palmerston Street. The May sunshine was as tender and gentle as all their life there together had been.

It was like Daniel to have said nothing till all was settled. For months now no one could doubt that *Hard Facts*, whatever else it might be, was something that would incredibly enrich those associated with it. As Theodore Chrystal had so punctually told Lady Pinson, it had become necessary to hire a rotary printing press in the heart of Manchester. Soon this press was devoted to nothing but the production of *Hard Facts*. At the end of the year a million copies of the paper were printed every week. The offices, too, had moved into hired rooms in Manchester. But all this hiring was soon to end. A site had been leased not far from the Cathedral, and Dunkerley and Satterfield were in daily consultation with the architect who was planning the premises that would be wholly theirs.

Things being thus, George Satterfield was amused to find

Daniel Dunkerley still living in Palmerston Street. He had
solved his own problems swiftly. His child Grace' was sent off
to a boarding-school in the Lake District. There was then but
himself to think of. He was quick, was George, to exploit a
situation for his own good; and when, among his business
acquaintances, he heard that Fred Mirfield, a cotton man who
had recently died, had not been so rich as was generally supposed, he saw how this might help him. He had known
Mirfield slightly, had been, indeed, once or twice to his house
at Bowdon. It was a nice little place. Nearly everything in it
was of the best, and the garden, a couple of acres, looked across
fine open country towards Knutsford. Mirfield's daughter,
Millie, he remembered as a woman of fifty, tall, thin, and as
fine as the old well-worn silver in the house. She was too old
for what George called to himself "nonsense." Mirfield had had
his horse and carriage; and when George heard that these had
been sold, the gardener dismissed, and the indoor staff reduced
to one girl, he made his call upon Millie Mirfield. The poor
thing, he found, had been thinking of the very idea that he
had now come to expound. But there had seemed to her something shameful in the idea of "taking in lodgers." George put
it in quite another way. He and Millie would be "jointly
responsible" for running the place. But it was really as a
lodger that he went there. He paid five pounds a week, had two
excellent furnished rooms, with the use of a bedroom for
Grace when she should be on holiday, and both he and Millie
Mirfield were satisfied. His rooms had a fine sweeping view,
good furniture, and what he considered to be first-rate pictures.
In fact, the finest of them were a Landseer and an Alma-
Tadema not in the best of taste. But, as George would have
said: Query what *is* taste? As for Millie, relieved of immediate
anxiety, she considered herself a lucky woman, and confided
this to God when she prayed in the church that stood on a
ridge looking magnificently across the great sweep of the
Cheshire plain.

It was in June, three months after *Hard Facts* was founded,
that George took his rooms in Bowdon, and, for town con-
venience, had himself elected a member of the Manchester

Constitutional Club. Daniel Dunkerley remained in Palmerston Street. He was a rich man already, and there were schemes in his head, known to none but himself and Alec Dillworth, by which he confidently expected to be richer yet. "When I set up house," he said when George Satterfield pressed him, "it will be a *house*. I can afford to take my time."

Didsbury. That was where he wanted to live. It was but five miles from the heart of Manchester, it was on the main road, and it was open country still. And, with the touch of romance that underlay his hard and practical mind, he remembered a day when Sim had taken him, a child, to Didsbury: a day in a Whitweek that seemed incredibly remote, a day of flowering hawthorns and laburnums, with double pink cherries glimpsed over an old brick wall, and the tender green of young beech misting the air. They had sat on the banks of the twisting Mersey River, and Sim, spreading out on its paper the bread and cheese he had taken from his pocket, said: "Now this is what I *call* a place to live in."

Well, thought Dan, when he heard that the White House was in the market, perhaps Didsbury would never be quite what it had seemed to his young eyes; but Dinah's eyes and Laurie's were as young now as his had been then, and, by gosh! he'd see that they had something better than Palmerston Street and the Stockport Road to rest upon.

When he first inspected the White House, the day was nothing like that far-off day in Whitweek. It was a day of March: it was the day, he remembered with a thrill of fate, that was the first anniversary of the birth of *Hard Facts*. Saying nothing to anyone, he had walked over to Didsbury alone. Off the Wilmslow Road he turned into a rough lane that ran down to the Mersey meadows. Almost, you might have been in the heart of the country. On his left was a long brick wall with the elephant-grey trunks of beech-trees towering above it, glistening with wet, their bare branches dripping upon the lane a distillation of the mist that crept over the landscape from the near-by river. On the right were the fields that belonged to the White House. He looked for a long time at the house, which stood on a grassy bank whence the view

would take in the not-far-distant tower of Northenden Church. It was a square, white-painted stucco house, bigger than he had remembered. For just a moment he had a sharp feeling of panic. "It's daft. It's damn well daft—from Palmerston Street to this," he said aloud. There was no one to hear him. Only the drip, drip of the mist in the lane broke the wintry silence. Then he pushed open the long white wooden gate and walked resolutely up the drive towards the house.

The lawyers had told him that he would find Mrs. Dobkin there. She had been for years old Slattery's housekeeper. They had told him about old Slattery, too: one of those tyrannous fools whom no one can live with. His wife had left him. His son, treated in his early twenties as though he were both an infant and an imbecile, had walked out and never come back. And now the old fool had died, as such old fools do, lonely, neglected, and forgotten. All—the house and the furniture—had been left to the son, now a man of forty and himself wealthy. He had written to the lawyers from South Africa: "Sell the lot. I never want to drink from a cup that touched his lips. I never want to stand in a room that his spirit darkened. I never want to see my face in a mirror that even for a second reflected his. And when you've sold it, don't send me the money. I wouldn't use a penny of his to save my soul from hell. Give it to the following charities."

These were lugubrious things to remember in the chill and damp of a March afternoon, with the day's short light fading fast. "Now if I were a lawyer," Dan reflected in his business-like way, "I wouldn't tell customers stories like that—not till after they'd bought the property, anyway." And then he was at the front of the house. A gravelled drive separated it from the grassy bank that sloped sharply down to the field. Beyond this field, though he could not from here see them, were the meadows through which the Mersey carved its swift tortuous way, and beyond these meadows, sure enough, he could see the squat sandstone tower of Northenden Church blocked against a pallor in the sky, which was all there would be today to show for sunset.

He liked the silence, the sense of space and isolation. He

liked the great trees, reaching the thin pattern of their winter boughs into the sky. Only the harsh rasp of the gravel beneath his feet broke the stillness. From the gravel two short flights of stone steps, one on either side of the portico which contained a handsome and highly polished mahogany door, led down the bank to a lawn, separated from the meadow by a half-circle of white-painted iron railings. There was a flower-bed or two, winter-bare now, in the lawn, and a weeping ash that would make a pleasant green umbrella to sit under on a hot day. Sitting there, he would be able to watch Dinah and Laurie in the meadow, tanning their skins with sunshine, riding ponies perhaps. Yes: ponies would be possible. And on this lawn Agnes could entertain people to agreeable tea-parties. He could see them coming down the stone steps from the gravel: some of the big advertisers George was after; Alec Dillworth, of course, who was so much more important than George or any of the rest of them suspected. Perhaps that young chap Chrystal, the parson. (That chap was going to get on, thought Daniel, who prided himself on being able to assess the poten-tialities of the people he met.) These to begin with. There would soon be others.

He was about to step under the portico and ring when a lighted window farther along the front of the house caught his eye. He walked towards it and looked into a room whose curtains had not been drawn. And his heart lifted within him. "I don't care," he thought, "if the Devil himself has been living in a room like that. It suits me."

It would have suited most people. He came to know it later as the small drawing-room. A fire burned behind a shining brass fender in a white marble fireplace. There were pictures, books, chintz-covered furniture; and a lamp was burning on a table near a chair in which an old lady sat. There was another small table before her, and on this were tea-things of silver and a plated muffin-dish. She sat between him and the lamp, her face in profile, and it was a homely, pleasing face. Mrs. Dobkin, no doubt. Mrs. Dobkin, if she would stay, looked the sort of person who would get on with Agnes, he reflected with satisfaction.

And then he saw that, as Mrs. Dobkin drank her tea and ate her muffin, she was reading a copy of *Hard Facts*. He turned sharply away from the window, his mind suddenly engaged with the phenomenon he had called into being. That room in which Mrs. Dobkin sat, and all the rooms in this great house whose whiteness was rapidly becoming a mothy glimmer as the last light drained from the west—all this could be his, probably would be his, because a million Mrs. Dobkins every week bought *Hard Facts*. When they had read it, it would go to light the fire, or line a shelf, or wrap a back-street butcher's meat. There was not a thing in it that anyone would want to keep to remember. It was perhaps the most transient and evanescent publication that had ever been given to the British people; but on the weekly recurrence of this triviality his strength and power were based. A million pennies a week. He had discovered that, with this hard fact as an argument, he could raise what money he liked where he liked. And the million pennies were not the end of it. The spenders of the million pennies were there as George Satterfield's backing when he sold his space to advertisers. And George certainly knew how to sell his space. Even to Daniel Dunkerley, who had seen it all coming, confidently plotted for it to come, there was something a little daunting in the result of this one year's work. And on that anniversary night, as he trod the gravel before the White House windows, there was for the first time a doubt, almost a twinge of shame, when he looked on the one side at what he was giving, and on the other at what he was getting. *But this isn't the end,* he reflected. *No, by George, this isn't anything like the end. They'll get something worth having. But not yet. Give me time. I must have time.*

Then he rang the bell, heard for the first time what was to be the familiar peal in the depths of the house.

"I'm sorry to disturb you at your tea, Mrs. Dobkin. I peeped through the window and saw you at it. Now please finish it, and let me help you to dispose of a muffin or two."

Mrs. Dobkin had been warned by the lawyers to expect a call. She had worried a good deal about the sort of caller it

was to be, and this pleasant speech, and Dan Dunkerley's smiling blue eyes, seemed to her better than anything she had expected. "Damn it all, Dobkin, draw the curtains before you guzzle, and guzzle in your own room." Something like that Mr. Slattery would have said. And here was this very young-looking man—just a boy she thought him—drawing the curtains with his own hands, returning to the fireplace, and saying: "I've left this call terribly late, Mrs. Dobkin. But it's not a bad idea to see a room by firelight and lamplight. The look of it that way is just as important as the way it looks in cold daylight."

He talked on; he even poured out a fresh cup of tea for her; he made her feel easy and comfortable. He himself carried the lamp when they made a tour of the house. It was a sketchy tour, because something had told Daniel, before his foot crossed the threshold, that this place would be his. And a casual glance over the principal rooms showed him that, if Mr. Slattery's temper had been vile, his taste had been faultless. Linen, glass and cutlery, pictures, books, furniture: oh, it was great luck, he reflected, not to have the bother of accumulating these things, but simply to take possession of a collection made by somebody who knew what he was after. It was all such splendid stuff that it would cost a pretty penny; but he thought with a grin of the million pretty pennies rolling in each week.

"And now, Mrs. Dobkin, the bathroom," he said. But, said Mrs. Dobkin, there was no bathroom. A house boy had carried up water every night before dinner to a tub in Mr. Slattery's dressing-room. Dan looked at her in mock consternation. "Then you must be prepared, Mrs. Dobkin," he said, "to see this house considerably torn about. I've never yet in my life had a bathroom, but, if you'll pardon the expression, I'm damned if I'll live in a place of this size without one. Indeed, without three. There shall be three bathrooms, and where they are to be we'll discuss later on. And another thing, Mrs. Dobkin. I don't know whether there is a private house in Manchester lit by electricity. But this one will be. We'll need our own plant." (He was half talking to himself.) "Very well. We shall have our own plant. And what is more, those bath-

rooms and that electric light will have to be installed within
the next two months. I can see I shall be pretty busy chasing
people about."

Mrs. Dobkin, thinking it all over when he was gone, decided
that the idea of chasing people about had seemed pleasant
to Mr. Dunkerley. And indeed it was. When his own rather
slow-moving mind was finally made up, nothing would change
the decision he had arrived at; and then it was a great pleasure
to him to chase people round, causing them to do in days what
he had thought about for years. Not that he had cogitated for
long about the bathrooms and electric light. The idea had
come to him in a flash. Agnes's birthday was in May. He would
give her this house, and, by gosh! it would be the sort of house
you didn't see every day. Three bathrooms and electric light!

Theo Chrystal wrote to Lady Pinson:

My dear Adela:—To see you and dear Sussex again will be
an inexpressible joy. Mr. Burnside is permitting me to be
away for the first fortnight of next month, and your command,
which you are so kind as to call an invitation, will be promptly
and happily obeyed. We will read Greek together again, and
you will enchant me with your music. After more than a year
in Ultima Thule I have earned a respite in Arcadia.

Even here, though, an Arcadian moment may be snatched.
You will be surprised to hear that at six this morning I was
walking along the Stockport Road, admiring the sunlight
gilding the by-no-means lovely spire of St. Ninian's. I could
not but think of May Morning as I once knew it during a visit
to Oxford and the young voices raised on Magdalen tower
in praise of beauty. The contrast was sharp, but one should
accept where one finds it such overflow of God's bounty as
He chooses to vouchsafe.

I had been invited by Daniel Dunkerley to breakfast at his
new house. You do not need to ask who Daniel Dunkerley is:
I have told you enough about him during this last year and
more! I perhaps misjudged him at the beginning. He certainly
has the power of doing what he sets out to do, and I suppose
he has already become one who, by his stewardship of riches,

should receive particular attention from those who would see riches rightly used—that is to say, for God's glory.

He has bought a large house at Didsbury, and it was his whim to invite a number of people to breakfast. At that hour of the morning there was nothing to do but walk, and I had arranged to go with Alec Dillworth and his sister Elsie, who had both been invited. I have told you a good deal about Alec, too: an utterly unpredictable person, madly joyous at one moment, depressed the next, and all these emotions struggling in a body as fragile as a tom-tit's. Outside St. Ninian's, where I had arranged to meet them, I found Miss Dillworth alone. . . .

"Alec isn't coming," she said simply. "He asked me to give you this note." She was dressed in white muslin, the flounced skirt almost sweeping the pavement. She wore no hat, and her red hair was in a loose pile on her head. A parasol of alternate green and white flounces dangled from her gloved hand. They had met often during the last year, usually at Alec's small house or at Mr. Burnside's; Theo had not before met her alone. "My dear Chrystal," the note said. "I'm an editor, not a lackey. Damn his new house. How he'll love showing it off and impressing you all with the great man he is! He talked to me about his library. I hope he'll paper it with pages of *Hard Facts,* just to remind himself what bunkum it's all founded on. Anyway, I sha'n't be there to pander to his vanity. I advise you to tell Elsie to get back home to bed, and to do the same yourself. However, if you want to go, she's a good walker."

Theo wanted to go very much indeed. "So, Alec isn't coming," he said. "He was all for it last night." She laughed, a sudden bright brittle sound in the street that was so enchanted by the quiet effulgence of the May sunshine. "Don't ever count on Alec," she said. "If it comes to that, I wouldn't be surprised to find him running after us at any moment."

Theo realized with a quickening of the pulse that the last thing he now wanted was to have Alec running after them. "Well, Miss Dillworth," he said formally, "what do you think? Should we go?"

"I'm going, anyway," Elsie said. "Please yourself."

So they set off together through the sunny silence that was broken now and then by the iron ring of clogs on the pavement as men and women passed them, bound for their work in Manchester. Most of them stared to see a young parson and a red-haired muslin-clad girl walking the streets at an hour so unaccustomed. From one group of shawled women came a gibe that Theo did not catch, followed by a gust of coarse laughter, and a shout: "Are you rescuin' 'er, mister?"

Theo was shocked. Elsie laughed—again that sudden brittle sound like thin glass breaking in the sunshine—and that shocked Theo more than the remark that had occasioned it. His cheeks burned, and his tongue was frozen. Elsie, who had eighteen years to his twenty-five, looked at him with adult compassion. "Don't worry about a saucy slut like that, Mr. Chrystal," she advised him. "I've heard worse things than that in my young life."

They walked on in silence then, and presently turned off the long dreary road into the leafy lanes of Burnage. Even the streets, even the Stockport Road, in the calm unsullied sunshine of the May morning had seemed to lie under a blessing; but now, among the rare houses, under the foliage of trees whose green was yet tender and virginal, with thrush and blackbird singing amid the boughs weighted with cherry blossom and lilac and hawthorn, Theo felt his heart uplifted and began to sing. He had a tenor voice of power and purity. He sang

> *Drink to me only with thine eyes*
> *And I will pledge with mine.*

To his surprise Elsie joined in. She sang the song right through with him, in a soprano voice as true as his own. He hadn't, somehow, expected her to know a song like that. What *did* he expect of her? What sort of songs did he expect her to know? He was aware of a puzzlement in his feelings about her. He looked sideways at her, striding along gamely at his side, and he was aware, as he had often been, of her powerful attraction. Yet there was something odd about her, too. It was a little thing, but he had never before known a woman walk in

the public streets without a hat—not, at any rate, when other-wise she was all dressed up, as Elsie was. And there were brief hints that Mr. Burnside had occasionally let fall. "I'd hate to hurt Elsie Dillworth. She's been hurt enough already." Dark saying of that sort. And that remark she had herself just uttered. "Saucy slut" was an expression he had heard often enough, but never from the women who were his friends. And what did she mean: "I've heard worse things than that in my young life?"

These things nagged in the back of Theo Chrystal's mind because Elsie looked as sweet as the flowering cherries, as virginal as the white candles burning on the chestnut trees, and he had a pleasant feeling that it would be easy to fall in love with her. They marched on now in silence save for the birdsong and the occasional cheerful clatter of a milk-float, and Theo allowed his thoughts to roam. There was nothing against marriage. It would be ridiculous on a curate's pay. All the sturdy common-sense of the bank-manager who had been his father told him that. But he would not be a curate long. He had, he knew, a pleasing way in the pulpit. Women liked him. It had been disappointing that the women who attended St. Ninian's hadn't liked him as well as the women in the South of England—women like Adela Pinson. But St. Ninian's wouldn't last for ever. It was, anyway, hardly his idea of a church. No: there would be preferment, a benefice somewhere more congenial to his talents. And there was that 150 pounds a year that was his private fortune. He had been surprised to be invited by Daniel Dunkerley to realize the capital and put it into *Hard Facts*. He had hesitated a long time about this. He had prayed about it, and he had even thought of consult-ing Mr. Burnside. But he had consulted Alec Dillworth in-stead. "Yes," said Alec, "every bean you've got. If you can borrow money to put in, do that, too. Get in now, and in a few years you'll be able to sell your shares for ten times what you give for them. But you'll be a fool if you do." He had done this a year ago, and had said nothing to any one. He felt sure that Adela Pinson would not like it; and in this perhaps he was right, though Adela Pinson's man of business would have

given his ears for so valuable a tip. Alec had promised with
a grin to keep the knowledge of the transaction to himself.
"My dear boy," he said, his little wrinkled face puckered by
mirth like a monkey's, "I would not be so blasphemous as to
emulate a famous performance and chase the money-changers
out of the temple."

"But, listen," Theo began earnestly, "money is a trust—in
my view, a sacred trust. Money confers a certain power, and
the thing is: how do we exercise that power? Now, for my
part. . . ."

Alec waved him away. "I know, I know. I could recite it all
for you myself. If you want money, my dear Chrystal, go for
it. I don't see any harm in it myself. I wish I could take the
plunge with you. Believe me, I wouldn't want to explain myself to any one. Now get out. I'm busy prostituting my soul in
order to enrich you."

For a flashing second, Theo thought there was a look of
contempt and hatred in Alec's wizened bony face. "Well,
thank you for the hint," he mumbled.

"Thank *you*," Alec said courteously. "You've given me my
theme for the Rev. Phillip Strong's next sermon: 'The Christian attitude to money.' " When Theo read the sermon he
realized that he might have written it himself.

Well, that all seemed, now, a long time ago. The unease
that had niggled at his mind for a few weeks troubled him
no longer, and he could with a happy heart occasionally make
a joke, for Adela Pinson's benefit, about the incredible production *Hard Facts*. At the moment, in the sunshine of this May
morning, the cheerful thought in his mind was that marriage,
whenever he chose to embark upon it, would not be, finan-
cially, too hazardous.

When Theo and Elsie Dillworth reached the White House
it was half-past eight, and Agnes Dunkerley was striding up
and down the gravel walk. Here were two of them, she thought,
as they came through the strengthening sunshine. It was, indeed, now quite warm. From a cloudless sky the sun shone on
the lawn, newly cut, on the brown-velvet texture of the wall-

flowers that filled the beds, on the half-circle of railings brilliant in a new coat of white, and on all the great trees that Daniel had looked upon in their winter poverty and that now were rich with leaves and clamorous with the noise of rooks. It couldn't have been lovelier, but the thought of breakfast filled her with apprehension. It would be "entertaining," that was the trouble. She and Daniel had never "entertained," and though all the people invited were almost as familiar to her as Daniel was himself, it was this idea that she was a "hostess" that fluttered her breast.

Theo shook her hand, with just that hint of an extra pressure, that infinitesimal prolonging of the grasp, that was his way with women whom he wished to please. Agnes liked it, as so many women liked it: that and the earnest deep look it was his custom to turn on their faces. "And how is Mrs. Dunkerley this most beautiful morning?" he asked. "And how is she liking this most beautiful house?"

He looked about him with appreciation: at the new white seats placed here and there upon the lawn, the gleaming stucco of the façade that had all been repainted, the door as rich and luminous as a well-groomed horse's coat.

"Oh, I'm sure, Mr. Chrystal, it's all only too good for a woman like me being what you know I was not much more than a year ago that foggy night as you well remember when you first called and Grace was coming in with the tripe for supper."

"Yes, yes, indeed," said Theo. "Great changes. Great changes. Not that I didn't see them coming, Mrs. Dunkerley. I may say that from the beginning I recognized in your husband a man who caused change to come about. Perhaps we have not yet seen the end of what it is in him to achieve. It is your privilege to forget what you were a year ago and to be always fitting your stride to his."

"But this entertaining, Mr. Chrystal! Honestly it frightens me out of my life! Food I've never cooked being served by girls I'm not to talk to Dan says but leave it all to Mrs. Dobkin."

Elsie Dillworth broke in with a laugh. "Well, really, Mrs. Dunkerley! That wouldn't worry me. I wish I had the chance. You can learn anything. I've learned a lot in the last twelve

months. I'd soon learn to be waited on hand and foot. Just
go on doing it till it comes natural. That's all there is to it."

"You're a pair of comforters, I must say," poor Agnes ran
on. "Apart from you two there'll be no one but our own
family, yet here I am scared it's just the servants."

Theo began to pace the gravel, with one of the women on
either side of him. "Servants," he laid down, "are in the
natural order of things, Mrs. Dunkerley. Indeed, we are all
servants one of another, each rendering his service according
to his station and ability. You are called now to the station
your husband has won for himself, and no doubt you will
not find it difficult to move comfortably in it."

"Well I hope so I'm sure but Dan just hates his bacon-fat
cold."

All her fluttering was needless. There was no bacon-fat.
There were no servants. Dan had told her nothing, but that's
how it turned out to be. Dan himself stuck his head out of a
window and shouted: "Hallo, Chrystal. Good morning, Miss
Dillworth. Where's the Editor?"

"He greatly regrets that he couldn't get here after all," said
Theo smoothly. "He asked me to apologize to you and Mrs.
Dunkerley."

"Like hell he did," Dan answered. "I know my Editor. Well,
come on in. Breakfast is ready."

It was a beautiful room. A long refectory table, brown as
a moorland trout stream, glossy as new gilt on a book's edge,
ran down the middle of it, and punctuating its length were
three porcelain bowls containing double tulips coloured like
honey suffused with vermilion. The lovely flowers bent their
heads over their own images which were flanked by silver
and porcelain laid out by someone who would have earned
Theo's approval as knowing the job that belonged to his
station. Old Sim Dunkerley, stiff and military-looking with
his new frock coat, his enormous skewers of moustache and
an orchid at his lapel, was standing by the sideboard talking
to George Satterfield, and Laurie and Dinah sat at the table,
looking somehow both intoxicated and subdued by the splendour about them. At either end of the table was an urn. Daniel

Dunkerley was standing before one. "Agnes," he said, "there's coffee in this urn and tea in yours. You look after that, and I'll look after this. Now help yourselves, please, from the sideboard."

Theo helped Agnes and Elsie to their chairs. He had already surveyed and approved the sideboard. "Now, Mrs. Dunkerley and Miss Dillworth, what shall I bring you?"

Agnes laid her hand on Elsie's. "It's so easy after all," she whispered. "Mr. Chrystal is a dear, I think."

George Satterfield, not to be outdone by anybody in the functions of a gentleman, was carrying thin slices of York ham for Dinah. "Laurie, my boy," he said, "you'll have to learn to do this for your sister, you know."

"Get me some," said Laurie irrelevantly. "I'm not going to school today. I can afford to be sick."

"Don't talk like a disgusting little glutton," said George severely. "You ought to send him away to school, Dan, as I've sent Grace. You remember my daughter Grace, Mr. Chrystal? You met her, I believe, the first night you were in Manchester. She often asks after the gentleman with the beautiful face."

"You must send her my devotion, Mr. Satterfield," said Theo, helping Elsie to fricassee of chicken. "Will you drink some of your own tea, Mrs. Dunkerley, or shall I bring you some coffee?"

At last he himself was seated, on Agnes's right. Elsie was opposite him. For her, he reflected, this must be a more difficult occasion than for Mrs. Dunkerley. She certainly could never in her life have been in a room like this or have eaten a meal like this. He recalled how, on that fantastic morning when *Hard Facts* first appeared, he had gone with Alec to bring books to his new house. He remembered the place they had called at, where he first saw Elsie, and the shiver of the spine it had caused him. It was not merely that it was dirty, smelly, with the walls polished by passing shoulders and the oilcloth worn into holes by trampling feet. It was not only the bedroom Alec had taken him into, where the bed, at noon, was a chaos of faintly odorous blankets, and the tattered lace curtains made a shame-faced effort to hide the squalid backyards the windows

looked upon. No: there was more in it than that. There was
a real sense of evil in that house. He would not have been
surprised to find someone hanging by a cord behind a door;
and when they had taken out the suitcases full of books and
turned a corner into another street that ran into the Stockport
Road, he felt he understood the way Alec, having dumped his
suitcases, stopped and wiped his forehead with a handkerchief,
though the day was not warm. Alec had suddenly turned to
Elsie and cried: "We're out! We're out!" as though they had
escaped from great peril or privation; and had placed a hand
quite roughly on each of Elsie's shoulders and kissed her. Theo
had felt there was a significance in the moment, but what it
was escaped him.

Well, he thought, looking now at Elsie so cool and, it
seemed, self-sufficing, in her white muslin, you are certainly a
wonderful improviser. You know how to take hold of each
moment as it comes and deal with it. It was now that Mrs.
Dobkin came into the room, sent for by Daniel, who thought
that this would be the moment to thank her publicly for the
good send-off she had given to his new way of living. He did
so, with a certain rough honesty he had that forbade him to be
merely ceremonially polite; and Mrs. Dobkin, used for years
to Slattery's grumbles and grudges, was pleased and fluttered
here and there behind the guests' chairs. She came to Elsie's,
and Elsie said: "Thank you, Mrs. Dobkin. That was the nicest
fricassee of chicken I ever tasted in my life."

Theo was enchanted. Certainly, my dear young woman, he
said to himself, you have never before tasted fricassee of
chicken. I doubt, indeed, whether you ever heard the word
till I asked you a moment ago to have some. He was pleased
with the way she had seized on the word and remembered it;
and then he wondered why he *should* be pleased whether
socially she were dexterous or clumsy. But pleased he was.
After all, he had brought her there—not by design but because
Alec was Alec; but, however it had happened, he felt responsible for her and glad that she did well.

And now, on the gravel outside the window there was the
crunch of wheels, and Theo saw a brougham go by, heard it

draw up beneath the covered portico. Daniel sprang up, dabbing a napkin to his lips and consulting his watch. "Sim—George—come along. We must be going."

Neither Sim nor George appeared to have expected the brougham. "Well, well. I have to make do with the Cheshire Lines Committee," said George, referring to the railway line on which he travelled daily from Bowdon. Daniel smiled like a conjuror with plenty more tricks in his hat and up his sleeve. "I told you, George," he said, "that when I moved from Palmerston Street I would move from Palmerston Street. That meant all that Palmerston Street was and stood for. I told you, Sim, when I first borrowed your bit of capital, that you wouldn't regret it. From now on you will drive with me to the office every morning. And remember, this isn't the end of any of us. I'm only thirty-three, and just beginning."

Old Sim stood there, rigid, unsmiling, trying to take in his stride a situation that threatened to overwhelm him. He gave Dan an unforgettable look, compounded of such love and confidence as he had never permitted to appear in his face before. His jaws worked as though he were about to speak; then he thought better of it, strode into the hall, slammed his tall hat on to his head, and walked out to the brougham. The coachman held the door open. Sim got in, and Dan, coming out a moment later, said: "No. George will sit there, Sim. You and I will face the horses."

It was a good thing that George Satterfield decided to have a look round the brougham before it started. It was he who discovered the old shoe tied to the axle by white satin ribbon. "That damn fool Dillworth is somewhere about," he shouted, cut the ribbon with a penknife, and flung it, flutteringly attached to the shoe, into a shrubbery. Alec emerged from the bushes. "A gesture wasted," he said. "It was to symbolize the marriage of *Hard Facts* to all the rich respectabilities."

George Satterfield, his sensibilities touched on the raw, was looking, his face burning with blushes, at the coachman, who was now aloft, aloof, and apparently unaware that anything out of the way was happening. Dan Dunkerley got out of the

brougham, and asked calmly: "Have you had breakfast, Alec?"

"No," said Alec. "The dogs have been licking my sores."

"Well, you can damn well do without it," said Dan. "There are plenty of oats in the stable, but we're not wasting them on asses. Get in, and come to the office. You've got your day's work before you."

"Sorry, Dan."

"It's all right. I expect it of you. These things get talked about. It means something to the paper to have an eccentric editor."

Alec sat beside the scowling George Satterfield. There was a spatter of gravel and the brougham drew away: into the leafy lane, into the Wilmslow Road, down the long straight way to Manchester. They were a silent company. Each in his own way was moved by the magnificence of Daniel's gesture: that house, this brougham, bowling along on the first of the countless times it was to take that road.

As soon as the brougham was out of sight a man appeared and began raking the gravel. Daniel had done a lot of chasing round. He had oiled many wheels.

Agnes Dunkerley persuaded Elsie to stay and explore the house and the few acres of ground. Theo said he must be getting back to Levenshulme. The enchantment of the morning's early hours was gone. The suburbs he passed through were full of the same birdsong; the gardens were still gay with flowering shrubs; and the sun still shone brightly; but the passing of an hour or two had rubbed the virgin bloom off things, and the day had a workaday feeling as though it had got up and begun its business. And there was more in it than this. Theo was aware of a disappointment that Elsie was no longer with him. He had looked forward to walking home with her. They had not had much to say to one another on the way to the White House. Now he thought of all sorts of things he would have liked to discuss with her. What was she reading? No doubt Alec was keeping her mind occupied with something. How was she getting on with her violin lessons at Mr. Burnside's? And what about her religion? He wondered if she had been confirmed.

He never saw her at St. Ninian's. That was one of the queer things about Mr. Burnside. You met so many people at his house that you never saw in church. He didn't even bother to ask them. Well, Theo decided, as he strode on his long thin legs through Burnage, something might be done with this music at Mr. Burnside's. He himself, though music had never made more than a superficial appeal to him, as Lady Pinson had quickly discovered, had had a certain proficiency with the piano drilled into him. Mr. Burnside played the cello, and if, by the coming winter, Elsie had made some progress with the violin, they might arrange some simple musical occasions at the vicarage. But as at last he reached the straight, grim Stockport Road, where no shrubs bloomed and the May sunlight served but to illuminate the repulsiveness of the thoroughfare, these promised delights seemed a long way off, and he felt an urgent wish to do something about Elsie Dillworth at once. In his room in Hardiman Street he ran his eye along the books which long since had replaced the china in Mrs. Hornabrook's cupboards. What sort of stuff would she like? It was tantalizing to know so little about one whom he had come so suddenly to like so much. He chose Tennyson's *Idylls of the King,* a book which he himself deeply admired. He wrote on the flyleaf in his thin ascetic-looking hand: "With Theodore Chrystal's kind thoughts to Miss Dillworth, sharer of a memorable morning. May 15, 1886." He wasted no time, but walked at once to the house Alec had taken and dropped the small parcel through the letter-box. He felt relieved now that he had done something definite; and, having eaten Mrs. Hornabrook's mid-morning stay-bit, he settled down with an easier mind to his letter to Lady Pinson. "Outside St. Ninian's," he wrote, "where I had arranged to meet them, I found Miss Dillworth alone." He considered this for a moment, and then tore up the page. He went on with his description of the occasion, leaving Lady Pinson to assume that Alec had been with them all along. Something suggested to him that the red-haired, green-eyed Elsie Dillworth, concerning whose antecedents he knew nothing that was not discouraging, would hardly commend herself to Lady Pinson.

Chapter Six

THANK God, Thank God, Thank God. So the wheels of the train seemed to say to Theo as they slipped over rails and ran him, leaning back in his second-class compartment, through the dingy slate roofs and smoking chimney-pots and yellowish brick that would soon give way to wider and wider glimpses of country, and, at last, to dear Sussex itself.

He had been in Manchester for fifteen months without once spending a day out of it. He had worked hard in his own way, though his total feeling now was of disappointment and discouragement. After all, a curate was in the hands of his vicar; of himself he could do little; and all that he would have liked to do at St. Ninian's was regarded by Mr. Burnside as not of much importance. The services lacked the colour and drama that Theo would have liked to impart. The priest lacked a good deal of the sacerdotal authority and importance that he felt he should have. The church—that is, the wood and stone known by that name—seemed to Mr. Burnside the least important thing in all his scheme of living and ministering. An unhappy sense that he was working under the wrong vicar was beginning to enfeeble Theo's endeavours and to discourage his temper. He had kept to many of his own plans. He had maintained his Friday fasts and his two daily hours of devotional meditation and reading. He had even added a little to his book on the authorship of the *Epistle to the Hebrews*. But he didn't like St. Ninian's; he didn't like Levenshulme; and he was enchanted to be hastening as fast as wheels could take him to Sussex and Lady Pinson.

He had the compartment to himself. Through the window, let down to admit the June warmth which flooded his face, he saw on back after back of the dreary little houses: *Hard Facts. Every Friday. Hard Facts.* It went on with a crazy insistence for mile after mile; and no one in England, he supposed,

76

would now have to ask what *Hard Facts* was. Theo had not
liked these advertisements on the backs of small houses. They
were everywhere: not only here in London but in most great
cities. They were, of course, George Satterfield's idea; and their
iniquity had not struck Theo till Alec Dillworth pointed it
out. "You see, my dear Chrystal, the poor devils can't object.
They don't own the houses they live in. They are owned
by dukes and pork butchers, deceased clergymen's widows, the
Ecclesiastical Commissioners and such-like. For a few pounds
a year paid by our George, these are only too glad to add insult
to infamy by disfiguring the very kennels the poor dogs are
permitted to live in. Beauty is truth, truth beauty, as I am told
you remarked in a sermon recently; and by the same token
ugliness is the devil's own lie. But you can plaster your mucky
ugliness all over the homes of the poor. They have no right to
protest, and no one else thinks it worth while to do so. I
pointed this out to our George, and said that as the occupants
of these houses are our most numerous readers, we should show
them some respect. He thought I was crazy."

Theo would not have seen the thing that way himself, but
he was impressed by Alec's earnestness. The little man, as a
rule, spoke cynically or with some flippant double meaning;
but this matter touched him on the quick. Theo himself,
repeating Alec's arguments, raised the point with George
Satterfield, who replied sharply: "Shareholders can question
the directors' policy at the annual meeting." That put Theo
in his place. George knew well enough that Theo was hardly
likely to appear in public as an investor in Dunkerley Publications Limited.

It was a rebuff which Theo was hardly likely to forget, for,
wherever he was, he saw the offensive streamers; but, if he could
not forget, he buried his memory pretty deep, reflecting that
the more than satisfactory state of the Dunkerley shares would
some day permit him to be a Christian almsgiver.

It was all very well, he thought now, as the train went ringing its iron way through opening suburbs, for Mr. Burnside
to say, as he had done, that to give alms was easy: to give oneself was the thing to aim at. "My dear boy, give all you can.

Give the shirt off your back. But really what is called charity doesn't amount to much, you know, in the eyes of God."

Here was another of those strange sayings that made it difficult for Theo to get close to the spirit of Mr. Burnside. This was so different from Lady Pinson's attitude, which, she had told him, had been suggested to her by her brother, the Bishop of Chanctonbury. She, like the bishop, gave away one-tenth of her income, after, of course, deducting her living expenses. What with a coachman, two gardeners, and three maids, these were high; and he had often heard her wish that she had been called to a simpler way of living that would permit her to give more.

"You see, Chrystal, hardly a penny in the pound of the millions distributed annually in charity is missed by the people who give it. When some wealthy manufacturer of a common article gives away tens of thousands, I wonder where he got it from? It seems fairly obvious either that he has charged the public too much for what he sells, or he has underpaid his workers, or both. So that what he gives is simply a part return of filched money. I admire more the man who wins his sixpenny bet on the two-thirty and stands his friend a pint."

No, I shall never understand Mr. Burnside, thought Theo, who tended to admire such ceremonies as the washing of the already carefully washed feet of the poor, giving them twopence and a piece of bread, and sending them on their way rejoicing. Not that Mr. Burnside was altogether without points that pleased him. He had been deeply touched when he mentioned to Mr. Burnside the matter of musical evenings, with Elsie Dillworth present. It was a warm night, soon after that inaugural breakfast at Daniel Dunkerley's new house. Theo had called late, letting himself in by lifting the latch of the never-locked door, and he had come upon Mr. Burnside alone in his study, with a book and a cat. When any one called and found Mr. Burnside reading, it was not his habit to place the book open on the table, reminding the caller that he was anxious to get on with it. He shut his book, put it in its place on the shelves, and turned to Theo. "Well, my dear boy, that's enough of that for tonight. Tell me all your news. What have

you been finding in the howling wilderness of my parish?"

Theo sat in one of the wicker chairs and accepted a pipe of tobacco. The gas was lit but the brown velvet curtains were undrawn and the windows were open upon the stuffy night. In the country Theo had loved the night, with the sudden calling of nocturnal birds, and the quiet talk of the trees, and the singing of water. Here he hated it. All the little lives that were out and about on their affairs during the daylight were clamped down now beneath their roofs, every street a swarm, the suburb a multitude, the city a host. Sometimes Theo was physically oppressed by the thought of this countless army, hidden behind every wall, ambushed in every street, invisible yet pressing so closely upon him. He had mentioned this oppression once to Mr. Burnside, who seemed to understand and sympathize with the feeling, but who confessed nevertheless that, for himself, it was the sense of all these lives with their hopes and needs and fears that gave his own life meaning and opportunity. "The howling wilderness of my parish." Yes, indeed, thought Theo. Yet in this and such places Mr. Burnside had spent all his life as a priest, neither attempting nor wishing to change his lot. Oases? Well, it was about an oasis that he had called.

"I wondered," he said, "if we might look forward to establishing something of an oasis next winter? Some musical evenings. I'm not too bad at the piano. You love the cello, I know, and I thought it would be a help to Elsie Dillworth with her violin. I don't know how she's getting on. Is there any chance that she'll be fit for that sort of thing by then?"

For a moment Mr. Burnside said nothing. He considered his visitor so carefully that Theo at last said, with a little unease: "I'm very fond of Alec, you know."

"Yes," said Mr. Burnside, "and you're rather fond of Elsie, too, aren't you?" As Theo did not reply, he added: "Well—yes —but don't get too fond of her, Chrystal my dear boy, unless you are prepared to get very fond of her indeed. Do you see what I mean?"

Theo saw well enough, but his mind shied off the subject with a polite equivocation. "Oh, yes. I like her. I think she's a charming girl."

All right, Mr. Burnside thought. If you're edging away from me, I sha'n't press the matter; and turning from that, he said: "I can't encourage this idea of yours, because I have other ideas about Elsie Dillworth. It's just a year ago now that I first began to teach her the violin. It was nothing but a casual impulse."

"Yes," said Theo with a smile. "You said it might be her way to heaven."

"Did I? Well—yes. She'd had a tremendous row with Alec. Did you know that those two sometimes fight like cat and dog? Perhaps I should say like tiger and lynx. No? Well, they do, you know. Usually about nothing whatever. They are two very remarkable people. Never forget that, Chrystal—whatever they do—whatever they may become. Well, so far as I remember, the row that night was because Elsie wasn't wearing a dress that Alec had bought her. Elsie stormed out of the house, and when I met her she was crying her eyes out. You see, it began as simply as that. She came along here with me and we drank coffee and ate parkin, and then I began to scrape on the fiddle for her. I do sometimes, though the cello's my real weapon. Like a child, she wanted to have a try, so that night I showed her how to hold the fiddle and the bow. I didn't ask her to come again. I never press people, you know; but well— yes—she did. The very next night. 'Let's have another go,' she said. It began like that, a year ago. Alec bought her a fiddle, though I may say I chose it; and she's gone into the thing head over heels. She's very talented. There's really nothing more that I can do for her, and that's not saying much, you know. It simply means that she's learned the barest elements. Do you go to the Halle concerts?"

"No. I'm not really musical. I was just taught to strum a bit, and I never got beyond it."

"I go whenever I can," said Mr. Burnside, "and I've been taking Elsie. I thought perhaps she or Alec would have mentioned that."

No; they had not mentioned it; and Theo was a little hurt to find that they had this secret from him. But with a sudden and rare imaginative flash, he understood that perhaps here

was an ambition being nurtured, a hope fostered, about which nothing would be said lest it fail.

"Well," said Mr. Burnside, "the point is that there are some excellent violinists in that orchestra who can take her on at the point where I left off. I know the best one of them all pretty well, and it has been possible to make arrangements for Elsie. There is a chance—just a chance, mind you—that she will develop into something good. So I think on the whole, my dear boy, we had better not make any arrangements for her. Her arrangements now must be in Simmons's hands. Still, if you ever care to come along and strum, as you call it, I'll be glad to join in."

This did not seem an alluring idea to Theo. He would much rather give his spare time to his book on the *Hebrews;* and, as he crossed the Stockport Road into Hardiman Street, the prospect even of this did not assuage a vague feeling of depression and disappointment.

And now there he was, speeding through the summer day, paler than usual from his stay in that drear Manchester suburb, but handsome as ever—"the gentleman with the beautiful face." So, George Satterfield said, he had been called by his daughter Grace—that child whom Theo had glimpsed once or twice before she was whisked away to Bowdon and then to school. Strange, he thought, how all these people had entered so deeply into his life in the fifteen months since he first knocked on Mrs. Hornabrook's door. By a mere chance, Mr. Burnside had asked him to call about some handbills. But for that, he might never have known the Dunkerleys and the Dillworths. He might never have been a shareholder in *Hard Facts,* or a contributor either.

The little houses were gone. The name no longer flashed with its idiotic repetition upon his sight; but here and there it flaunted in the middle of a field, on a hoarding as big as the side of a house. *Hard Facts.* Even now, he could barely realize the hard fact that week by week an article from the pen of Theodore Chrystal, B.A., B.D.—though not signed by that name—graced the pages about which, more than once, he had

so scathingly written to dear Lady Pinson. It arose out of his saying jokingly to Alec Dillworth, when Dan Dunkerley was present: "Well, Alec, I reckon *Hard Facts* owes me a guinea. Dr. Strong's sermon this week is nothing but the ideas I gave you the other day on the responsibilities of wealth."

Daniel Dunkerley prided himself that *Hard Facts* paid for what it used (though, whenever possible, it paid at a price cut down to the bone). "Is that so, Alec?" he asked, and Alec said that it was. There and then, Dan wrote a cheque for a guinea and handed it to Theo, who accepted it as part of a good joke. But the matter quickly passed beyond joking. "While we're at it, Dan," said Alec very seriously, "let me tell you this. I've been editing this paper now for over a year. It's no part of an editor's business to write his own contributions, especially when the editorial salary happens to be five pounds a week. I'm writing you three articles for every issue. You can pay me for them, or get someone else to do them, or find another mug. For myself, I'd rather go on with my present pay and put the articles out. That would give me time to do other things besides handle your garbage. After all, I *am* a writer."

There was a moment's thundery silence. Dan's blue eyes went very hard and his face very red. He tried to restrain himself, but could not. He rose suddenly and banged his fist on Alec's desk. "Damn you, Alec!" he shouted. "Why do you try day after day to undermine my self-respect? Again and again I have to stand up for you to George Satterfield, who'd like to throw you out into the street——"

"Where I came from. Go on. Say it," said Alec, whose face was white and furious.

"—and all I get is your constant gibes and ridicule. If you don't like the paper why in hell don't you leave it?"

"Because it's a soft job," Alec announced. "I don't mind editing your damned paper, but if you expect me to praise it, you'll have to go on expecting."

"I don't want you to praise it. Shut your mouth about it. That's all I ask."

Theo picked up his hat and began to make for the door. Alec cried: "Don't go, Chrystal. While you're here, let's settle

a point. Those articles I spoke about, Dan, are going to be written out of this office. I'll see you and Satterfield in hell before I sweat my guts out for you any longer. Dr. Phillip Strong, D.D., to begin with, would suit Chrystal here down to the ground. He could do it on his head before breakfast. Well, let him try his hand at prizing a bit of wealth out of *Hard Facts*. It'll be an enlightening experience for him."

Dan sank back into his chair. "Alec," he said, "you may thank your God that I'm very fond of you, damn fool though you are. But don't presume on it too often. Well, Chrystal, what do you say? Two guineas a week. Not bad for a thousand words."

Theo's methodical and mathematical mind worked like lightning. Two guineas a week was more than two thousand pounds paying five per cent. It was more than his salary as a curate. It was nearly as much as his investments had been paying before he capitalized them all and turned the money in to *Hard Facts*. And simultaneously another part of his mind was saying: A million readers a week! A million souls to influence! The sermons need not be rubbish. He could put all he knew into them. Surely it was his duty to seize this chance!

"I'll think it over," he said. He didn't think for long. Once or twice since then Alec had adjured him: "Remember you're Dr. Strong, not the Rev. Mr. Chrystal. Just play down a bit, my dear boy. Come to earth." And obediently Theo had come to earth.

Merriman Beckwith, Q.C., had a habit in court of holding his hands behind him and with great frequency using them both to flip his gown up above his backside. It used to be said that he charged five guineas a flip; and, whether this were so or not, he had plenty of guineas to dispose of. This was fortunate, for the young Beckwiths were many. During twenty-five years Mrs. Beckwith bore fifteen children. Of those who survived, Adrian Beckwith, Bishop of Chanctonbury, was the oldest, and Adela Pinson was the youngest. In that June, when Theodore Chrystal was hurrying towards Lewes, Adela was thirty-one, Adrian was fifty. Theodore Chrystal was twenty-five.

All Sussex—all southern England—was simmering under the midsummer heat. Outside Lewes station the Bishop's coachman had drawn up horse and brougham in a shady spot. Inside the station Adela and Adrian walked a platform mercifully darkened by its canopy. He held her arm. He was deeply attached to his only sister, and he was not unaware of the tragedy her marriage had been. You would not have taken them for brother and sister. Adela's face was haphazard and irregular. Beautiful chestnut hair and grey steadfast eyes were her most attractive features. Adrian's close-cropped hair was an iron-grey stubble on a head as round as a shot. His short, thick neck, his small well-carved nose, a certain sensuality of the mouth, the rounded stubborn chin: all made one think of a Roman emperor. Indeed, it was said among those privileged to be jocose about him that his domestic chaplain, using a pen-name, was the author of a book popular at the time, called *At the Mercy of Tiberius*.

Old Merriman Beckwith, retired now, and a widower for many years, lived at Lewes, and brother and sister had chanced to call upon him on the same afternoon. Adela had called because she would be going to Lewes station to meet Theo anyhow; and Adrian because he knew this. It would be, he decided, an opportunity to see and appraise the young man of whom he had heard a good deal. Nevertheless, he affected surprise at finding Adela at their father's.

"But I told you, Adrian, that Mr. Chrystal would be staying with me and that I was meeting him today."

"So you did. So you did. It had gone clean out of my mind."

He persuaded her to send her carriage away. "There's no need to keep the horse standing about for hours, my dear. I shall be passing Cotter's Court, and you and Mr. Chrystal can use my brougham." As they were pacing the platform he asked with a twinkle: "You don't mind my having a look at him?"

"He can stand inspection," Adela said shortly.

Yes, thought Adrian, when Theo alighted a few moments later. He certainly can.

Taller than the Bishop, Theo was Greek to his Roman. He took off his hat and bent over Adela's hand. His fair curls shone.

The beauty and delicacy of his profile could not be hidden. Adrian Chanctonbury thought: Put him in a fashionable West End church and there'd be no holding him. He's the sort women go for.

Theo was well aware of the purple beneath the formidable chin, the gaiters on the rounded calves, the cross shining at the end of its chain. He was in no doubt who this was, but affected a pleased surprise when Adela said: "This is my brother."

They shook hands. "You have done me the honour to write to me, sir," said Theo. "It has been a great help." He added with a smile: "One needs it, you know, in Manchester."

"Some do and some don't," said the Bishop. "I imagine Burnside is self-sufficient. Didn't you think so?"

They were making their way out of the station. The question came abruptly, almost as a rebuke. "Well," said Theo, "I suppose he's the stuff saints are made of."

The Bishop opened the door of the brougham, saw Adela in, and climbed after her. "Don't you believe it," he said, presenting his well-upholstered posterior to Theo's gaze. "Burnside isn't raw material. He's a finished article."

Theo seated himself and the carriage started. "I didn't know you knew Mr. Burnside," Theo said. "He's never mentioned it."

Adrian permitted himself a smile. "He wouldn't," he said. "I imagine he doesn't altogether approve of me. Nevertheless, we were at Christ Church together. He was in his last year when I went up. We became very friendly." He stopped suddenly and placed an affectionate hand on Adela's arm. "My dear, this all seems a terribly long time ago. To think that you were still a babe in arms when I came down from Christ Church."

"Don't side-track yourself," said Adela. "I can see that Mr. Chrystal is terribly interested in what you were saying about Mr. Burnside."

"There's precious little to say. He took Orders at the earliest possible moment, was a curate in the East End of London and in Salford, and then became Vicar of St. Ninian's in Levenshulme. He's been offered several fine benefices and one

deanery, but he wants to stay where he is. That's about all, except that he's the only man I know who refused a fortune."

"Now this is something new," said Adela. "You've told me all the rest before."

"Oh, yes. Burnside's father was immensely rich. A tea-merchant in Mincing Lane. And till he came up to Oxford Burnside knew what to do with money. Knew only too well from all I heard. Yes—dissipation. During his first year at Oxford he was converted, as surely, absolutely and suddenly as Saul on the road to Damascus. His father died soon after he had taken Orders. Burnside was an only son and came in for something like fifty thousand pounds. He gave it all away—every penny."

The countryside, drowsy with summer, spun past the open windows. Honeysuckle hung upon the hedges. The elms were like great ships becalmed, motionless and mute. The horse's hoofs beat musically upon the white dusty road, and the wheels purred with sleek content. Fifty thousand pounds! Fifty thousand pounds could buy all this. Theo thought of Levenshulme on a summer's day: the burning pavements, the arid houses, the afternoon wilting in the treeless streets. He thought of Mr. Burnside with his window open upon the breathless night, the moths batting into his gas-globe, his cat at his feet. Fifty thousand pounds!

"Yes, we had great arguments about it," the Bishop was saying. "A priest can do a lot with fifty thousand pounds. I told him so. I remember his answer well. 'My dear Beckwith, when I was commanded—as I was—to become a fisher of men, nothing was said about golden bait.' I had to leave it at that."

"Do you think he decided wisely, sir?" Theo asked.

"It depends, young man, on what you mean by wisdom," said the Bishop. "You hear people talk about worldly wisdom, as though wisdom were something sold in various grades and qualities, to be used for various purposes. If a priest took that view, then obviously he would not decide as Burnside did. Equally obviously, Burnside being what he is, there was no other course open to him than the one he did in fact take. . . . Well, Adela, my dear, here you are. You must bring Mr. Chrystal over to tea some day while he's here."

Dinner would be in an hour's time. Adela suggested to Theo that he should rest till then. His portmanteau had been taken up to his bedroom, and when he followed it he found a shallow tin bath on the floor and several large copper jugs containing hot water. Cotter's Court was not so up-to-date in its plumbing as the White House, Didsbury, now that Daniel Dunkerley had taken it in hand. Sitting on the bed, pulling a clean shirt over his head, Theo allowed his thoughts to wander: to Levenshulme, to Didsbury, to the Bishop of Chanctonbury leaning back looking like a priest-emperor, and laying down the law so pontifically and imperially. "If a priest took that view, then obviously. . . . Equally obviously, if. . . ." Yes, thought Theo; beautifully balanced and cancelled out, meaning nothing. Well, if that's how one becomes a bishop, it's no wonder Mr. Burnside is a suburban vicar.

Dressed, he stood at the window. "I've given you the best view in the house," Adela had said. Theo would have called it one of the best views in England. He had seen it often enough, and on winter days in Levenshulme, when he looked between Mrs. Hornabrook's brass-bound curtains to the back of the Palmerston Street houses, it sometimes swam back into his imagination with a nostalgia almost unbearable. The house stood on a shelf half-way up the southern acclivity of a shallow valley. To the right, the valley narrowed to a mere wooded gulch that climbed to the downs. Below the house, it broadened into fertile meadows, watered by a flashing stream, pastured by cattle, punctuated by a farmhouse or two, and shaded here and there by groups of noble beeches. Looking to the left, one saw the view closed by a snug village. At this time of year the church tower was hidden by trees; but Theo had seen it in winter time, square, homely, pleasing, with the smoke of the Greyhound Inn rising above it like perpetual incense. And all this little valley—fields, farms, inn—belonged to Adela Pinson. Even the church belonged to her in a sense, for hers was the right of choosing the parson and the privilege of paying him.

From Adela Pinson's own room, in the west end of the house, the view was directed fully towards the village. She had moved

into this room after her husband's death, for one thing because it was as far as she could get from the room she had shared with Sir Brian, and for another because the village it looked upon was her dearest concern. Farms, land, and all sorts of other tiresome business she was prepared to leave to her agent, but people were her affair. "You look after the tenements and I'll look after the tenants." She was a good woman. In her own way, according to the light of her times, she did look after them. There was one thing she would have liked to do for them: give them a new vicar.

For generations Pinsons had held the living: sons, brothers, nephews, and uncles of the reigning Pinson. Only once in Sir Brian's time had the living been vacant, and then it happened that the Pinson male relatives had ceased to exist. The old family had come to the end of its tether. Sir Brian was the last of them, and he had chosen a man who would be, at need, congenial company. The Rev. Henry Herwald could shoot and ride, drink his glass and tell his story at dinner, and he had been much at home at Cotter's Court. Adela had not made him welcome. She thought him most things that a priest should not be. But she had a tender place for him in her heart, remembering the bitter winter day when Brian was buried. In the grandiose fashion that the Pinsons had always used, the coffin, looking absurdly small, was put upon a farm cart and drawn over roads clinking with ice to the church already so plentifully adorned with stones and tablets and effigies recording the virtues of Pinsons—so many Eustaces and Brians since the time of Eustache de Pinson who was the first to be granted this patch of Sussex land. The coffin was carried in from the cart and placed upon a catafalque, and she had stood there in the freezing church, heavily veiled, with her brother Adrian holding her arm, wondering why the service was so long in beginning. She had looked up, and through the darkness of the veil she had seen Mr. Herwald, curiously dim and distorted, his face convulsed by emotion, tears unashamedly streaming down his cheeks; and she, herself moved by nothing but a rapture of relief that she dared not face, said in her mind: "He loved him. He loved him." And she felt somehow glad, as though it ex-

punged her own secret treason, that there was someone to love the poor corpse, now so harmless and pitiful upon the bier.

It was soon after this that a slight stroke caused Mr. Herwald to reel and fall during a Sunday morning service. He recovered and went on with his work, but it was clear that he was not as competent as he had been. Adela suggested to him that he should employ a curate. He had objected till she said that she would pay him. That was how Theodore Chrystal came to Little Riddings and attracted the attention of a woman who felt that in two years of marriage all her youth had been burnt up and her innocence defiled.

Adela was so much younger than her brother Adrian that his friends, ever since her childhood, had seemed to her rather like honorary uncles than contemporaries. She could not remember a time when she had not known Richard Newstead, who was now a Fellow of All Saints College, Oxford. He held this position as "founder's kin." It was a delightful arrangement. Because an ancestor, centuries ago, had been founder of the college, Richard had the right to free rooms therein, with a garden-view from his window, a lovely hall to dine in, a common-room to talk in when he felt like talking, which was rarely, and a modest, but sufficient income. In return for these benefits, he had nothing to do except take a nominal interest in the affairs of his college, criticize its port, and obstruct its reform. To even such enterprises as these he brought small enthusiasm. "Leave me alone and I'll leave you alone" was his attitude to his college as to everything else. He collected Greek coins, and it was said that on the basis of these he was writing a book upon the Greek colonization of the Mediterranean coasts and islands. He had laid down a few rules for the conduct of life. One was: "An hour's exercise a day is necessary for the moving of a man's bowels. Beyond that, exercise is barbarous." In obedience to this rule, he would leave college at three precisely, winter or summer, hail, rain, snow or broiling sun, and walk upon the Woodstock Road re-entering the portals of All Saints as the Oxford clocks were striking four. He had also said: "A dog is fit to share the exercises of a man's

body, a cat the exercises of his mind." Therefore, on leaving
the college, he would call at the Mitre where his bull-terrier
Mr. Gladstone was kennelled in the yard. The walk completed,
Mr. Gladstone would be returned to his kennel, and Newstead would expect to find his Persian cat Dizzy awaiting him
with the tea and toast in his rooms. Only Dizzy knew whether,
in fact, a pen had ever been set to paper on the subject of Greek
coinage and civilization. He was a beautiful smoky-grey creature with staring orange eyes, and looked far more likely than
his master to compile a work of erudition. Whenever Newstead
left Oxford, Mr. Gladstone travelled with him in a crate in
the railway guard's van, and Dizzy, in a large wicker basket
lined with quilted pink silk, in his own compartment. At this
moment, while Theo Chrystal was preparing to go down to
the drawing-room, Mr. Newstead and Dizzy were walking
upon the lawn, and Mr. Gladstone was gnawing a bone in the
stables. It might almost have been Queen Victoria's own arrangement for them. Presently, Theo saw Adela join Mr.
Newstead on the lawn and heard her call: "Lottie, come and
take a turn with us in this beautiful evening. Mr. Chrystal
will be down in a moment."

Theo was disappointed. There was so much that he had
wanted to say to Adela, and that he would have preferred to
say to her alone. He had expected to be the only guest, but,
when he came to think of it, Adela Pinson was the sort of
woman who would never allow herself to be in a position
which might be misconstrued, by however far-fetched infer-
ences. He remembered that, in the days when he gave her
Greek lessons, they always sat, in the winter months, in the
large comfortable hall, where servants came and went, and,
in the summer, at the open French window of the drawing-
room, where a gardener might pass at any moment. He wondered rather impolitely who the slovenly looking old buzzard
with the Persian cat might be. Lottie, who now joined the
others on the lawn, he knew well enough. She was Lottie
Chambers, who ran some sort of club for working mothers in
the East End. She was a raw-looking old Scot, as poor as a
church mouse, but with an infinity of aristocratic friends and

a genius for extracting money from them. He had heard old
Herwald say that there had been a good deal of unpleasant-
ness between Sir Brian and Adela about the size of some of her
cheques written for Lottie Chambers. Well, he thought, I
hope these are the only two, and that we'll be able to get rid
of them now and then. He gave a last look at himself in the
mirror, fixed a smile on his face, and went down to join the
others.

Adela Pinson had thought Theo pale-looking and tired
when she met him at Lewes station. Now, bathed and changed,
and feeling the comfort of being at his journey's end, he looked
a different man. Throughout his life he was tall and straight
and thin; then, in the morning of his youth, he had a classic
beauty, untouched by thought or care, that no painting or
photograph could catch. It needed the three-dimensional
treatment of sculpture to reproduce the purity of the profile
and the shapeliness of the golden head. I am really seeing him,
Adela thought with a quickening of the pulse, for the first time
since all these months—over a year. Oh, it seemed an endless
age! When she presented Theo to Mr. Newstead she was
pleased with the old man for saying: "I, too, collect Greek
coins, my dear Adela." Not that *his* pulse-beat quickened, or
Lottie Chambers's either. The profound selfishness of the one
and the selflessness of the other had carried them far beyond
the point where a face meant much. But Adela, who had been
looking forward to the meeting with mixed feelings, knew suddenly that this was a moment she would never forget: this
kindly light of the Sussex evening, with the roses at their best,
and the madonna lilies that grew under the wall of the house
scenting the air, and the fish moving lazily in the little pond
near which she stood, and Theo coming towards her with a
shadow that touched her feet while he was still a long way off.
She tried desperately to seem casual, no more pleased with him
than the politeness of a hostess demanded; but her heart would
not be still. She was glad when the parlour-maid beat upon the
mellow gong and Mr. Newstead brought her back to earth by
saying: "Dizzy hopes that that means, among other things, fish."

Secluded as Mr. Newstead's life at Oxford was, he could not avoid undergraduates altogether. Had it been possible, he would have done so. The purposeful ways of the young made him feel useless, and because he *was* useless, he resented this feeling. He tried to get even by being rude to them, questioning everything they said, and giving them to understand that till a man was fifty he had much better keep his mouth shut in the presence of mature minds. If he could be offensive to the young in a dead language, why, so much the better. Many an Oxford reputation for wit and learning was based on little more.

Though he had given Adela a pleasant word on being introduced to Theodore Chrystal, he was annoyed that anyone so young had been included in the party. Adela should have had more sense. The boy's presence was bad enough, but when Dizzy leapt upon Theo's lap in the dining-room, Mr. Newstead felt that treasonable happenings were afoot. He did not speak, but walked round the table and lifted the cat off Theo's knee. "Thank you, sir," said Theo. "I don't like cats."

He could hardly have outraged Mr. Newstead's feelings more deeply in an hour of speech. It was bad enough that Dizzy had preferred an alien knee; for a man to say he didn't like cats was worse; but to include Dizzy among cats in general was worst of all. This was to strike at an inner principle of Mr. Newstead's life: that anything he did, or anything that belonged to him, could not conceivably be in the common run of things but derived a sanctity from his association with it. He happened to be left-handed, and had seriously put forward the opinion that there would be a universal improvement in craftsmanship if all men were left-handed.

Both Theo and Mr. Newstead thought it a dull dinner. They were wary of one another with instinctive dislike, and left the conversation more or less to Lottie Chambers. It developed into a rather tiresome monologue on the tribulations of pregnancy in the East End, and the need for more and more money to counteract the enterprise of aggressive husbands. Theo was glad when Adela rose and went with Lottie into the drawing-room. She placed a decanter and a box of cigars on the table

before leaving. "I hope these will be to your taste," she said.

"I expect," said Mr. Newstead when the door was closed, "that that remark was addressed to me. One rarely finds that the young have the head to enjoy port or the taste to enjoy a cigar. You bear me out, I take it, Dizzy?"

Dizzy had leapt upon the table, miraculously avoiding in his landing, as only a cat can, the clutter of knives and forks, plates and glasses, that he could not possibly have seen when he took off. He did not heed Mr. Newstead's remark, but gave an absorbed attention to a creamy sweet that Miss Chambers had left untouched.

"Dizzy is a gourmet," said Mr. Newstead, "and I hope the young of today realize that that is not the same thing as a gourmand. But perhaps I am mistaken, and you will join me in a glass of port? Or a cigar?"

Theo said he was not interested in either; and Mr. Newstead ventured that possibly the junior common-room at Selwyn was not the best breeding-ground of palates. Perhaps not even of prelates, he added, snatching greedily at his suddenly seen small joke.

He sniffed his wine with gusto, crackled his cigar at an appreciative ear, and lolled in his chair as he exhaled the first incense. Sir Brian, who had chosen both the port and the cigars, had not made a mistake. "Well, young Chrystal," Newstead condescended at last, "what do you want to make of your life? Has youth any ambition nowadays?"

"I have always thought," said Theo carefully, "that I would like to be a Boswell, but so far I have been unfortunate. Johnson was slovenly, rude and a bore, but these defects were counterbalanced by qualities. His cat Hodge would bear me out, I think."

Adela and Lottie Chambers had not sat long in the drawing-room. They had passed through the French window and Theo now saw them walking upon the lawn. He deferentially placed the decanter a little nearer to Mr. Newstead's elbow, and then, without a further word, joined the ladies.

Bats were threading an erratic pattern upon the saffron sky, and the tremolo of a small owl sounded from a cedar. *The old*

fool, sitting there swilling and filling the room with fug. Theo was boiling with young indignation, but this was no moment for speech. This was a moment to thank God for, and to store in the imagination against the dark days ahead in Levens-hulme. Neither Adela nor Lottie wanted to talk, either. The three of them silently paced now to the west, where every leaf and twig was a silhouette against the luminous pulsing of the midsummer night, now to the east where the cedar was gathering its cloak about it and slipping within the embrace of the dark. The lawn had been mown that afternoon, and the wounds of millions of beheaded grass-blades sent up a smell of sacrifice.

They came at last, as by common consent, to a pause, standing together looking upon the darkling circle of water in the fish-pond. Theo broke the silence by saying simply in a low voice: "He made summer."

The night, and the fragrance of the wounded grass, and Theo's voice saying these few simple words, were a powerful magic to Adela. How she had loved this Sussex house and garden! But always she had been denied the final seal of peace. For two years that two-and-twenty would not erase she had suffered and endured; and memory since then had been tyrannical. It had had the power, in her most tranquil moments, to intrude and destroy, and sometimes she thought it would drive her out at last, like Eve from Eden. But now she knew that this would not happen. She laid her hand lightly on Theo's arm. "Let us go in, Theo," she said. They went in together, and Miss Chambers followed.

They came into the drawing-room through the French window as Mr. Newstead came in through the door. A maid followed him. She shut the windows and began to light the oil lamps that stood on standards here and there. "My friend Daniel Dunkerley," said Theo with a laugh, "would find Cotter's Court dreadfully antiquated. Oil lamps, indeed! He'd soon have them out of the way and electricity installed."

Adela had sensed the antagonism of Theo and Richard Newstead. She was glad of a topic which, she hoped, would keep their minds interested. "Tell us about him, Theo," she

said, and, turning to Newstead: "This Daniel Dunkerley, Richard, is the mind behind this ridiculous paper called *Hard Facts* that's spreading like a plague through the country. Theo knows him well."

"I don't know," said Theo traitorously, "whether there's a *mind* behind the paper at all. It's hardly likely that Mr. Newstead has come across *Hard Facts,* but if you have, sir, what do you say? I have heard the editor himself refer to the paper as garbage."

Mr. Newstead was in a thoroughly bad mood. He had sat for some time chewing over the suave insult that Theo had addressed to him. Then he had taken Dizzy up to his bedroom and put him to bed. Now he was ready to deal with this young man, to controvert everything he might say, and expose him to Adela Pinson for the nincompoop he probably was. He lay back in an easy chair, his finger-tips together, and a ridiculously small foot clothed in a shiny pump jiggling and jerking. "If Mr. Chrystal is, as I assume, a friend of this Mr. Dunkerley," he began, "then I fear he only confirms my opinion of modern youth by speaking of his friend in terms calculated to bring him into contempt."

"Oh, I'm sure——" Adela began, but Mr. Newstead held up a fat peremptory paw and continued: "As to whether I have read this paper, the answer is Yes. As to whether there is a mind behind it, I am afraid I must differ from Mr. Chrystal, for the answer again is Yes. Do not be led into the assumption, my dear young man, that a fool can lead the public by the nose. There may be a great deal of mind behind a great deal of nonsense—or garbage, as another of your friends so elegantly calls it."

The fat little sloven sat there like a Buddha, and Theo had not the heart to be annoyed by his self-satisfaction. "And what would you call it, sir?" he asked.

"That," said Mr. Newstead, "is beside the point. The important thing is that, seeing we are now fools enough to teach every dock labourer, navvy and servant-girl to read, there is a lot of brain in a man who realizes the level at which the intelligence of these people works. We pour out the national rev-

enue in order to produce reading-machines. If we leave it at that, as we are content to do, then a Daniel Dunkerley is inevitable. I may, and I do," he added—and he would have been happy had he realized how hard he was hitting!—"I may, and I do, feel contempt for those who write for him. Presumably, they are at least semi-literate and should know better. But I feel some admiration for the man who has them, like his readers, harnessed to the creation of a fortune."

It was all so rotund and flowing, and he had got it off with so little interruption, that he felt pleased with himself, and forgiving. If only the senior common-room at All Saints would hear him as patiently! "Now, young Chrystal," he said condescendingly, "we shall be pleased to hear something about this Daniel Dunkerley. After all, he is a portent—more so, no doubt, than an immature mind can realize—and it is one's duty to understand a Napoleon of the Press even though his *Grande Armée* marches in the gutter."

Theo could not now resist a gust of laughter. "Really, Mr. Newstead," he said, "my intention was just to talk about a man I chance to know. You make it sound very solemn—as though I were under some historical necessity to enlighten my comtemporaries. Dunkerley's quite a simple person, I believe. You talk about mind. Well, frankly, I don't agree with you. A good deal of resolution and perseverance—even ruthlessness—yes. But not what I, anyway, understand by mind."

"I might ask you," said Mr. Newstead, "what you *do* understand by mind, but I shall refrain." He looked as though he thought Theo should be thankful for his forbearance. "You are wandering again into general issues. Give us some concrete facts about this man."

So the conversation drifted into safe waters. Theo told them about Dunkerley's house, with its new bathrooms and electric light. Lottie Chambers applauded, and wished her own place in the East End could be fitted up in the same way. "I wish you'd try and interest Mr. Dunkerley in our work, Mr. Chrystal," she said. "I'm sure it would make an excellent article for his paper. Perhaps he'd open a fund to give us baths and modern lighting. The drudgery we'd save!"

Well, now at last we're happily away, Adela thought, and those two won't be at one another's throats. Really, I hadn't noticed what a crotchety old bore Richard has been turning into for years past. I've been seeing too much of old people. All my friends seem to be Adrian's contemporaries, not my own. Even Lottie, dear soul, is nearly old enough to be my mother. She felt a sudden nearness to Theo, a need for the refreshing influence of his youth and beauty. Her husband had been old, her friends were old, and she had been taking it too much for granted that she was old herself. The night was now dark, and in the room shadows filled the spaces between the kindly and gentle effulgence of the lamps. She sat withdrawn in reverie, leaving the conversation to the others. She was thinking of the beautiful days she and Theo had passed in this room together— just the two of them—learning Greek, listening to music. It was a bit traitorous, she thought, to wish Lottie away, but really she did, and Richard, too. Richard was very tiresome. It was a pity that the conveniences had not allowed her to ask Theo alone. She was amusing herself with a fantastic thought of getting rid of Richard by causing a telegram to arrive concerning the discovery of important Greek coins at Smyrna. Would he at once rush away, or were his Greek coins, as she half believed, little more than a few he had bought from London dealers? Really, she was thinking the most idiotic thoughts. She was nodding, drowsing. It was all this heat of the long summer day, and the tiring journey into Lewes, and the even more tiring call upon her very old father with whom she had not been happy and at ease since he arranged that marriage with Brian Pinson.

She came to with a start, hearing Theo say: "Yes, a most beautiful girl." That she had pulled up on the edge of sleep was so obvious that Richard Newstead at once rose. "Adela, my dear," he said, "you have had a hard day. You must be tired out."

Adela apologized. "I'm sorry. It must be the heat. Really, I only nodded. I knew what Theo was saying."

"He was telling us," said Newstead, "of a Manchester Venus, the lovely sister of the brilliant poet who edits *Hard Facts.*

Really, I had not known that our industrial districts were so rich in beauty and talent. However, we must not impose these travellers' tales upon you. I wish you good-night, my dear."

He kissed her fingers and waddled off to where the candle-sticks stood on a table in the hall. Theo and Lottie Chambers, each tired from a journey, were glad enough to follow his example. But Adela now felt suddenly wide awake. It was only ten o'clock. She drew a chair nearer to the lamp, hoping to read, fearing she would not be able to do so. It was only too true that the imagined face of "a most beautiful girl" swam between her eyes and the page.

Old Merriman Beckwith, at eighty-five, had a housekeeper, a valet, and a gardener-coachman to look after him in Lewes. The valet was the only one of the three who had any influence with the old man, and he had not much. "It's no good talking damned nonsense to me, Robinson. There's never been any damned nonsense in my life so far, and it's not going to begin now." This was the attitude whenever anything was suggested that he did not approve of, and he approved of very little that did not suit his own obstinate humour. He was the more insistent that there had never been any damned nonsense in his life because there had been one supreme piece of damned nonsense—if one might so describe an utterly headlong, head-strong action that all his friends and relatives disapproved of.

He was a barrister with a moderate practice, but the name Merriman Beckwith, painted in a list of many others on a board outside a door whence you heard the cool splash of water in Fountain Court, didn't yet amount to much. However, young Mr. Merriman Beckwith—fairly young: he was thirty-three—had nothing to worry about. He was a bachelor, and intended to remain so. His father had recently died, and he had five hundred a year under the will. That, and his earnings, kept him handsomely.

It was a spring day. He had been briefed that morning to defend in what promised to be a profitable slander suit, and as the parties on both sides were not only wealthy but famous—they were, indeed, a popular dramatist and one of the best-

known actors of the day—the case would have wide publicity. What more could a rising young barrister ask?

He stepped out of his chambers into the mild spring air, intending to walk over to the Cheshire Cheese for lunch. He came to a halt outside the door, arrested by the lovely quality of the morning. He had looked upon the scene times out of mind, but now, suddenly, he seemed to see it with eyes new-washed: the cool grey stretch of pavement, the ripe colour of the brick, the blotched trunks of the plane trees on whose boughs the new leaves of this year were unfolded among the macelike nuts of last year's fruit, the virgin blue, unspeakably tender, of the sky from which the sun sparkled down on the flashing water of the fountain and the iridescent necks of the pigeons strutting and crooling.

As young Beckwith stood there looking at all this with new delight, a girl came from the direction of the Embankment and walked slowly towards the fountain. It was the quality of her walk that first caught his eye, and he was never to cease to love it. For all the rest of her life, he could see Elizabeth come into a room with delight, and he was never tired of watching the effect on those who saw her for the first time. It was as though one who came with such dignity and tranquillity must have something momentous to say, so that one waited for her first words as one might for those of an actress obviously en-trusted with some weighty matter.

Though a bachelor, Beckwith was not inexperienced. He demanded three things of a woman: she should look well, she should move well, and she should speak well. For him, whose own fine voice had helped him to such success as he had gained, and was soon to help him to so much more: for him, the voice was almost more important than anything else. He wondered about this girl who looked and moved so well. How did she speak?

This desire—almost a compulsion—to hear her voice caused Beckwith to approach when the girl came to a stand alongside the fountain and began to scatter crumbs for the pigeons. He stood near her for some time, watching with delight the grace-ful flutter of her fingers and the animated loveliness of her

face. Presently, he casually said: "Don't you think they get abominably overfed?"

She did not resent his speaking to her. She looked at him with a friendly disarming smile and said: "Oo, na-ow! I expect the pore things is often 'ungry."

Beckwith winced. It was like a smack in the mouth. He bore it manfully. She was indeed very beautiful. "Well, I'm hungry myself," he said. "I was just making for my lunch. Would you care to join me?"

He held his breath. Would she turn virtuous and indignant? She gave him the same sweet and utterly friendly smile. "If you like," she said.

He had no "intentions," honourable or dishonourable. She was an unusually beautiful woman, and it would be agreeable to eat a meal with her, despite the cut of her poverty-stricken clothes. She was frank about everything, including herself. She was the only child of a street-corner green-grocer in Lambeth, a widower. Beckwith never pretended to himself that he felt any distress when this parent died a year after he had become engaged to Elizabeth. They were engaged for two years, and during that time he hardly saw her. He won his slender case brilliantly and became a much-sought-after man. Elizabeth was living in Brighton with a widow of the most perfect discretion. "You needn't try to teach her anything except the daily fashions of your life and how to speak." Those were his orders, and they were carried out.

As Adela Pinson sat in her drawing-room that June night she was thinking of this story. Neither her father nor Elizabeth herself had ever tried to conceal her origins. Adela knew only too well that a lot of nonsense is talked about origins. She had adored her mother. Elizabeth's marriage had been a brilliant success. From such a woman, Adela was thinking, a bishop, a colonial governor, a few men distinguished enough in their walks of life could spring. And, as his letters might have warned her, Theo Chrystal was interested in a beautiful girl of no class at all in Manchester. And what was there against it? With painful honesty, she said to herself: Nothing.

Chapter Seven

WHEN the Bishop of Chanctonbury and his sister had called that afternoon on their father, the old man had not been feeling well. The weather was trying. He was too old now to be comfortable with extremes. Excessive heat or cold searched him out. His valet Robinson had wanted him to stay in the drawing-room, the coolest place in the house, with green sun-blinds shading the windows. But he insisted on going into the garden. Wearing a rustling suit of tussore silk and a Panama hat, he reclined in a bamboo chair beneath the lime-tree that he had planted forty years ago. The tree was in flower and the bees were invading it in diligent armies. All those little wings—each so fragile—combined to produce a powerful dynamo-hum. The whole tree seemed to vibrate, and this, with the scent of the flowers, drowsed him in body and mind. He had brought out some papers with him, intending to refresh his memory for the next chapter of the book he was writing: a book dealing with the celebrated cases in which he had been involved. These papers concerned the case of Tanner v. Urquhart—that slander case whose brief came to him the morning when he first set eyes on Elizabeth. *The greatest day of my life.* He had often said that. The day when his career as a lawyer and his private concerns had both turned a prosperous corner.

He laid the papers on the table beside his chair, threw off his hat, and leaned his head back so that the plentiful white hair made an aureole for his tanned face against the crimson cushion. He gave himself up to the drone and hot murmur of the afternoon. It was of Elizabeth he began to think—not of Tanner and Urquhart, both gone, like her, long since into the silence. He remembered bringing her to this house. He remembered the blowy November afternoon when he had planted this lime-tree, boring a deep hole with a crow-bar to take the stake to which he tied it. He was as anxious about it

as an old hen. Whenever he came down here from London he would renew the ties, cocking his head from side to side to see that the trunk was rising straight. Then at last he forgot to do this, and looking at the tree one day he saw that the ties were gone, and the stake had rotted below ground and fallen askew, and the tree was springing straight and clean out of the strength of its own roots feeding deep and wide in the earth. And that's how Elizabeth was, he thought, opening his old pale blue eyes for a moment and letting them rest on the white dazzle of the house front. She had soon been able to do without him, but she never had done without him. She was a wonderful woman.

He wished he had had a daughter like her. A beautiful woman was a great comfort about the place, and a great inspiration. Adela was always plain. When she was twenty-one they had had a party for her, here in this garden. It was just such a breathless day as this, and the tea was laid out on a great circular table running round the lime-tree. It had been impossible for him to be there at the beginning, and when he arrived he stood for a moment looking from the cool of the drawing-room into the hot light of the garden, full of muslins and silken parasols and blazers and white flannels. There was a great to-do of talk and laughter, and young Sanderson was carrying a plate of sandwiches and a cup of tea across the lawn, dodging in and out among the guests. A grand boy, young Sanderson, and heir to a fortune. But he wasn't seeking Adela. He was seeking Elizabeth. The pink pearl rhododendrons were at their best, a rising bank of them; and Elizabeth was standing against them, wearing white. A white cartwheel of a hat shaded her face; her white dress was a bell of flounces from waist to feet, and white gloves protected her arms from the burning light. He felt his heart turn over at the sight of her—so tall and fair and utterly self-possessed. There was no one there to touch her.

Young Sanderson placed a chair for her near a green iron table. She sat down and her dress settled slowly about her feet in a white foam. Even from where he stood, Beckwith could see that young Sanderson was adoring her like a dog. She

smiled and rested a hand lightly on his arm and spoke, and he got up and began looking about the garden. Beckwith could guess what she had said: "Find Adela, there's a dear boy." It was at that moment that Adela surprised him at the window. "Oh, Daddy! I'm so glad you've come," she said. She hooked her arm through his. "Let's go out now, and I'll give you some tea."

"But, my dear, what are you doing indoors? It's *your* party."

"Oh, no," she said, without any envy or malice at all, but quite simply, "it's Mamma's."

He looked down sharply at this rather short plain daughter of his, and there was suddenly a pain behind his eyes. "Why, you goose——" he said, and could say no more. He patted her arm and took her through the French window, and he and Elizabeth, Adela and young Sanderson, somehow crowded round the small green table, laden with sandwiches and trifle, ice-cream, cake and fruit.

Even under the lime-tree the air burned like hot brass. The old man stirred uneasily, half-asleep. I suppose it's like this for Ben all the time, he thought. Sir Benjamin Beckwith. Something to do with the administration of Bengal. And a punkah-wallah would come and keep the fans moving.

They were all gone. Only Adrian and Adela remained in England, and these did not bother him much. So far as Adrian was concerned, so much the better. The old man thought him a bore. But he would have liked to see more of Adela. Since her marriage her visits had been few. He knew why. She didn't hate him. He supposed she was incapable of hating anybody, but she had not forgiven him for the pressure he had put on her to marry Brian Pinson. He could only guess what had gone wrong with that marriage—she hadn't told him a thing—but against the measuring-rod of his own complete success in marriage he was able to sense a disastrous failure.

It was Benjamin who had sent Brian Pinson to him. Pinson, after leaving the university, had not spent much time in England. Most of his life had been passed in the East. He had made some spectacular journeys; he had put his name to books about

them, written badly by some newspaper hack in Hong Kong. No doubt, old Beckwith now reflected, he had picked up some spectacular vices. Benjamin had met him in Bombay just before his father, Sir Eustace Pinson, died. Then, when Brian came home to enter upon his inheritance, Benjamin had urged him to call at Lewes, so near to Cotter's Court.

That was how it began. Adela was mistress of the house then, and it happened that she was alone when Brian Pinson casually called. Beckwith remembered how that night she had reported to him on the meeting. She hadn't liked the man. She didn't know why. Yes, he had been amusing and entertaining enough, full of stories of where he had been and what he had done. He came again in response to a formal invitation to dinner—a man of forty-five, small, wiry, tough as hide, but hide that had been too long in the sun and had the juice dried out of it. It was clear that he was attracted by Adela, and this surprised Beckwith, because few men took notice of her. She was a little too short and a little too plump and a little too plain. Her awareness of her own defects made her socially awkward, so that she acted like a gauche girl. She was young enough, but you would have taken her to be much younger. It was only when all the mischief was done that it occurred to Beckwith that Brian Pinson had seen in her a young reluctant virgin to be despoiled. Perhaps he would not have guessed even so much if Benjamin, after the marriage, had not begun to learn some unpleasant facts about the man's reputation. "You will want to keep an eye on Adela and her husband," he wrote. But, bless my soul, what can you do in a case like that? The only comfort was that Pinson had died so soon, and intestate.

The old man drowsed and slept; and was awakened by the tinkling of china as Robinson placed a tea-tray on the table. "His lordship has just arrived, sir," he announced, and there his lordship of Chanctonbury was, propelling his gaitered legs across the lawn. A damned uncomfortable outfit it must be, too, on such a day, the old man thought.

"Sit down, Adrian my boy," he said, rousing himself with a faint crackle of his silk suit. "Adela's coming, isn't she?"

"Yes, I believe so."

"About time, too. It's six months since I set eyes on her. And now, I expect, she's coming into Lewes on some other business and just cuts me off ten minutes of her time. You, too. You don't exactly pester me."

Adrian murmured soothing words and commented on his father's look of robust health. "Ay, looks, looks. I suppose I look all right. But I'm not so good as I look, let me tell you. If I were sixty years younger, I'd call it stitch. Now I shouldn't be surprised if it's angina."

Adrian did not take this seriously. Indeed, he passed it over altogether. He sat down alongside his father and asked: "Has Adela ever said anything to you about marrying again?"

The old man's heart bumped. This was something he had always longed for. And let her choose for herself this time. He would feel as though a sin had been expiated. "No," he said crossly. "Why should she say anything to me? What do any of you say to me? I tell you I haven't seen her for six months."

The Bishop balanced a calf upon a knee and clasped it with both hands. "There was a boy called Chrystal," he said. "Used to help old Herwald. I never met him, but I know he and Adela were very thick. Excuse the word."

"What's wrong with it? It's good English."

"Well, he went to Manchester as a curate, and now he's coming down here to spend a holiday with Adela. He's arriving this afternoon."

"Which explains why she can spare a minute to see me," the old man grunted. "Well, that's a thin story, I must say."

"Not so thin as all that," Adrian said. "They used to read Greek together when he was here, and they've corresponded regularly while he's been away. She's talked to me a lot about him. I think there's something in it."

Old Beckwith ruminated for a moment. "A curate, eh?"

"I was a curate myself once," Adrian said humbly, fingering his cross with one hand, hugging a gaiter with another.

"Well, I hope he's a better-looking one than you were. I used to be ashamed to be seen about with you."

Adela came then, and he thought there was a flurry of excitement about her as she kissed him. He had her for just a

moment to himself before she and Adrian went. He put an arm through hers. "Well, my dear. Everything all right with you? No news? Nothing I can do for you?"

How he would have rejoiced if she had confided in him! But she only patted his hand affectionately, and he hoped the affection was more than a gesture. "News?" she said. "No. The same old round, Daddy. Just a widow with ten thousand things to look after."

"Oh, well——" he said, rather hopelessly.

"Adela, my dear, we must be going." It was Adrian's sonorous voice calling down the short drive. She kissed him hastily and hurried after her brother. He felt empty and lonely, just as the green-grocer in Lambeth had felt, no doubt, after Elizabeth had gone away to Brighton, to learn to talk like a lady.

He had tried to give that young fool Adrian a hint about his condition, and it had been wasted. Well, he wasn't going to bother any of them with his worries. Stitch! That was a good one. He recalled the first time the agony had come upon him. It was the night when he had returned from Brian Pinson's funeral. It was in this room where he now sat with the green-shaded lamp lit on his writing-table and the window flung wide on the night. Little breezes, exhaling the stored heat of the day, stirred the curtains. Riding had always been the exercise he liked best, and he had ridden back from Cotter's Court that day. He had gone gingerly, for here and there in the side-roads where little traffic had passed the frost made slippery patches; but when he came to the main road where wheels all day long had been breaking up the ice, he allowed the horse to canter. It was a horse he was not much used to. He had liked the look of it, coveted it, for a long time, and now it was his. Sombre clouds drifted across the sky, pressed low on the lifeless winter landscape. The light was nearly gone: an orange bar smouldered among the ashen grey low down in the west. He was a mile or so outside Lewes when a dog ran yapping from a cottage garden. The horse stopped, laid back its ears, and suddenly lashed backward at the dog with its hoofs. Beckwith,

accustomed to a horse that took no more notice of dogs than of midges, was disconcerted, and as the dog, untouched, came up again snarling and snapping, he leaned down and wiped at it with his crop. This sudden motion pleased the horse as little as the dog had done. For a few moments it fretted and fidgetted to and fro on the road, then bolted. In all his years of riding, Beckwith had had the luck never before to be astride a horse doing an honest-to-God bolt, as frightened and intractable as though man had never entered into its life. He found it a rather terrifying experience, but that was because of his age and his failing strength, and his apprehension of what might happen if the horse in this condition should reach the town streets. But he subdued the beast, brought it to a stand, trembling and lathered, on the town's outskirts. He leapt down from the saddle, trembling and lathered himself, and, being near home, led the horse to its stable.

When he got up after dinner he found that his legs were still weak beneath him. The study upstairs, with the lamp lit and a fire burning, was soothing. He had intended to write, but, instead, sank into a chair by the fire. Suddenly his whole being reeled. He felt as though a hand of steel had gripped his heart and squeezed it. "I am going to die." The words formed clearly in his mind. Surely this sharp agony, piercing in fiery rays through his chest, making his arm seem like a limb of fire, could mean nothing less. After the first revolting shock he was hardly conscious. He felt as though he were drowning, waves of pain washing his unresisting being to and fro. He was cold as death. And then he was clinging to life again, like a drowning man who finds his fingers miraculously clinging to a rock. The waves were dripping off him, falling away one by one back into the hellish abyss of pain whence they had leapt. To his surprise, he was able to wipe his forehead with a handkerchief. The fire began to warm him. He looked at the clock and saw that not more than three minutes had passed since he had sat in his chair. He felt as though he had wandered in the shadows for hours on end.

That was the first time, and now he kept always in his waistcoat pocket a phial of nitrite of amyl pearls. He had used them

twice, crushing a pearl into his handkerchief, breathing the
sweet relief that sent his enemy headlong. But he had not
ridden again. It was mortifying, for Adela, who did not ride
at all, had offered him the pick of the horses in Brian Pinson's
stable. "No undue exertion and plenty of bed." That was the
prescription from the first doctor he had consulted in his life.
Well, he could live without exertion, and there'd be plenty
of bed when he was bedded down in the earth for good. Till
then, he'd take his seven hours as he'd always done, no more
and no less. He didn't count those afternoon hours when he
drowsed in his chair in his study or under the lime-tree on the
edge of the lawn.

He stood at the open window, and the lime-tree was very
lovely. The full moon was rising, and the shadow of the tree
was the only stain on the milky radiance of the lawn. He had
thought of putting a fountain on the lawn. It would be a tall
single jet in a circular basin, like the one in Fountain Court,
where he had first talked to Elizabeth. If only he had planted
a plane instead of a lime! But there it was. It had been a lime,
and there was never a fountain, though he and Elizabeth had
talked about it so much. It was these hints Adrian had let fall
that turned his mind tonight to those early days with Elizabeth.
A young parson, named Chrystal. It was a nice name. He hoped
Adrian was right about it. He would rejoice to think that
Adela knew those breathless delights that had been his and
Elizabeth's. He remembered the day when he went down to
Brighton after the ending of Tanner v. Urquhart. The sun
shone, and the phrases of old Justice Hendry still echoed
musically in his ears. "But the defence of my—er—hrm!—young
and—er—learned—and if I may so say—brilliant and witty
friend Mr. Beckwith. . . ." Elizabeth was waiting for him. He
remembered it all: the saddle of mutton and red-currant jelly,
the apple-pie and cream, the white clouds bowling over the sky
that canopied the immense prospect from the Devil's Dyke,
where they lay and let the sun soak through them, and lazily
talked with their fingers interlocked on a cushion of thyme. He
sat up and pulled a grass-blade and tickled the delicious red-

ness inside her nostril. "Am I wonderful? Am I young and—er—hrm!—learned and brilliant and witty?" He looked fascinated at the violet tinge of her closed eyelids and saw a tear squeeze its way through. He bent down passionately and tasted the salt of it as he kissed it away. He raised her up with an arm behind her back, and she looked at him with eyes sparkling from tears still unshed. "Yes, you're wonderful, darling," she said. "But, you see, I can't believe it. I can't believe any of it. I can only believe that I'll make a terrible mess of things and that you'd better go away while there's still time."

Ah! that was a wonderful day! He hoped Adela would know some days like that.

He ambled over to his table where the lamp made a circle of light on the papers he had spread out ready for work. As always, he laid the handkerchief and the phial of nitrite of amyl ready to hand. Then he sat down and took up his pen, his mind moving back into the far-off days of Tanner v. Urquhart. It had been an amusing case. Both the parties were so shrewd and witty. Never had the papers enjoyed such a galaxy of epigram and repartee. But it was no good. He couldn't deal with it tonight. It was all too much mixed up in his mind with Elizabeth and Fountain Court. He would go out. Let Robinson think what he liked: he would go out into the garden and cool his mind in the moonlight.

He went softly down the stairs, enjoying the sense of conspiring with himself to defeat the watchful Robinson. Anyway, the fellow should be going to bed by now, if not already there. He left the front door open behind him, so that there should be no betraying click, propped it open with an absurd brass dog kept there for the purpose. The rhododendrons that Elizabeth had loved so much were a dream in the samite moonshine: a great bank of the ghost of opals, without fire or iridescence. He sat in the wicker chair under the lime and could almost hear the crust of the world gently contracting as the fiery heat of the day gave up its breath. He thought that he might still build the fountain. On such a night as this, with the jet collapsing into the basin, and all those dreaming flowers for background!

He thought of nothing else but the bomb of anguish that exploded suddenly in his breast. Instinctively his hand went to his waistcoat pocket, and his last conscious thought was: *I'm finished. I left them on the table*. He held on to the arms of the chair and shuddered in agony.

Robinson blew out his lamp, went to draw back the curtains from his open window. He looked out on to the bluish light falling upon the lawn, with the black shadow of the tree at the heart of it, and then started with consternation. The light tussore silk bundled into the chair was unmistakable. He was about to run from the room when a terrible shout froze him where he was: "Robinson!" And then: "Elizabeth! Oh, Elizabeth!"

Adela could hear Mr. Newstead moving about in the room over her head. She could even hear the rumble of his voice as he said a few good-night words to Dizzy. Then there was perfect quiet in the house. A maid looked into the room, and was about to withdraw when she saw her mistress still sitting there. "Come in, Alice," Adela said. "Put out all the lamps except this one. Then you can go to bed. I sha'n't want anything else."

When the door was shut, her own words seemed to echo in the quiet room, and they were words without sense or meaning. There was so much else that she wanted, and there seemed so little likelihood that it would ever come her way. A profound discontent with her life fretted at her heart. Ever since Brian had died she had persuaded herself that there was some purpose and reality in the comings and goings to the village, the calls on the cottagers, the burnishing of brass in the church, and the pouring of armfuls of lilies into the vases on the altar. But she was more and more aware that all this was only a busy effort to fill a void. The cottagers, she said to herself in her moments of frankness, could do without her very well, and no doubt would prefer to do so. Any verger could polish the brass, and the lilies praised God better growing in the garden then perishing in a dribble of water. All that she did seemed to her no real enlargement of her own life, not even an expression of

such life as she had. She could even envy Lottie Chambers, wearing out her days in the squalor of Limehouse. Limehouse, she thought, was perhaps not unlike Levenshulme, judging from what Theo said about it. And, of course, that was the whole trouble: she wanted to be in Levenshulme with Theo Chrystal. Or anywhere with him. Levenshulme just happened to be where he was. Levenshulme, Limehouse, or some rustic parish full of cows and corn and apples and clean running water: it would be all the same.

Well, she had her practicalities, too. There was nothing to be gained from sitting here letting vain imaginations spin through her head. She took up from the table under the lamp the task she was engaged on. She was translating into English verse Ronsard's *Sonnets for Helen*. (She remembered how, years ago, young Sanderson, who had come to Lewes to play tennis, had given her a little book called *My Favourites*. His friends had filled in their favourite flowers and names—most of the girls had written George, which was Sanderson's name —and seaside resorts and poets. Her favourite poet, she had written, was Ronsard, and George Sanderson had said lightly "Good lord! Who's he? Never heard of him." "His *Sonnets for Helen* are the most wonderful love poetry," she anwered naïvely. Sanderson had laughed gaily. "Then I must get to know the old chap," he said. "But, you know, Miss Beckwith, the thing to do with love poetry is to live it, not read it.")

The book fell open in her hands. *"Lorsque le Ciel te fit, il rompit le modelle."* How translate that? *Live it, not read it.* Yes, but how did you begin to live it if you were a woman, and not so young, and not so handsome? The book slipped to the floor. She let it lie there, blew out the lamp, and opened the window into the garden.

Theo had asked to be called at six. He must not, even during this holiday, neglect the two hours of prayer and devotional reading with which his day began. But it looked like being for him a short night. He felt wide awake and did not undress. He took from his suitcase his Greek Testament and a brown, stained edition in Latin of St. Theresa's *Way of Perfection*. He

placed these in his methodical fashion on the table by the bed.
He blew out his unnecessary candle. The curtains were drawn
back and the full moon of midsummer had begun to climb.
There was an easy chair near the window and he sat in it, his
arms resting on the sill, looking out into the garden and listening to the diminuendo of Mr. Newstead's retiral next door.
He felt an irking sense of grievance that his holiday was to be
jarred upon by this obnoxious specimen of university bore.
Miss Chambers one might get on with, though she was not his
idea of sustaining female companionship. It ocurred to him
suddenly that there were two queer things about his life. He
had, almost since he could think—certainly ever since he had
decided upon the Church as his calling—told himself that he
would never marry. Yet for years now he had written to a
woman almost every day. All the time he was at Selwyn he had
written to his mother. Ever since he had been in Manchester
he had written to Adela Pinson. And at this moment he felt
an irresistible desire to write to a woman. He got up and took
a pad of paper from his bag and a stub of pencil from his
pocket, and then, sitting again, where the moonlight just fell
upon the page, he wrote: "My dear Miss Dillworth."

He was surprised at his own almost involuntary reaction.
He gazed at the words just visible on the moon-blurred sheet,
and a host of images rose up before his mind: the grey aguish
streets of Levenshulme in a winter dusk; his own little room
with the curtains drawn and the fire shining and Mrs. Hornabrook bustling in to change the velvet cloth for a linen one
and serve "summat t'ate"; Alec Dillworth's thin enthusiast's
face; a spring morning on the road through Burnage, with
Elsie Dillworth, hatless, walking with him to Dan Dunkerley's
new house at Didsbury. It was all charged with an extraordinary nostalgia. He thought he had hated the place. Now he
knew that it had treacherously stolen into his heart, taken
possession, and left him, here in this lovely house lapped in
quiet, lonely and homesick. This final word of his reflection
startled him. Homesick for Manchester? He looked down at
the sheet resting on his knee and continued to write: "I've told
you often what a lovely place this is, and you will be surprised

to know that my feeling on this first night here is that I miss you all very much."

All. . . . He was aware of the almost imperceptible pause before he inserted that word. He had not meant to use it. He did not want to use it now. "I miss you very much." That is what he wanted to write. And that explained everything he had been feeling about Manchester. A wild impulse suddenly flooded him to tear up the sheet and begin again: "Darling Elsie—How I miss you!" But he merely ran his pencil in an irritated line through what he had written, threw the pad back where he had taken it from, and went to stand at the window.

He did not know that that morning the view from the window had been obscured by a tangled growth of clematis and Virgina creeper. Adela, looking into the room to see that all was in order, had told the gardener to clear this away. He had done so, climbing to the window on a ladder, and he had left the ladder where it stood. The moonlight showed it to Theo as he idled restlessly there looking down; and, feeling sleep to be far from him, he clambered over the sill, ran lightly down the ladder, and breathed deeply the clear still air. He stood stock-still, leaning against the wall at the foot of the ladder. He could not, at that first encounter with the superb serenity of the night, bear to disturb it by so much as the whisper of his footsteps brushing the sleeping and enchanted grass. The bats were gone. All movement and all sound seemed to have been sucked out of the world, and yet he could hear as it were the majestic and frightening sound of nothing. That, he thought, was what Baudelaire had heard, and he murmured to himself: *Entends, ma chère, entends la douce Nuit qui marche.* But it was not in such a place as this that Baudelaire had written. He had written leaning from a city window over a mean street. It was the sort of poem Alec Dillworth might have written in Manchester.

Still leaning against the wall, he fumbled in his pockets, charged his pipe with tobacco, and struck a match. It was the leap of the small flame that caught Lady Pinson's eye. She had been walking quietly on the grass, and now, standing in the

shadows of the cedar, she could just make out Theo's form, leaning back in the darkness under the wall of the house. As he sucked upon his pipe, the matchlight flared, subsided—flared, subsided—with the intake and exhalation of his breath, and his face dawned and died upon her vision: the high white brow, the clinging golden hair upon his hatless head, a fleeting irradiation within the band of darkness. Her breath came painfully. She wondered what to do. She would stay just where she was till he had either climbed back to his room or walked out of her sight. As she thought this, he stepped into the moonlight and began to walk towards the cedar. She had not realized that her white dress, gleaming in the darkness, had betrayed her. "Is anyone there?" Theo said as he approached. "Ah, Adela, it's you. I thought I was the only one keeping such late hours."

The night compelled him to speak quietly. It was conspiring to make them seem conspirators. "I was restless," she said. "I tried to read, but couldn't."

She came out from the layered shadows of the tree, and they stood side by side in the moonlight that made her seem insubstantial and him a column of solid black topped with a shining head. Without a word further, with a mutual understanding, they began to move away together—away from the house, towards the drive that ran through half a mile of field and spinney to the high road. She could hear a slight suck and gurgle in the bowl of his pipe, so quiet was the night. Before them now was the stretch of open field, bleached and lunar, with the dark fleece of the spinney ahead laid across its shoulders. "Adela," he said suddenly, "you've always been so good to me. I want to tell you something, and ask your advice. You know, there's no one else, no one at all, I rely on as I do on you."

Oh, God, stop him, stop him, she prayed. If he wants to marry her, let him do so. But don't let him talk to me like this. He makes me sound as though I were his mother or grandmother. Oh, God, deliver me.

"I believe I'm in love," he said.

A bubble of sound exploded softly in the spinney. Then another and another, all on the same sweet low wooing note.

They stopped walking and leaned on the iron railings that edged the drive. "It's the nightingale," Adela said.

"I've mentioned her in my letters. She's a poor girl, not even educated, but very beautiful."

"Listen a moment. Don't you love that prologue? Now he's going right into it. We always want to speak quietly on a night like this, but the nightingale sings at the top of his voice." Sing, bird, sing, and stop him from talking.

"Don't you think," she said, "half the enchantment is that we don't see him? We see the blackbird and the thrush, and even when the lark's half-way to heaven we glimpse the speck of him. But who's ever seen a nightingale? I never have. It's as though the night itself were singing its heart out."

Then she was silent, and Theo, too, had for the time nothing more to say. The vibrant *roulades* of melody surged upon the air, and, listening to them, his mind was busy fitting in the appropriate passages from the poets. His emotions were rarely expressed at first hand. Baudelaire had described for him the quality of the night; and now he called in the services and Keats and Swinburne. He listened at second-hand to the gorgeous confluence of joy and sorrow pouring from the dark secret places of the thicket up into the gracial and unresponsive immensity of the dead sky.

They stood there for a long time, until the fiery song was expiring in a few pulsing embers of sound. Then another sound began to gain upon their ears. At first they could not believe it, then Adela said "Wheels?" and Theo, looking ahead, glimpsed the headlamps of a carriage. "Good gracious," he said. "It must be midnight."

A premonition of ill seized Adela's heart. Perhaps God had chosen his own way to deliver her.

The approaching chariot of fate did not seem frightening, or even notable. It was an old four-wheeler cab. It lumbered towards them slowly. A faint steaming showed from the nostrils of the decrepit horse. Robinson, hearing the great shout which was the last sound produced on earth by Merriman Beckwith, had called the housekeeper and had run with her

into the garden. He left the old man in her charge and himself went to summon a doctor. Thence he went to a livery stable, and with some difficulty persuaded the proprietor to produce two old cabs and two old horses and two old drivers. All this took time, and it was past eleven o'clock when the vehicles rolled away, each driver carrying a note that Robinson had written: one to Lady Pinson and one to the Bishop of Chanctonbury. "My Lady:—Mr. Beckwith was taken very ill suddenly tonight. I cannot give you any information as to the nature of the illness, for I left the house, as soon as my master was found lying in the garden, in order to send this message. But he was unconscious, and your ladyship may wish to return with the person who brings this note. I have informed His Lordship of Chanctonbury."

So the conscientious Robinson had written, saying briefly all there was to say.

Adela handed the note to Theo, who was able to read it by the clear moonlight. "Get in," he said, opening the cab door. "I shall come with you."

Even at that moment, she could not dismiss the thought of the sensation, perhaps the scandal, at Cotter's Court in the morning. Two beds unslept in. Lady Pinson and the Reverend Theodore Chrystal disappeared! "Shouldn't we leave some message?" she asked. "Get in," said Theo, masterfully in control. "You've got no time to waste. I'll see to all that."

He opened a gate leading from the drive into a field, told the cabman to drive through and turn his horse, and when the cab was back on the drive again he shut the gate. "This is a matter that needs speed," he said to the driver. "Go as quickly as you can, short of killing that poor beast. Lady Pinson's father is perhaps dying." Then he joined Adela in the cab and they rolled away.

However warm two days may be, one must die before the other is born, and in that interval death is very chill. That moment was upon them now. The news itself had made Adela feel cold. She knew that his hurry through the night was useless, that she would find her father dead, and death still had terrors for her. She had met it only once, when her husband

died, and then it had come with so deep a sense of relief that she was moving now to an experience she had never had before. Real though the estrangement had been between her father and herself, this moment rubbed a sponge over those spoiled months and years. The differences had been of understanding, of adjustment to living, not the profound spiritual difference that had separated her from her husband. She was thinking only of the things she and her father had loved together: Elizabeth, and the home in Lewes, and the walks on the lean, windy downs. All those things seemed now an incredibly long way off. Her father's death snapped the last frail thread that bound her life to so much that was so lovely.

Suddenly she shivered violently, from the cold without her and within. Quite clearly, Theo heard the castanet-clatter of her teeth. She drew nearer to him, as though to find warmth from the contact. "You must put my coat about you," he said. He pulled off the coat and placed it round her shoulders. She protested feebly. "It's getting very cold. You'll miss it." He laughed in his strength, full of pride that she had drawn towards his warm masculinity. "Me? On a midsummer night? I've never had a cold in my life." And not knowing that he was torturing her, he said: "Lean against me if it makes you feel warmer." She leaned hard against the white sleeve clothing his left arm, and to ease things and make her feel more comfortable he placed it round her. "There," he said. "Is that better?" She answered with a little animal grunt of contentment. He leaning back in a corner, she leaning upon him, the cab swinging out of the drive into the road to Lewes.

And now Adela scarcely dared to breathe. She was thinking no longer of her father, less of the husband she had shrunk from with body and soul alike. She was thinking only of the dear intimate quality of this moment. Not thinking of it so much as giving herself up freely to it, with a sensuous delight that would have startled and disconcerted her if indeed she had been thinking rather than living instinctively. Theo's left hand rested lightly on her waist. She longed to put her own hand upon it and press it there. She was warm now, with a warmth engendered in herself. Her breasts were taut with

longing. She gave a wriggle which brought her closer upon
him, and then, with half her being crying "Don't, don't!" and
the rest of her borne irresistibly down with longing for the
kind of love she had never known, she took hold of his hand,
rejoicing in its long cool thinness, raised it from her waist, and
frankly pressed it against the tell-tale swelling of her breast.

Then, indeed, the part of her being that was anchored to
old loyalties and unselfish impulses started back aghast. She
remembered Theo's voice saying: "I want to ask your advice.
I believe I'm in love." She felt cleft in twain, and, as if she
were waking in fright from a dream, she sat bolt upright,
pulling her body away from the disastrous intoxicating contact with his. His hand fell limply down, and now each was
leaning back in a corner, each looking out of a separate window at the silvered hedges sliding by and the trees sleeping
where they stood. But the avowal had been complete, irrevo-
cable. Nothing, Adela thought, nothing can be the same between us again. I have destroyed myself.

For a long time neither spoke. Theo was trying hard and
honestly to see what he should do with the situation so as to
inflict the least hurt upon her. He was profoundly shocked.
Not in a stupid way. His mind did not say: "How shocking of
her!" and recoil from her; but he was shocked, jarred, by the
suddenness and complete unexpectedness of what had happened. He had never laid a hand upon a woman, and that a
woman should herself lay his hand upon her in that way
rocked him to the foundations. He had sometimes wondered
whether Lady Pinson loved him, but had dismissed the idea
as incredible. He was certain that he did not love her. He
admired her, had a deep respect for her, and was, too, material-
istically aware of the advantages her friendship could bring.
One second of time had now swept all these considerations off
the board. It is not surprising if a happening so complete and
unmistakable should have left him for a moment without
bearings.

The best in Theo rose to the surface in that moment. He
understood now that she loved him, and that being so, there
was nothing here, he felt, that he could not comprehend and

pardon. A great pity for Adela filled his heart. He blamed himself for the blindness which had led him to make her confession possible. The quality of the night, the emotion of his own begun confession of love, this sudden tragic news from Lewes: all had conspired to undo her, and he had done nothing to help her.

For a long time he watched the frosted silk skeins of the telegraph wires dipping between the fingers atop the posts; then he stretched out his hand to where hers lay white and forlorn on the rusty old leather seat. He pressed her hand once, briefly, warmly, reassuringly, and said: "The best thing will be, Adela, as soon as daylight comes, for me to go to the livery stable and get them to send over a letter to Cotter's Court. It should get there before anybody's up, and I'll explain everything."

"Yes, that would be best," she said faintly, feeling deathly cold again, but thanking him in her heart.

They said nothing more about it. It didn't sound as though *these* words were about it; but Adela knew that they were, that they wiped up the whole matter.

Old Beckwith was dead all right; and Theo explained to the Bishop of Chanctonbury that in the circumstances his visit to Cotter's Court must end at once. He did not stay even for the funeral, and with a great gladness of heart found himself boarding the Manchester train at St. Pancras.

Chapter Eight

NOT a word was spoken. The occasion was too serious, almost solemn. There they were, the four of them, driving away in the brougham from the White House, Didsbury, after Dan Dunkerley's inaugural breakfast: Dan and Sim facing the horses, Alec Dillworth and George Satterfield gazing backward along the unwinding road. These two sat away from one another, each close into his own corner, not liking one another. But at the moment Alec was not thinking of his dislike for George Satterfield. He was keeping his face as solemn as the other three faces, but in his heart he was writhing with laughter. The mild sunlight was blessing the earth; the trees crowding close to the road as they passed through Fallow-field were lit up with red and white and yellow blossoms, and swifts were skating in majestic arcs upon the blue plane of the sky. And here we are, thought Alec, moving through all this like mutes going to pay our respects to a corpse. He felt that they should be leaning out of the window and cheering, or blowing trumpets, or throwing confetti. But no. There was old Sim, yellow gloves, skewers of moustache, the flower at his lapel, the Malacca cane in his hand, gazing straight before him out of his ice-blue eyes as though he were some fantastic aristocrat on the way to the guillotine. There was Dan, his round healthy normal face set into an expression of almost holy devotion: worshipping Mammon, already, so soon, thought Alec. And there was Satterfield, neither daunted like the old man nor dedicated, to whatever unworthiness, like Dan, but just plainly and vulgarly stuck up. Ah well, thought Alec, they'll soon be used to it. Soon it'll mean no more to them than the morning bacon; and by then, of course, there'll be something else, something new and wonderful all the time, to keep on reminding them that they're richer and richer, more and more successful.

He would have liked to shake them all up in a bag, do some-

thing rude or shocking to bring them to their senses; but he bore down the impulse and sat quiet, looking like an intelligent handsome monkey. He had now arrived finally at his editorial costume. The uniform, with *Hard Facts* on the collar, had been a passing if irresistible joke. The exaggerated Byronism that succeeded it, and which had pleased George Satterfield, was abandoned when the offices moved from Levenshulme to the heart of Manchester. While the new building was going up, the work was done in a fine old house in St. John Street, and here Alec was to be found giving a modified version of the first Byronic flourish. He wore a black felt hat whose brim was only mildly exaggerated, a soft white shirt with a bow tie which, while carelessly knotted, was not outrageously large. For the rest, he was toning down, seeing clearly enough the significance—or utter insignificance—of Dunkerley's grandiose visions, but keeping his mind to himself and his conduct fairly free from offence. He was better off than he had ever hoped to be; he would be better off yet; and there was Elsie to think about. Whenever a temptation stronger than usual to play the fool assailed him, he could now put it aside with that reflection: there was Elsie to think about.

There had, if it came to that, *always* been Elsie to think about. His mind, which photographed experience with extraordinary fidelity, could always roll the film back to the moment when he first realized that Elsie needed him. He would be seven at the time, and she six. It was a winter night of piercing cold, and he, Elsie, and their mother were together in the kitchen. The fire was lit, and to his infant mind the sordid little room seemed cosy and desirable. He was sprawling on a rag mat by the fender, with a book on the floor. It was a Bible, the only book in the house, a colossal volume that caused him to totter as he reached it down to lay it on the mat. He had only just discovered this treasure. He could read, and as this was the only thing there was to read, he read it. And there were many pictures. Some of them were gentle and soothing: shepherds carrying lambs on their shoulders; angels kneeling with stiff calico wings by a manger in which a baby was

sleeping with a piece of round shining tin behind its head.
Some were horrific: an old man with a knife uplifted to stab
a little boy lying on a pile of wood; a youth with a great stone
in his hand smashing in another boy's head; lions eating men
and women in an immense shadowy building whose upper air
was as thick with angels as the sky above a wood with rooks at
eventide. Alec found it all profoundly moving. It released his
imagination on the maddest flights; and he began to read carefully from the first page. *In the beginning God created the
heaven and the earth.* He wriggled with ecstasy to see how
long—endless it seemed—the book was. All that to read: night
after night after night.

Elsie was under the table, squatting on her haunches, rocking herself to and fro, clutching to her breast a bundle of rags.
The top of the bundle was vaguely a sphere and a piece of tape
tied beneath it could be reckoned a neck beneath a head. From
this neck the bundle flowed down in a tatter of what Elsie held
to be her baby's clothes. This baby was named Bim, though
no one knew why, and for a long time Bim, Elsie, and Alec
had shared a bed. They would all three have been in this bed
now, for it was fairly late; but Mrs. Dillworth, who had made
up her mind that she would not go to the pub on the corner
that night, knew that this was one of the nights when it was
no good making up her mind. She would find herself in the
pub whether she wanted to go there or not. She had had a hard
day, what with scrubbing offices before nine and doing a family's wash in Burnage after that, and thinking all the time of
her husband serving the first fourteen days he had ever been
sentenced to. In these circumstances, she knew that before the
evening was much older she would find herself in the pub. She
had not at that time lost all sense of what she owed to her children. She felt that if she went to the pub they must go with her.
All day long they had been left to fend for themselves; and
they would have been safe enough in bed. But this did not
seem so to Mrs. Dillworth's mind. They might be alone all
through a winter's day, but she drew the line at leaving them
alone throughout a winter's night.

She had been sunk in torpor in her chair since seven o'clock.

At nine she rose, pulled on an old coat and a battered hat, and said: "Now, you two. You come with me. I'm going out."

Elsie crawled from under the table, hugging Bim. Alec was so absorbed that he literally did not hear the words addressed to him. His mother took him by the collar and pulled him to his feet. "Going out," she said briefly.

He looked at her stupidly, dazed with the immensity of the journey back that his mind had made. Then he sagged again to the floor, announcing simply: "Go on reading."

"I can't be bothered; I'm too tired. Let him do what he damn well likes. Let him burn the bloody house down," the woman thought wildly, enraged by life and by her own weakness to deal with it. She took Elsie's hand and whisked her out of the room. Alec was hardly conscious of the front door's bang. *God created the great sea monsters.* His imagination was rushing through primeval chaos, watching it fill up, day after day, with the flaming sun and the tender ghostly moon, every creeping thing moving through the grass, and birds flying among the trees that had magically matured, and great sea monsters with scintillating scales cavorting and spouting in the brand-new deep.

What brought him back to a sense of his surroundings was the cold. The fire had gone out. The house was not only cold: it was terribly quiet. A profound sense of his abandonment fell on the child's heart. He missed his father whom he had not seen for a week. He had no idea where his father was, and had the man been present it would have meant no more than harsh words and occasional blows. But Alec missed him, because his absence breached the familiar, the accustomed, in which a child's mind finds its sanity and repose. Now that the fire was out—both the fire in the grate and the fire that had warmed his imagination—the room, seeming so cosy an hour ago, was suddenly harsh and forbidding. There was no light now save that which fell from a tin lamp hung to a nail on the wall, and this filled the room with unmoving shadows. The worst thing of all was that the window was uncurtained. Beyond it was a small square of backyard. Who might now be in that backyard,

peering, himself unseen, into the kitchen, noticing with a bloody relish that in it was one small boy, unprotected?

Alec ran in panic to the stairs. Bed, with his head under the clothes, was the place for him. He was half-way up in the pitch darkness when a white form wavered and surged towards him. It was an old dress of his mother's, hanging there on a hook. He had seen it scores of times, but what did that matter? It was waiting for him, and he had better be quick to save himself. He turned, rushed through the kitchen into the passage, opened the front door, and found himself in the street.

Now he could pause to take breath. He was on familiar ground. The streets, by day and night, were known and dear to him. It was snowing, and the undersized waif, without overcoat or hat, was happy. A great sense of escape, of freedom, flooded him, and he stood stock-still, looking up into the grey immensity above the cañon-walls of the street, rejoicing in the white flurry and dither of the snow. As he stood there, his small mind was aware of the majesty of the silence, the awe and beauty of the myriad flakes spinning through the void to kiss the earth so quietly and die.

It was near to Christmastime, and at the heart of the grey-white vista before him was the cheerful orange smudge of a corner-shop window. It seemed magnificently heartening, though its magnificence was indeed a comparative matter. One oil-lamp which furnished all the light was set behind a shield of red paper, and through this the muted glow fell upon coloured paper festoons, some glittering glass baubles of red and blue, a meagre pyramid of oranges, and tall glass jars filled with sweets. The dark green of holly leaves, lightened by berries like beads of scarlet sealing-wax, filled in the background and formed a frame for a home-made notice that wished young Alec, gazing entranced through the glass, A Merry Christmas.

Now that he was out of the spell which the pictures and his reading had thrown upon him, he knew where his mother was. She had gone to the Bull. He had a precocious knowledge of these things. He knew that the Bull shut its doors at eleven, and that he need not expect to see his mother till then. He could go to the Bull and wait for her, but he did not want to

do this tonight. He had never before been out alone in a snow-storm; it would all be spoiled if there were any one with him.

Long afterwards, Theo Chrystal was to reflect—in very different circumstances, in a summer night of moonlight and nightingale-song—that Alec Dillworth, in Manchester, might have written the line: *Entends, ma chère, entends la douce Nuit qui marche*. Alec could not have written the line that night, but none the less his young heart was moved by the spirit that would have made the line possible. He turned now, with his back to the small window, noticed how the light fell in a tender warm suffusion upon the snow immediately before him, and looked up again at the relentless silent multitude of flakes, marvelling that things so light could fall so swiftly. He held out his hands, like a shabby infant Francis of the gutter, luring these fragile birds into his palms. One after another they settled, and in settling were gone. There was nothing at all but a wetness on his hands.

It was now that he was aware of footsteps shush-shushing through the snow, and saw Mrs. Goostrey, muffled in a cape and hood, coming towards him. She and Mr. Goostrey managed, they alone knew how, to snatch a living out of this little shop. Alec was not aware of the pathos of his appearance—so white and undersized, standing there with the snow thickening upon his hair and shoulders, his hands extended palm-up in the immemorial attitude of those who beg for alms. Mrs. Goostrey, a warm-hearted woman who was returning from a Wesleyan class meeting where Christmas hymns had cheered her, swooped upon him like a benevolent eagle having the best intentions towards a small shivering lamb. Her arms went right round him, scooped him up, and carried him through the private door alongside the shop-window. "Arthur! Arthur!" she called, butting open the kitchen door with her plump knee. "Look at this shivering morsel! One o' them Dillworth kids. Frozen stiff. His father in gaol an' all, an' his mother in t'Bull, Ah shouldn't wonder."

Mrs. Goostrey's philanthropy exceeded her common sense. She did not know that she had driven an arrow through Alec's

young heart. So that was where his father was! He knew, with a swift inescapable knowledge, that it was true, and everything in him shouted in protest. "Oo, you bloody ole liar!" he cried, wriggling free and confronting her angrily. "My father's gone to Ardwick to see about a job."

Mr. Goostrey, large and placid, took off his spectacles, laid down the evening paper, and looked up from his comfortable arm-chair by the fire. "Ay, ay, Ah shouldn't wonder, lad," he said. "Ay, Ah've 'eard that's just where 'e is." He gave a warning and reproachful look to his wife, who went through the passage and could be heard flapping the snow off her cloak at the front door.

"Well, it's seasonable weather aw reight," she announced, returning. "Let's 'ave a cup o' tea."

"Ah've got it ready," said Mr. Goostrey. "Ah could do wi' a sup mysen."

The tea-pot was on the hob, a cloth was on the table, with places set for two. Mrs. Goostrey laid for Alec, and produced a large cake from a cupboard. These preparations, and the comfortable presence of the two old people, the hospitable warmth of the kitchen which was decorated with evergreens and streamers more lavishly than the shop, might have cheered Alec's heart but for the poisonous knowledge that Mrs. Goostrey had dropped into it. Quick beyond his years, he had seen and understood the glance that Mr. Goostrey gave his wife, and he knew that now both of them were playing a part, both of them knew that his father was in gaol, and that his passionate lie was not believed.

Mrs. Goostrey cut a formidable slice of cake and placed it before him. It was rich and brown and stuffed with fruit. He sat there full of an odd reserve, like a wild young trapped thing that will not come to terms with its captors. The cake was good, and the tea warmed him, but his heart did not thaw. He would not give himself to Mr. and Mrs. Goostrey. When he had eaten half the cake, he put the rest into his pocket. "That's for our Else," he explained. It was the first word he had granted them after his outburst at the woman.

"Why, you poor thing," Mrs. Goostrey cried. "You eat that

cake now—every crumb an' morsel. If you want some for your
sister, I'll cut it for you."

And so she did, wrapping it in a piece of paper, and drop-
ping it together with a small bag of sweets into his pocket. But
she could not win his good will, and when he was gone, with a
grave announcement that he must now be on his way, she said
to Mr. Goostrey that she "couldn't mak head nor tail" of him.
Mr. Goostrey was pulling heavily on his pipe. His small flesh-
embedded eyes saw more than his wife's. " 'Appen, lass," he
said, between puffs, "tha's given 'im a bit of a shock like. Ah
shouldn't wonder."

The snow was still falling, but now Alec did not linger to
admire its beauty. The streets were empty. His feet made no
sound. There was never much traffic here, and the notion
came to him that he would like to go to the Stockport Road,
where, usually, there was a good deal. It would be interesting
to see carts and horses moving through the storm, with no
sound coming from wheels and hoofs. A few corners turned,
and he was there. Now the spectacle was more impressive, for
the road was wide and he had a longer view to east and west.
But either way, it closed in a deepening darkness, with snow
drawing a wavering curtain upon the view. And there was not
much traffic. A lorry went by, with its vast horses treading as
quietly as Alec had once seen swans treading the water of a
lake, and a cabby, with a cloak of snow laid upon his shoulders,
whipped his horse along, looming into view, and being there,
and passing from sight all in a few silent muffled seconds. The
roof of the cab was iced like Mrs. Goostrey's cake.

As he thought this, Alec remembered Elsie, and turned at
once back towards the Bull. The pub stood on a corner, and
its lights were not like the muted light that fell through the
window of the Goostrey shop. There was a big gas lamp over
the door; from this and from the windows a hard white light
lit up the whole corner. As he approached, Alec saw by this
light that the snow was dotted with figures gesticulating wildly.
Shouts and screams reached his ears; and he stopped when he
was a hundred yards away, arrested by the drama of the spectacle. He had never been to a theatre, but this was a scene of

theatre that he was looking at now: the stage illuminated amid surrounding darkness, the actors at grips, the audience dimly discerned, in diminishing clarity, receding from the fringes of action. Upon the stage the snow was falling through the bright light, and amid its whirl and dance the principals were whirling and dancing, shaking fists and shouting abominable words. All this, too, had its macabre beauty that registered faithfully upon Alec's imagination; so that always thereafter he was able to live again in that pulsing moment as he advanced over the dumb white pavement and recognized his mother in one of the two prancing figures of malediction. Her hat was askew over one eye; her hair was down, and in one hand she held the deadly weapon of a furious and drunken woman, a hat-pin. This long slender stiletto, hilted with a bead of jet, was the fascinating focus of the drama to the spectators who stood with shoulders hunched under the falling snow.

The other woman was young, with raffish good looks. She moved slowly round in a circle, her eye warily on Mrs. Dillworth's hand, and opposite her Mrs. Dillworth was slowly moving in this same circle, half-crouched like an animal waiting to spring. The dialogue was monotonous. "You old cow. You old gaol-bird's cow," the young woman repeated again and again; and Mrs. Dillworth as tiresomely kept on saying: "You two-and-sixpenny whore. You two-and sixpenny whore." So they went, beating out a track in the snow like circus-horses pounding the tan of the ring; and occasionally they would be drawn out of their orbit, rush together with incoherent shrieks, and then break away to tread anew the ritual, fascinated pattern of this dance.

Alec had approached to the outer ring of spectators. He stood in a dark doorway, and the snow came on heavier, so that now he was watching the drama through wavering gauze. The crowd became impatient for the kill and began to shout: "Go on! Kill t'little bitch!" "Knock t'owd cow down. Stamp on 'er." " 'E *is* in gaol." " 'E bloody well isn't."

So that was how it began, Alec realized. There had been an argument in the pub about his father. And then the scene suddenly dissolved. He saw the audience at first slowly, then

more swiftly, vanishing one by one into the mysterious darkness behind the white curtains, and even the bemused women, rapt in their fatal hatred, at last became aware of some new element in the occasion. It was a policeman—as simple as that—materializing out of the night, a stolid blue figure, mottled with white on head and shoulders, advancing with no hurry or agitation right into the middle of the scene. The younger woman saw him first and ran like a gazelle. Mrs. Dillworth, clutching her hat-pin, stood alone, looking about her stupidly. The policeman walked up to her and saw what was in her hand. He roughly pulled her hat straight, and said: "Put that where it belongs." With fumbling fingers she obeyed. "Now get along home, you silly old fool. You ought to know better." She went, and the policeman followed a little way behind her, and then the stage was empty again, save for the snow which persistently and contemptuously fell, unheeding whether upon passion or emptiness.

Alec never forgot how in the hush of that moment Elsie came to him. She had been swept out of his mind by the new excitements of the drama, and then there she was, walking across the white empty stage with Bim held to her breast. Their mother, so long as pride of anything was left in her, was proud of Elsie's hair. It was long, down to her waist, and it was never confined by any ribbon. It hung in a shining sheet of orange-gold down her back, and Mrs. Dillworth would brush and brush at it till every fine silken hair gleamed. This banner, this golden aureole, was about her as she crossed the road, and the light from the pub lamp and windows fell upon it. She was like an angel, Alec thought, like one of the angels in the big Bible. He said: "I got some cake for you."

They had nothing more to say to one another. They sat on a sheltered doorstep and Elsie ate the cake. Then Alec took out the sweets and they began to suck them. As she was doing so Elsie fell asleep with her head on Alec's shoulder. It was thus that they were found by Mr. Burnside. Newly come to the parish, it was the first time he had seen them. As he stopped and looked down at the children, Alec put a finger to his lips. "She's asleep," he whispered hoarsely.

"Well, young feller," said Mr. Burnside, "I'm afraid we'll have to wake her up. She'll get too cold, you know, sleeping there. And so will you. Shall I take you home?"

"No," Alec answered firmly. "My father's in gaol and my mother's tight."

He nudged Elsie, and she woke up, her strange green eyes, bemused by sleep, slowly taking in the pair of long black legs set like twin pillars before her. She looked up into Mr. Burnside's face, and what she saw there by the light of the street lamp, pleased her. She got to her feet and instinctively put her small frozen hand into his. "Cold as paddocks though they be . . ." he murmured, his heart rent with pity. The children went with him gladly. He thawed them out by his study fire, gave them hot drinks, and knelt before them to pull off their boots and stockings. When their hands and feet were warm, he wrapped them in blankets and left them to sleep there on the floor. In the morning, under a heavenly blue sky, he walked them through the crisp snow back to their mother.

That, as Alec remembered it, was the first time he had been aware of Elsie's need of him. His sense of this need found a pathetic expression: he never again, if he could help it, stayed at home when Mrs. Dillworth took Elsie out at night. There was, too, his own need of Elsie. There were only two bedrooms in the Dillworth house, and Alec and Elsie slept in the same bed till he was twelve years old. Hers, because of the circumstances of his life, were the only woman's limbs he had ever felt warmly upon his own. In the cold winters they would lie wrapped together, and on hot summer mornings, when sometimes she would leap out of bed before him and throw off her shift before dressing, he would look with admiration at her long slender legs, and the immature buds of her breasts, and the gold streaming down her back. The life that stunted Alec's body was unable to check the beautiful growth of Elsie's.

It was at this time, when he was twelve, that Alec's schooling ended. He was sent to work with a grocer on the Stockport Road. He was there at eight in the morning, sweeping out the shop, polishing the brass, cleaning the pavement, shining up

the window. He had wondered what he would have to do for
his four shillings a week, and found there was little he didn't
have to do, from carrying goods to customers' houses to peel-
ing potatoes and washing dishes for the grocer's wife in the
kitchen behind the shop. The shop shut at eight at night, but
that wasn't the end of it. Now there was "tidying-up," and
chopping firewood ready for the kitchen range in the morning, and this and that. It was a six-day week, and the grocer
was resolved to get his eight-pennyworth of blood and energy
a day.

Alec didn't mind. It was a new experience, and his restless
inquisitive brain was always responsive to change. He was
looking forward to telling Elsie all about it. The great moment of every day to him was when he lay in bed alongside
Elsie and poured into her ear all his doings and imaginings.
That night, he found that blankets and a sheet had been laid
on a couch in the never-till-then used "best room." Here,
Elsie was told, she would sleep in the future.

When he had gone to bed, Alec felt an extraordinary sense
of loss and frustration. He turned to this side and that, but
he could not sleep. His mind was over-charged with matter
that found no safety-valve of expression, and his body was
restless for familiar contacts. At last he rose and, clad only in
the shirt which he did not change night and day, he crept
downstairs and into the "best room." Elsie was in bed. The
linen roller-blind was up and the street lamp, planted on the
pavement not a yard from the window, laid the black cross
of the window-frame, filled in with pale yellow light, upon
her as she lay. He whispered: "Are you asleep, Else?"

She was not. She threw back the bed-clothes, hitched herself towards the wall, and Alec climbed in beside her. It was
a narrow bed; there was not really room in it for the two of
them; she put her arms round him to prevent him from rolling out on to the floor. All the pain and bafflement of his
mind flowed away. He felt happy and released and began to
pour out the story of his day: the wonders of Mrs. Church-
man's kitchen, with a tank alongside the fire-range, so that
you had but to turn a tap and hot water flowed out. The

splendour of a house he had called at in Burnage. "A bear,
Else, a real great big bear, standing up inside the door, holding a brass tray, an' a girl with a white cap—a real servant—
who said 'Madam' to the woman." There was another house
where he had been given a penny tip; and now his imagination sketched the marvellous day he and Elsie would have
when penny tips should have mounted to half-a-crown. They
would go in to Manchester and have tea and buns in a shop,
and then they would go to a music hall; or they would buy
buns at Mrs. Goostrey's and go right out into the country—
to Marple, or perhaps to some place incredibly remote, like
Disley.

Elsie said nothing. The talking was always Alec's part of
their association. She only gave him a hug now and then or
crooned a small ecstatic assent to his adventurous imaginings.
Her voice gurgled in her white throat like honey.

Suddenly, Alec heard this voice for the first time. Thousands of times he had heard Elsie laughing and talking; but
this was something different. For years now he had been devouring the great Bible. The voluptuous roll of words enchanted him, already was touching the secret places of his
heart wherein an unborn poet groped in darkness. He would
recite long passages from the Song of Songs, with the words
"my sister" threading in and out. Now he looked at Elsie,
with the pale wash of lamplight lying upon her, and said:
"Else, your voice sounded like honey, and your throat is as
white as ivory. Your throat is an ivory flute full of honey,
wrapped up in tissue of gold."

He felt free and elated when he had said this. It was the
first time in his life that beautiful words had risen up to obey
him, to make an image of what was in his mind. They were
but an echo of other words, long familiar; nevertheless they
enchanted him and gave him a feeling of joy and power. He
jumped off the couch and screeched "An ivory flute full of
honey," forgetting Elsie, seeing only the image, hearing only
the words. At the sound of his voice, his mother came from
the kitchen and flung open the door. Mr. Dillworth, gross
and brutal, with a brass-buckled belt loosely about his waist,

lumbered after her. They looked at the skinny boy, poised in his shirt in the glass-filtered lamplight, were motionless for a moment, and then Mr. Dillworth advanced and took him by the neck. He almost dislocated it as he flung him from the room. Alec fell in a heap at the foot of the stairs, crashing his skull on the lowest step. This dazed him, so that he was slow to rise. It gave Mr. Dillworth time to unfasten the belt, take it by the leathern end, and lash with the brazen buckle. The blow caught Alec's buttocks as he at last found his feet and began to rush up the stairs. The pain went through him like a sword, and his father's voice pursued him. "If I find you in Elsie's room again I'll beat the lights out of you."

Now at last—only now—with that voice and its implications in his ears, Alec shivered with shame as he pulled the bed-clothes over his head; and he knew that he could no more go to Elsie's room again than Adam could return to Paradise. His father's words whirled before his eyes like a flaming sword.

Throughout the next five years Alec Dillworth found all sorts of jobs to do. He did not stay anywhere for long, and there was only one fixed point in his life. That was Mr. Burn-side. The point was fixed, but Alec's approaches to it were erratic. Mr. Burnside tried for a time to make their relation-ship constant. He suggested meetings at regular times for talk and reading, but Alec, agreeing to these suggestions, would never abide by them. Mr. Burnside became reconciled to the spasmodic incalculable nature of the friendship. Alec would turn up in his study at most improbable moments. Mr. Burnside had even come down of a morning and found the boy asleep there in his chair. The best he was able to do for Alec was to incite him by talk whenever they met. He lent him many books; half of them never came back, but he didn't worry about that. Alec had discovered the public library and was reading widely and wildly, and Mr. Burnside did his best to control and co-ordinate this irresponsible raiding of the boy's mind. There was a time when Alec became obsessed with the idea of Oxford. He had but a vague grandiloquent notion of what Oxford was or what was done there, but the

thought filled his head that without Oxford he could do nothing.

Mr. Burnside, comfortably stretching his toes to the fire, drew on his pipe and said: "You know, Alec, an awful lot of nonsense is talked about Oxford. I was there, and I know. One lives there more or less alone, and reads more or less what one likes—just as you're doing anyway. There are a lot of men there called tutors. Each student has his tutor, who is supposed to be a wise fellow able to help and direct the young. You go to your tutor's rooms and talk about this and that. The most valuable part of Oxford life is this talking with one's tutor. Just as you and I are talking now. Well, what's wrong with going on as we are? Consider me to be your tutor. Come to me whenever you like and talk to me about anything you like."

That, more or less was how it worked. They were five valuable years for Alec. But he had his secrecies and reserves. He never allowed Mr. Burnside to see the poetry he was beginning to write.

Elsie went to her first "place" when she was fourteen. As fate would have it, it was at the house in Burnage where the gymnastic bear had charmed young Alec. It was now Elsie's business to be "a real servant," to wear a little white cap and call her employer "Madam." Her employer was fascinated by the child's grace and beauty. Coming back to the house, she never failed to feel exalted at this golden apparition which appeared in answer to her ring, the absurd little goffered cap perched aslant on the pile of burning hair, the white apron, the unspoiled loveliness of an opening flower. She had a son of nineteen, and one evening she heard him, in the hall, give a howl of dismay. Coming hastily from the dining-room, she saw him nursing his face from which blood was streaming. Elsie, with her little cap tumbling off and her hair disordered, was holding the brass tray that she had snatched as a weapon from the bear's paws. She could have hit him with the flat of it, not hurting him much; but she felt so outraged that she had wanted to hurt him as much as possible. Swinging the

tray as hard as she could, she slashed his face with the edge of it. An inch higher, and his eye would have been out. As it was, the flesh on his cheek was cut through to the bone, and he bore the scar to his dying day.

The woman of the house bound up the wound and then went with him to a doctor to have it stitched. When she returned, the cap and apron and one or two other things she had bought for Elsie were decorating the bear. The cap was on his head; the apron was tied round his middle; a grey satin dress was draped over his arm. Elsie was not rancorous. As soon as the door had shut behind the pair, her sense of outrage evaporated and her rough humour took charge. So she decorated the bear, packed her things, and hid her big tin trunk behind some shrubs near the garden gate. Late that night, Alec helped her to retrieve it, and they carried it home, singing.

During the next couple of years, Elsie had many adventures which did not differ materially from this one. Except that she did not continue to maim people. She came almost to expect men to handle her, and she developed a laughing and tolerant, rather than a violent, fashion of keeping them in their place. At the beginning, she would tell Alec of these scrimmages and encounters, but his rage frightened her. She feared that he would turn up at the "place" and do more damage than she had done with the brass tray; and so this side of her life became secret and withheld.

She was sixteen when she became a parlour-maid at Sir Charles Frome's. Sir Charles, a childless widower of fifty, who had a charming house in the suburb of Bowdon, where George Satterfield was later to settle, was a cotton merchant, an official of the Chamber of Commerce, a city councillor, a magistrate and a church-warden. He was grey-haired, good-looking, beautifully dressed, with austerity and probity written so deeply all over him that if he were an actor, acting a combination of all the parts life had assigned him, he could not have done it more perfectly.

For a day or two, Sir Charles Frome knew nothing of Elsie Dillworth's arrival in his house. She had been engaged by the

housekeeper who kept her at first in the background, to see how she "shaped." But Elsie had glimpsed Sir Charles once or twice, and she rejoiced to feel that now she had found a "place" in a million, a place where everything was quiet and ordered and decorous, where there was only one man in the house, and he seeming so aloof and reserved that probably he would not even be aware of her presence.

Elsie had to rise at six in the morning. She did so on the fourth day after her arrival in the house, washed herself in the basin on the washstand, and then began to brush the hair that was her pride and delight. She sat in a chair, bent forward, pulled the hair right over her head so that she was hidden behind a golden veil reaching to the floor. It was a May morning. The sun was shining on the garden that glistened with dew, and the blackbirds and thrushes were singing loudly in the blossoming trees. Elsie had never felt so happy. She went to the window of the attic, cut into a slope of the roof and so low that she had to kneel to see the beauty of the world. She hadn't much time for looking out of the window, so as she knelt there she continued to brush her hair, gazing through the silken mesh that tumbled over the window-sill and down the front of the house.

This was the enchanting apparition that met the eye of Sir Charles Frome. He was an early riser; he was proud of his garden; and on such a morning as this always walked in it for a while before doing the hour's work that came before his breakfast. He was walking now in a short avenue of pleached limes, and between the limes and the lawn that reached to the flower-beds under the house wall was a bank of azaleas and rhododendrons. Therefore, it was not easy to see him from the house, and Elsie, in fact, did not see him; but, as he turned in his slow pacing, he saw the red banner that streamed down into the morning, with the sunlight glancing and glinting upon it. He stood stock-still, instinctively seeking the concealment of a tree trunk. He watched a pair of white and exquisite arms weaving a pattern up and down upon the banner of hair. Not the scent of the flowers, or the song of the birds, or the shining of the sun, but this moving poem of a

girl's hair and arms seemed to him the spirit and essence of
the morning. He watched till the arms ceased their weaving,
till the hair was slowly drawn like a precious carpet through
the window, and then he went to his study, feeling deeply
moved by the beauty of what he had seen.

Beauty had played little part in the life of Sir Charles Frome.
There was the garden, but that was the gardener's affair, and
Sir Charles was hardly aware of it except as a place in which
he could think quietly of agenda and minutes, annual meet-
ings, interim dividends and what not. To all these matters,
and to the business affairs of the Church, he brought a cold
and punctilious honesty. He and his wife, dead now for two
years, had dwelt together like a pair of polar bears in an arc-
tic waste of righteousness. She had been, as he was, a public
figure in the life of Manchester, a woman all compounded
of blue books, white papers, and red tape. She was scarcely
to be met not hurrying, with a black despatch-case, from a
committee to a council or from a convention to a conference.
Her keen grey eyes were set above a Wellington nose so thin
and sharp and bony that it could have been used to chop up
frozen meat. Sir Charles Frome, who expected all his feelings
to be in order, expected to feel a sense of loss when she died.
He was surprised to find that he felt nothing of the kind.
There was not much difference between reading an agenda
to himself and discussing one with her.

One reason why Elsie felt so exalted as she knelt at the attic
window that May morning was that she was to be permitted
for the first time to attend Sir Charles Frome at breakfast. The
housekeeper was pleased with her: she would do. Sir Charles
breakfasted at seven-thirty. His carriage was at the door at
eight, and he was in his room at Comberwait and Frome's, in
Portland Street, at nine. There was no reason why he should
be, except to "set an example." He and Lady Frome had lived
in the belief that men needed an example and that they were
well fitted to provide one.

Elsie was already in the dining-room, anxiously checking
up everything on the table and sideboard when Sir Charles
came in. She was trembling a little, but she did not know

that he was trembling, too. One glance had shown him that the apparition from the window was now in the room. He had seen nothing but her hair and her arms. Now her arms were hidden by the grey print sleeves of her dress, and all the hair that had streamed and glistered at the window was tightly bound upon her head and topped with a small white cap. He could see now that she was tall, evidently long-legged, with a lovely face. He could not trust himself to speak to her. He did not say so much as "Good-morning." He felt in the cold recesses of his heart a vague sense of outrage. She had struck at him so suddenly, had so swiftly breached the cold formalism of his nature, that he resented and feared her even while he was aware of the trembling flutter of unaccustomed desire.

It was only at breakfast that Elsie was for any length of time in his presence. That first morning she was timid, a little nervous, disappointed that Sir Charles was so moody and dumb. She might have been serving oats to a clothes-horse, she said to herself, for all the kick there was in it. But her womanly intuition was sharp, and her senses were in the moment of their awakening. As day by day went on in this fashion she realized with a shock that this august person, living in this fine house, with a housekeeper and coachman and gardener to do his bidding, was for some reason or other afraid of her. She was not acute enough to know that this frozen stream had been atrophied for so long that it was bitterly resenting the spring's kiss. She thought in her simplicity that warmth and kindliness would be welcomed.

The morning sun was streaming through the window, falling upon Sir Charles Frome's grey hair and tightened face when Elsie said, filling his coffee-cup: "It's a lovely morning, sir. Cheer up."

Incredible words to be addressed by parlour-maid to master! "Don't open your mouth unless you're spoken to." Those were the housekeeper's orders; but orders of this sort were no good to Elsie Dillworth. It was not in her nature to stand round like a statue watching this poor grump sink deeper and deeper into misery.

She was right by his side; he could feel the warmth of her body, sense its curves, as she poured the coffee. He was a notorious martinet; his house and office staffs feared his barked commands, for his human contacts were as sterile as his humanitarianism was fervid. A surge of resentment made him flush all over. Never before had a servant had the insolence to address a human word to him. "Cheer up!" He was about to snap and hector when something suddenly melted in him, as though ice had cracked. He wanted to put an arm about her, pull her to him. Not to do so was torture, but the habits of a lifetime were not to be overcome. But he managed to smile. "Yes," he said. "It *is* a lovely morning."

They were the first words he had spoken to her. She looked at him, at the smile on his face. "That's better," she said, as though she patted a child's head. She would never be afraid of him again. She was the only person who ever had the intuition to divine that Sir Charles Frome was a frightened and frozen mite.

Now that the thaw had begun, he was more deeply frightened than ever. Bliss was there to be freely gathered, but now he began to scheme to possess it furtively. The idea of Sir Charles Frome marrying his parlour-maid scared him stiff. He had not the courage to carry off a fine independent human gesture. But once the first barriers were down, he permitted beauty to gnaw at him, resenting its intrusions. He had called all other parlour-maids by their surnames, but he called her Elsie. "Elsie," he said one morning, "I was walking in the garden early one morning, and I saw you brushing your hair at the window." She noticed that he was moistening dry lips. "I'm always out there on fine mornings at six."

He got up and went. She understood him clearly enough. Well, if the sight of her hair pleased him, why not? And every day she streamed it through the window, and Sir Charles feasted his eyes on that banner hung out to the morning and on the arms, white and undulant as swans' necks, that weaved upon it. But this never brought him the joy of that first unpremeditated occasion. It made him self-conscious when he met her, and he resented her appearing to be quite unself-

conscious, as though she wanted and expected nothing of him, when he knew that he wanted so much of her.

He had never laid a hand upon her, hoping yet to pull himself free of the toils. He could tell his housekeeper to send her away, but this idea was the most frightful of all. The battle between his lust and the comfortable undisturbing frigidity of his life till now reached its climax one day when he was walking through the parched June streets of Manchester and saw on a hoarding an auctioneer's announcement of a number of small houses to be sold. One was in a back street behind Oxford Road. "I could walk there from the office any afternoon," he thought; and came to with a start, realizing that for some time he had not been reading the poster, but just standing there gazing through it and beyond it at a small house, in a region where no one knew him, and in the house was a bedroom, and in the bedroom Elsie Dillworth's hair was streaming not down bricks and stone but down white limbs whose visioned beauty set him trembling there on the pavement in the hot June street.

At the auction it was announced that the little house had been privately disposed of; and with all the privacy and discretion that wealth can command it was furnished. Now Sir Charles Frome was in full gallop and there was no drawing back.

Elsie was allowed a half day off every week, and in these summer days she would spend this time walking on the highways and in the fields towards Knutsford. She rejoiced in the wide sky above her and the tangles of meadow-sweet, campion, and ragged robin that filled the hedge-bottoms, the amethyst lakes of bluebells in the hollows of the woods, and the coots bobbing their white-blazed heads on the reedy meres. This summer was the best time she had ever known, she thought, what with a nice bedroom and good food and this lovely country at the door. She thought her employer a queer, moody but harmless old thing; something even of tenderness was in her feeling for him.

She was still so much of a foolish child that she had a child's

habit of piling her arms with wild flowers that she would dis-
card before the afternoon was done. On a Saturday towards
the end of that June she lay on the grass at the edge of a mere,
all her limbs stretched in glad acceptance of the sun, the flopping straw of her hat pulled upon her face to protect it from
the glare. The sleeves of her dress were short, nothing but
puff-balls of transparent gauze upon her shoulders. Sir Charles
Frome, who had observed her habits, found her there. She was
unaware that he stood looking down at her as she lay upon
her back, with one knee drawn up and both her arms flung
wide. Within the crook of one elbow was a sagging bunch of
bluebells, and the inside of the elbow of the other arm was
canalled with veins as blue as the wilting flowers, as shadows
on snow. All about her were wide-open buttercups. She was
lying on a golden bed alongside the water that flashed in the
sun and moved back in arrow-headed ripples from the thrusts
of the coots. He knelt suddenly and kissed her on the silken
blue-threaded flesh within her unencumbered elbow.

Elsie knew at once whose shadow this was arched over her.
She did not sit up. She did not remove the hat that hid her
face. She was languorous, drenched with sunshine, and she
thought it pleasant to be kissed. Save for Alec's fierce posses-
siveness, she had lived a life without affection. There had been
no affection, nothing but light sexual skirmishes, in her rela-
tions with men thus far. There was something different about
Charles Frome. She sensed the battle in him: all those elements
that were fighting to tear him away from her as well as those
that left him helpless as a steel chip within the power of a
magnet. She felt a great pity for him. She wondered what he
would do now.

He did nothing. After that first kiss, he recoiled as though
the sweet flesh had scorched his lips. Presently, she pulled off
her hat and looked at him. He was sitting with his hands
dangled down between his knees, his head sunk, his eyes mood-
ily contemplating the grass at his feet. She tried to draw his
eyes upon her, but he would not look. "Why are you afraid
of me?" she asked.

She could not get over the strangeness of it: that a man who

seemed to her so full of authority should be afraid of her. It gave her a sense of power, and this was her undoing. To be able to straighten out such a tangle as Charles Frome was clearly in her innocent mind a high responsibility. Life had never before given her Yes or No such significance. To be significant to any degree was something new to her, and the excitement of it disposed her to use her power mercifully. She was at first hardly aware of what Sir Charles Frome was mumbling, sitting there with his heart thumping and his words coming thickly and uncertainly, for he was not used to speaking such words as these. They had nothing to do with declaring a dividend or appropriating ten thousand to a sinking fund or supporting "all that the last speaker has said in favour of a measure so clearly of the greatest benefit to those not so fortunately circumstanced as most of us here." He could have handled all that easily enough, hand on lapel, and fine grey head thrown back; but now it was a matter of just one person not fortunately circumstanced, and a little house in a rather furtive back street, and an allowance of three pounds a week.

As he went on, Elsie sat up, the better to get the drift of his mumblings. Presently she understood, and she sat there, the hat flung aside, a hand pressed down into the grass on either side of her, and the blue flowers filling her lap. She looked the youngest and loveliest thing under God's heaven, something to be wooed with rapture; and the choked and stumbling voice of Sir Charles Frome was an indecency staining the bright air about her. At last he stopped, turned upon her the nauseating brown eyes of a dog that expects a kick, and to his own shocked surprise found one of her thin warm hands lifted and placed upon his. She did not look at him. She was staring over the sun-glistered water and the rising green beyond as she nodded her head and said simply: "All right. Cheer up." She sprang up then, spilling the flowers from her lap, not seeing them, treading upon them as she went away, leaving him hunched there like a man who has been flogged.

It was with regret that the housekeeper told Elsie she must go. She liked the child, and she did not understand Sir

Charles's objection to her. But there it was. He had reeled off a catalogue of offences that seemed to her mostly imaginary and ended with an order that could not be argued about. Elsie Dillworth must be given a week's notice. When the week was up, a four-wheeler drove to the house, Elsie's box was strapped on the top, and she set off on the drive towards Manchester. Sir Charles was not present. The housekeeper was pleased that he had instructed her to pay for the cab. There was something so young and appealing and, apparently, defenceless about Elsie that the old woman, as the girl stood by the cab door wishing her good-bye, suddenly hugged her, with a tear squeezing out of her eye. Elsie patted her shoulder. "It's all right. Cheer up," she said and climbed into the cab. A long white-gloved arm fluttered toward the housekeeper as the cab went round the twist in the drive, and Elsie was gone.

She sat back in the cab, thinking of what was before her. She had been told that she would find everything in order in the house. All she would need to do was buy food, and she had been given the money for this. She opened the snaps of the little red leather purse that Sir Charles had given her and looked at the three golden sovereigns it contained. Never in her life had she possessed so much money. She examined the coins one by one, entranced by the spectacle of St. George, so well mounted, so well and truly ramming a spear in at one end of a dragon and out at the other. And that, of course, was what gold pieces could do. There was no end to the dragons they could run through the vitals.

Rolling in a cab towards her own house, she felt almost prim, almost like a young married woman going to take possession of her home. That, Sir Charles had impressed on her, was how it was to be. She was to consider that to all intents and purposes they were married. Tonight he would be with her. He had told his housekeeper that an engagement would keep him out of Manchester. Not that he would be with her on many nights. He would visit her occasionally in the afternoons. But she was to consider this their wedding night. And some night, she thought, really would be their wedding night. She felt confident in her power over him.

The July noon was stuffy in the street when the cab pulled up at her door. She felt a pang of disappointment as she got on to the pavement and looked about her. It was such a street as she had been born in, such a street as she had always known till she went to her first "place." Dusty garbage wilted in the gutters. Dirty children squalled and squatted, and slatterns with hands on hips stood at doorways and stolidly stared at nothing. The houses were unkempt and furtive-looking, bleary-eyed old houses that life had knocked about too hard and for too long. This one before which the cab had stopped, and which Elsie now verified as No. 47, differed from all the others in having at the lower and upper windows curtains whose cleanliness, elegance even, marked it out from all its neighbours, had made it for some days the cynosure of a lewd curiosity, and now drew all stares upon the trim young woman alighting from the cab. Sir Charles Frome was a most inexperienced amorist.

A latch-key was with the three sovereigns in the red leather purse. Elsie, aware of an intent watch upon her from doorways and windows, opened the door, the cabman dumped her box into the passage, the door shut, and she was alone. Then her heart, for the first time since she had engaged herself in this adventure, misgave her. She leaned against the wall of the passage, the hat in her hand trailing on the floor, and felt her heart fluttering like a frightened bird. Here, everything was so still: outside, everything was so menacing, with a menace that was but too familiar to her: the menace of the rancorous and vicious poor. She had read with her short lifetime's knowledge all that was written in those silent staring figures.

She put her fears by and looked about her. The passage was newly decorated with a dark varnished wall-paper. Its floor and the stairs were laid with a red strip of carpet, figured in blue. This, to begin with, was an unaccustomed embellishment in such a street. She opened the door of the front room and started back in surprise. It was empty. It had not even been decorated. Dirty paper had curled back and hung in folds where walls and ceilings met. The fireplace was full of

rubbish. The net curtains she had observed from outside were simply a cloak, a screen, concealing emptiness.

The walls of the back room had been stripped and painted white. Inside the full net curtains were curtains of blue velvet, and the two easy chairs and couch were upholstered in blue velvet, too. There were a few cheap prints on the wall, a highly polished dining-table and chairs, brand new from a multiple furniture store, a newly black-leaded grate with a brass fender and black wool rug. Elsie thought the room elegant, and, better-pleased, went through it to the small kitchen. This, too, had the air of having come straight from the hand of a multiple store, as it had; but it was clean and complete, and Elsie at once put a light to the fire in the range. No doubt Sir Charles tonight would want something to eat.

Upstairs, she found that the front bedroom, like the front room downstairs, had not been furnished. The pristine curtains were a blind. In the back bedroom, white like the room downstairs, the floor was covered to the skirtings with a pale green carpet. The heavy velvet curtains were pale green, and a pale green linen bedspread was on the double bed. A wardrobe and a chest of drawers with a small swinging mirror upon it completed the furnishing.

This was all. It did not enter Elsie's little head to notice the stark utilitarian economy of the whole outfit. There was nothing so daft and useless as a bird in a cage or a fish in a bowl. There were no flowers on a table, no note on a pincushion saying: "Welcome, my little love." There was nothing but two rooms and a kitchen in which Sir Charles Frome had decided to hide a woman.

Sir Charles had drawn up in his mind the agenda for this day. In the strain of these clandestine arrangements, his mind had not functioned as clearly as it was used to do. When he told Elsie that he would be with her that night, he had forgotten a long-standing engagement for the afternoon. Canon Sherwood, the vicar of the church where Sir Charles had for many years been a church-warden, was to unveil a mural tablet, commissioned long ago by Sir Charles, commemorating

the virtues of his wife. So harassed had Charles Frome become that it was only as he sat at breakfast on the day when Elsie was, a few hours later, to drive away in the cab, that this engagement came suddenly flooding into his mind. It almost overwhelmed him. It brought sharply back the image of Alice Frome as she had for so many years sat opposite him at this table, absently picking at her food as she sorted her letters or thumbed and pencilled a pamphlet. She sat there now like Banquo's ghost, the chilly memory of a woman who had given him everything she had to give. She had poured out lavishly her frozen apples and Dead Sea fruit.

Elsie came into the room. The morning sun, lancing through the window, lit her up like a supple flame. She looked so red with that untempered light upon her that he shuddered as at the sight of the devil. He did not speak to her, and she, who most humbly respected his moods, did not speak to him. For a moment he was tempted to tell her that something had now happened which would make it impossible for him to be with her tonight; but he could not do this, for her attraction was as strong as his loathing for her at that moment was deep.

When his brougham was at the door, he outlined to his housekeeper the day's programme. The brougham would bring him back from town to Bowdon in time for the three o'clock service in the church. Thence he would return home, eat his dinner at six instead of seven-thirty, and be driven into Manchester. He had a train to catch at eight o'clock, and he would not be back that night. To himself he added that when the brougham had driven away from the station he could either take a cab or walk to the little house where Elsie would be waiting for him.

There were not many people in the church. Alice Frome was not a woman whom many human hearts cared to recall now that she was two years dead. No friend supported Sir Charles. He was alone in his pew. Behind him a few people scattered here and there emphasized the emptiness of the building. The afternoon sun struck through a stained-glass window and threw its colours upon the cold white marble of

the tablet in the wall on Sir Charles's right hand. Incongru-ously, a line learned in he hardly knew what remote and irrelevant time, spoke on the lips of his memory:

And threw warm gules on Madeline's fair breast.

It was so startlingly inappropriate to all he remembered of Alice Frome that suddenly his heart was swamped by a wave of pity for this woman now gone beyond the concerns of her fussy ineffectual life. He had never loved her; certainly he had never before pitied her or thought of her as a being who needed pity. But now for the first time, and too late, he saw her as she was, seeking to warm the chill of her life with a little bustling bonfire of paper scraps. The Vicar's voice was so-norously engaged in eulogy. "Love of humanity . . . selfless devotion to the outcast and unfortunate . . . the beloved helpmeet of our brother who now alone, as when fortified by her love, wages a ceaseless war for the deepening and human-izing of our common life."

There were so many tablets upon the walls, commemorat-ing so much dust that for a moment had spun in the brief gleam of life and now was still! Sir Charles, sitting in his pew Sunday after Sunday, had learned the words of many of them, unconsciously, by heart; but who these people were, what they had meant and done in their lives that were so lamen-tably less durable than these stones and inscriptions that re-corded them, he did not know. So, he reflected, standing as the organ moaned and the thin scatter of congregation joined with the choir in singing "For all thy saints who from their labours rest"; so, it seemed to him, catching through an open window the green of trees and the loud happy cries of the birds; so it would be with Alice. Already all the furniture she had used to fill the dusty empty rooms of her life was re-furbished and used by others who were as good as she at moving and proposing, seconding and amending. Soon she would be forgotten by all save himself, and for him the mem-ory would be of little beyond a polar probity, a chill and ethic rectitude. Again that wave of pity for the dead woman en-gulfed him. It was as noble an emotion as he had ever felt;

and as he knelt while the Vicar uttered a concluding prayer, he thanked God that, even at the eleventh hour, he had been shown his way.

That night, arrived at the station, he travelled to Liverpool, stayed at the railway hotel, and felt in the morning an upsurging of strength. He had conquered! When his mind turned to Elsie Dillworth, it had no pity for her. She was the devil, and he had had the strength to put her behind him. In a sense, he said to himself, she was better off than before. She had a house for which she had no rent to pay and he would pay the rates himself. A clean break, he said. A clean break. No excuses or explanations. Parleying would mean putting himself back within the devil's reach. He would never see the girl or communicate with her again.

When Elsie had finished her inspection of the house she went out, turned into Oxford Road and walked towards town. She was aware of the covert glances that watched her proud young figure going down the sordid street. It was one o'clock, and she gave herself a meal in an eating-house near St. Peter's Square. Then she did her shopping. The thoughtfulness of the provision that had been made for her in the house could not have been bettered. In the kitchen cupboard she had found everything save perishable food. There were tea and sugar and coffee, pepper and salt, rice, dried fruits, pots of jam, fish-paste, and, as she said to herself, goodness only knows what all. She bought a cabbage, pork chops, two loaves of bread and a quart of milk, to hold which she had brought a screw-stoppered bottle. She did not hurry over this business. She was unused to being alone and at liberty in the city and made use of her opportunity. She dawdled so long before the shop fronts that it was four o'clock when she returned to her house, promising herself the refreshment of a cup of tea, for the afternoon was hot. At the door of the next house a girl who looked little older than herself was leaning against the wall. She seemed to Elsie to be inappropriately dressed for the time of day, for she was wearing a pink satin dressing-gown, with pink mules on her feet, fluffed with blue feathers.

As Elsie, laden with her goods, struggled to extract the latch-key from her purse, the girl came up and said: "Let me help you, duck," taking, as she spoke, the cabbage in one hand and the milk bottle in the other. When the door was opened, she followed Elsie into the house. She cast her eye appraisingly at the new carpet and the newly papered walls, and said: "Nice place you've got here, duck, I must say. Stylish, I call it."

Elsie did not know what to do. Sir Charles had instructed her: "You will keep yourself to yourself. Have nothing to do with the neighbors." But Elsie was a good-hearted child: she found it difficult to be rude, and this girl looked kind enough. "Ah, well," Elsie thought with a little burst of rebellion, "a fat lot *he* knows about living in a street like this." Keeping to oneself was easy with an acre or two between you and the next neighbour. Let him try it here!

The girl had shut the front door. She followed Elsie into the back room, threw herself into a chair and stretched her nude legs towards the fireplace. The dressing-gown sagged open above her waist, and with something of a shock Elsie saw that she was wearing nothing but this one garment. The girl perceived her surprise, and said: "It's so damned hot, duck. My name's Gert. What's yours?"

Gert was fair, fat, and rather pasty-looking. Elsie was not displeased at having someone to share her tea, and as she clattered about in the little kitchen behind the back room Gert shouted conversationally. "A bit of all right I call this place, Else. You should see old Ma Adams's next door. Theatrical digs. Digs all right. Every damn thing digs you. The springs in the chairs dig you in the backside, the lumps of flock in the mattresses dig you in everything they can reach, and old Ma digs out every bloody brown you've got. That was Terry's little joke. He's a caution."

Gert laughed immoderately as she recalled Terry's sparkling sally. Elsie came in with the tea things on a tray. They drank tea and ate a rich cake that Elsie had found in a tin. "Terry's our funny man," Gert explained. "A fair caution. You ought to come and see our show. Twice nightly."

"I'd love to," said Elsie, "but I couldn't possibly tonight. I must stay in." She added innocently: "I'm expecting a friend."

"All right, duck. You don't have to explain to me," Gert said magnanimously. "You don't get paid in gold bricks in our job, and just between you and I, I do a bit myself. Well, thanks and ta ta." She adjusted her dress before leaving. "See you again. Look in next door about eleven if you want a laugh. You should see Terry cooking a kipper. He says: 'Look! This bloody herring's split its sides with laughing!' Always the same thing, but it's not what he says; it's the way he says it. I think that's so true in our profession. Well, au reservoir, duck, as Terry says."

Elsie did not leave the house for three days. She could not understand what had happened. That first night she did not go to bed at all. The pork chops burned on the kitchen range. The potatoes and cabbage boiled dry. The dining-table, which she had carefully set, even running out at the last moment to buy flowers for it, seemed to grin at her mockingly. She had been so afraid that Charles would come while she was buying the flowers. She arrived back panting. But there was time and to spare. She forgot the cooking food till the smell of its burning filled the kitchen. Then, with tears of mortification in her eyes, she poured the whole lot into the garbage-pail.

She went into the empty front room, the better to hear the sounds of traffic in the street. A box was there, and she pulled it to the window. She sat, a forlorn abandoned young creature, peering through the net curtains which hid her but permitted her to see the fading evening light that fell upon the unkempt road and furtive houses. The traffic there was little enough, but when, rarely, the sound of cab-wheels broke the stillness, she would start up with her heart beating and peer sideways through the snowy gauze to catch the first glimpse, to be ready to rush to the door should the horse's hoofs slow down their beat. But the cabs went by, and the squalling children were one by one hauled out of the gutters; and soon the dusk came,

and the darkness, and still she sat upon the box, not now looking out, but with her elbows on her knees and her chin sunk
into the cup of her palms. She did not get up when she heard
Gert and Terry festively arrive next door. The uproarious
home-coming of these late workers somehow put a term to
the day, made her think of it as at last dead and done with,
extinguished whatever spark of expectation remained a-glim-
mer in her heart.

She was not able to analyze or assess the emotions by which
she was desolated. She had been expecting Charles Frome
with no lover's fervour, and she would have been puzzled to
say why his not coming left her feeling so bereft. It was her
pride that was in the dust. She had seen him stricken, and all
her young generosity had been touched and melted. Out of
pity she had offered him all she had, and now, for what reason
she did not know, it was treated as though it were nothing.

She went at last into the other room, sat on the couch with
her head back, and spent the night in uneasy slumber. It was
six o'clock when she woke. Already sunlight was flooding
upon the blind unopened eyes of the street. The air smelt
to her, as she stood timidly at her front door, clean and sweet
in that brief moment before the stain and soilure of the day
had breathed upon it. She took it down gladly into her lungs,
went in and breakfasted on tea and the remains of the cake,
and felt better. In the mornings one always felt better. Impossible to believe that a shining morning has an evil trick
up its sleeve. Perhaps, thought Elsie, there would be a letter
explaining all. And surely all could be explained. The full,
romantic life (as she naïvely conceived it) of a man like
Charles Frome must hold each day a dozen contingencies,
an endless shift of concerns, of which she could know nothing.
She was humbly willing to accept any explanation, and surely
an explanation would come.

She was on her box again, in a livelier mood now, as the
postman went rat-tatting along the street. She started up as
he drew near, went even into the passage to catch the letter
as it should fall through the box, and felt a chill of fear when
the hob-nailed footsteps clattered by on the pavement and

receded to extinction. Only then, she decided to go to bed. She stayed there all day, eating nothing, sleeping fitfully; and at six o'clock hope again came to her foolish heart. She must be ready for Sir Charles. Something had detained him last night; he had not had time to write; he would come tonight. She bathed in the tin bath in the kitchen, ate a little food, and waited. She did not sit up that night. A hard spark of rebellion in her was blowing up to a flame. She began to feel not only cheated and defrauded but insulted and belittled. She had offered so much that a keen humiliation made her burn as she admitted, finally and frankly, that it was all rejected.

The weather remained torrid. A sky of brass burned over the shabby street, and with all the windows open, Elsie felt nevertheless that she was living in an oven. She wanted, too, to be with people again, hoping thus to shake off the dark apprehensions which gnawed behind the optimism of her youth. She had not been eating much; she was surprised to find that her legs were a little uncertain as she turned into Oxford Road. She went to a cheap and glittering café, and at once felt better. The seat was comfortable; the hot tea soothed her overstrung nerves; there were lots of people talking and laughing. She sat there for an hour, submerging herself in the normal.

She was about to leave when a cheerful strident voice cried: "Well, duck, where've you been hiding yourself? 'Struth, you don't half look like something the cat brought in. Been bad?"

Elsie had not herself been aware of her haggard look. Gert flopped into a chair alongside her. "This is Terry," she explained.

Terry was a thin cheeky-looking youth wearing a striped blazer and a straw hat decorated with a green and white band. "This is Else, Terry: the girl from next door to Ma Adams's," Gert said.

Terry did not appear to be interested. However crashingly he might bring down the house in the theatre or privily sparkle in Ma Adams's rooms, here he was as dumb as a cod and about

as funny. He poured his tea into a saucer and sucked it noisily.
Only one word did he utter. "Tea!" It was to be gathered
that you could keep all China so far as he was concerned,
with Ceylon's isle, India's coral strand and Mincing Lane all
thrown in.

"Don't take any notice of Terry, duck," Gert exhorted
Elsie. "I think it's damn bad breeding if you can't be common polite unless you're half canned. I've said it before and
I say it again, and if he thinks I'm going to traipse round four-
ale bars at this time of day he's bloody well mistaken." She
raised her cup. "Well, here's to Tommy Lipton, duck. The
man who invented the drink that cheers you up without
pinching your virtue."

Elsie had finished her tea, but Gert poured a cup from her
own pot and ordered an extravagant quantity of jam tarts
and doughnuts. Elsie's meal began all over again. They had
not got far into it when Terry rose, threw a half-crown on to
the table, said: "That'll pay for it," and departed.

"My God," said Gert, "he'll end up absolutely pickled puce.
Men! Well, duck, we can get along without 'em—in between
spasms anyway, and I've got one coming on. And how *are*
you, duck? I must say that cup o' tea has made you look a bit
better—less like the end of a month's honeymoon with San-
dow."

Elsie said that she was feeling very well indeed, but Gert
did not accept this as a hundred per cent. She looked at Elsie
with a critical eye which in the last few years had looked at
many a ticklish situation. "That place of yours has been like
a morgue these last few days," she said, "and when I came in
here you looked like a corpse let out for an airing. What you
want is some fun and games, duck. You come and see the
show tonight."

Suddenly this seemed to Elsie an idea packed with allure-
ment. She had never been to any sort of entertainment in a
theatre. It would be just what she needed, something that
would shake her out of the doldrums, put a puff into her sails,
and show her which way she should go to get clear of her
clogging anxieties. She thanked Gert, who handed her a free

pass marked "Second House." "Terry's always better in the second house, duck," she explained. "He'll be as canned as a cuckoo, awash to the ear'oles. We'll have to take him home in a cab."

That is what they did. Gert and Terry, Elsie and Mr. Bentley, shared a four-wheeler. Who Mr. Bentley was Elsie did not know. During the interval of the show an attendant had come to Elsie's seat in the stalls and whispered that Miss Swayne would like to see her in the dressing-room. It took her some time to realize that Miss Swayne was Gert, whom she had hardly recognized on the stage, anyhow, so bright with paint was her pasty face, so dark were her eyes with kohl, so unexpectedly pleasing was the negligibly clad dancing figure now for the first time revealed. It was exciting to be here in the stuffy dressing-room, where Gert's clothing, and the clothing of two other girls, was now hardly even negligible, where gas buzzed in two round wire cages over spotted mirrors and the choked air was fogged by cosmetics, scent, and bottled beer. Mr. Bentley was serving the beer, with a dressing-table for buffet, expertly drawing corks, and pouring, and froth-blowing, and handing with a melancholy bow to the ladies. He was young and dark, with a silky drooping moustache. He wore a tight frock coat with satin lapels, and, achieving what was perhaps the only joke of his career, he wore in one lapel the touch of blue silk ribbon that indicated a teetotaller. His feet were encased in patent leather buttoned boots, and for some reason he wore, there indoors, a tall silk hat. "Have another glass of water, dear," he would say, handing the foaming beer. "I'll join you."

From all except Mr. Bentley, who maintained a morose unsmiling face, the sally was greeted with laughter each time it was uttered. Elsie heard it uttered eight or nine times. She herself was pressed by Gert to "take to the water, duck," and she drank one glassful which she didn't much like. She had to admit, though, that she felt, as the first gassy onset on her vitals passed away, cheered and that the second half of the show seemed better than the first.

She was invited to the dressing-room again when the curtain fell. Mr. Bentley was still there wearing his hat and handing round "glasses of water." No doubt it was a good joke: he did look absurdly like a temperance lecturer; but the other two girls seemed to have tired of it. They were anxious to be off, and soon only Gert, Elsie, and Mr. Bentley were left. Gert was pulling on a stocking and Elsie was drinking another glass of beer when Terry came in, rocking a little on his feet. Mr. Bentley handed him a drink which he threw quickly down his neck and said: "C'mon, Gert. I've ordered a cab."

Gert was soon ready, and they found the cab waiting at the stage door in a side-street. Mr. Bentley had a bottle in each of his trousers pockets, one in the inside pocket of his coat, one in the tail pocket, and one under each arm. Gert gave the cabman Ma Adams's address, but Mr. Bentley countermanded this. "Drive South," he ordered with a vague grandiosity. "Drive South, an' when you're South, turn an' drive North again." He seated himself in the cab at Elsie's side, removed his silk hat for the first time, and with a wild cry hurled it through the window of the cab. Then he began to sing a song which said: "We're southward bound, and since the whole damn world is round, you can travel as long as you damn well like, and you're always southward bound."

Terry disputed this, and said there was the North Pole, wasn't there? If you went right on you'd be bound to reach the North Pole some time, and how could you reach the North Pole without travelling North?

Mr. Bentley, whom, Elsie gathered, neither Gert nor Terry had ever met before, said Terry was incapable of understanding a great fact of geography and philosophy. "Fact of the matter is," he said gravely, "we shall none of us see our homes again. The South, my friends, is unattainable. Likewise the East, West, and North. We shall go on and on. We are now in search of the unknown. Our bones will bleach where we drop."

They were passing through Fallowfield, and the cabman called down through the trap: " 'Ow much further?"

Mr. Bentley sprang upright, thrust his head through the

trap and shouted in a ringing voice: "To the South. To un-
imaginable longitudes. To uncharted latitudes. Where's my
hat? Stop! Stop the cab! Where's my hat?"

Gert was collapsed with laughter upon the seat. Mr. Bentley
withdrew his head through the trap and glared at her wildly.
"Where's my hat?" he demanded. "You're sitting on my
hat."

"For Gawd's sake, Mr. Bentley, give us a glass of water,"
Gert said feebly.

It seemed a good idea to Mr. Bentley. He recovered his
temper and took a corkscrew from his pocket. There were five
small explosions. Bottles were handed round. Mr. Bentley, dis-
daining the trap, leaned his long length through the window
and handed one to the cabby. "Remember the course, captain,"
he said, "and keep your eye on the binnacle. S.S. by S. Take a
bearing on the Southern Cross."

"I've got a bearin' on the Southern Cemetery," the cabman
answered. "No further than that this night, laddie."

"Mutiny! Mutiny!" Mr. Bentley cried. "Enterprises of great
pith and moment their currents turn awry, and lose the name
of action."

He came back into the cab and leaned his head on Elsie's
shoulder. "Direct the fellow home," he said sadly. "The breed!
The breed! The great breed is passing from the earth."

Elsie wanted to go to sleep. If you have never drunk a glass
of beer in your life, it is not a good idea to drink three within
a couple of hours. She thought vaguely that this Mr. Bentley
was a caution. He had now abandoned all interest in the journey South, and leaned his head again on her shoulder. Terry
had told the cabby to drive to Ma Adams's. The whole evening
was going flat. The horse was trotting sedately back through
Fallowfield. Terry was silent. A gentle snoring came from the
corner where Gert had suddenly passed out. There was only
one bottle of beer left. It was in one of Mr. Bentley's inside
pockets. Elsie could feel it pressing into her breast. Mr. Bentley sighed and snuggled closer. He put his arms round her.
She thought he, too, was asleep.

But when they reached Ma Adams's, he seemed the only

one of the four thoroughly awake. He paid the cabman. He rapped smartly on Ma Adams's door and saw Gert and Terry safely within. While he was doing this, Elsie was fumbling in her red leather purse for the latch-key. She had never felt so clumsy. The purse fell to the ground.

It was nearly one o'clock. The intemperate heat of the day was still oozing out of the stones of the street. There seemed to be not a whisper anywhere in the world, and a full moon flooded its light upon the dead chimney-pots, making the roofs shine like escarpments of dull silver. Upon this silence broke the tiny metallic tinkle of the latch-key, fallen out of the purse, striking upon the pavement. Mr. Bentley looked down and saw it lying at his feet. All through the evening, though he had done little to show it, he had been most disturbingly aware of Elsie. It was not his fault if he mistook her status. A good-looking girl who went round with Gert and Terry, who appeared to have her own house and her own latch-key: what would you? It was the most natural mistake in the world.

When Elsie woke in the morning, Mr. Bentley was gone. She lay for a long time with the light of the summer day beating through the window, her mind seeking to piece together the adventures of yesterday. It all came rushing back upon her when she saw Mr. Bentley's last bottle of beer standing on the mantelpiece. Tired and bewildered, she got out of bed and picked it up. There was a golden sovereign beneath it. And lest she should feel thirsty, Mr. Bentley had considerately left the corkscrew.

Elsie did not think any more about the corkscrew till Mr. Bentley called again. That was a week later. It was a strange week. That morning when she woke up alone in bed, hardly aware whether she had dreamed that someone had shared it, that some strange, disturbing, and bittersweet experience had exalted the night above all nights she had known, was a Sunday. She saw Gert and Terry, each carrying a large suitcase, go down the street. They were bound for the railway station, for a Sunday journey to the digs of some other Ma Adams, for another stage on their pilgrimage to those heights of theatrical

distinction they were never to attain. They had played their
part in her own drama, and now they were walking off the
stage. She never saw them again.

But Elsie did not think of it in such terms as that. She was
sorry to see them go, because they were the only people she
knew here, but as the day went by she ceased altogether to think
of them. As the day went by, and as the week went by. . . . She
had plenty to think about, goodness knows. In the mornings
she would go out and do her simple shopping, take a turn in the
streets, eat her principal meal in a café so that she need not be
bothered with cooking; and then for the rest of the day she
would stay indoors. She thought round and round her problem. So far as she could see, there were three courses open to
her. She could apply for another "place." But she had been
sacked from Sir Charles Frome's, and that meant that she'd get
no "reference"—or so she thought, not knowing that the housekeeper would give her the best in the world. She could go
home and say that she had been sacked. This was something
she would do only in the direst need. Home, to Elsie, was a
brutal place, where a prodigal daughter would hardly find forgiveness. Thirdly, there was Mr. Bentley's sovereign under the
beer bottle.

Elsie knew well what the sovereign meant. Even before she
had gone to her first "place," she was aware of the profession
of one or two women living in her own street. The theory of
all that was familiar to her. Obstinately she refused to acknowl-
edge that, even now, she knew anything of its practice. As if
symbolically, she left the beer on the mantelpiece, and the
money beneath it. What, then, of this three pounds she had
received from Sir Charles Frome? Her little head dazed itself
with sophistries. That was another thing, she said. There, she
would have been utterly the giver out of her great pity for the
man's torment.

By the end of the week her mind was tranquil, for she had
come to a decision. What money she had left, she would spend
on a cab to take her and her box home to Levenshulme. It
would be horrible, ignominious, but it would have to be done.
Alec and Mr. Burnside would do something for her. She would

say nothing about this week: let it be assumed that she had driven from Bowdon.

Happy in this resolution, she was preparing herself an evening meal on the Saturday night when there was a knock at the door. This was so startling, so unaccustomed, an interruption of her long solitude that her heart fluttered, and for a moment the wild notion held her that Sir Charles had come at last. But it was Mr. Bentley. He had a new silk hat, and he was sober. He was carrying a little black despatch-case. He raised his hat and smiled. Now that he was not, as Elsie put it to herself, "under the influence," he was not a bad-looking young man. The fleck of blue ribbon was gone from his button-hole. He seemed altogether sensible.

Nevertheless, her instinct was to send him away. But he spoke so pleasantly, was so anxious to be assured that he was not intruding, that she admitted him. He put his hat and despatch-case on the hall-stand that filled half the passage and followed her into the sitting-room at the back. He at once put an arm about her and tried to kiss her. He had come with the intention of repeating when sober the delights he recollected from last Saturday night. Elsie gently but firmly put him aside. "Look," she said. "There's a drink upstairs. Go and get it. On the mantelpiece in the bedroom."

It was some little time before Mr. Bentley came down again. As Elsie had intended him to do, he found the corkscrew, the bottle, the sovereign, just as he had left them. He sat on the bed, puzzling out the implications of this. When they fully broke upon his mind, by no means a dull one, he gave a low whistle. Then he pocketed the sovereign and went slowly and thoughtfully down to the sitting-room. He and Elsie exchanged a long glance. He said inadequately: "I'm sorry. I was tight."

"I know that," she said. "So was I." And more briskly: "Well, have a bite of food. And then you'd better be going."

Mr. Bentley seemed overwhelmed by the generosity of her forgiveness. "Look," he said. "Come out and eat a meal with me. We'll go somewhere first-rate. And then we'll go on to a show. It'll do you good."

The idea of behaving himself, spending a sensible evening

with this lovely girl, seemed suddenly commendable. He looked so anxious, crestfallen, as he awaited her reply, that she laughed gaily. "All right," she said. "Cheer up."

He was expansive, almost garrulous, as they dined. They took their meal in the grill-room of the best hotel in the city. Mr. Bentley drank nothing but water. Elsie followed this excellent example. "I ought to leave it alone altogether," Mr. Bentley explained. "When I've had a few, I go as cracked as a cuckoo. My job leads me into it." He explained that he was a writer of gossip about the theatre, and that this involved too much giving and taking of drinks. Not, of course, that he was going to remain a gossip-writer. He was going to write books, or plays, or both, lead a sensible life, swear off the drink. He appeared, indeed, this evening to be an ambitious, exemplary young man. He had a free pass for the theatre, which was no distance away. They had but to walk across a street and they were there. Had they walked across the street five minutes sooner or five minutes later, much might have been different in the life of Elsie Dillworth. As it was, they crossed just at the moment when Mr. Dillworth, who liked to spend his Saturday nights in town, emerged from a bar and let the swing-door fall behind him. He stayed rooted where he was, out of their sight. At first, seeing them come out of the hotel, he could not believe that this was Elsie, whom he thought to be menially slaving at Bowdon. But beyond a doubt it was. His furtive mind was furiously working as he watched them cross the road and go into the theatre.

Mr. Dillworth was out of work. This was a condition he liked to be in. A wise man, as the fool esteemed himself to be, could always pick up a bit here and there. His life involved much hanging about and waiting for this and that. It was no hardship to him to wait for a couple of hours till the show was ended in the theatre. A lot of time could be spent over a drink or two.

In the theatre, Mr. Bentley suddenly remembered that he had left his despatch-case on the hall-stand in Elsie's house. He said it didn't matter: he would call for it on Monday; but Elsie,

who was wise enough to suspect that it had been left there as an excuse for another visit, said that she would be gone by Monday. Mr. Bentley was grieved to hear this, and wanted to know how, when, where, he could see her again. She had had enough of Mr. Bentley and of all that was associated with that dreadful house. She evaded his questions, and he was intelligent enough to know that this adventure was now ended.

"Well," he said, when at last they came out into the street again, "I'd better come along for that bag and then say good-bye."

They went in a hansom cab. Elsie would have liked to leave him on the doorstep, hand him his despatch-case, and say good-night; but he was a dexterous young man, and, having paid the cabman, he inserted himself into the passage. She wanted this matter to end graciously, and so she did not quarrel with his presence there.

Mr. Bentley left an hour later. It had been altogether an evening of good resolutions and good fulfilments. The hour had passed in friendly talk, mainly about Mr. Bentley's ambition. He even read some passages from the manuscript of a novel which was in the despatch-case. Elsie politely put her hand before her red tongue and white teeth as she yawned. She didn't want him to see how bored she was, but she did wish he would go.

His departure was dramatic, for no sooner was the front door opened than a strong hand seized him by the collar and sent him spinning into the middle of the road. A burly form brushed by him into the house, and before he could pick himself up he heard the door bang. He heard, too, a cry from behind the door. He was no hero. He brushed the dust from his clothes with his fingers, picked up his despatch-case, and moved smartly away towards the Oxford Road.

A candle was burning in a holder on the hall-stand. By its light, when the door banged, Elsie beheld her father. She backed swiftly towards the foot of the stairs, looking with terror upon his gigantic shadow wavering upon the door. He lurched towards her, and the cry Mr. Bentley heard in the

street was uttered as she fled up the stairs. He aimed a blow at her, crying: "You little whore!" but he was unsteady on his legs. He overbalanced and crashed face-downwards on the lowest steps. She stayed for a moment, her hand at her trembling mouth, looking down at him. Then, as he staggered to his feet, she ran on, reached her bedroom, and locked the door.

Now, indeed, she was at the end of her tether. She lay on the bed and cold shivers of horror swept her from head to foot. She could hear her father panting heavily like a wild, winded beast on the landing. Presently he began to beat upon the panels. She feared he would break down the door, and she rushed to the open window and gazed out distractedly into the silvered wash of the night. Elsie, alas! was no athletic heroine of romance. The sight of the drop daunted her. She did not masterfully knot the bed-sheets into ropes and swarm down to freedom. She merely felt choked with the terror of her situation, trapped beyond hope of escape. She threw herself again upon the bed. The banging upon the door stopped, but she could still hear the man's heavy breathing. She could picture him sitting there, leaning against the door.

All night long she did not sleep. By four o'clock the room was full of the grey of dawn. She looked dazedly at Mr. Bentley's bottle of beer, vaguely shaped against the wall. She got off the bed and lifted it by the neck, unconsciously weighing its strength. What she should do when she had escaped from that house she did not know. There would be no going home now. But escape she must. Grasping the bottle, she stole to the door, knelt, and pressed her ear to a panel. She judged he was asleep. She could just make out a gentle breathing. If he remained asleep, so much the better.

She turned the key, and began to open the door inch by inch. The weight at once told her that he was still leaning against it. She tried to do the job so delicately that he would ease back into the room without waking. She had placed the bottle on the floor as she took the weight of the door against both hands; but all her efforts were useless. Suddenly a great snore shook his body awake. He sat up with a start and glared

at her with bloodshot eyes. She snatched up the bottle, cleared his body as lightly as a bird, and flew down the stairs. She pulled at the front door, and realized that not only was it fastened by the catch, but that her father had shot the bolts at top and bottom. She strove as in a nightmare one strives to cry and cannot. He was lumbering down the stairs behind her. Then, feeling the bolts stiff and unyielding in her hand, knowing that she was without hope, she felt sweep over her a relaxing of the tension that had so cruelly stretched her in body and mind for these last few weeks; her till-now-unacknowledged sense of all the wrong that had been done her burst like an abscess suddenly lanced. Everything cleared up in one dynamic moment of action. She hardly knew she had done it till he was lying at her feet, motionless, with the blood streaming from a gash in his temple. Then, when the way was open before her, she did not go. She knelt at his feet, cradled his head in her arm, and cried: "Father! Father!"

All the nightmare quality was gone from the moment. Elsie's mind was clear now of everything but prosaic fact. She remembered how, years before, she had struck with a brass tray at a youth in her first "place," and how his mother, going with him to the doctor's, turned at the front door to say: "You'd better watch your temper, young woman. One of these days it'll be murder."

She wondered if she had killed her father. He was lying still. Not a sound escaped him. His face was bristly, its skin greyish. He looked altogether repulsive. She knelt at his side and put her ear to his chest. He was breathing. She went to the kitchen and warmed some water, brought a flannel and a towel, and ripped a piece from another towel for a bandage. She washed and bandaged the wound, cleaned up the mess, and then, feeling sick and empty, made some tea. She was sitting at the kitchen table, drinking the tea, when she looked up and saw him standing in the doorway. He was a terrifying apparition. His mean, bloodshot eyes glared at her from beneath the bandage, and his hands moved, in a gesture she had known since childhood, to unfasten the brass-buckled belt. Her

hand, raising the cup to her lips, trembled, and the tea spilled down on to the table. He grinned, pleased with his effect, and said: "Give me some tea." She refilled her own cup, and he advanced to the table, emptied it at a swig, and said: "Attempted murder. Do you know that? Attempted murder." He saw that his words had terrified her, and raised his voice menacingly: "One word from me to the police. . . ."

She was shivering with fright. "No, no!" she cried. "I didn't mean . . . I didn't realize. . . ."

With one hand on either post of the doorway to which he had returned, he hung sagging there with his yellow teeth bared and a red blot spreading upon the bandage.

"You didn't realize!" he said. "Well, well. Realize this, my girl. I'm ill. I must rest. I'm going to bed. I may be weeks getting better. You'll have to keep me and feed me. . . ."

He grinned again as the thought of this holiday he promised himself spread in his mind. He wasn't feeling too bad. This wasn't the first time—not by a long way—that someone had crowned him; but, by God, he swore to himself, never before had a crowning given him such a glorious opportunity as he had now. It would teach the little bitch a lesson.

"You bring me up my breakfast in an hour's time," he said threateningly. "And at one o'clock you bring me my dinner. An' then we'll see."

"I can't do it," Elsie cried. "You don't understand. I've only got a few shillings left. I'll take you home in a cab. I can do that. I've just got the fare."

The idea of going home did not please Mr. Dillworth. There would be no meals in bed at home and precious little sympathy. He turned and without another word lumbered up the stairs. Standing at the stair's foot, Elsie heard him climbing into her bed.

An hour later she took him his breakfast. That fastidiousness of words that was a worm in Alec Dillworth's heart was, in Elsie, a fastidiousness of person. Now she was revolted. She could have retched as she looked at this hulking mass that was her father. She had never seen him in bed before. He had stripped to the shirt. As he sat up, snarling to her to put the

pillows behind him, this fell open, revealing the black hair
matted coarsely upon his obese body. Unshaven and unwashed,
crowned with the blood-soaked bandage, he looked obscene.
She placed the tray upon his knees and longed to rush from
the room, but there were things to be said.

"Father."

He was wolfing the food, and looked at her slyly sideways.

"Father, I can't give you any dinner. There's nothing in the
house, and I've got no money. Let me take you home."

He looked at her for a moment with a sort of venomous
patience; then his face suddenly suffused with passion and he
shouted: "Money! Go and get money!"

Still she did not understand and her temper began to rise.
"Where from?" she cried. "D'you think I can go out and pick
up money in the streets?"

"Yes," he said. "Where else, you murdering little whore?"

Then she understood, and she walked quietly out of the
room. She did not blame him. She could see all that had happened in his base mind, all that must have flooded through it
as he watched her bring Mr. Bentley home and as he waited
there for an hour in the midnight street. He did not think he
was imposing this on her. He thought that she had already imposed it on herself and that now he could profit from it. It was
her own passion, too, that had laid him low, left him helpless
on her hands. Or was he helpless? How ill was he? She did not
know; but the white bloody head was terrifying. She thought
of him staggering out into the street with it, accosting a policeman. "My daughter . . . tried to murder me." He was capable
of it. She knew that. And he was capable of sustained and
brutal violence. The buckled belt had been his wand of authority all through her life and Alec's. Flight was all that now
seemed open to her. But whither? Her whole story now, from
the moment she had left Sir Charles Frome's house, was too
dubious, too much open to the worst interpretation. Her
thoughts trapped her, hedged her in with no loophole save
Alec. And what could she tell him? Nothing would explain
her position but the truth, incredible as it was; and if she told
him that, what good could come of it? She saw, indeed, much

evil: saw a flaming Alec raising hell's diversions either at Sir Charles's city office or at the house in Bowdon. He would be wild and ungovernable. She feared what might happen there.

A tapping upon the ceiling rescued her for a moment from these harrying thoughts. She dragged herself up the stairs, and her father feebly motioned to her to take the tray from the bed. He lay back and moaned faintly, whether in pain or pretence she did not know. "Draw the curtains," he said in a hoarse whisper. "I must sleep. I'm bad—bad . . ."

She drew the curtains across the window and looked once at the tangle of hair, the bloody splodge on the pillow. She hated him with a deep bitter hatred and wished he would die there where he lay.

All day long he and she went hungry. Whenever she looked into the room he did nothing but whine and moan. At nine o'clock she went out into the street. Across the way another girl was leaving a house. The two met, and the other girl said: "Hallo, dear. You going to town, too?"

Elsie went to town, too. She did not know that in the unfurnished front bedroom her father was peering through the net curtains. He watched the two girls go side by side down the street, then returned with satisfaction to bed and fell into an untroubled sleep.

When Mr. Dillworth's holiday had lasted for a week, he began to be troubled in mind. Life was elysian: plenty of food, plenty of bed, and a few drinks in the evening. His bandage was gone. His wound was healing beneath a star of sticking-plaster. But this happy state of affairs, he knew, could not last. He was married. There was already a sufficient reckoning to pay at home, and the longer he tarried the heavier it would be. One morning, Elsie, returning from shopping, was surprised to find a four-wheeler at the door. Her father stepped out of it, said to her roughly "Get in," and crowded her to the cab door so that she had to get in whether she wanted to or not. The cab at once moved away. Mr. Dillworth knew nothing of Sir Charles Frome; he did not know that Elsie had a rent-free

house. As it appeared to him, she was wasting money. If there
was rent to be paid, let her pay it to him and Mrs. Dillworth
for the use of the house in Levenshulme. This seemed a sensible arrangement to Mrs. Dillworth, too. It lasted until Alec
became editor of *Hard Facts* and took a small house for himself and Elsie: that is to say, for little more than six months.

Throughout that winter the close and subtle bonds that
held Alec and Elsie together endured such tension that they
hated one another. Neither would speak to the other if it were
possible not to do so. When they did speak, words were as
dangerous as a flame to petrol. At any second there might be a
flash, and more than once Alec ran out of the house lest the
flash should become a consuming flame. It was at this time
that Mr. Burnside and Daniel Dunkerley found him most un-
manageable. As for Elsie, her open giving nature became surly
and withdrawn. Daniel Dunkerley never knew how deep was
the private hell from which he lifted Alec Dillworth, or that,
while Alec might curse him for having destroyed his dreams,
he blessed him for deliverance from his nightmares.

There was a night when Elsie, walking along the Stockport
Road towards town, was accosted by Alec, who stepped suddenly out of a side-street. She was surprised to see him, for he
had avoided her as though she were plague-stricken. It was a
miserable night, dewed by a fine drizzle of rain. In the light of
a street lamp she looked at Alec's face, always white, now contorted like that of a beast in agony, and at the grey webs of mist
settled upon the wool of his coat. He must have been standing
there for some time. He must, she reflected with a painful
irony, have studied her habits as Sir Charles Frome had done
before finding her lying in the sun by the Cheshire mere. And
then, thinking of that day and this, of the midsummer sun, the
dancing water, the flowers and birdsong, and of this trudging
through the bleak wet night of the city to which that moment's
impulse had led her, she felt a swift revulsion against all that
was young and sane and generous in herself. Never again, she
thought, would a movement of pity find encouragement in
her breast.

She looked angrily at Alec, feeling a bitter seniority of

knowledge and experience. "What do you want?" she demanded sharply.

He seized her wrist in his thin bony claw. The grip had the strength of a maniacal intensity. "Don't take any one home tonight," he said.

She did not answer him, but pulled her hand with difficulty away. She began to walk on through the drizzling night.

"Did you hear what I said?" he called shrilly after her.

She gave the laugh like brittle breaking glass that was to fascinate Theodore Chrystal, a laugh so different from the sweet gurgling in the throat that once had delighted Alec. She stopped and looked at him, and something in his stillness, his intent white regard, made her begin to move back towards him. But he did not wait for her. "I've warned you," he said, and like a shadow he was swallowed by the darkness of the street.

It was nearly two hours later that she returned in a cab, and as she and a man alighted at the door, again that shadow brushed by them and disappeared. "I've warned you," he said. And what he meant she realized a little later when she stood again at the door, and out of the darkness a knife whizzed and pierced the wood behind her. With wide fascinated eyes, as the man was running down the street, she looked at the haft still quivering from the impact that had embedded the delicate point in the wood, and wondered whether it had been intended for him or her. It was a matter her mind never decided. She pulled the knife out of the door, snapping off the point. The bright splinter of steel caught the light, embedded there as, come what might, the hard point of these months would be for ever embedded in her heart.

Chapter Nine

ON that May morning when Alec drove to town from Didsbury, Theodore Chrystal returned early to Levenshulme, leaving Elsie Dillworth to explore the new house with Agnes Dunkerley. He had been exhilarated by Elsie's company as they walked together singing through Burnage, and he had found the return journey dull without her. Against the insistence of all his cautious instincts, he had decided to do something which, he hoped, would stimulate in Elsie the feeling for him that he had for her. He chose the timorous method of sending her a book—a book undeniably respectable, beyond reproach: Tennyson's *Idylls of the King*.

Elsie did not return from Didsbury until six o'clock. Alec was back in the house by four. He found the small parcel on the mat, picked it up, and took it into the sitting-room. He made himself some tea, and for a time looked at the parcel propped against the tea-pot. As editor of *Hard Facts*, he had no difficulty in recognizing Theo's handwriting. He felt an itch to know what Theo Chrystal was writing to Elsie about, or sending her: an itch that became a pain, an imperative command.

For fourteen months now he and Elsie had lived in this little house. They had been happy together in their way: a way of rather high tension, subject to dangerous vibration at a rude touch. Elsie had regained her gaiety; she had found a calling. Nothing had pleased Alec more than the passion she had shown for the violin. He was not musical, but he was always pleased to go with her and Mr. Burnside, or with her alone, to a Halle or any other concert. His satisfaction was two-fold: Elsie was developing her *daimon;* and, he believed, a passion for an art would lessen the danger of her seeking passion elsewhere. He wanted the company of no woman but Elsie; he saw no reason why she should want the company of any man but himself. That was the truth of it; but what he said to himself

was that life had hit Elsie too hard; he must see to it that no
more blows reached her.

He told himself that he had a right to know what Theo
Chrystal was up to. He didn't much like the young man.
Theo was older than he, but Alec always thought of him as
a raw young creature. He felt that he, and Elsie too, had been
born knowing many things that it would take Theo Chrystal
a lifetime to learn, if he learned them at all. Yet there were
admirable things about Theo. He would get on. Alec had
sensed beneath Theo's ascetic façade the pliable and insinu-
ating qualities that would worm their way through all the
loopholes of a successful career. So far as *that* went, good luck
to him. The world, as Alec saw it, was a conspiracy against
the poor and unfortunate, and if they could best it, he was prepared to cheer them on. Theo was poor enough. Any advantages he had, he had devised out of his own spirit, such as it
was.

He snipped the string of the small parcel. *Idylls of the King.*
On the fly-leaf: "With Theodore Chrystal's kind thoughts to
Miss Dillworth, sharer of a memorable morning. May 15,
1886."

Alec began to flip over the pages. "Morning shadows, huger
than the shapes that cast them." "Travail, and throes, and
agonies of life." "Blackening against the dead-green stripes of
even." Good lines. He had read the *Idylls* more than once, but
now, leaving the littered table, he moved to a comfortable
chair by the dead fireplace and began to read again. He forgot
Elsie, forgot Theo Chrystal, forgot the inscription which
linked their names on the fly-leaf he held in his hand. Soon he
was as deep in the book as he had been in the Bible that night
long ago when his mother took Elsie out into the snowstorm
and, following them, he had seen the fight in the snow-dumbed
street and sat in the doorway with Elsie's head on his shoulder.

Elsie let herself in with her latch-key and found him sitting
there. For a May day, the warmth, even at that hour of late
afternoon, was unusual. She was a little tired with her long
walk back from Didsbury, a little inclined to be petulant.
But to Alec, looking up suddenly from his book, she was en-

trancing. She was so tall; she held herself so well within the white flounced dress; the parasol of green and white that dangled from her hand looked like an immense flower. Tennyson's Elaines and Lynettes seemed suddenly far-off and paper-white. "Let me get you some tea, Else," he said.

The state of the room offended her. The years she had spent in service had given her a sense of household propriety, and this was deepened by an instinctive wish to have everything as different as it could be from the home in which she had been brought up. All this meant nothing to Alec. He had not put a cloth upon the table, and, pouring tea as he read, he had swamped his saucer and the table as well. He had a habit at mealtimes of crumbling food with one hand as he held a book with another, and Elsie looked with displeasure at the tea-soaked remnants of cake broadcast upon the table. To make things worse, a length of string and a piece of sodden brown paper were added to the litter.

"I've had tea," she said shortly. "I'd better clean up your mess."

Seeing that she was displeased, he grunted and picked up the book again. Elsie laid her parasol on the couch, took the brown paper between thumb and forefinger, and, holding it away from her to keep the drips from her muslin, she began to carry it to the scullery. Then she saw her own name written upon it in a hand that was unknown to her. She said nothing, but took a tray and a dish-cloth into the sitting-room, wiped the mess from the table, and, to give point to her actions, brought out a cloth, furniture polish and her housework gloves. As she polished the table, she said quietly: "What came for me while I was out?"

Alec looked up with a start. Only now did he remember what he had done, that he had forgotten to burn the paper, that he had intended that Elsie should not see this book. His pale face coloured deeply. "Oh, it was this," he said, and handed her the book. "I could feel it was only a book, Else, and you know I can never resist a book. Forgive?"

Elsie was reading the inscription. He tried to decipher her look, but it was inscrutable. She said nothing, and Alec could

feel that taut nerve between them vibrating. "I'm going for a walk," he said, and went out.

In front of the new building the hoardings were still up. Valuable hoardings. George Satterfield could have sold the space again and again and had it by now plastered from end to end with bills and posters. Instead, he had had the boards painted white, and on this virgin surface red letters announced here and there H A R D   F A C T S. Reiteration was the keynote of all Satterfield's advertising ideas. It was inconceivable that any one in Manchester, and more than a few people in England, had not by now heard of the paper and understood its status. None the less, George Satterfield continued to whisper it, shout it, bellow it, whenever and wherever occasion offered. He would, had it been possible, have written it upon the face of rivers and the rotundities of clouds.

The streets were quiet. Manchester became empty enough by six, but the air was clamorous with the noise of bells. The cathedral bell-ringers were engaged in one of their crazy endurance festivals, and the sound of the bells soared and tumbled, crashed and surged, setting a maelstrom of sound awash about the new offices of *Hard Facts*.

Alec pushed open a wicket gate in the hoarding. Within a complicated web of scaffolding and platforms the new building rose before him. The façade was finished; the roof was on. The windows, row upon row, were eyeless sockets. The main entrance gaped doorless, but already in the lintel of Portland stone the name *Hard Facts* was deeply incised and gilded. Alec smiled. O more than happy name! With what satisfaction must George Satterfield have told the workmen to write it in gold! But there was still so much emptiness, the place yawned and gaped so, that the letters looked to Alec like flecks of gold in the teeth above a skull's vacant mouth.

He went through the doorway into an interior that smelt excitingly of dust and varnish, wood-shavings and drying plaster. This entrance hall was an impressive place. No doubt, before the work was finished, sub-division would reduce its splendour. Now you could dump into it several establishments

as big as the premises on the Stockport Road where *Hard Facts* had its beginning fifteen months ago. The place echoed in the fading light as Alec walked on the mosaic of its floor. In the middle, forming a circle in red, was again the magic talisman: *Hard Facts*. Standing with his feet upon this solid earthy assurance, he lifted his eyes. The great stone staircase, with its mahogany rail, spiralled upwards, corkscrewing the sides of the well which reached out to daylight far above him in a dome of glass. In the plain whiteness was inserted a ruby pattern: *Hard Facts*.

Alec rocked with laughter. "My God!" he thought. "Even the angels, looking down, are not denied enlightenment."

It was fantastic, monstrous, and absurd. And somehow frightening. Alone in the great raw building, with the light waning and the cathedral bells filling the air with a clamour of mockery, there, at the bottom of that pit, pinned between hard facts over his head and beneath his feet, he was oppressed by a sense of his nothingness, of his capture and mutilation by Daniel Dunkerley's grinding machine. He longed for some reassurance, some vindication of his own being, and now he ran quickly up the stairs to seek it.

"You go to the first floor, Alec, and have a look at the corridor that runs off to the left," Dan Dunkerley had said.

All along one side, the corridor was pierced with unglazed window-gaps, opening on a well. Bags of workmen's tools, piles of planks, an odorous litter of pine shavings, filled the long perspective. On the other side was a series of doors, and chalked upon them were names for the sign-writers' instruction. On the central door of the last three he read: Editor, Mr. Alec Dillworth. On one side of this was: Editorial Secretary; and on the other: Editorial Assistants. All that was sceptical in him, all the untamed animal part of him that Daniel Dunkerley alone recognized and feared, and Mr. Burnside understood without fear: all this made him want to laugh as he had laughed standing beneath the dome. But something else in him, all that had been friendless and homeless, exposed to the ills of chance and change, and therefore exposing Elsie too, was suddenly moved to the quick. He passed his long thin hand up and down

the smooth mahogany of the door, permitted himself a wry grin as he wondered whether this name too would be written in gold, walked two or three times by the door, warily, like an animal reluctant to enter a cage; and finally pushed the door open.

It was a big room. Three windows pierced one wall. Here he was above the hoarding level. He gazed out upon the darkening town, his hands resting on the sill. A few cabs went by, the sound of their wheels drowned by the cascades of noise beating down from the cathedral tower. The lights were going up along the streets and flowering in innumerable windows. He watched for a moment the omnibuses and lorries, the sauntering lovers, the hurrying men and women with work to do. He loved the city, the quick, warm pulse of its life, its myriad contacts, the heat of its summer streets and the enchantment of its brumous winter dusks. Leaning out, he felt a rich satisfaction stirring the upper layers of his being, but his eyes were hot with unshed tears as he turned once more to the room, murmuring angrily: "All this will I give thee if thou wilt fall down and worship me."

This was a compact little suite, he saw now. Doors from his room led to the rooms on either side. He went into them and noticed with satisfaction that they were smaller than his. What he was going to do with an "Editor's secretary" and "Editorial assistants" he was not clear. He supposed it meant for one thing that letters would now have to be answered instead of being thrown into the waste-paper basket, and he thought this an unnecessary elaboration of his present method, which worked well enough. In a corner of his room there was another door which he had not yet opened. He did so now, and found himself in a small cabinet with a wash-basin in one corner and a mahogany-seated water-closet in another. Hereupon, his gravity again broke down. "My God!" he cried, "what a thing it is to be an editor." He turned a tap and water flowed into the basin. He laved his hands, dried them roughly on his handkerchief, finished them off with rubbings on his trouser-legs, and then solemnly and ritually stood up to the water-closet. He pulled the chain, and a daunting roar and

swoosh answered him. It drowned even the cathedral bells. It sounded as though every wall in the building were packed with water-pipes, and every pipe was pouring in its contribution to a symphony of roarings, chucklings, gurglings and drippings of water. Alec listened with satisfaction, turned, and saw Daniel Dunkerley watching him from the middle of the editor's room. Alec grinned. "The Editor," he said, "is now christened, inducted, installed, and invested. And no one in this building will ever in future need to ask whether the Editor is In or Out."

A lantern swung from Daniel's hand. The darkness had deepened and the lantern made a pool of light at Daniel's feet. He did not take up Alec's freakish remark, but asked gravely: "Well, Alec, what do you think of it? Will you be all right here? Will you be happy and comfortable?"

Ah, thought Alec, that is something you're asking now, my friend! Happiness? Comfort? Perhaps even the overlordship of these rooms, with the world's most vocal plumbing thrown in, could not be guaranteed to produce these. But he said nothing of this to Daniel. Daniel was in his solemn mood. He was the Man with a Mission. After all, Alec reflected, this was Dan's big day. This morning he had given his first breakfast party at the White House. He had driven to town for the first time in his carriage. And now he had come to gloat upon this building that he had caused to rise and to dream of loftier and loftier flights of fact and fancy. And so Alec suppressed the flippancy that tended always to assail him in the presence of Dan Dunkerley's ambitions, and he answered quietly: "Thank you, Dan. It's really very fine."

Dan held the lantern aloft, casting its light into the corners where now the shadows were settling thick and fast. "Yes; you should be comfortable, Alec," he said. "That's a nice fireplace there. You'll be cosy on a winter's day. I've been chasing people round a good deal, you know, to get things right for you. I *think* of you, you know, Alec."

"I'm sure you do, Dan. Thank you."

"I want you to furnish the room yourself. Don't you see— that will make you feel at home. Get your sister to help. And,"

he added with a smile, "the bills had better come to me, not
to George Satterfield."

. Alec was moved by this. "More chains on the leg. More ropes
on the wrist," the bitter core of him was saying; but a more
prosaic voice assured him: "You're not so damned important.
There are plenty of men could do the job better than you're
doing it. Be grateful, you skunk. Dan's a good man. Thank
your God that he likes you."

"That's very kind of you, Dan," he said.

"Not a bit. Come and have a look round. And mind your
feet."

Inside the building, it was now quite dark. Dan held the
lantern low as they went back along the corridor. "Let's go
right out to the top," he said.

They went up the stone stair, flight after flight. Here and
there Dan paused, leaned on the rail, hung the light out over
the well, and peered down into the now impenetrable gloom
of the entrance hall. "Hi, there! Hi, hi!" he shouted each time
he did this, and seemed to get pleasure from hearing his voice
beating about in the tube of darkness and sending back ghostly
volleys: *Hi, hi!*

There was a lot of builder's junk lying about on the topmost
floor. They picked their way delicately among it till they
came to a small iron staircase, and when they had mounted
this Dan pushed open a door, saying: "Well this is it, Alec.
This is the top of our world."

They stepped out on to the leads, and instantly the tumult
of the bells beat upon them. They were as high as the belfry,
and all the air was vibrating with the rush of brazen sound. To
Dan, it seemed to give a quality of exaltation to the moment.
The sky was full of stars, and Alec looked at Dan standing by
the parapet with his bare head silhouetted against them and
the rush of music all about him, his face uplifted, and the
tiny light of the lantern burning in his hand. His figure
seemed suddenly to Alec to be poignantly, unbearably, sym-
bolic. The great city stretched away at his feet, to the plains of
the west where the new moon was now sinking, to the bold
hills and the bare uplands of the east. There he was, above it

all, one of earth's lords and masters, destined, Alec felt, to be
more so as the years went by, and his light was a fag-end of
candle in a tin case. He walked a few paces and stood by
Dan's side and looked down at the moving lights in the street
below. "Dan," he shouted, for shout he must to make himself heard, "how much finer men are than the things they
do."

Dan was in no mood for subtle implications. He laid his
hand along Alec's shoulder and shouted: "Some men, Alec.
But not everybody. Not us. Gosh! The things we're going to
do!"

And when at last they were back in the hall again, he elab-
orated this. "Don't think all this," waving his hand to the
darkness above and below, "is just for *Hard Facts.* We
shouldn't need all this for one paper. But we're only beginning, Alec. There's a lot in front of us."

Alec voiced a thought that had troubled his unfinancial
mind all through the evening. "I don't know where you get
the money from, Dan."

Dunkerley laughed. "Well, that's not your side of the worry,
Alec. And at the moment it's credit, not money. If any one
wanted me to pay cash down for this lot, we'd be on the streets
tomorrow."

But before the year was out, the streets were being comfortably warded off by *The Little One,* printed on cheap green
paper, and *The Littlest One,* printed on cheap pink paper, and
British Youngster, printed on cheap white paper. *Gosh! The
things we're going to do!* They made Alec sick, as he thought
of his big Bible; but that night all this was hidden from him.
He felt an unaccustomed warmth of affection for Dan Dunkerley as they stepped through the hoarding into the gaslit
street.

Dan said: "Look, Alec. The brougham will be waiting for
me in St. John Street. I can drive back along the Stockport
Road and drop you near your place."

He spoke almost with diffidence, and Alec thought: "Poor
old Dan! He's trying his best to act as though his horse and
cart are already part and parcel of him. But really he's like a

child who wants to share a splendid new toy, partly from generosity, partly to show off."

"No, thank you, Dan," he said. "I've got a call to make."

He watched Dan stride away through the lighted thoroughfare, then turned into the small ill-lit streets of the Shambles. It always pleased him, this surviving bit of ancient Manchester, these old shops and inns crowding round the foot of the cathedral like chickens under a hen's wings. It was getting late, but there was still a ray of yellow light rising up out of Mr. Suddaby's cellar. He ran down the steps into the cave of secondhand books, sniffing with pleasure the familiar smell of old leather, dust, a gentle emanation of disintegration and decay. You seemed, down here, to be inside the damp crust of the earth, so that, even in midsummer, it was never really warm. He was not surprised to find, when he had threaded his way through the avenues and corridors of books and come to the fireplace where the old bookseller's chair stood on a faded mat, that there was still a bit of fire burning. Mr. Suddaby, thin and silvery, with a skull-cap on his head, was emptying the sodden leaves from his teapot on to a page of the *Manchester Guardian*, and as Alec came up and wished him good evening, he dumped this extinguisher upon the few dying coals.

"Well, my young editor," he chaffed him, "my moulder of the public, I suppose you're too important a man now to come and see me at a respectable hour. What you will be like when you get into that vulgar dollop of building they're putting up I don't know."

He shrugged himself into his overcoat, removed his skull-cap, and put on a silk hat. He took an ebony stick from a stovepipe standing by the fireplace. "I'm going," he announced firmly.

The coat and hat extinguished him as effectively as the wet tea leaves had extinguished the fire. He tottered about, putting out the gas-jets one by one. "Just one minute, Mr. Suddaby," Alec pleaded. "I want a bit of music, that's all. Something good for the violin. I don't know anything about it. You must guide me."

"Oh, I must, must I?" said the old man with a pretence of

severity. "If I'd had the guidance of you, you'd be working for the corporation street cleansing department rather than doing what you're up to now. Ah, well. Music, it it? We don't go in for music here, you know. Still, there's a fag-end or two." He rummaged in a box under one light he had left burning. "Here you are. Take this. No, no. Not a penny." His old eyes lit up with their quizzical gleam. "You exploiter of proletarian ignorance and laziness! D'you think I'd touch your tainted gold? Besides, that music's been there for a year and would stay there for years more. And how much longer d'you think I'm going to live, eh? Not long, you can bet your boots. Well, then. I've got enough to see me through and buy myself a funeral. So why should I go on worrying my head with pay, pay, pay?"

He put out the last light and followed Alec up the steps to the open air. He turned up his coat collar, looked up at the stars piercing the indigo of the narrow strip of sky. He said irrelevantly: "Just about here, you know, young Dillworth, Bonnie Prince Charlie once stood, looking up at these same stars, when he was on his way in the '45 through Manchester to Derby. He lived to look on the stars for a good long time, but some of the Manchester boys who marched with him were not so lucky. There was young Deacon, for one, who lived with his father Dr. Deacon in Fennel Street. Butcher Cumberland laid hold of him and he was disembowelled at Kennington. They sent his head back here, and it was stuck on a spike on the Exchange. When old Deacon would pass that way, he would pause for a moment, look at the curls he used to stroke, and raise his hat."

The cathedral bells, that had been shouting all this time, suddenly stopped and the night was quiet. In the silence, in the dark narrow street, Alec shivered. He had not heard that story before, and it was the sort of story that pierced to the quick of his pictorial imagination. He could see the young man marching behind the skirl of the Jacobite pipes down the long vista of the Stockport Road, and see, too, the ghastly end of it: the bloody head on the spike, the father saluting in gallant sorrow the mutilated mask of the son.

"So you see, young Dillworth," Mr. Suddaby was saying, beginning to move on through the night which was turning chill, "when you hear all the stuff about Prince Charming, remember that at any rate his head did stay on his shoulders, and that other people were not so fortunate. They are a good lot, taking them all in all, those other people. Win or lose, nothing can be done without them. They deserve something pretty good. That's a hard fact I commend to your editorial attention. Some day we may need a people educated enough to distinguish between running after romantic illusions and getting on with their own job of living."

He stopped and held out his hand. "Well," he said, "here endeth the lesson." Alec could see his eyes smiling in the dusk. "Now I must be off home to my steak and onions and a good read of Shelley. You can't beat either."

And as, a moment ago, Alec had watched Dan Dunkerley depart, so now he watched Mr. Suddaby. Clutching his roll of music, he felt as though he had been assailed from all hands.

The music was a peace-offering for Elsie. He had felt small and mean as he thought of what he had done with Theo Chrystal's gift. Now he was eager to see Elsie again, to thrust the music into her hand. But when he reached home she was not there. *The Idylls of the King* lay upon the sitting-room table, opened so that he should see at a glance that the fly-leaf with its inscription had been torn out. It was lying in the cold fireplace, where a match had been set to it. For a moment, Alec, with his hands on the mantelpiece, looked down at it, black but intact, with the words still legible on the charred curling sheet. "Theodore Chrystal: Miss Dillworth." He took up a poker, stirred the page, and it dissolved to dust.

Elsie had waited for Alec to go out. Then she had taken up the book. Theo Chrystal had wondered whether this would be the right sort of book for her; he knew so little of what she read or thought or did. However, he had at least had the sense to know that, even if she read nothing at all, a gift was a gift; and to make a gift was what he had in mind.

The book meant nothing to Elsie. The very names puzzled

her: Guinevere, Pelleas, Etarre. How did one pronounce such names? She read nothing—nothing, that is, that Theodore Chrystal would have called anything. No doubt, Theo had thought that morning, Alec helped her, put her reading on the right track. He was mistaken in this. Alec did not care two pins what she read or whether she read. Every week he gave her a copy of *Hard Facts*. She read it with interest from cover to cover, accepted with faith the silliest things it said. She was occasionally touched by a thought in the Rev. Phillip Strong's article. She did not know who Phillip Strong was. The identity of a contributor was safe with Alec. She had come, now, to like *Hard Facts*, to look forward to the moment each week when Alec would lay it on the table. She could not get over the wonder of his being the editor of this paper. Alec would watch with amusement the concentration of her lovely face as she turned the pages. If she wanted this stuff, let her have it. He wouldn't have her different: she was Elsie.

Thus, it was not the book, it was the gift, and the inscription of the fly-leaf, that Elsie was considering as she stood there with the *Idylls* in her hand. After breakfast that morning, she had been glad when Mrs. Dunkerley suggested that she should stay and look at the house and garden. She did not want to walk back with Mr. Chrystal. Superficially, her beauty was lazy and slumbrous, but beneath this she was highly charged with emotion, and she was a sensitive receiver of the emotions of others. It had not taken her many minutes to divine the discomfort of Sir Charles Frome the first time she met him, and much brutal experience had not deadened but sharpened her apprehensions. But now she was a guarded woman. What lay so dangerously close to the slumbrous surface was kept in check. She had learned not to smile and speak her old childish encouragement: "Cheer up!"

She had been aware, as she and Theo walked together through Burnage, that in her companion there was a heightening of emotional feeling towards herself. She had met Theo often enough, with Alec or Mr. Burnside, once or twice alone. This May morning was the first time he had sent out the tingling messages she so sensitively received. She had liked him

from the start. Before she had gone to her first place in domestic service she had been no one; one of innumerable children playing in Levenshulme gutters, hopping over the
chalked squares of the pavements, swinging on ropes from
lamp-posts. Then she became "the girl" in a succession of
middle-class houses, and the girl learned to take for granted
the small respect that she received. Upon this followed the
disastrous interlude into which Charles Frome's awakened
pity had pitilessly plunged her. Alec had pulled her out of that
hideous swamp. She had just had time to feel a little cleaner
and to be aware of walking on firm ground again when she first
met Theodore Chrystal. It is small wonder that she liked him.
He did not know it, but he was the first man she had ever met,
of something like her own age, after too many years of insult
or indifference. She was not yet used to being spoken to as
Theo spoke to her. His manners were beautiful, and no woman
could fail to be aware of his face and form. All the same, Elsie
was like a young animal that has seen the knife and smelled
the blood and has yet miraculously escaped from the place of
slaughter. She was not yet ready to trust her own emotions.
Therefore, she accepted Agnes Dunkerley's invitation with
pleasure, and the two women spent the day among wonders
new to them both, exclaiming with glee at water running into
a bath, clapping their hands at light filling a room at a touch
of a switch, looking with awe into a stable where, in an exciting
atmosphere of ammonia and hay, a groom was rubbing down
the flanks of a horse.

And now, Alec being gone, Elsie stood with Theodore
Chrystal's gift in her hand. "A memorable morning." Suddenly, she felt unutterably weary. She was, in years, hardly
more than a child, but oceans of experience flung a bitter
drenching wave upon her as she held Theo's naïve gift in her
hand. He would have been surprised to know that in that
moment he appeared to her as someone infinitely young and
innocent, with years to go before he could hope to come up
alongside herself. He knew nothing of her and nothing, she
guessed, of what life was all about. Her mind approved of
what Alec had done. She decided that she couldn't bear to have

any irruption of passion into this small circle of safety where
she had precariously arrived. She would just do nothing about
the gift and let Mr. Chrystal draw his own conclusions. She
tore out the fly-leaf and put a match to it in the grate. Alec
would see and understand. There would be no need to say
anything to him, either. She went to the cupboard where her
violin was kept and set off for the lesson with Mr. Simmons.
The light was beginning to fade as she hurried through the
streets, hugging the violin-case to her side with more passion
than she would have felt had a young parson's arm been tucked
there. It was Alec, not Theo Chrystal, who had bought her this
fiddle. Now she was happy and released. All the disturbing
complications that had appeared in the offing as she pondered
Theo's gift sailed away and dipped beneath the horizon. She
was left alone to think of her music.

You could go so long, Elsie thought, perhaps, if you had bad
luck, you could go right through life and out at the other end,
wherever that might lead to, without understanding the
things that were happening inside you. Looking back, she
could see now that something had always happened to her
when she heard music. She had thought at the time that this
happened to everybody. Now she knew that it didn't. There
was a boy in the street where she had spent her childhood
who used to play the mouth-organ. That was the first music she
could remember. The boy was a Pied Piper who could make
her stop whatever she was doing. She would slide round
corners and down back lanes till she came upon him, the
small instrument sliding across his mouth, his foot rhythmi-
cally tapping; and she would stand there and gape at him till
the music ended, the spit was shaken out of the organ, and
wiping it on his trousers seat the boy would shove it into his
pocket, grin at her, and depart. Not knowing it, they were
doing much for one another. He was her first musician. She
was his first audience. He became a star attraction of the
music-halls, but she never knew that.

She followed the German bands from pitch to pitch through
the streets of Levenshulme; and on Sunday nights outside the

Bull the Salvation Army band lifted her soul to heaven. When she began to work, she listened entranced, from her place in the kitchen, to piano-tinklings in parlours; and in the last "situation" she had before going to Sir Charles Frome's something happened that she was never to forget. One Saturday night a few guests were invited to the house for a "musical evening." Among them was her mistress's father, an old blind man. Elsie was told that at nine o'clock she was to carry a tray of sandwiches and coffee into the drawing-room. The "musical evening" began at eight. When everybody was assembled and the party had got under way, Elsie tiptoed into the hall to listen. A rumbustious bass shook the plaster; her mistress and a baritone sang a few duets; there were some pianoforte solos. Elsie enjoyed it all without discrimination. It was all "music" to her. At a quarter to nine she stole back to the kitchen, made the coffee, saw that her tray was all in order, and then carried it to the little table outside the drawing-room door. When the clock in the hall said nine, she knocked at the door, picked up her tray and entered.

She was at once embarrassed by someone in the room exclaiming "S-sh! S-sh!" She was frozen by this reproof coming upon her in the presence of so many people. She stood inside the door, holding the heavy tray, looking about her. It was a winter's night. A fire was burning. The flames of two candles burned steadily on the open upright piano. Near the piano was a tall standard lamp, its light suffusing a shade of golden silk. Everything in the room was quiet. Elsie was aware of a sense of expectancy. The guests were all seated, except the old blind man, who stood with the light of the lamp shining upon his fine carved face, his white hair, his eyes which looked unseeingly across the room. A fiddle was tucked under his chin. His right hand hung down at his side, holding a bow. Elsie's mistress was at the piano, her hands waiting on the keys. She was looking up into the old man's face. Presently he raised his bow and gave a slight nod.

Elsie had never before heard the violin played, and it was her fortune that the first time she heard it, it was played by a great amateur. It was a small perfect thing—a Brahms valse—

tender and warm. Elsie could not move. She gazed at the calm mask of the blind man, at the fingers magically distilling a sweetness that entered into her bones. It turned her bones to water, and there was a creeping sensation in her spine. The charming reiterated melody went on, and she felt tears gathering in her eyes. Never before had music made her feel thus. It had made her want to dance and sing, to march or clap her hands. But this music made her feel so happy that she wanted to cry. She could feel the tears absurdly streaking the sides of her nose and she could do nothing at all about it. The tray was in her hands and she dared not move to put it down. She held it stiffly out, fearing that her tears would fall upon the coffee cups and sandwiches.

Then it was over. The old man did not move for a moment, but still stood looking rapt across the room, and no one clapped as Elsie had heard them clap for the baritone and the piano-player. They all seemed slowly to come awake with a sigh and a stirring. The old man relaxed into the chair placed carefully near him, and Elsie's mistress got up from the piano-stool. She saw the child standing just inside the door with the heavy tray in her hands and the tears smudging her cheeks. She went across to her and smiled kindly. "It's all right, child," she said, thinking the tears flowed from embarrassment. "It's all right. Put the tray down now. It's not your fault. You just happened to come in at the wrong moment."

Where their gods were concerned, the Dillworths were secret children. Elsie never spoke of that night, not even to Alec, but the scene remained in her heart like a lighted shrine, and it was of this that she was thinking much later when Mr. Burnside played the violin for her. She had come back to Mr. Burnside the next night. Her words sounded casual to him, but to her own heart there was a fearful expectancy in them as she said offhandedly: "Let *me* have a go."

Chapter Ten

NOW that the visit to Cotter's Court was so suddenly and dramatically ended, with his holiday barely begun, there were all sorts of things that Theo Chrystal could have done. He could have gone into Somerset to see the people he had known as a boy, or he could have fulfilled an old intention of visiting the remains of the great Cistercian abbeys in the North of England. He could even have worked at his book on the authorship of the *Epistle to the Hebrews*: certainly not St. Paul, he said to himself. But who? He had complained often enough that only lack of time prevented his making some progress. Now the time was his, and the one thought in his head was to be back among the bricks of Levenshulme, baking in the midsummer heat.

As the train sped north through the uninspiring plain of central England a mood of depression settled upon him. His profoundest and most characteristic instinct was of prudence, of seeing his way all around and well ahead, of destroying nothing that might be a weapon in what he saw as the arduous and difficult fight before him. He had flown violently into the face of this principle that had governed his life, and now came the reaction, with foreboding of evil. To put it in its frankest way, Adela Pinson and all she stood for had been the best card he had to play. He wondered now whether this had been thrown away for ever, whether all that he had to do would have to be improvised out of circumstances as they arose. Unpromising enough the circumstances were likely to be.

The day was oppressively hot. At Derby he got out of the train and walked up and down the platform, hatless, pale, pondering his future. It was a subject never far behind the front of his mind. A cold hard gleam of ambition to succeed in his chosen walk of life was his warmest fire.

Once Derby was left behind, his mood began subtly to change with the changing scene. The monotony of the Mid-

land plain gave place to the mounting grandeur of the Peak. Streams flashed and leapt in the sun. Cattle stood knee-deep in them beneath the green shade of the alders, lazily whisking the flies from their twitching hides. The land rose in gentle swells, and then in nobler escarpments, climbing steeply to the burning blue of the sky. The grey solidity of farms and cottages huddled beneath the outstretched arms of elm and sycamore, the unmortared walls drawing their firm but erratic patterns upon the flanks of the hills: all this came upon him with the impact of newly perceived beauty. He had seen it but twice before: when he was, for the first time, going north to join Mr. Burnside, and that had been on a winter's day of mist and gloom; and when, but a few days before, he was travelling south. Then he had been so excited by his escape from Levenshulme that he had hardly noticed the land he was running through.

He could analyze more clearly now the reason for the joy he had felt in escaping to the south. He had been running away from Elsie Dillworth. She had never thanked him for that small gift he had sent her in May. She had not even mentioned it, though they had met several times since then. But they had not met so often as they had been accustomed to do. He had a feeling that both she and Alec were standing off, finding excuses for being engaged. With Alec, it was the work for *Hard Facts,* though, goodness knows, he had always taken that lightly enough. With Elsie, it was music. There was always a lesson with Mr. Simmons, or a concert, or a small party where a few musical friends were gathering together.

All this shook Theo profoundly in what was a sensitive part of him: his self-esteem. He remembered what an outcast Alec had seemed the first day he met him at that crazy party which launched *Hard Facts.* He remembered the sordid and brutal room from which he had helped Alec and Elsie to remove the books. He saw himself in the favourable light of a friend in need to the Dillworths. He had not yet seen the meaning of Mr. Burnside's answer to his suggestion that new ways might be found of helping Alec and Elsie. "Well, I'm not sure, Chrystal. Frankly, you know, I don't think much help can be

given to people who always want help. If I can do a bit to keep the ring for Alec and Elsie, I imagine they'll do the sparring."

Well, there it was. He had felt, after that walk with Elsie in May, that he was outside the ropes. It had not taken him long to decide that perhaps this was as well. His cautious disposition, recalling the girl's background, was a little startled at his own rashness in having attempted to start something that might become serious. "Don't get too fond of her, Chrystal my dear boy, unless you are prepared to get very fond of her indeed." That was Mr. Burnside again.

How fond of her was he? Having fled, it did not take him long to find out. Poor Adela herself, overcoming the inhibitions of a lifetime, had given him the final enlightenment. And yet, going back now as quickly as the train would take him, even in this uplifting landscape, he could not overcome the hesitations that plagued him. At Millers' Dale the train stopped again. He made a sudden decision, pulled down his bag from the rack, and got out on to the platform. He stood there till the train had curved out of sight, then humped the bag into the blinding sunshine outside the station.

There was no need, he thought, to rush so impetuously back. To leave the train in that way seemed itself impetuous; in fact, it was nothing of the sort. It was an assertion of Theo's habitual restraint, a playing for time, a postponement of decision. The train had stopped in the heart of what, he remembered a friend had once assured him, was the loveliest and most varied county in Britain. He had time on his hands. He would here continue his holiday and think over the situation.

No one but himself had left the train. Outside the station the day burned down upon this unknown countryside, and he stood there wondering what to do. There was no one in sight. He thought that perhaps he had better leave his luggage there and walk till he found a cottage that would house and feed him. His problem was suddenly solved for him. A trap with its new varnish flashing in the sunshine came at a good lick towards the station approach. The driver pulled up his horse

in a little flurry of white dust, wiped his brow, and shouted: "Are you the gentleman for Castleton?"

Theo shook his head. "No," he said, "and as far as I can see there's no gentleman for Castleton here. I'm the only person who left the train."

"He was coming from London. I was to meet him here and take him to Castleton," the man persisted.

Theo decided what to do. "Well," he said, "he's not here, as you see. But you can take me to Castleton if you like. Is there a good inn there?"

"Ay, there is that. That's where I'm from. This man was going to stay there."

"Well, I'm afraid there's a long time to wait for the next London train. Can you take me?"

"Ay, I suppose so," the man said doubtfully.

He got down from his seat and helped Theo to hoist his luggage into the trap. Then they both climbed in, and the fresh little horse went briskly away.

In the sunshine and the winy northern air, Theo felt ease of mind returning. The driver fell into abstraction, absently stroking from time to time with his whip the horse's shining sides. The dust rose under the wheels, but they were always a foot ahead of it. Larks soared and sang, invisible against the sky's aching blue. As far as Tideswell, they followed the high road, but left it at Lane Head and went due north, stirring the thicker dust of a lesser road. Now, thought Theo, I am learning. Now I am beginning to discover that "the North" is something more than that stewpot Stockport, simmering in a pit of smoke beneath a railway viaduct and than Manchester smeared over the great plate of its plain.

They clattered through Little Hucklow, with the land rising boldly up to Hucklow Moor on their left and to Abney on their right, and went by farm and field and cottage, all air-washed and invigorated.

"It's glorious country," Theo shouted.

"It's aw reight," the driver conceded. "But tha should see it in t'winter."

However, this was not winter. This was glorious summer;

and here was Castleton, a grey and decent village lying on the
edge of the wide green Hope Valley, threaded by a glancing
stream.

A telegram had been received to say that "the gentleman
for Castleton" had been detained in London, and Theo was
shown up to his waiting room. Methodical as ever, he unpacked his things at once, laying on the table by his bed the
Greek Testament and *The Way of Perfection*. He stood, arrested, with this book in his hand, thinking of the last time
he had unpacked and laid it on a table. That was at Cotter's
Court. He had not read a word of it there: events had swept
him along too swiftly and dramatically. And this moment, he
now felt, standing there with the book in his hand, in a
strange room, with the drowsy afternoon sounds of an unknown countryside drifting through the open window, was
itself a part of this dramatic space of time in which he found
himself enclosed. It had all been part of one flight and return—
a return that he had arrested, it is true—but the return, sooner
or later, was inherent in the whole quality of the movement
in which he was involved. The mood of elation that the drive
had engendered in him went suddenly flat. He felt tired, as
though all the emotions, all the unsolved questions of the last
few days, had come in that instant to a head. There was an old
wicker chair, chintz-covered, near the bed, and sinking into
it, he put his fair curls back upon the bizarre pattern of par-
rots and vine-tendrils, and was soon asleep with *The Way of
Perfection* still held in his hand.

When he awoke, he wondered for a moment where he was.
Through the open window sounded the slow slop and shuffle
of cattle moving to a byre for milking. Theo got up and looked
out at their feet splaying in the dust, their udders too heavy
to swing, their placid eyes and the knobbed vertebrae of their
backs. A child whittling a stick followed behind them, swal-
lows wheeled with shrill cries through the street; opposite, a
dog lolled its tongue in a doorway's narrow shade. It was peace-
ful, idyllic: he was glad he had come. He sluiced his face in
the wash-bowl and went down to tea. It was a formidable

"stay-bit" that would have pleased Mrs. Hornabrook, he thought, as he tucked into the ham and tongue, the bread-and-butter, jam and cake. And thinking of Mrs. Hornabrook, he thought again of Levenshulme, which meant Elsie Dillworth. He got up with resolution, went again to his bedroom, and sat down to write.

My dear Dillworth:—You think I am in Sussex, but here I am in Derbyshire—almost on Manchester's doorstep, you might say. I have just been looking at the map on the wall in the dining-room of this inn, and I was surprised to see how easy a journey it is out here. I ought to have done more of this. I ought to have taken an occasional refreshing day in this magnificent countryside. I'm surprised that more Manchester people don't do it. I'm surprised that *you* don't do it. I've never once heard you speak of coming out into Derbyshire. Mr. Dunkerley's imposing Didsbury mansion seems the limit of your rustic peregrinations. And that, I imagine, does not appeal deeply to you as I understand you.

Well, then, why not Castleton, my dear Dillworth? Hop into a train, and in no time at all you will be at Hope, where I could meet you, and we could walk back here together. Make it a few days. Make it a week. Surely, Mr. Dunkerley owes you a holiday. I haven't known you take one since *Hard Facts* started. What do you say? Come before this glorious weather breaks. Send me a telegram and I'll see that a room is kept for you at this inn. This air would not hurt Miss Dillworth either.

I left Sussex because my hostess's father died suddenly. I should have been a nuisance there in the circumstances. I believe you have two "Phillip Strongs" in hand at the moment, so I need not to worry about that.

In the expectation of seeing you soon, I am,

Yours very truly,

Theodore Chrystal.

It was not till he had been out and posted this that he wrote another letter.

My dear Adela:—In the greatness of the sorrow that came so suddenly and tragically upon you and your brother, what

could I do? I am glad that you approved my going away at once for, despite the beautiful kindness you have always shown me, I felt that that was a moment when I had no claim to consider myself other than an intruder.

It was my intention to return at once to Manchester and throw myself into the work of the parish, hoping that in this way I should to some extent overcome the deep depression into which these events have brought me. But on an impulse I decided to stay here in Derbyshire, where a short rest will permit me to go back more tranquillized. Among these rude moors and rocks I shall not forget dear Sussex, nor, I fear, shall I find anything to compensate for the loss of the delightful days to which I had been looking forward. As it is, I have the memory of one perfect evening to store in my heart.

But enough of me. What can I say to *you*, so cruelly stricken? Little enough. You have your faith. There is that consolation. It is not as though I had to think of affliction falling upon a heart unfortified and unprepared. You have the strength to bear whatever God, in His inscrutable providence, lays upon you. That is your comfort—and mine. As a priest, I pray God to bless and keep you. As your unchanging friend, I beg you to consider me at your service, now and always.

Believe me, dear Adela, as ever yours,
Theo Chrystal.

When the telegram came, Theo could hardly believe that this had happened. You sent a letter, baited with one phrase which was the essence of the matter, and heaven's delight fell into your lap. Standing within the cool dusky porch of the inn, with the midsummer blaze filling the street, he felt his heart beating strongly. This had never happened to him before. It was the consequence of holding this piece of paper in his hand. He wondered if he would have felt as strangely moved had it come from Alec. But Alec had been busy. He had asked Elsie to send the telegram, and so it read: "Arriving Hope with Alec 3:15. Elsie Dillworth." He had written to *him*. The answer was from *her*. This seemed to Theo to be a moving

personal point. It was Elsie who was coming, bringing Alec with her.

It was ten o'clock. He was in no mood to stay any longer indoors. He ordered some sandwiches, put them in his pocket, and set off, hatless, swinging a large stick. Was there ever such a morning? he wondered. Sometimes at Cambridge, lazing on the river, with all the small dragonflies like winged tubes of blue brittle glass filling the air and the midday sun spilling everywhere the scent of wild mint, he had been visited by rapture, by a sense of life's sheer beauty and joy and goodness so strong as to be almost mystical; and at times—as once in Salisbury Cathedral where he had wandered alone listening to the clear disembodied loveliness of unseen boy's voices lifted in melodies that seemed meet for Heaven—he had been reduced to tears by an apprehension of beauty and mortality commingled. But never, he thought, striding along the road to Hope, had life seemed so uplifting, so little anchored to the dusty concerns of mortal flesh. The very name of the ground he was walking on seemed part of the moment's glory.

"What do you call this place?" he shouted gaily to a passer-by, knowing well the answer.

"The Vale of Hope," the man answered, wondering at the youth's radiant face.

The Vale of Hope! I'm walking through the Vale of Hope! Lovely and inspiring name, with the sky blue above, the pastures fat and watered, and the dear summer dust whitening the hedges, and the larks singing like mad. And all round this enclosed and paradisal plain the hills stood up, their edges, where they touched the sky, blurred and uncertain in the heat of that perfect day.

It was a day, thought Theo, that he would never forget. Every moment of it seemed memorable, yet he wanted those moments to rush by. Lovely as all was, he would annihilate all if he could, and bring himself in one swoop to 3:15.

He passed through Hope and climbed to the summit of Win Hill where a breeze was stirring. He stood for a long time, looking down at the placidity of the valley where numerous waters met, a bowl of glistening green under the inverted blue

bowl of the sky. He sat on the short springy grass. At the inn they had packed food enough for three men. He ate a sandwich, filled and lit his pipe, and in deep content leaned back upon a sun-warmed stone. He thought with impatience: They won't have left Manchester yet.

Looking back the way he had come, beyond Hope, beyond Castleton, he could see the rise of the land through which the pass of the Winnats dropped steeply. He had wandered through it the night before. It had been almost dark, and in that deep fold of the land, that narrow twisting gulch, with immense limestone boulders strewing the sharp acclivities that ran up to cut battlements against the strip of sky, in the utter silence, no bird singing and nothing stirring save his own feet on the track, half rock, half turf, he had felt a breath of evil, a taint of tragedy, so that he was glad when at last the lights of Castleton bloomed below him through the dusk and a voice gave him good-night.

Later, in the inn he had found a guide book and read how, many years before, a boy and girl who had run away to be married were returning that way to Castleton, and at a bend in the gulch they were seized by five ruffians, dragged to a barn, and murdered. Their wandering horses were the first dumb evidence of the tragedy. Now, on Win Hill, with the daylight burning down, he thought again of that melancholy tale: the young lovers, and the jingling harness, the lights of the village just round the bend with promise of bed and bliss, and the sharp, villainous, brutal end. The woes of lovers dead and gone must fill the world, he thought; but the sun shone as though they had never been. For today's lovers there was always today. He had brought with him William Law's *Serious Call to a Devout and Holy Life*. Leaning back upon the rock, he began to read, but soon he found that he was turning page after page with no apprehension in his mind of what his eye scanned. He dropped the book into the close turf and fell asleep.

He sat up suddenly, rubbing his eyes. For a moment he wondered where he was, a Cambridge punt, the Sussex downs, the

last few days, jumbled in his mind. Then he remembered, and looking down into the valley he saw a train moving out of Hope station, drawing a scarf of steam behind it. He leapt to his feet, ready to run down the hill, leaving book and stick on the grass; then thought to pull out the great gold turnip that his father had bequeathed him. 1:35. Oh, this day was leaden! But it passed as all days pass, and half an hour before the train was due he was sitting on the station platform, flushed with impatience, browned by the sun, his blue eyes a deeper blue in the rich colour of his face. At 3:10 he said: I shall shut my eyes and not open them until I hear the train not only arrive but stop.

It happened that the compartment in which the Dillworths were travelling stopped right against the seat. Before the train was at a stand, looking out they saw him there, his chin sunk upon his breast, his thin brown hands clasped upon the crook of his stick. As they tumbled out, he opened his eyes, and there she was, almost as though she were tumbling into his arms. She and Alec each carried an ancient and dilapidated Gladstone bag. It would be difficult for Theo to realize this, but (save for Elsie's stay in "places") neither of them had ever spent a night away from home. They had never needed luggage, and Alec had hastily salvaged these two bags from a second-hand market. Printed on his were the initials C.M., and on hers E.R. He introduced himself to Theo as Christopher Marlowe, in attendance on Elizabeth Regina.

She, too, thought Theo, was tall and thin and had red hair, but never, let the poets dribble about her as they might, could she have looked like Elsie Dillworth. With the Gladstone bag in one hand, she carried her violin-case in the other, and Theo hastened to relieve her of this burden. "Oh, no. No thanks, Mr. Chrystal," she said. "If you want to carry anything, you can carry this." She clung to her precious burden and handed him the bag plastered with labels of hotels in Venice and Nice, Florence, Lisbon, Rome. "They'll think, in this pub of yours," said Alec with a grin, "that they've landed a travelled woman."

And she's never been outside Manchester, the poor soul, the darling, Theo was thinking. He himself had never been out of England. The names shining on that bag in this little Derbyshire backwater station were as exciting to him as they could possibly be to her. *Some day we'll see all these places together.*

"It's just a forecast," Alec was saying as they stood at the barrier and he fumbled in his pockets for the tickets he had lost. "Some day, she'll see all those places—won't you, Else?—when she's a world-famous violinist on tour."

He found the tickets, and they wandered out into the road. I hadn't thought of that, Theo's restless mind was saying. I know so little about her. This music. I don't know what it means to her. I don't know how much it weighs. I don't know whether she has a great talent or just plays the fiddle. Suddenly, he felt humble, and that was unusual with him. Suppose she really was a violinist with the future Alec had laughingly sketched? What then? Where did a curate fit in?

But this was not a day when youth could for long entertain such thoughts as these. She was there, and the sun was shining.

"Alec, how long can you stay?" Theo asked.

"Oh, about a week, more or less. It depends on whether I can stand the country. It may drive me mad. I may decide to go back tomorrow. I'm a townsman, you know."

"I'm glad Mr. Dunkerley was reasonable."

Alec shifted his bag from one thin hand to another. "Well, you see, we're building up more of a staff now. In the autumn we shall be moving into our stately pleasure dome. We're training the people we shall want. There's an assistant editor for one thing. It'll do him good to shovel the manure on his own for a week. To tell you the truth, I didn't tell Dan Dunkerley I was coming. No one knows where I am. An editor, after all," he said, with dignity, "should be allowed to make decisions."

"The firm seems to have plenty of money to spend nowadays," said Theo, more to make conversation than for any other purpose. "It's time Mr. Dunkerley raised your pay."

"That's all right," Alec answered easily. "I've seen to that. You must forgive me, Chrystal, if I chewed the fat more than I should about old Dan. I'm like that. I'm ready to slander anybody behind his back and insult him to his face. Well, Dan's all right. If my pay was an office-boy's, so was everyone else's. He had to see his way. Now that he sees it, he's been handsome enough. So it's good-bye to Levenshulme for me and Else. Now what is that?"

He took the stick from Theo's hand, and with the crook pulled down the trailing tendril, with its dark green leaves and ruddy-yellow flowers.

"That? Why, that's honeysuckle."

Alec broke off the flower, smelled it, held it curiously in his hand. "Honeysuckle," he said. "I've never seen honeysuckle before. A strange name, rather beautiful. I suppose it suckles the bees on honey," he said gravely, "as a woman's paps suckle a child on milk." He turned the flower over and over, then handed it to Elsie. Theo wanted to blush; but really he wasn't interested in the honeysuckle. He asked: "You don't mean you're leaving Levenshulme, Alec?"

"Why, yes, indeed we are. We shall take a small house in Burnage with a small garden. And we shall look for a small girl to cook our small dinners and sweep the place up with a very small broom. Her name will be Thumbelina Small. Altogether we shall begin in a small way."

Burnage. Well, that wasn't so bad, Theo thought. For a moment he had been in a panic, picturing Elsie whisked away to some far suburb. But Burnage was all right.

"You see, for one thing," Alec was going on, "Else and I have a father for whom we entertain no small hatred. At the moment, he's serving a small sentence for burglary."

Theo laughed gaily. This was carrying the small joke much too far. He had often wondered what might be behind the hints Mr. Burnside had let drop concerning the Dillworths. He knew that their childhood had been grey and unhappy; their parents, now vanished, had been undesirable. But he had never imagined them as criminal, and he did not now believe Alec's words. So he laughed and said: "Don't be

so absurd, Alec. One of these days someone may take you seriously."

Alec stopped in the road and faced him squarely. "Don't *you* take me seriously?" he demanded. "Don't you think I'm fit to have a burglar for a father? Huh! You don't know you're born, Chrystal. You ought to be still on the titty-bottle. Let me tell you my father's a bloody swine and my mother's a boozing old bitch. How's that for filial feeling, eh? Well, that's how I feel. I'm shifting Else where they're not likely to find her, and if one of them *did* by chance wander into our house, I'd do my best to throw him out and break his neck."

Theo realized with a great shock that Alec was speaking the truth. In that mid-afternoon hour of blazing sunshine, with all the birds silent, they had come to a stand, looking at one another on the dusty road between the powdered hedges. Alec had gone white, and Theo looked sickly. Strange, he was thinking, even in that tense moment, what qualities of silence Elsie had. She had spoken hardly a word since arriving at Hope. She had marched along, straight as a young willow-wand, listening to Alec but putting in no word. Even when he publicly proclaimed these things that were tormenting Theo, she looked proud and aloof as though none of it concerned her or could in any way touch her; and now, as the two young men faced each other in the road, she said nothing and looked nothing. She stood a little apart from them, gravely turning the honeysuckle over and over in her hand. It seemed to Theo an age before Alec directly appealed to her. "Am I telling the truth, Else?" She said with a smile: "Oh, yes. But what does it matter?"

Alec picked up the Gladstone bag that he had rested at his feet. "All right, then," he said with a return to gaiety. *"En avant, camerados.* Let us continue this small journey. But you should know, Chrystal, the sort of people you're going about with."

Theo could not so easily shed the moment. He was still shaken. "What does it matter?" They were, he thought, an incredible pair of people, and he remembered what Mr. Burnside had said about keeping the ring for them. By God, he

found himself blaspheming, they *do* know how to fight! And at the thought, the mingling of pity and horror that had frozen his inexperienced mind, resolved and flowed into channels of admiration. "By God!" he suddenly shouted aloud, bringing his great stick down with a thwack into the dust. "I *do* admire you, Alec! Did I ever tell you that before? I do admire you. I do." He added awkwardly: "And you, too, Miss Dillworth."

They all three stopped again at that outburst. Elsie said nothing, but in her enigmatic smile Theo read pity and almost contempt for youth so retarded that it must needs wonder at mere necessary courage and hardihood. Alec was more emotionally moved. His face worked strangely and he said with difficulty: "Thank you, Chrystal." And then, with his twisted grin: "Damn it, you *ought* to admire us. The Dillworth kids are something special."

Round a bend of the road they could see white dust rising higher than the hedges and hear a bleating and baaing of sheep. When they were past the bend, Theo was thankful to the sheep for providing relief from the moment's tension. They filled the road from hedge to hedge and were so many that the head of their procession was out of sight beyond another bend. Over the host of them rose their unceasing quavering cries and the white cloud that their small trotting feet kicked from the earth. A tongue-lolling dog with one blue wall-eye walked at the shepherd's side and from time to time threw a bark unnecessarily into the heaving mass that jostled heavy fleeces and dung-caked reesty tails along the road. They were bound for a washing-place. There was no getting past them. Theo thought he would never forget the smell of them and the smell of the hot summer dust, or the sight of the yellowish undulating chock-a-block mass, stained here and there with an ochre brand, or of Elsie looking with a child's pleasure on a sight which she could never have seen before. He couldn't sort out his feelings about her. Looking at the sheep with her lips half-parted in a smile, she seemed a child; but he sensed knowledge and experience that made him feel altogether beyond any understanding of the depth of her. Her

own question recurred in his mind: What does it matter?
The day was good, and she was here, and now, clear of the
sheep at last, they strode into the inn where tea was waiting.

Tea, Elsie thought, is the first thing. It was a hot day and
she was tired from the unaccustomed journey. She ate as
heartily as Alec or Theo, who both laid with conviction into
the cold meat and pickles. But she was through before they
were, and said: "I shall go up to my room." Theo sprang up
to open the door: it was the sort of thing Alec never did.

Her room was little more than a large cupboard, but she
entered it with awe. The inn, to her, might have been one of
the world's famous hotels. She had never before been away
on a holiday; never before, except on that one morning at
Dan Dunkerley's new house, had a servant laid a meal for her,
as the prodigious rustic tea had been laid. This, now, was the
first room that had ever been ordered, booked, for her, and
she gave it her respect. There was a bed, and a chest of drawers
with a mirror standing on it, and a wash-stand. Her bag was
on a chair by the bed and her violin-case on the floor near it.
Standing in the china bowl on the wash-stand was a large
copper jug, wrapped in towels which had become warm from
the hot water within. She was pleased with this attention. It
was the sort of preparation she herself had often had to make
for a visitor to one of her "places." It was nice, she thought,
to be waited on, to have people doing for her the sort of things
she had so often done for others. She did not know that Theo
Chrystal had arranged these matters, that the inn's normal
attentions did not run to hot water and clean towels at tea-
time, and that he had, out of his own store, placed the per-
fumed soap in the dish, removing the piece cut from a slab
of hard yellow.

Elsie washed herself and lay on the bed, with her white arms
under her red head. The room was cool, though small.
Through the window she could see the wide green spread of
a tree which she did not know to be a sycamore, and beyond
that the land rising to the moors. It was a sort of country she
had never known except in imagination, different indeed from

the green pleasant flats, studded with reedy meres, that made up the Cheshire plain into which she had wandered from Sir Charles Frome's house. She had held her breath, frightened a little, when the train, before reaching Hope, plunged roaringly into the tunnel beneath the High Peak.

Through the iron spokes, a fanlike radiation from a half moon at the foot of the bed, she could see the red paper crinkled in the fireplace, the china dogs, collared in gold, facing one another on the mantelpiece from either side of a glass case enshrining a composition in shells and seaweed. Over this a text in brilliantly coloured letters, framed in oak, assured her that "The strength of the hills is His also," and on the wall above the chest of drawers an immense steel engraving showed pigmy men labouring up and up on a tower of Babel whose unfinished pinnacles were lost in the immensity of heaven. Her floor was of bare boards, scrubbed white, with a strip of carpet at the bedside.

So there Elsie lay, warm, relaxed, content, accepting these humble blessings which seemed to her sufficient. Alec, it is true, occasionally, half-seriously and half in teasing, presented to her mind a picture of life different from this: a picture of a famous woman living in a world made up of first-class railway carriages and luxurious steamer saloons, hotels of fabulous grandeur and concert-halls filled with tense expectant faces which broke up, when she had finished playing, into agitated enthusiasm. There were artists' rooms in continental springs, full of orchids and mimosa, which were things that she, who had looked today so happily at the honeysuckle, could not imagine. There were jewels, too, and furs impregnated with expensive perfumes, and all these things were the care of a maid, a mythical majestic being rustling in stiff black silk whom Alec called Hortense.

"Of course, I sha'n't be with you, Else. That'll be the devil of it. You'll be beyond me. I shall have to stay in England and grind my living out of Dan Dunkerley's machine. Hortense will have to look after you. She'll be utterly devoted."

And, as though the pyramid of nonsense he had erected had been substantial, Alec would look woebegone and forsaken,

and she would say: "I'm not leaving *you*, Alec. You know that. Not for anything." And then he would look happier and say: "Good old Else. You know, I believe I only create these ideas in order to torture myself."

But theré were moments, she would admit, when she allowed herself to wonder whether her life might not be different from what it was. Not the sort of life to which Alec's fancy added details day by day—("I forgot the lovers, Else. There'll have to be lovers. You will repulse them all. There's that fat dark fellow Van der Poorten Schootz, the Amsterdam diamond merchant")—not that, but perhaps some life to which her violin would carry her, where she would be a person in her own right, living a life erected out of her own integrity. It was not in such words that Elsie shaped her thoughts; indeed, she could hardly be said to shape them at all; but Mr. Simmons, hard, tyrannical and sparing of praise, nevertheless was pleased with her, thought that if she worked hard for an immense time someone better than himself—someone in Austria whom he wouldn't even name—*might* think she was worth taking further. Out of such cautious hints and veiled admissions, the child permitted herself to build a picture of a future that was humble enough.

She was still humble where the violin was concerned, where all that had to do with music was concerned, but she could be rebellious about other things. She felt now a mood of rebellion where Theo Chrystal was concerned. Here she was on firm ground, both of knowledge and intuition. She did not suppose it was in a mere flash of impulse that Mr. Chrystal had asked Alec and her to join him. She would have to walk warily—the more warily because she knew in her bones that she liked him. She felt that she could easily go right over the top. And she didn't know whether what she could do and what she ought to do were the same thing. The drowsy warmth of the day, the tiredness of travel, overcame her. She fell into a sleep full of crazy dreams; of Hortense saying firmly to Mr. Van der Poorten Schootz that he could *not* come in, while in a room full of opulent anonymous flowers Alec and Theo Chrystal were struggling together like furious cats on the carpet.

"I'd like to take you up the Winnats pass," Theo said to Alec. "The time to go is just at sundown. You get a real feeling of the creepy crawly place then."

"Elsie won't come," Alec said. "She'll want to be practicing her fiddle."

Theo, with the match half-way to his pipe, looked surprised and disappointed. They had finished tea and were standing in the porch, looking out into the quiet village street. "But surely while she's on holiday——" he began.

"Look here, Chrystal. Just now the girl in there asked me what time I wanted to be called tomorrow. She said: 'I don't have to call the parson. I hear him stirring about at six o'clock.' I've no doubt you get up early to do your devotions."

Theo blushed, and Alec went on: "All right. All right. I'm not laughing at you. It happens that I believe in vigils myself, though perhaps you don't understand that. Well, since you're not giving up your own devotions this holiday, you mustn't expect Elsie to. She practices every night. I've asked the landlord if he minds, and he says it's all right."

"Where *is* Miss Dillworth? Couldn't we go for a walk now before supper?"

"No, we can't. I've just had a peep into her room, and she's asleep. I sha'n't disturb her."

"How good is she with the fiddle?" Theo asked. "I mean is it just a pastime or will she make a career of it?"

Alec looked defensive. "I don't know," he said. "I know nothing about it."

Theo had a feeling of being rebuffed, of having been put off as he would himself have put off any one who impertinently pried into his morning devotions. "Well, look," he said. "Let's arrange about tomorrow. How would you like to come into the Speedwell mine?"

"Never heard of it," said Alec.

"It's an abandoned working that goes into the mountain. I don't know anything about it except what they tell me here. It's just a show-place now."

"We'll see what Elsie says. Let's leave her to her sleep now and have a walk."

It wasn't an altogether pleasing walk, Theo felt. He had imagined, when he held that telegram in his hand, that once Elsie arrived they would be together all the time. The abrupt and purposeful words at the tea-table, "I shall go up to my room now," were a surprise, and Alec's announcement that she would want to be by herself every evening disappointed him. "I am going to ask Elsie Dillworth to marry me." The thought was at last clear and hard in his mind. Even the revelation that Alec had made on the way from the station had not shattered it, though it had shaken it for a moment. He was conscious now of pride that he had had the resolution to hold to his purpose. It would mean staking all on his own power, cutting himself loose from everything that came within the title of influence and patronage. He was surprised that this left no uneasiness in his heart or mind. Indeed, it gave him a feeling he had not experienced for a long time: a feeling of freedom and joy and rectitude. If only Elsie had been with them now his heart would have soared. As it was, he made conversation with Alec.

"Well, Alec, how are things with you? You've had time now to settle down in the editorial seat. How d'you feel about it?"

"I feel," said Alec, "very much as I imagine Mr. Burnside would feel if he were lifted out of Levenshulme and had his backside planted on to the bench of Bishops or on to a chair in the offices of the Society for the Propagation of the Gospel."

"Well, those are jobs that have got to be done," Theo said sententiously. And half in jest he added: "I for one sha'n't say no when I'm offered a bishopric."

"Oh, you'll be offered it all right," Alec replied easily. "You've got all the grease necessary to run smoothly in that groove. But I'd never have taken this job with Dan Dunkerley if it hadn't been for Elsie. I had to provide for her. It gave me a chance of keeping her away from our bloody parents. But do you think I *wanted* it? Good God, man: I'm a writer."

Theo had heard him say so before, caught again the fierce pride with which the word was uttered. "Well, Alec," he said, "plenty of writers have had to earn their living uncongenially

while waiting for success. There's nothing to stop you from writing, is there?"

"Oh, nothing, nothing," said Alec, "except spending eight hours a day in a refuse tip."

"Really, you know," Theo urged in a reasonable voice, "you've got a lot to be thankful for. Aren't you inclined to be a little intolerant, Alec?"

Alec winced like a horse touched on raw withers. "Intolerant?" he shouted. "Of course I'm intolerant, you damn fool! Didn't your university teach you the meaning of words? What does intolerant mean except that there are things you damn well won't put up with? How do you think anything ever got done except through people who shouted: 'We won't put up with it any longer! We won't! We won't!' How did any piece of crookery and palming off on the people get abolished except through intolerant fools like me? That's what's the matter with you and all your bloody gang. You tolerate, tolerate, tolerate! Has the Convocation of Canterbury ever announced that *Hard Facts* is dishwater and that no intelligent person should read it while there's Shelley and the Bible in the world?"

Theo had stopped and looked aghast at Alec, standing there white in the road, almost shaking a fist under his nose. He would not have known what to do had it not been for that last rhetorical question, which struck him as such a rich absurdity that the only thing to do was to laugh aloud. His clear ringing laugh seemed to bring Alec to his senses. He took out a handkerchief and mopped his forehead. "I'm sorry, Chrystal," he said. "But there are times when I feel trapped. But it's my own fault. I chose it myself. Lend me your stick."

He reached up into the hedge and pulled down the vines of the honeysuckle. He gathered a great bunch of the flowers and said: "They'll smell grand in Elsie's room."

Watching him at his task, Theo was aware of the process that had worked itself out in Alec's mind. The outburst of rebellion against his ineluctable fate had been a treachery to Elsie. "I chose it myself." And he chose it for Elsie's sake. He must not forget that. What he had chosen he must bear with-

out complaint. These wild scented wayside flowers were his
peace-offering to Elsie. Theo wished that he had thought to
take her the flowers himself. Looking at Alec's thin fingers
holding that foaming cup of blossom, at his sensitive nose
going down into the heart of their fragrance, he felt a sharp
momentary disturbance. He wondered for the first time
whether in this matter of Elsie he had taken sufficient account
of Alec.

Theo's mind amused itself with the question: "I wonder
what Adela would say if she could see me now?"

It was the first time he had thought of Adela since writing
to her immediately on his arrival at Castleton. The letter had
purged his mind of her. Now her memory returned only to
give point to a moment which, even to Theo himself, seemed
incredible. With a pipe clenched in his teeth he was valiantly
knocking out *There's no place like home* on the piano in the
bar-parlour. With tobacco smoke wreathing about her like
incense, Elsie Dillworth stood at his side, playing the violin.
The bar-parlour was crowded by an entranced audience. They
applauded with hands and voices when the playing ended,
thumped with beer-pots on tables, demanded more. Theo and
Elsie obliged with *Annie Laurie*.

Theo had gone out alone. Elsie had joined him and Alec
at supper at seven o'clock. Then Alec had said that he wasn't
going to walk any more that night, and Theo, feeling a little
disgruntled by the way these Dillworths hung together, set
off to the Winnats. Borrowing his emotions as usual from the
poets, he murmured to himself:

> *It is a beauteous evening, calm and free,*
> *The holy time is quiet as a nun,*
> *Breathless with adoration.*

The hot fret was gone out of the day. The grey solid houses
of the village were beginning to be webbed with twilight, and
in the narrow pass of the Winnats gloom was settling fast. He
did not stay on the track but struck up the sharp escarpment
to the left, clambering among age-old boulders and tough

turf that had taken the frosts and thaws of centuries. He came
out among the crenellated crags that fringed the pass like high-
lifted castle walls, and there he sat down while the light faded
to a clear lucent green in which one star throbbed and
trembled.

> *Bright star! Would I were steadfast as thou art!*
> *Not in lone splendour hung aloft the night. . . .*

Oh, damn the poets! I don't want to think about them. I
want to think about Elsie Dillworth.

Here was the end of the first day, and he'd seen almost nothing of her. The day had been, he thought unromantically,
just a sandwich, with a snatch of Elsie crushed in between
two meditations upon the mountains. A short walk from the
station, a half hour at table: that was all he had had of her;
and for the most part she had been inaccessible even to speech.
Her face had been as smiling, reserved and enigmatic as the
Mona Lisa. . . .

It's pictures now! Poets or pictures all the time! Let me
think of Elsie Dillworth as she is: tall, straight, red and white,
following the bleating sheep with a childlike pleasure that
half opened her lips and showed her white teeth gleaming.
Well, he thought, that was something he had. That was one
picture that was his for good.

Are she and Alec utterly inseparable? Shall I never have a
moment with her alone?

There were more stars in the sky now, and the pass at his
feet was becoming so dark that he decided to go down while
he might still see something of his way. He did not expect to
see her again that night. She would finish her practice and go
to bed. As he drew near to the inn, he heard through the crystal
of the night air the music of a violin. He had never heard
Elsie play. Strange, he thought, that it has never entered my
mind to wish to hear her play. I have never thought of her
and her music as one thing; but if she is a player at all, then
she is her music and her music is she.

A door, dusky midnight blue, led into a yard that was at the
side of the inn and turned round to the back of it. In the angle

a great sycamore was growing, its leaves devoid now of all individual being. Above the dark wall they rose in one ebon
silhouette carved upon the night sky. Theo tip-toed to the
angle, looked up at the back wall of the inn, and saw a window
faintly lighted. Evidently no more than one candle was burning in the room, but the light was enough to show him Elsie.
As Sir Charles Frome had done on a summer's morning, so
now on a summer's night Theo instinctively blotted himself
into the shadow of the tree trunk, though all was so dark down
there that he did not need to do so. The curtain had not been
drawn and the window was flung open. He could see Elsie
from the waist up, and in the faint golden light she seemed
insubstantial. Her hair was nothing but a bright blur round
the pale oval of her face which bent lovingly upon the fiddle,
caressing it beneath the tender shadow of her chin. She had
changed. She was wearing a white dress. The lawn sleeves, he
could see, were full but caught firmly at the wrists. The light
made this gauzy stuff shimmer as her right arm dipped and
thrust across the strings of the violin.

There rushed into Theo's mind a moment that seemed to
him now to belong to a time incredibly old, remote and forsaken; yet it was but a few days ago: the moment when he had
stood in the garden at Cotter's Court and he and Adela had
listened to the nightingale. Did ever, he wondered, nightingale pour such music as this into the enchantment of the night?
He was aware even as he listened, even as his heart was bewitched by the mingled strength and tenderness of the music
that soared out from the little chamber, that he knew nothing
of what he was hearing. He did not know who the composer
was, whether it was an inspired improvisation, or even whether,
so poor was his technical knowledge, the performance, to a
musician, would seem glorious or faulty. He only knew that
he felt a shiver of the spine such as affected him when for the
first time he came upon a great line of poetry, something which
in its total unquestionable impact made the heart accept it as a
breath of immortality.

So, listening to Elsie Dillworth playing like a bird singing
its heart out in the night, he felt that he needed no more

equipment than a sensitive human breast to feel that it was being stroked, soothed, excited and exalted by something beyond the ordinary. It happened that the candle was so placed that now and then her arm swept across its light, and the lawn of the sleeve shimmered as if the arm itself were mantled in radiance. It was as if she were flashing a sword; and the music was a sword that pierced to his heart and made him tremble with humility. So this was Elsie! This was the reality behind the aloof young smiling face. It was something as deep and ancient as he had from time to time sensed behind the taut ironic mask of Alec. He had thought of Elsie as a citadel to be reduced. Now, as his limbs trembled, he realized that she was terrible with banners and that it was he who was conquered, abject and worshipping before power of a sort that could never be his.

The music ended on a note, high, clear and pure, that seemed to pass slowly into the night and end as part of its being. The flashing arm dropped to the girl's side. She stood for a moment with her head still lovingly arched over the violin as though listening to God knows what last dying echo of enchantment. Then, so quiet was the night, Theo heard a great sigh float from her like a moth; the rigid form liquefied into rippling lines; she laid down the violin and came and leaned upon the window-sill.

Leaning back into the angle of the wall, his hands touching the smooth bark of the sycamore rising like a pillar before him and the darkness of the night softened by no more than a premonition of the rising moon, Theo felt nevertheless that he must be visible. He longed to hear her speak, call to him in a voice that would be low, in the confidence of this silence. She knelt upon the floor, leaned her elbows on the window, and held her face from chin to temples like a chalice in her palms. She looked out at the tree whose topmost leaves, could Theo but have seen them, were now shining with a faintly bluish light. For five minutes she stayed there, not moving, as though the night had bewitched her; then she moved back into the room and he saw her take up the violin again. At the

same moment a shadow slid into the yard, and though he could not see him clearly, he knew that this was Alec.

Theo felt a pang almost of jealousy shoot through his heart. He felt as smitten as though a rival for Elsie's love had stolen upon the scene. When was he to have a moment alone with her, he wondered? Could he not have even this moment of darkness and silence when she did not so much as know that he was there?

He watched Alec's frail figure tip-toe through the yard and come to rest against the wall on which Elsie's window looked directly down. Once Alec had settled there, he was as invisible as Theo himself. And while those two waited, as taut with expectation as the strings of the fiddle, the music again poured out of the little room. This time it was all gaiety and caprice. There had been an autumnal solemnity, a pomp of doomed splendour, in the music Theo had first heard; but this was all springtime, flashing with wings and young water. It was brief, gay and lyrical, ended so soon that Theo was left sorrowing at the passing of it almost before he knew it had begun.

Then Elsie came to the window, still holding the bow and fiddle, and called softly down into the darkness. "Alec!"

There was no answer for a moment, and she said again: "Alec! I know you're there."

Then Alec stirred away from the wall and answered her in the same hushed conspiring voice: "Well, Else. That was grand."

"Why, Alec! What's the matter with your voice?" she asked.

"You know damn well. I'm crying."

"But, Alec, what's there to cry about? It was nothing but dancing and singing."

"Aren't dancing and singing something to cry about in this bloody world?" Alec asked roughly. "There's so little of 'em, Else."

Her laugh tinkled down to him. "All right. I'd better play you a Dead March. Then you'll split yourself laughing."

Theo could just make out Alec rubbing his sleeve across his eyes. "Look, Else. Come down and play in the bar-parlour. All the boozers are crowded at the foot of the stairs with mugs in

their hands, listening to you. The landlord would love it if you'd come down."

Theo was shaken with indignation. That Elsie—Elsie as he had known her at any time—should play in a bar-parlour was an idea that revolted him. But that this new Elsie whom he had got to know within the last half-hour: that *she* should play to a room full of beer-swilling sots was something that seemed like a desecration. He waited to hear her firm refusal.

"But, Alec, what a glorious idea!" she cried, and whisked away at once from the window. Alec ran eagerly out of the yard. Theo stood for a moment planted where he was, baffled by the enigma of the Dillworths. Elsie playing like an angel, Alec weeping like a sorrowful faun; and then the pair of them rushing off to appear in a room full of tobacco smoke and beer and village topers: it was beyond him. He felt he would never understand them.

When Theo came out from the yard, the village street was serene under the flat light of the climbing moon. He filled his pipe and walked slowly past the front of the inn, feeling deserted, an outsider, uncertain of where he stood with anybody. He felt he would like to take a walk in order to sort out his emotions, but he was held by a deep reluctance to move far from Elsie. Suddenly he turned about, walked through the inn door, thrust his stick into the hall-stand, and, still grasping his pipe in his teeth, swung open the door of the bar-parlour. He had once before glanced into the room, though he had not entered it. He knew that to one side of the fireplace there was a yellowing upright piano with pink pleated silk behind fretwork in the front of it. Hardly pausing now to see who was in the room, seeing only that the piano stool of worn button-studded leather was empty and that Elsie, fiddle in hand, was standing near it, he strode to the stool, threw open the piano, and slammed out the opening bar of the first popular melody that came into his head. It happened to be a rousing one: "Marching Through Georgia." He was aware that Elsie's violin had taken up the tune, that a silence had fallen upon the bar-parlour, and that the state of the piano combined with his

execution, which was little more than a vigorous vamping, was producing sounds that must be excruciating to Elsie's ear. But something pushed him through. The performance ended, and in a daze he heard the "Bravos!" the pot-thumpings, the excited clatter of men who were getting what they liked. He swung round on the stool, and Elsie was saying: "Splendid, Mr. Chrystal! I didn't know you played," and Alec was shouting: "A pint, please! A pint for Mr. Chrystal!"

On the piano was a round flat projection convenient for housing the sustenance of the artist, and on this a pint pot of beer was put down. All round the room drinks were being renewed, pipes were being charged, and there was a general air of settling down to make a night of it. Theo, with a recollection of that undergraduate tramp when he had learned to intone in churches and wet a dusty throat at wayside pubs, took a swig, smacked his lips, stuck his pipe back into his mouth at a cocky angle, and said to Elsie: "What shall we give 'em now?"

Every one at once began to shout his favourite, and for the next hour these favourites were dealt with by Theo with a thumping heartiness and by Elsie as best she could in the circumstances. She finished up by playing, alone, the "Londonderry Air." It was beautifully done, thought Theo, but wasted on this half-drunk audience, sunk by it into maudlin sentimentality. Time she got out of this; time she went to bed. He noted with satisfaction that it was ten to eleven. It was then that Alec, who was slightly excited by drink, shouted: "I shall now recite 'The Derbyshire Ram,'" and, standing by the piano, proceeded forthwith to do so. Theo had not heard "The Derbyshire Ram" before, and he felt that with Elsie present he did not want to hear it again. He was deeply annoyed with Alec as gust after gust of laughter greeted the ribald sallies of the old ballad. He stole a glance at Elsie, standing in a corner of the room, excited, with lips parted and eyes shining, and he saw that she was enjoying this roistering salacious tale as much as anybody.

Alec ended amid a burst of applause that was punctuated by the landlord's cry: "Time, gentlemen! Time, gentlemen, please!"

Elsie had slipped from the room. Theo said: "I'll take a breath of air, Alec."

Alec went with him. They walked gravely up and down the street in the moonlight. "You see, Chrystal," said Alec, managing his words and his feet with some care, "the great heart of the people. The throbbing heart of humanity. Good for poets and parsons. I shouldn't be surprised, Chrystal, if that's the first time you've come into touch, man to man, with Jesus Christ's clientèle. We'll make something of you yet."

Alec said: "I can't do it. I can't do it, I tell you. Why didn't you tell me there were all these damn steps?"

"I knew nothing about it," Theo answered, himself annoyed at Alec's unreasonable annoyance.

Elsie said nothing. She was standing at the top of the steps, looking down with grave speculation into the darkness.

"Heights and depths are all the same to me," Alec went on obstinately. "A couple of months ago Dan Dunkerley took me up on the back of his new white elephant. I wanted to fling myself over into the street. And down there I'd scream. I'd feel the walls were closing in on me."

The man with the lantern, custodian of this old Speedwell mine, now a show-place, stood by patiently, awaiting their decision. They had brought him out from a near-by cottage. "A hundred steps," he said, adding with relish, "into the bowels of the earth."

"I dislike bowels," said Alec. "Come on, Else. Let's have a walk."

He turned towards the sunlight filling the morning, but Elsie continued to gaze as though fascinated at the steps that lost themselves so swiftly in the pit. "I shall go down," she said.

"You, sir?" the man asked.

"Yes," said Theo, "I shall go too."

Now he was praying that Alec would not change his mind. He had not expected this. He had looked forward glumly to another day which would bring him no nearer to Elsie. "Come, Alec," he urged with false heartiness. "Everybody who visits

Castleton must go into the Speedwell Mine. The guide book says so. Even Byron when he was here went down."

The man with the lamp pricked up his ears at the name. It was part of his worn and tattered recitation. "That's right, sir," he confirmed. "Byron, peer and poet. He died later, fighting the Greeks."

"Did he?" said Alec with a grin.

"Yes, sir, fighting the Greeks."

"Thank you," said Alec. "I must remember that. It's not widely known." He turned on his heel. "Well, Proserpine," he shouted over his shoulder to Elsie, "you and gloomy Dis can descend to your underworld. Me for the fields of Enna." He strode defiantly away.

Elsie turned with a smile to Theo. "What's he talking about now?"

"Just an old tag from Milton," Theo answered.

"I don't know half the time what he's talking about," she said. "Was Milton a poet?"

"Yes," said Theo gently. "I'll tell you about him some day— shall I?"

"If you like," she said. The words breathed warmly on his neck. The man had shut the door behind them. They were on the steps, he in front, holding the lantern low; then Theo, and behind Theo, Elsie, with her hand on his shoulder. Theo continued to talk, because all his being thrilled at her warm breath falling in this dank tunnel upon his skin. "Doesn't Alec ever tell you about the poets and things of that sort?" he asked.

"Oh, no," she laughed. "He never bothers his head about me one way or another." She added gravely: "There's no need to. We understand one another." She gave a little shiver and said: "It is cold down here."

"Yes," said Theo. "I feared it might be. I brought this cloak for you to wear when we get to the boat."

"Oh! I thought that was for yourself."

"No. It is for you."

"Thank you," she said.

He was glad that she did not protest, that she so naturally ac-

cepted this small attention; and she was glad that he had thought to bring the cloak for her. Alec would not have done that. It would never have entered his mind. He would simply have damned himself, when it was too late, for *not* having brought it.

Elsie removed her hand from Theo's shoulder. This incident of the cloak was so small; it could be, in other circumstances, so meaningless. But she knew that it was not. When Theo said: "No. It is for you," she felt his excitement radiating into her fingertips and read immensities into the simple words.

Since last night she had moved ahead in her liking for him. She had never before seen him in a mood which convinced her of its spontaneity and frankness. He had always been a young parson, inclined, as she put it to herself, to watch his step. She remembered how he had talked to Agnes Dunkerley that morning in the new house at Didsbury. "Servants are in the natural order. Indeed, we are all servants one of another." She had heard a good deal of talk like that from Theo: parsons' talk, as she mentally dismissed it. She supposed he had to do it, though Mr. Burnside never talked like that. It had spun a veil of convention between her and Theo. She couldn't see him clearly through it. But last night she had felt a new tenderness for the good-looking boy so abominably thumping on the piano, the more so because she guessed he had not wanted to be there, and had come only because he thought that in some way he was bringing protection to her. Her bedroom at the inn was next to his. The morning sunshine, streaming through her window as it never did in Levenshulme, had awakened her early. She had heard Theo moving about in his room, had caught the sustained murmur of his voice, and had guessed that he was praying aloud. She could picture him on his knees at his bedside, and she tried to shut out this image from her mind and to stifle his voice by pulling the sheet over her head, for a delicacy forbade her to eavesdrop upon so private a moment. But the voice went on, a falling and rising monotone, and the picture of him persisted in her mind. She felt a pity for him, as for something young clinging for comfort to vast cloudy skirts.

She fell asleep again, and at eight o'clock a maid came into the room with the shining ewer wrapped in a towel.

"Good morning," said Elsie. "Thank you for looking after me so well."

The girl seemed for a moment surprised that any one should go out of the way to thank her; then, as Elsie swung a leg out of bed, she grinned in a friendly way and said: "Stay where you are for a bit, miss. Your tea and biscuits are just coming."

She had left the tray on a table outside the door, and now brought it in and laid it on Elsie's knees. "This is lovely," Elsie said. "I've never had tea in bed before. Thank you again."

"Oh, don't thank me," said the girl. "Thank the young parson. It don't run to morning tea an' hot towels here as a rule, I can tell you. He ordered 'em special. He don't have 'em himself."

All this was the background of Elsie's thought as Theo said: "It is for you." And as the perturbation of his mind came tingling out of his body she withdrew her fingers from his shoulder and said: "Look! We're down! I can see the water."

The lantern-light fell in an oily gleam on the narrow canal and showed the boat waiting there at the foot of the steps. "One hundred steps down. We are now in the bowels of the earth," their conductor announced. He cleared his throat and began his familiar tale. "The Speedwell Mine, on whose exploration we are about to embark. . . ."

Elsie was looking at him wide-eyed, ready to take in his romantic chronicle, but Theo, pressing a shilling into his hand, said: "Let us go quietly—do you mind? I think we should prefer that."

The man got into the boat. Theo hung the cloak on Elsie's shoulders and handed her in after him. "It will be better," said the man, "if we all sit so that we can look back the way we come. You will find it a very pretty sight."

But Theo was in no mood to stare at Elsie's neck or to have her staring at his. Saying nothing, he sat facing her. Behind her was the guide who had extinguished the lantern and lit a

candle stuck to the boards between his feet. They were in a tube of rock floored with water, so low that Theo instinctively kept his head lower than it needed to be, so narrow that there was no room to propel the boat with oars. Pressing with his hands upon the wall on either side, the man began to move it slowly forward.

Alec was right, Theo thought. This is indeed the realm of gloomy Dis; and he wished there were a little more light for him to look upon the fair face of his Proserpine. Huddled in the cloak, with the candle behind her, she was nothing but a black silhouette upon the pale yellow light that gleamed fit-fully upon the rocky walls sliding by. Her face was all but in-visible; there was not enough light to awaken a gleam in her eye. But he noted with pleasure how the light caught her hair, making it shine like fine-drawn gold wire.

He leaned towards her, and because of the utter silence which his fortunate shilling had procured, a silence unbroken even by the sound of a ripple, so gently was their guide pushing the boat forward through the water, he asked in a whisper: "You're not cold?"

Elsie leaned her head towards his. Their foreheads almost touched. "No," she said. "Thank you for bringing the cloak."

Oh God! he thought. What agony this is! They were closer together than he and Adela had been in the cab. Now he under-stood the torture Adela had endured, understood how the longing for physical touch had overcome her and caused her to press his hand upon her breast. Beneath his eye he could see Elsie's hands folded together like white flowers in her lap. He longed to take them in his own. As if divining his intention, she drew away, sat straight up, and began to rub her hands to-gether.

At the man's feet there was a box of candle-ends, and now he lit one from the candle burning in the bottom of the boat and stuck it, as they passed by, upon a rough ledge of rock on his right hand. For years, down here in the darkness, this per-formance had been going on, so that these ledges, spaced here and there through the tunnel, on each of which he reached out his hand to place a light, were encrusted with thick grey gob-

bets of wick and wax, looking like twigs and the slimy excreta
of evil birds who nested in the darkness. But soon the effect
of these points of light, reaching back and back through the
darkness, unwavering because the tunnel was utterly windless,
and setting ripples of light on to the water that the boat's
passing had disturbed, was so charming as to cause Elsie to
clap her hands with delight and call upon Theo to turn his
head and look.

He did so, and found it indeed a beautiful spectacle, the
more so for being staged down there beneath the sunny earth
and for the profound silence in which these small flowers of
light bloomed in the abode of Dis.

"I must look at this while I can," he said. "It is charming,
and I don't suppose I shall ever be in the Speedwell Mine
again."

So, crouching low, he came over from his seat and sat beside
Elsie on hers. She moved across to make room for him, and was
aware again of the currents shooting between them as, on the
narrow thwart, they could not but sit with warm thigh to thigh.
She sat defensively silent, and Theo felt a dryness of his lips and
throat. She could not fail to notice the huskiness of his voice
as he said: "It's a pity Alec didn't come. He would have enjoyed
this. He would have loved Proserpine's flowers." And when
she asked him what those were, he told her the old fable,
speaking very quietly. But she knew and he knew that his
words were only a veil hung for a moment between them and
the reality of what they were thinking, and Elsie was less surprised than Theo when he took her hand and held it in both
of his. He could feel his own limbs trembling, but was not
prepared for the violent agitation that tingled to him through
her fingers. She was shuddering as if with deathly cold. She
did not draw away her fingers. She turned her head and, with
eyes now more accustomed to the darkness, looked with sad
speculation at the pale glimmer of his face. He chafed her hand
between his, then held her fingers tight. She continued to
shudder, looking back now down the long perspective of
twinkling lights.

Theo could not understand the fear that took hold of him.

He was amazed at Elsie's physical reaction to his first touch. He knew that it was not cold but heat that was shaking her, and this should have gratified him. But he thought he would never forget the sadness of that look she had turned upon him, as if from a distance he could not hope to bridge, as if her mind for some reason he could not guess would never sanction the eagerness of her body. He was perplexed and alarmed and wished their first approach had been in the sunshine. His spirit was oppressed by the presence of the mute Charon at his back silently pushing them over this irksome Styx.

"Aren't we nearly there?" he asked with unintended sharpness.

"Ay," said the man. "Listen!"

From far off came the rumour of falling waters, and momently now its sound increased till the tube they travelled through was full of its noise and vibration.

We must be an immense distance under the earth, Theo thought. One hundred steps down, and then this canal had run straight in, with the land rising sharply above it to a mountain's height. Now what had been a vague and indistinguishable increasing roar became recognizably the sound of water spouting and falling. His mind punctually supplied the quotation:

Where Alph the sacred river ran
Through caverns measureless to man
Down to a sunless sea.

The boat grated alongside a rough wooden jetty. "Well, we're here," said the man. Deprived of his smooth story he had not many words, and seemed to wonder if he should speak at all.

Theo released Elsie's hand. She had ceased to shudder, but her limbs seemed rigid. He stepped first out of the boat and leaned down to help her on to the wharf. Two souls arrived in Hades, he thought. We're as happy as that.

The light of the candle which the man carried threw a fitful and insufficient gleam upon the immensities that enclosed them. Bosses of moisture-dripping rock, vast configurations of stone carved by water through frostless centuries, caught for a

moment the light, then, as the man's hand moved here and there, lost it again. The cavern in which they stood was of no great size, but the chill of lightless aeons was in it, and the majestic thunder of the water. It slid in an icy river out of the rock, gleamed darkly for a moment on the cavern's floor, then plunged over a rocky lip into a profundity that the eye could not measure. A frail wooden fence was on the edge of this abyss, and there the three of them stood, the man holding out his spark to suggest rather than plumb the void into which the water boiled endlessly down. And as beneath their feet on the quaking ground there was depth that seemed measureless, so above their heads, piercing the rocky roof, was a vastness of space beyond calculation.

Shrouded in Theo's great cloak, Elsie, a child of the streets and their mean securities, stood with one hand on the rail, affrighted by the sublimities that assailed her eye and ear. Theo could see that she felt small and weak and wretched; and his mind went back to the music that he had heard last night as he stood beneath her window. She belongs to all this, he thought. This is full of the spirit that is in herself; but she needs an arm to lean on. A compassion for her smallness and loneliness flooded him; and he was glad when she turned and laid her arm on his and walked back to the boat.

What they had seen and felt, and the silence of the tunnel through which now they were once more moving, laid a quietness upon them. They sat side by side, and their eyes, turned back towards the falling water, rested always on darkness, for the boatman picked the candle-ends from the rocks, blew them out and dropped them into the box at his feet. There was something inexpressibly melancholy in these frail glimmers dying one by one, in this slow withdrawal from the indifferent majesty of sound and sight which desired no eye to see it, but would thunder eternally on in lightless oblivion.

By the gleam of the lantern which the boatman had left at the foot of the stairway they climbed the hundred steps, and when the door at the top was opened the full blaze of the July noon made them blink. Alec was lounging near the entrance

and came forward with what Theo thought was a keen in-
quisitorial look. But he said nothing except: "Well, I suppose
you haven't found the bowels of the earth as warm as bowels
usually are. We'd better get back now and have something to
eat." He lifted the enveloping cloak from Elsie's shoulders and
handed it to Theo. Then they trudged away together down the
sunny road. They passed a letter-box let into the wall of a
farm building, and Alec dropped a letter into it. "I have been
acquiring a slight sense of editorial responsibility," he said.
"While you two have been cavorting, I've written a note to
Dan Dunkerley, letting him know where I am."

"Oh, Alec!" Elsie exclaimed. "Now he's sure to call you
back."

"Possibly he will," Alec answered; and Theo knew that there
was no "possibly" about it, that Alec would certainly be recalled, and that he had posted his letter in order that he might
be.

"That should reach Dan by the first post in the morning,"
Alec said. "So we shall soon be put out of our misery. If he
wants me, he won't write: he'll send a telegram. We shall know
before this time tomorrow."

He seemed in high spirits and ate generously of their midday
dinner. Neither Theo nor Elsie shared his ebullience, and
Elsie said the afternoon was too hot for walking. She would
go to her room and rest.

The afternoon post brought Theo a letter. The handwriting
told him that it was from Lady Pinson, and he was disgusted
with himself at the reluctance he felt to open it. Alec, on some
pretence of having work to do, had gone to his own room. A
queer idea these Dillworths have of a holiday, Theo thought.
He thrust Adela's letter into his pocket, took his massive stick,
and set off on the familiar road to the Winnats. He clambered
half-way up the side and lay down on a sun-warmed limestone
rock.

I don't want to think about Adela, he said to himself. Not
now. Not till there is some shape in things, one way or the other.
He did not understand Elsie. He had held her hand and she

had not only permitted him to do so but she had been, he knew, deeply moved. Yet she had not encouraged him; she had not given him so much as a smile—nothing but a strange unfathomable look in which fear and pity were blended. And now she was eluding him, and Alec was staying near her like a fierce little chaperon-dragon, and he had written such a letter to Dan Dunkerley, Theo did not doubt, that tomorrow the pair of them would be off to Manchester. He wished he had been more emphatic, but what could you do or say with a boatman sitting at your back? I might, he thought with a wry grin, have thrown the fellow over his own precious waterfall.

He took Lady Pinson's letter from his pocket and opened it.

My dear Theo:—Thank you for your letter. I cannot tell you how valuable your sympathy is to me at a time like this. I am not referring particularly to my father's death. After all, he was an old man. There were reasons why I had not seen much of him during recent years, and now that the shock of the *suddenness* of his end has been survived, my life goes on much as before. Mr. Newstead went away at once, but Miss Chambers remained with me till after the funeral. Now she is gone, too.

No; it is not to all this that I am referring, but to something that I hesitate to allude to at all. I need not be more explicit. I only wish to say that had you chosen never to write to me again I should not have been surprised and would have had no just reason to be resentful. But you *have* written, and I am deeply grateful that you have not left in my heart a feeling of offence unpardoned.

Dear Theo, I want to say this: that I would not be ashamed of what happened if it had not happened *after* you had begun to tell me about yourself and Miss Dillworth. You did not mention her name, but there was no need for you to do that. It is difficult for me to write this, but I must say something to relieve my heart of the shame I feel. I want you to know that I wish you happiness. I can guess that you were going to ask my advice as to whether you should marry a girl who, as you said, is not perhaps of the station people would expect you to choose your wife from. Do not have any hesitation. Marry

where your love is. You would not marry a person of scandalous life, and nothing else matters. I need not tell you why, but I have reason to know how happy and successful a marriage can be between two people of different stations, provided there is *goodness* on both sides.

There is nothing else I want to say, dear Theo, except this. You are poor, and so is she. So are many of the best people I know, like Lottie Chambers. I am rich, and by my father's death senselessly richer than ever. Can I do anything, unobtrusively, perhaps through Mr. Burnside, to make things on that side more comfortable for Miss Dillworth? It is difficult, but you must think of a way; and you must know, dear Theo, that whatever I may be able in the future to do for your career will be done as though there had never been any threat to the perfection of our friendship. That you permitted it to be only a threat that came to nothing is another reason for my signing myself

Ever yours most gratefully,
Adela Pinson.

Theo folded the letter thoughtfully and put it in his wallet. He felt, for once, humble. It is a love-letter, he said to himself. If she had written in burning phrases, it could not have been more undoubtedly a love-letter.

That night Elsie played without an audience. Alec and Theo together climbed the shaly shivering slopes of Mam Tor. They had little to say to one another. They sat on the summit watching the wide bowl of country below them fill slowly with shadows. Alec was edgy. He complained of Theo's pipe fouling the evening air. He complained of the country itself. "I'm a townsman, Chrystal," he said. "A little bit of this goes a long way with me. I hate to watch a day bleeding to death, as we're doing now. I prefer to watch the lights come up and the night beginning to live."

Theo did not answer. He was thinking of Elsie and of Adela's letter in his pocket.

"In town, I wake up at night," Alec persisted. "You can do

things at night that are not possible in the day. The only time I ever tried to kill a man was at night."

He looked sideways to see the effect of this on Theo. Theo's face was unmoved. "A murder can get done in the country as easily as in the town," he said. "There was the case of the runaway couple clubbed to death in the Winnats. The murderers were never found."

"Damn the Winnats," said Alec. "I'm talking about me. I'm telling you I once tried to kill a man. Aren't you interested?"

Theo looked at him indulgently. "You don't look a murderer, Alec," he said.

"I should imagine few murderers do," Alec answered testily. "If ever you see a man who has 'murderer' written all over him you can bet your boots he teaches a Sunday school class, is kind to canaries, and takes up a cup of tea to his wife every morning. The fact remains that I once tried in cold blood to kill a man. I threw a knife that missed him by inches. I'd practised for a week on a back door."

Theo was still unimpressed. "The poor fellow must have annoyed you very much," he said lightly, tapping out his pipe on his heel.

"I didn't like the way he was treating Elsie."

Theo would not allow his perturbation to appear. "I find that a good reason for wanting to kill anybody," he said. He got up and began the slippery descent of the hill.

Elsie knew that Alec was not in the yard tonight. She was playing to no one but Bim, unless the people from the bar-parlour were listening. She did not care whether they were or not. She had again put on her white dress. It was a point she could not explain to herself, but always before playing she was under a compulsion to wash carefully and dress in her best clothes. Bim was propped against the pillow. He was the only doll Elsie had ever had. Years ago, Alec made him and christened him, and Alec never forgot the night when he had sat on a Levenshulme doorstep in the snow, and Elsie had slept with her head on his shoulder, her hair tumbling in a fiery pall protectively over Bim.

Bim was never washed in those days. He was a disgraceful and dirty object, but it wasn't difficult to keep him clean. His outer being was but one sheet of rag wrapped over many rags inside, and with the head delimited from the body by a close-pulled tie which once had been string and was now blue silk. This outer sheath of Bim was now often washed and his raggy entrails were renewed; but he remained Bim, for whom Alec would from time to time buy a new ribbon, and the ribbon at this moment, as Bim sat up in bed while Elsie played, was decorated with a brooch in which one real diamond twinkled in the candleshine. It was the only jewellery Alec had ever bought. In his imagination, even Hortense was secondary to Bim, for Bim had never left Elsie's side in all her wanderings from "place" to "place." He had even shared her tragic sojourn in the small house that Charles Frome had provided.

Theo could not know of this vital imaginative background of Bim, so that Elsie's words conveyed nothing to his mind when she stopped suddenly in her tracks the next morning and exclaimed: "I've forgotten Bim! He's in the bed!"

It was again a day of grilling heat. Dan Dunkerley's telegram had come, and as Theo had expected there was a rush to pack bags and be off. It was characteristic of Alec, Theo thought, that, though he had obviously planned this and expected it, he had not taken the precaution to have the bags packed and the bills paid. The bills were the worst part of it. There was not much for the Dillworths to pack, but at that inn the writing of accounts was a laborious matter. Theo had made up his mind the night before that if Elsie went he would go too. At last they were off, with a narrow enough margin for catching the train, and as they were hurrying through the hot sunshine Elsie stopped and uttered the cry that Theo found meaningless: "I've forgotten Bim!"

Alec had been in high spirits, but now he flamed into annoyance. "Oh, damn and blast you!" he cried. "You'll be forgetting your fiddle next." But Elsie had her precious fiddle safe. She was carrying it herself, and Theo was burdened with his own large portmanteau and Elsie's Gladstone bag. He was shocked to hear Alec speak in that way to Elsie, and hardly less

to see that she took it as a matter of course. "Who is Bim?" he
asked. "Is there anything I can do?"

"No," Alec answered surlily, "there isn't. You two go on."
He turned and began to run back towards Castleton. Theo
picked up his ponderous burden, and he and Elsie set off together ."Who is Bim?" he asked again.

She answered shortly: "A bundle of rags." She seemed in a
bad mood.

"Couldn't we have written to have it sent on?" Theo asked.
"No. We couldn't."

Theo was deeply puzzled. "Well, I don't know," he said with
a sigh. "I don't think I shall ever understand you two."

"No," said Elsie. "I don't suppose you will."

They said no more, and, each of them burdened now with
two cases, for Elsie had taken up Alec's Gladstone bag to give
him fleetness of foot, they trudged on to the station. Why isn't
Alec frank with me? Theo wondered. If he had told me what
he intended to do, we could have had all this stuff sent to the
station in advance on a handcart. He hated to see Elsie labouring in this way through the heat, and he was temperamentally
given to planning and arranging. The Dillworths were a dis-
orderly couple, he thought.

It was only when the train drew into the station that Theo's
heart gave a sudden leap as he saw that this annoying diversion
might work to his advantage. He hoisted the cases on to the
rack of an empty compartment, put Elsie in, and then stood
with the window down, leaning out to wave to Alec and show
him their position when he arrived, but hoping all the time
that he would arrive too late. He was aware that his stance at
the window prevented Elsie from leaving the compartment if
she wished to do so. And she did. When the engine gave its
first panting cough she put an arm right round him and tried
to pull him aside. "Let me get out," she said. "I'll wait for
Alec. We'll come on the next train."

But Theo stayed planted where he was. The train was already moving when Alec rushed into the station, waving a
bundle of rags. Theo saw him try to mount the train, saw a
porter seize him and pull him back. All this time Elsie's arm

was tight round him. He turned slowly within that disturbing girdle and saw her eyes close to his. Her hat had been thrown on to a seat. Her hair was a little loosened and her forehead was pearled with sweat. She looked at him with that same frightened glance that had puzzled him the day before. But she did not release her hold, and when he put an arm round her waist and drew her to him he was surprised by the passion with which she took his lips.

Standing between the seats, they remained locked in one another's arms, pressing limb to limb and face to face till a swerve of the train threw them apart. Then they sat, facing one another. Not a word had been spoken. Elsie was the first to break the silence. "It was me you wanted to come to Hope— not Alec. Wasn't it?" she said.

Theo nodded. "Thank you," said Elsie politely. "I wanted to be sure of that. What did you want me for?"

"I wanted to ask you to marry me," Theo answered simply. The train had stopped at the next station. There was no one on the platform but one girl, and she did not get into the train. They watched her standing there as they rolled slowly by. "If I had never seen you before in my life, and if you were standing there like that girl as I passed by in a train, I should never forget you. I should jump out at the next station and come back, and if you were gone I'd search the world for you."

"What do you see in me?" she asked wonderingly.

"All that I want."

"How can you want a woman like me?"

"I don't want a woman like you. I want you."

She turned on him then that look of pity and hopelessness that had perplexed him before. "You know nothing about me," she said. "If you knew one half of it, you'd know that I am the last person you should dream of marrying."

What am I sitting here for, talking? Theo wondered. That wild embrace had shown him what to do. He crossed over and sat beside her, put his arm about her, and pulled her down till she almost lay across his knees. He could feel again the trembling that had shaken her in the Speedwell Mine. "You love

me," he said. "When I touch you you are helpless." He bent
and kissed her again. Her arms went round his neck, and she
hung there with her sky-green eyes looking with naked passion
into his.

"Yes," she sighed. "I am helpless when you touch me."

"You love me." It was not a question, but a victorious assertion. He placed a hand upon her breast, and his pulses raced
as he felt its warm resilience. She struggled upright, breathing
heavily, and pulled his hand away. "Don't! Please don't!" she
begged him. She straightened her hair and managed a wan
defenceless smile. "I didn't think," she said, "this was how a
parson proposed."

"For God's sake," said Theo, "don't call me a parson—not
now. I'm a man."

Something of the cynical Dillworth grin lightened her face.
She looked at his hand, vibrating on his knee. "Yes," she said,
"I see that. But you're asking me to be a parson's wife, and
say what you will, that's something special, or ought to be.
Have I got to have sense for both of us?"

"I don't know what you mean," he said rather testily. "Do
I have to go round explaining my wife, apologizing for her? If
you and I want to marry, what has it got to do with anybody?"

"You'd find out," she said, "that it had a lot to do with many
people. You don't know a thing about me, and there are
plenty of things you ought to know."

Theo took hold of her again, and asked ardently: "Elsie.
My love. Do we need to know anything more than that we
love one another?"

She shook him off and moved over to the opposite seat.
"Yes," she said sturdily. "Many things."

She felt sick with longing for him. She wanted to shout all
that he ought to hear, tear it out of her breast and throw it at
his feet. Then she would know; then she would be able to
give herself to him with a passion that would devastate him.
Either that, or bear as best she could the bitter knowledge that
he had not loved her enough.

There was a long silence between them. Theo knew nothing
of the shattering debate that was passing in her mind as she

sat with a pale set face watching the hot countryside slip by the window. She knew that she could not do it: not now. She could see with sharp imaginative clarity the horror and grief that her confession would write upon his face. No; she could not tell him now: it would be like cutting a loving child to the heart. She felt worn out by the struggle within her mind: immensely old, soiled and sinful. She allowed her head to lie back; her eyes closed; and tears squeezed themselves out and hung like dew on the lashes beneath the translucent lids. They were her undoing; for Theo, who had been watching her in silence, unable to account for her swift alternations of warm surrender, temporizing, and complete aloofness, at once crossed to her side, gathered her again into his arms, and kissed her eyelids. "Elsie! My darling! What have I said—what have I done—to hurt you?" he murmured.

She relaxed in his arms like a child which has been a man for an hour, and has given up, and fallen exhausted into a mother's embrace. There was no passion in her now: only a great ease after tiredness, a tranquillity and trust so deep that she soon slept quietly on his shoulder. Theo cradled her gently in his arm, kissed her now and then on the forehead, and felt deeply moved to see how, every time he did this, a smile passed over the sleeping face like a sun ray over a clouded field. He was content to hold her thus, to let all passion sleep, watching the gentle rise and fall of her breast, so close to his own.

Chapter Eleven

"THIS," said Alec to Elsie, "is a great waste of money. I suppose in a year or so now Simmons will be sending you to this chap in Austria, and soon after that you and Hortense will be gallivanting all over the world. As for me, I don't propose to end my days in Manchester. So why have we done it? Why couldn't we have stayed where we were?"

"I've loved doing it, anyway," said Elsie.

"Miss Small," Alec shouted through the open door, "you may come and clear away."

Miss Small, who was small even for her fourteen years, came in with a grin on her plain pudgy little face. She thought Mr. Dillworth was a caution, but she liked being called Miss Small. It was better than her real name, Sarah Longbottom, which the children in her street were accustomed to interpret rudely. And she liked working for Mr. Dillworth and his sister. This was her second "place," and she had not been happy in her first. That had been in a house where three lodgers came in at all sorts of odd hours, expected meals at different times, and wanted fires laid and lit at inconvenient moments. Sarah's mistress had been terribly afraid of offending "the young gentlemen" and had chivvied Sarah from morning to night.

When she had gone to work for the Dillworths at the little house in Burnage Lane, the child had been amazed, on coming down the first morning, to find Mr. Dillworth on his knees at the kitchen grate, lighting the fire. "Hallo, Thumbelina," he said. "You're up early."

"That's *my* job," she said stoutly, pointing to the grate.

"Don't you believe it, Miss Small," Alec answered. "You get the breakfast ready. That's enough for you to be getting on with, you sparrow."

So it had gone on. Mr. Dillworth always lit the fire, and she was always allowed to have her breakfast when *they* were having theirs, which was a nice change, because she had been ex-

pected, in her last "place," to wait till all the young gentlemen
and her employer had finished, so that sometimes she was still
hungry at ten o'clock. Altogether, Miss Small was in danger of
becoming a hero-worshipper, what with Mr. Dillworth being,
as she put it to herself, "such a one," and Miss Dillworth being
so beautiful.

She came in now with devoted alacrity, piled the crockery on
to her tray, and panted off to the kitchen. She loved to pant.
Alec thought it, he said, her most endearing characteristic. As
an ostler suggests a vigorous enjoyment of his task by hissing, so
Miss Small by panting managed to convey an immense willingness to labour for those she liked, a suggestion that she was
giving her all, and even a little more.

A few moments later Alec set off to town and Elsie went out
into the small back-garden. It was nine o'clock of a charming
morning in September. The dome of the sky was filled with a
light mist, stained by the blue behind it. It was like seeing a
blue petticoat through a skirt of grey gauze. Thumbelina
Small, peeping through the kitchen window, thought Miss
Dillworth looked lovely, standing there with her face raised to
the sky. Elsie herself was thinking how great a difference a
little space could make. Burnage and Levenshulme lay almost
side by side, but in Levenshulme nothing of a morning like
this could get through to you. You wouldn't see a tree or a
flower or a drop of dew. Here, all was changed. The garden was
enclosed by a high brick wall that gave it privacy. It amounted
to nothing more than an oblong patch of grass, a path surrounding it, and, between this path and the wall, a narrow
flower-bed running round the garden on three sides. But this
was enough for wonder, for in the middle of the grass-plot was
a crooked apple-tree that now was heavy with russet fruit, and
in the flower-beds Michaelmas daisies were in bud and goldenrod was massed in yellow clumps. The air smelt singularly
sweet and clean, with a premonitory touch of autumn sharpness, and on every bud and flower and leaf the dew threw out
sparkles of red and blue fire. The mist thinned as Elsie stood
there, drifted away like slow smoke, and the light of the tem-
perate sun fell on the bloom of the goldenrod. She saw then

that two butterflies were alighted there. They had been invisible to her with their wings closed, but now they opened them to the caress of the sun. She stood entranced. Never had she seen such bewitching creatures. She was so near to them that she could see their peacock markings, the feathers of tender down upon their wings, the delicate twitching of their antennae searching out into the astringent air. Oh, to have such jewels in one's own garden, and to have Theo's letter in one's pocket! She trembled with happiness and fear. All was so beautiful! All so fugitive! The butterflies rose in the air, eddying in imperceptible currents, fluttering together amorously, and disappearing over the wall where a great beech whose roots were hidden from Elsie's sight lifted its shoulders and spread its cloak of gold and russet brown against the deepening blue of the sky.

A bench had been built round the apple-tree, but the tree grew out of the ground at an angle so steep that half the seat could not be sat on. But from the other half the tree grew comfortably back, and sitting there leaning against the trunk Elsie took out Theo's letter. It had come yesterday while Alec was out, and she was glad of that. Alec was not reticent about letters. He would have questioned her remorselessly.

She had never expected to receive a letter from Theo. It was all part of the coil she found herself in, so dreadful and so delicious. Sometimes she prayed for resolution to end the whole matter, to put it to the touch once for all. Sooner or later that must come, but she shrank from it as from suicide. Her love had been a torment. She had always liked Theo, but, hardly knowing that she was doing it, she had fought against the liking, aware at some unplumbed level of feeling that it was charged with the chance of tragedy. It was not till she had put her arms about him to pull him away from the railway carriage window at Hope that the flood was loosed in her and she felt that she was lost. It was as though her flesh had touched hot iron and adhered to what scorched it. She felt she could not pull herself away without leaving her living flesh behind.

She remembered how she had slept in Theo's arms, and how

he had gently awakened her in the dirty station at Levens-hulme. There seemed, then, nothing to be said, for everything had been said without words. They had carried the bags to her house, and then Theo had said simply: "Well, there it is, my darling. We are engaged to be married."

"No."

"Yes."

"Theo, you don't understand——"

"Ah, you have not called me Theo before. I never knew my name sounded so lovely. Now all you have to say is: Theo, I love you. I will marry you."

She couldn't stand there bandying words with him at the front door in that terribly public street. She looked at him despairingly, mutely begging him to have pity upon her, and all he gave her was a smile of confidence and triumph. "Theo, I love you," she said.

"And I will marry you," he prompted.

But she did not say it. She turned swiftly into the house and shut the door.

She thought it was in many ways the most terrible day she had ever lived through. Alec had come home in a raging temper. He threw Bim at her, shouting: "There's your bloody doll. A nice thing for me to carry through the streets!" When they quarrelled, they quarrelled bitterly, and they quarrelled that night, as people who love one another will quarrel, torturing themselves with the knowledge that it was all about nothing, that nothing—nothing whatever—could easily divide them eternally. Finally, Alec had wandered off aimlessly into the street, and she had gone supperless to bed, with her head splitting in the heat of the night.

It was not often that she or Alec troubled Mr. Burnside in those days, but she had gone to see him the next morning. She was still angry with Alec and he with her. When they were at this emotional pitch they could not bear to eat together. As soon as he was dressed he walked off morosely to town, and Elsie did not bother to prepare food for herself. She went to the vicarage, carrying her fiddle with her. Mr. Burnside never asked her to play to him, but she knew that he loved her to do

so, both because music was a passion with him and because he liked to know how she was progressing. He showed no surprise at seeing her after an absence of several months and invited her to join him at breakfast. He looked at her keenly. "You look very tired, my dear," he said, and she answered simply: "I feel as if I'd be glad to die."

"You mustn't do that just yet," he said with a smile. "Simmons would be too disappointed."

He poured her some coffee and saw with pleasure that his remark had brightened her sad face. "What does he say?" she asked eagerly. "For all I know of what he thinks, I might as well be working for a stone monkey."

"He is not displeased with you. That is as far as he goes; but, for him, that's going farther than I should expect."

"H'm," said Elsie. "To me, it sounds more like a kick in the behind than a testimonial."

Mr. Burnside considered her carefully as she dug into an egg. "I think," he said at last, "that I shall be justified if I break a confidence. It is always dangerous to praise or encourage a fool or a mere pretender, but there are people who would be all the better for a bit of appreciation. I think you are one of them, Elsie."

She grinned at him frankly. "There are times," she said, "when I could smash my fiddle on Mr. Simmons's head. I may do it yet. He's just like God, taking all the music of the angels for granted."

"There you have the advantage of me, my dear," said Mr. Burnside with a gentle smile, "for I don't know whether God does that or not." He crumbled a piece of toast and added: "Indeed, I know singularly little about God."

He filled her coffee cup and went on: "But about you I do know something, and I think it will be all to the good if I tell you that your affairs are going on well. It will cost a bit, you know, to send you to Austria, and the hopeful thing is that Simmons has been here to see me, to ask how we can raise the money."

She had stopped eating. She was sitting with her hands folded in her lap, watching his face with a child's grave attentiveness.

But her heart was in a tumult. All that had seemed to have the dazzle of a fairy-tale, and a fairy-tale's mad improbability—foreign lands, popular applause, even Hortense, even furs and jewels—slipped perceptibly a step nearer to sober reality as Mr. Burnside spoke. It had long been a bright cloud on the far horizon; now, when it should have been falling upon her in refreshing dew, it struck her heart with the piercing chill of winter rain.

"How long should I be away?" she almost whispered.

"I can hardly tell you that," said Mr. Burnside. "But it could hardly be less than a couple of years." He thought she looked almost haggard, and said encouragingly: "There would, of course, be holidays. We sha'n't work you to death, my dear."

Then she smiled again. Holidays and Theo! "What a fool I am!" she cried. "It sounded at first like a sentence."

"It is characteristic of you artists," said Mr. Burnside with mock severity, "that you take the cash side of things for granted. You haven't even bothered to ask whether I have succeeded in raising the money that Simmons thinks will be necessary. No doubt you believe this is something that the world owes you and should do gladly for you."

"Well——" Elsie began; but Mr. Burnside, filling his pipe, interrupted. "I'm not sure you would be wrong. Anyway," he added triumphantly, "I've got the money."

"Then I really am going?"

He lit his pipe and led the way to his study. He settled himself in one of his creaking wicker chairs and said: "Play to me, my dear."

It was some months since he had heard her, and he was deeply moved. He had himself played the violin from youth, and now, with his grey head sunk on his breast, he could do no more, and no less, than recognize that she had begun with an equipment of spirit which he could never hope to attain. To this, he recognized as he listened, the gruelling work Simmons had imposed had added a technical discipline which, if pursued, could hardly fail to make the girl a master. He did not speak for a time after she had finished, then he took up the question she had asked at breakfast. "Yes," he said, "you

are really going." And he felt a great sense of elation, of achievement, because it was he who had put her foot on to the first step of the path, and if this was not the way to save a soul, what was? She had never thanked him. She hardly ever, now, came near him; but he could do without that.

She put her fiddle into its case, wondering how to raise the matter that had brought her there, for it was not to play to Mr. Burnside that she had come.

"Sit down, Elsie," he said. "Don't have any *fear* about your music. Don't worry if Simmons doesn't praise you. He doesn't praise anybody. You have made wonderful progress. I know enough to take the responsibility for telling you that. Go on working as you are doing now, and you will be all right. And now," he added with a twinkle, "I'm going to read you a little lesson in human gratitude. Perhaps, as I say, the world owes you a lot, provided your music in turn repays what it owes. But all the same, 'the world' is rather a loose expression, and when it comes down to brass farthings it means one or two individual men or women. I don't want you to rush round thanking them. They would be annoyed indeed if they knew that I had mentioned their names, but all the same I am going to. It need go no further than between you and me, but it is always excellent to thank in our hearts those who do good to us. You have never even wondered, I imagine, who is paying Mr. Simmons. Well, Mr. Dan Dunkerley is. Then there is this question of Austria, which is a far more serious matter. I wrote to a lady whom I have known for a long time, though I haven't seen much of her in recent years. Her brother and I were at Oxford together. I thought she would be interested for two reasons. For one thing, she's very rich and very generous, and for another she's musically inclined. Mind you," he added with a smile, "she's no artist. She tinkles on the piano as I scrape on the fiddle. But all the same, she loves music, and she is the woman you are indebted to. Her very kind letter reached me only this morning. I mean Lady Adela Pinson. You may have heard young Chrystal speak of her. He's been visiting her lately. You won't mention this to anybody, particularly to him.

Lady Adela, for some reason or other, especially asks me not
to let him know that she is doing this. Remember her in your
prayers, my dear, if you ever pray. She is a good woman."

"Is she *very* rich?" Elsie asked.

"Yes, and her father's death not long ago has made her richer
than ever."

"She must be very old if you and her brother were at Oxford
together."

Mr. Burnside burst into a laugh. "Bless me," he said, "I'm
no Methuselah, even if my hair is the wrong colour. As for
Adela, I used to think of her as a child in those days. They
were a large family. My friend was the oldest of the lot and
she was the youngest. You're lucky to get your money before
she marries again and has a family. She's a widow, you know."

"Then she's—marriageable?"

"She certainly is. I've always hoped she would marry again.
She's a woman made for marriage."

"If I became a great violinist——"

"You *are* a great violinist, Elsie."

"Listen," she said with the gravity of a child. "I'm going to
say something serious. How could I marry if I had to travel all
over the world?"

"I've no doubt your husband would be only too happy to
travel with you."

"But what if he had work which kept him here in England?"

Now Mr. Burnside saw that there was some serious matter
afoot. "What are you trying to tell me, my dear?" he asked.

"Mr. Chrystal wants to marry me, and I love him—terribly."

For a moment Mr. Burnside was too dumbfounded to speak.
He looked at her standing erect before him with that quiver
of excitement in her body that the idea of Theo induced, as
though she felt his hands stroking her. She thought she had
never seen a face so full of pity and despair as Mr. Burnside's
was, his teeth gripping his pipe so tightly that his jawbones
stood out white and his hollow temples pulsed in and out.
"God help you, child," he said at last. He rose from the chair
and began to pace the room. Elsie stood at the window, look-

ing sideways through it to where this little by-street joined
the Stockport Road. Behind her the slow slush slush of Mr.
Burnside's worn felt slippers over the worn carpet went on as
though it would never stop. At last she could bear it no longer.
She turned and faced him and asked sharply: "What do you
mean—God help me?"

"Tell me," said Mr. Burnside, "what exactly is the position
between you two? You say Mr. Chrystal has asked you to marry
him. What answer have you made?"

"I have told him that I love him."

"Have you told him that you will marry him?"

"I haven't said Yes or No."

"Why not?"

"Well, surely to goodness," she burst out, "you know——"

"Yes, my dear," he said with infinite compassion, "I know.
I know everything about you. I wish to God I didn't. Then I
could keep my mouth shut."

"There's no need for *you* to worry," she said, pitying his
distress. "I'm used to worry, and I shall worry through this.
I haven't told him I shall marry him."

"I wish you hadn't told him you loved him."

"Good God, Mr. Burnside," she cried with deep sincerity,
"could I have done less?"

"It would have been better to say nothing till you were ready
to say everything."

Seeing the misery in his face, she summoned her gaiety and
cried: "Cheer up! I shall tell him everything, don't you fear,
and then, you'll see, it will be all right."

"God grant it may."

"Would *you* mind? Would you think I was all wrong for a
parson's wife?"

He considered the question anxiously for a moment, then
said: "I wish you hadn't asked me that."

"I would like you to answer me, all the same."

"Very well. To begin with, I think you are a splendid
woman, Elsie. You do realize, I believe, that nothing that has
happened to you in the past gives me any feeling of dislike or
hostility to you?"

She nodded, and he went on: "Nothing of all that would give me a moment's hesitation in expecting the happiest result from your marriage to a man with your own outlook on life and your own aspirations. Even in those circumstances there would be some danger for there would always be Pharisees to despise you and stone you if the facts about you became known. The danger, however, wouldn't be so great for you because the world tends to overlook things where artists are concerned. I don't say that that is good, because it is not usually a case of understanding and forgiving, but rather of a sloppy acceptance of any sort of conduct on the part of those who are considered to be eccentric."

He paused for a moment, lit his pipe, and asked: "Is all this tiring you? I've never spoken to you like this before. I don't often speak to anybody like this."

She asked him to go on, and he said: "Well, eccentric and scandalous conduct wouldn't suit you, anyhow. Don't think I'm suggesting that your conduct has been either. I'm merely trying to give you what I think would be the world's view. And all this is assuming that you married someone to whom the world's view alone mattered. But you ask me whether I think you would be all wrong for a parson's wife. And I do. You will probably have a career that will separate your life almost entirely from your husband's. That is one thing, but not the only thing. There is the Church's point of view to be considered. I think a parson should marry a woman who holds his own faith and is a member of his own communion. If, in addition to her not being even this, there have been such unhappy facts in her life as there have been in yours—why then, the world being what it is, the chances are that those facts will come out and the consequent scandal will ruin the husband's life. Do you see any hope of happiness in such a situation?"

He spoke with his head in his hands, gazing at the carpet where through years his feet had worn it threadbare. He felt, in anguish, that he would remember the grey criss-cross of it to the day of his death. He had been speaking very quietly, but now he stood up and cried aloud: "And yet, child, you are so in my heart that, God forgive me, I'd take the chance."

Elsie rose and picked up her violin case. She was deathly white. "Thank you," she said. "You have been very frank."

He laid a hand on her shoulder. "And terribly unkind."

"You certainly didn't use an anaesthetic."

"What will you do now?"

"I shall marry him, if he still wants to marry me when he knows everything."

"Are you strong enough to tell him?"

"Not at the moment. But I hope to be."

"Would you like me to do it for you?"

"No. He would hate you. If he's to hate anybody, let it be me."

She held out her hand, and this was the first time she had ever done so. He clasped it while he said: "Despite everything, you are so young, my dear. As an old man—an old loving friend—I beg you not to delay in doing what you have to do."

"I'm not in any hurry to break my heart."

"In these circumstances," said Mr. Burnside, "three months is a terribly long time, and I shall be doing violence to my conscience and to my common sense in giving you so long. I have a responsibility to Chrystal as well as to you. In three months' time, if you have not told him, I shall do so myself. Till then, I shall say nothing, but I am a fool to give you that much."

"This would be a gorgeous world," she said, "if it were full of fools like you."

When he heard the iron slam of the gate, he stepped to the window and watched her slim figure moving through the shadowed street towards the Stockport Road where full sunshine lay. At the corner she collided with Theo Chrystal, who, Mr. Burnside thought, had evidently been coming to see him. But he did not come. He and Elsie stood for a moment talking with animation in the bright sunshine, then side by side they disappeared round the corner. Mr. Burnside's heart was heavy with foreboding as he turned back into his shabby room.

That was two months ago—two months for Elsie of living at a tension she had never thought she would be called on to endure. She knew that this was all she was fated to have: this

exaltation of body and spirit that must soon, now, come to a climax, snap, and leave her, as she thought, exhausted and done for. She had no doubt that Theo would retreat in horror from the whole situation, once he understood what it was; and she asked herself again and again whether it could be love that consciously doomed the loved one to so terrible a disenchant-ment? But she was possessed; she could not act differently any more than a honey-bee can cease to suck because winter must come; and whenever she was in Theo's arms unreason took control and whispered that even yet—despite all—the doom would be averted.

To lose a week out of so short a time was almost more than she could bear, and she wondered whether this was a trick of Mr. Burnside's to keep her and Theo apart. There were three decrepit old women and one small crippled child whom the Vicar had sent to Blackpool to snatch a week's good air before the winter came on, and he had commissioned Theo to attend this pathetic handful of holiday-makers. For the first time since he had come to Levenshulme Theo had showed open resent-ment of his vicar's wishes, expressing the view that the old people were well able to look after one another and the child, and that he could be doing more worth while things in the parish. For the first time, too, Theo was made aware of Mr. Burnside's anger. The old man was afflicted by resentment against what he considered his own weakness. Never before, so far as he could remember, since he had had an adult mind had he allowed himself to act flatly against his own best judg-ment. He could see nothing but sorrow for young Chrystal coming out of events which he himself should have prevented from reaching their present pass. He did not much like the youth, but for the last few weeks he had felt a great tenderness for him, a pity for the raw inexperience clothed in so beauti-ful and assured an exterior. He looked at Theo as one might look at a lamb gaily gambolling along the road to the butcher's knife. He would have fallen at Theo's feet if the young man had been the sort to take Elsie, career or no career, Church or no Church; but he knew that Theo would never do this, and to that extent the blow that was about to fall was not from

without, but from Theo's own hand. Out of all his self-ques-
tionings, this was the only consolation that Mr. Burnside could
offer to himself: that it did not essentially matter whether the
knife fell now or in a few weeks' time, and whenever it fell,
Theo would strike the blow.

Torn as he had been for weeks past by these conflicts, he
was intolerably jarred by Theo's disparagement of the small
task placed on his shoulders. "What is for the good of this parish, Mr. Chrystal," he said, "is for me to decide; but Jesus
Christ decided long ago that willingness to give *personal* love
and attention to the poor and unfortunate is a mark of those
who presume to work in His name. I could give these people
their fares and lodging money and sweep them off my hands
and out of my mind if I wanted to. That wouldn't be doing
much, because it isn't even my money: it's blood-money sub-
scribed by the rich. But there is a little something that we,
as Christians, can add to it, and that is what I am asking you
to do."

Theo was covered by confusion. His face flushed. He was
ashamed and stammered an apology. Mr. Burnside, who had
never before seen him lose his self-assurance, felt his anger fall
away and a surge of tenderness come over him. He placed his
hand on the youth's shoulder and spoke with the old accustomed gentleness: "Come, Theo. This isn't for *me,* you know.
Either we believe that Christ's words meant something or we
don't. And His words are quite clear: Inasmuch as ye have
done it unto one of the least of these my brethren, ye have
done it unto Me."

When Theo was gone Mr. Burnside stood haunted by the
words he had uttered, for was he not conniving at a deed which,
soon now, would rock this young egoist to the foundations?

Sitting under the tree, with a dapple of sunshine on the page,
Elsie opened the letter. She had read it before; she felt she
would read it many times:

Elsie. My dearest Elsie. My darling Elsie. My sweet and
adorable Elsie. I have tried them all over, and scores of others,
but not one of them says more than Elsie, because Elsie says

everything that matters to me. I have just come in from walking on the beach with my three old ladies and my one small child. When I look at the old ladies I think of your beautiful youth, and when I look at the child I think of your inscrutable maturity, and so, whatever I look at, I think of Elsie. So you see there are compensations, even here, where I live beside an ocean that offers no alternatives but sea and Sahara as the tide flows and ebbs. No rock or pool or cliff. Nothing but a monotony which is now water and now sand. My child has a bucket and spade and unendingly constructs fortifications in the hope of at last making one that the tide will find too much for it. My old ladies are far beyond delusive hopes. They do nothing—nothing whatever but sit on the sand in the mild sunshine with their boots off, luxuriously stretching their toes. "Resting their feet," as they call it, is clearly to them life's supernal joy. I brought a few light novels with me, thinking they might like me to read to them. They were polite enough not to object—they object to nothing, the poor dears: they are utterly docile—but, oh! they were bored! So now we no longer read. We move from our lodging-house meals to the sand and from the sand to our lodging-house meals, and the days go by. Thank God, the sun shines daily. What I should do with them if rain kept us indoors I shudder to imagine.

Elsie, what a terrible, what a dreadful thing this is that we mean when we speak of social classes! I did not choose the way I should be brought up, neither did these poor souls. Our lives in the beginning—and it is the beginning that means so much!—were utterly out of our own hands and control, and the consequence is that they and I are more separated from one another than we would be if they were Greeks and I a Hottentot. How does one break down this terrible barrier? I long to talk to them, and cannot. I long to find something that interests them and me equally, and cannot. What, I wonder, does Mr. Burnside expect me to do? There are a few people who are able to get outside this prison of self in which I find myself shut and bolted and able to live happily only with the prisoners condemned to my own cell. Alec is one, and you are

another. Mr. Burnside, too, I suppose. So, you see, it need have nothing to do with "class."

Elsie! What a strange letter I am writing to you! I intended it to be a love-letter. But what is a love-letter save a letter to my love, and what should I tell my love except all that is in my heart? It will help you to know how I long for your dear presence in which all these coldnesses of my heart disappear. We shall be married, despite all your warnings that I must not take it for granted; and then you will teach me the secret of melting off this polar ice-cap that seems to fit me so terribly closely.

How astonishing that I should choose *you,* of all people, as my father confessor, for I have never before written or spoken to a soul about my consciousness of my own defects. You alone can save me. I feel it in my bones. When I know you inside out, even this awful secret you threaten some day to reveal, and when I accept you not for what I believe you to be but for what you are—and that, I know, is essentially love and goodness— why, then my own salvation will begin.

Forgive this letter. If it has done nothing else it will have shown you that I am not happy away from you. Send me a little note to say you are thinking of me, and believe me, my darling, ever your devoted lover,

Theo.

When Theo returned from Blackpool he found a letter awaiting him, containing an invitation to a lunch to celebrate the opening of Dunkerley House. This was to be a different affair from the grotesque ceremony that launched *Hard Facts* so little time before. The latest copy of *Hard Facts,* even now lying on his table, differed in no essential from the number which, that foggy morning, he and the others had held while the photographer pressed his bulb. But in the meantime the all-powerful god Success had smiled, and so this card which Theo was turning over in his hands was of beautiful translucent pasteboard, gilt-edged, charmingly printed, and half a dozen of Manchester's most distinguished names appeared in the list of those who would propose toasts or respond to them. A sheet of paper heavily embossed with "Dunkerley Publica-

tions" and the address was enclosed with the card, and on it was scribbled: "Dear Chrystal: Come along and have a look at the buildings any time. D.D."

Theo had brought his charges home in time for lunch. The afternoon was his, and, with a great sense of relief now that his custodianship was ended, he walked to town.

Though the official opening had not yet taken place, Dunkerley House was now finished down to its smallest nail and last lick of paint. The new stone shone whitely in the mild autumn sunshine. Theo stood looking up from across the road at the storeys rising one above another, at the long ranges of windows, and, above all, the flagstaff which held against the luminous blue sky a flag that idly from time to time distended itself in a little wind to disclose in yellow on a red ground the name *Hard Facts*. He was impressed. For all his labours—and really they did not come to much—on the authorship of *Hebrews,* he was not by temperament or equipment a scholar. His gift was for administration: he would have made—and perhaps should have made—an excellent man of business; and so the spectacle of Dan Dunkerley's solid achievement, palpably there to be seen and touched, to run one's head against, in stone and brick, glass and wood, stirred in him a feeling of admiration. But he was intelligent enough to recognize this for what it was, and, smiling to himself, he said that it was not only the heathen in his blindness who bowed down to wood and stone. This great building, which had even a certain beauty, if only because of the sunshine falling with so mellow a caress upon its new white stone, was nothing but the temple of a triviality, the body of a negligible, an even contemptible, mind.

A hand fell heavily and heartily on Theo's shoulder, and he turned to find Dan Dunkerley at his side. "Well?" Dan asked, and there was so much pride and pleasure, so much even of a naïve childlike satisfaction in the tone, that Theo had not the heart to give voice to his doubts and allowed nothing but congratulation to appear as he said: "You are no doubt feeling proud, Mr. Dunkerley, and indeed you have every right to be."

Dan seemed reluctant to cross the road. He stood at Theo's side looking at this crystallization of so much hope, so many

labours. His dark blue eyes shone with an enthusiast's passion. There was even a catch in his voice as he said: "A great many years ago now, Chrystal—the night I first clapped eyes on my wife—she asked me why I liked being in crowds. I said there might be a fortune in understanding what a crowd was thinking. Well, you see——" He allowed a wave of the hand towards the building to complete the sentence. Then he added defiantly: "And it makes no difference when Alec Dillworth assures me that all I have understood is that a crowd doesn't think at all."

Alec's view, fundamentally, was so much Theo's view, too, that he had nothing to say, and Dan Dunkerley went on: "Yes. That's a long time ago—or seems like it. It was one of Agnes's rare nights out. Usually, she stayed in, looking after young Grace Satterfield, her brother's child. You've met her, I think? Young Grace, I mean."

"Yes," Theo said absently. "Once or twice." Then, his face brightening to laughter: "Yes, indeed. Our first meeting was most unromantic. It's just come back to me. I ran into her in the street on a foggy March night. She was carrying a paper of fried fish or something of the sort that smelled to high heaven. It was my first night in Manchester. It all helped to build up an unforgettable impression."

"Ah, well," said Dan, "I don't suppose you'd know young Grace now for the same girl. She's at a good school and she's turning out all right. Well, come along now. Let's explore what Dillworth calls the entrails of the white elephant."

In the front hall a grizzled commissionaire came to attention. As they climbed the stairs Dan said with satisfaction: "There, but for the grace of God, goes old Sim. I always think that as I come in, Chrystal. It gives me pleasure. The old man, you know, really has a good deal of business sense. His job is supplies. He looks after the ordering of everything, from newsprint to steel nibs and pen-holders, and he's a regular hound at running down any sort of waste." He pushed open a door inscribed with the name of Mr. Simon Dunkerley. "Good afternoon, Sim. You know Mr. Chrystal, I think?"

The old man got up from a huge flat-topped desk on which

everything was arranged in neat order and bowed in the stiff fashion which Theo did not know was caused by his living within a steel tube, as a caddis grub lives within a bit of hollow wood or straw. Everything in the room looked new and smelled new. Even Sim looked new. He had a childish pride in his new status. But his language was as old as on that night when Theo had first heard his voice issuing from the small house into which Grace Satterfield had disappeared. "All well?" Dan asked.

"It had bloody well better be," Sim growled, "or I'll want to know why. I'm on the track of one or two things, I can tell you. Come and have a look round, Mr. Chrystal."

Theo stepped further into the room, on to the new carpet, and contemplated the new filing-cabinets, the new curtains, the new pictures on the wall. One was *The Thin Red Line,* another an engraving of Florence Nightingale as the Lady with the Lamp. Theo stopped before this, and Sim said: "Yes, that's the bloody woman. A serjeant of dragoons. I'll tell you about her some day."

"But not now, Sim," Dan begged. "We're busy."

It was a nice room, Theo thought. Though this was but September, a fire was lit and there were bronze chrysanthemums in a cut-glass bowl on the table. "From Dan's house at Didsbury," said Sim.

Out in the corridor, Theo was again puzzled by the complexity of his own thoughts. Fundamentally, this was all nothing, a bubble posed on the weekly reiteration of the meaningless. But, all the same, you couldn't get beyond certain solid facts. There was old Simon Dunkerley, happy in his way, handsomely housed, and, as Dan had said, he might have been doing the job of that commissionaire downstairs. And if it came to that, the commissionaire himself, to say nothing of hundreds of other people, and news-agents and bookstall-keepers up and down the country, were all beneficially affected by the existence of *Hard Facts.* It was perplexing. How much of the work of the world, Theo wondered, was based on the existence of nonsense, how much necessary bread was derived from the punctual provision of the unnecessary?

These thoughts were dispersed as soon as he entered Dan
Dunkerley's room, for there George Satterfield was waiting,
and evidently he was in a bad mood. He greeted Theo with no
more than a casual nod, and at once burst out: "Oh, there you
are at last, Dan. I've been waiting. I've got a bone to pick
with you."

Dan flung his hat on to a hook and seated himself in a red
leather chair in front of his red leather topped desk. "Sit
down, Chrystal," he said. "Well, George, pick away at your
bone."

"It's about these invitations to the lunch."

"Well?"

"I thought you and I had decided on the people who should
be asked?"

"So we did."

"Well, then, why go behind my back?" He was very angry,
striding up and down the room.

"You'd better explain yourself, George. I don't know what
you're talking about."

"I've just been into Dillworth's room, and on the mantelpiece there's a card of invitation to Mr. Dillworth and Miss
Elsie Dillworth."

"Any objection?"

"Yes, the strongest objection. We agreed to ask Alec Dillworth. Nothing was said about his sister."

Dan fiddled with the furniture on his desk. "Listen, George.
Be reasonable," he said.

"Query what is reason?" Satterfield burst out. "Is it reason
to ask a woman like that to a gathering that we want to be,
above all things, dignified and *comme il faut*? I object most
strongly."

Theo felt his ears burning and his face white. He got up.
"I'd better be going," he said.

"Sit down," Dan commanded. "This doesn't concern you.
Just wait a moment and we'll go round the building. Now,
George. I asked Miss Dillworth because I didn't for a moment
think you'd object. I was not trying to slip something past you.
I honestly thought that she would naturally be included with

her brother, just as the wives of all heads of departments are included with them. I didn't want to offend Alec, for one thing because I like him, and for another because he's a damned good editor. And all that is my side of things. The way I see it, as this concern develops Alec is going to be even more valuable than he is now, and I tell you I don't want to offend him. And the dead certain way to offend him is to throw any slight on his sister. I should have thought even you would have realized that by this time. Another thing. Let me tell you that when you ask Elsie Dillworth you're not asking rag-tag and bobtail. You're asking a remarkable woman, one you'll be damned lucky to get to any of your shows in a few years' time. I issued that invitation, and it stands."

Theo could have got up and applauded as he heard Dan utter these words, saw his stubborn chin thrust itself out, and watched his closed fist come down on the blotter. Even George Satterfield seemed for a moment non-plussed; but only for a moment. "What she is now," he cried, "is one thing, and I'm not at all impressed by fiddling like you are. What I'm talking about is what she once was, and that's as well known to you as to me. And to many others. Are we to ask some of the best-known women in Manchester, respectable married women, to meet a young——"

Dan Dunkerley had risen in his wrath. His eyes were blazing. "Silence!" he thundered. "I will not hear you."

Satterfield looked at him in amazement, and Theo, too, who had always considered him to be at best an industrious and obstinate man, was surprised at his tone and air of authority. Many were to know it later.

Satterfield hesitated for a moment, but was overcome by the threat that hung palpably in the air. It was from this moment that there was one final and unquestionable authority in Dunkerley Publications. Dan's face, which had reddened with his anger, slowly paled. He asked: "Is there anything else, George?"

"No, I don't think so, unless about hiring those new hoard-ings."

"Very well. I leave that to you. Settle it for yourself." He

remained standing till George Satterfield had left the room, then sat down and said: "Now, Chrystal, we'll have some tea sent up here to fortify us for our tour."

Even on so formal an occasion, and one to him so momentous, Daniel Dunkerley would not wear the uniform of well-dressed men of his time. Agnes, sitting on his right hand, thought that this gave him distinction. She remembered how, years before, at that dance in the Athenaeum, he had not been wearing evening clothes like the other men, and now he alone of all the men present, so far as she could see, wore a short black jacket and a bright blue tie in a low turn-down collar. She looked to her right and her left down this head table and saw that her brother George and old Sim and all the rest of them were wearing frock coats and up-standing cutthroat collars with ties of grey silk. There were six other tables running away at right angles from this one, and all the men sitting at them were dressed in this same way. She felt glad that Dan looked different. He *was* different. She had always known it, but only during the past eighteen months or so had she realized how different he was. She was still a little frightened by this new life she was called upon to lead. When Dan had asked a month ago whether she would like to say a few words at this inaugural lunch she had almost collapsed with terror. Her garrulous gadabout tongue was her cross, and she knew that, even if she could induce it to speak at all, it was not to be trusted. She said so to Dan, and he asked simply: "Well, why don't you *do* something about it?"

"What on earth can I do?"

"Use commas and full stops," he said, grinning.

"But I'm serious, Dan. I do want to speak nicely."

"Well, then, just listen to the way Mrs. Dobkin speaks."

How like Dan that was, she thought. George, she was sure, would have been disgusted with the notion of learning from one's own housekeeper—or from any one else's, for that matter. But Dan was right. Mrs. Dobkin never said too much or too little, and she said it slowly and clearly. Agnes was learning to do the same. She was making progress. She was training herself

to say, whenever possible, a simple Yes or No, rather than launch into a torrent of words.

But thank goodness, she thought, I am *not* to speak here today. All these people! Each of these six tables running away in front of her eyes had ten on either side of it, and there were twenty at this top table. She thought it foolish and affected of George to have brought his daughter Grace. Her own little Dinah was much too young, and Dan would not hear of Laurie being present. Laurie was away at school. It was hard to be without him, and she would have liked to have him for just this one day. But Dan said that when you were doing a thing the great idea was to do it, and at the moment what Laurie was doing was being a schoolboy. George, however, thought differently about Grace and begged special leave for her to be present. All that would be different, Dan said, once George had sent Grace, as he intended to do, to Cheltenham.

George sat on Agnes's right hand, and Agnes turned her head to look at Grace who was next beyond him. Well, you must admit, she thought, that if he wants to display his daughter she certainly is worth putting on show. She had always been a serious child, and now, at thirteen, she had an almost adult gravity. She was very fair. Her hair was the colour of ripe straw and her eyes were the blue of chicory flowers in a shapely oval face which certainly, Agnes conceded, never came from the Satterfields. She was her mother's child: Agnes could remember what a serious person Louie Wrathmall had been. What was enchanting about Grace was the combination of her flowerlike beauty with an unexpected earthly common sense. When she turned her startling eyes upon you it was not with the fluttering lashes of a woman who knows what they can do, but with a steady candid regard which seemed to be considering what she should say and how most honestly to say it. Agnes was fond of Grace and proud of her, and had no doubt that she was making an impression on young Mr. Chrystal who seemed to be talking to her as seriously as if she were one of his grown-up parishioners.

The tables looked beautiful, with golden chrysanthemums in the vases; and the air was full of an excited hubbub of con-

versation. This was ended suddenly when Dan gave a nod to the toastmaster who stood behind his chair and the gavel rapped smartly on the table. The voice was stentorian: "My lord, ladies and gentlemen: pray silence for the Reverend Theodore Chrystal, who will say grace."

It was difficult, Theo was thinking, to imagine that this was the child whom he had met in the foggy damp of a Levens-hulme street little more than eighteen months ago. He had seen her again the next morning, and he remembered now that she had been photographed with the rest of them. Last May, when George Satterfield had been present at Dan Dun-kerley's breakfast, he had referred to the child. "You remember my daughter Grace, Mr. Chrystal? She often asks after the gentleman with the beautiful face." These were all the contacts he had had with her, and they seemed now, as he talked with Miss Satterfield on his left hand, to have been with someone else.

He thought her a lovely child. "Not Angles but angels," his filing-cabinet mind said promptly. She was like that: what was usually called "the best Saxon type." But she was not just a type; she was a real little person with her common-sense, candid conversation. She remembered him well and recalled that foggy evening, and even humorously referred to her odorous burden of tripe.

"I expect you find life very different now," Theo suggested.

"Yes and no," she said in the considering adult way that he found attractive. "I was always a happy child. I don't think where one lives makes any difference to that—do you?"

"No. But perhaps how one lives, and with whom one lives, makes a difference."

"Well, I live more or less with myself, always, wherever I am," Grace said. "And," she added with a smile, "I've always found myself pretty good company. If people bore me, I just go away from them, and then it's all right. I can do that just as easily at my school in the Lake District as I could in Levens-hulme."

"That's a wise attitude," Theo said, thinking to himself

that this was an extraordinary conversation to be having with a child who looked no more than fourteen. Grace, in fact, was thirteen. She had left off her school uniform for the day and was wearing a long dress of a filmy blue material. Her poke bonnet was of the same stuff, lined with pleated white silk, tied with blue ribbon under her chin.

This was not the child one would expect George Satterfield to have, Theo thought. He wondered what kind of woman her mother had been. Grace had turned to talk to the man on her other side, and Theo, with the loud clatter of conversation in his ears, amused himself with speculation on the developing fortunes of the Dunkerleys and Satterfields. He had seen little enough of Dan's son Laurie, but remembered him as a pleasant enough boy who was being prepared for one of the public schools. No doubt in the fullness of time he would marry this attractive cousin, and the Dunkerley Dynasty would be under way. And Simon begat Dan, and Dan begat Laurie, and Laurie took unto himself Grace and begat perhaps Simon the Second. And no one, looking at Simon the Second, would ever think of the Stockport Road and the little printer's shop and papers of tripe and old Sim damning and blasting the fog. Nothing would be apparent but the accomplished fact, the success, the product rounded off in the customary mill of Nannie, school, and university. That was how it went. And Theo for one thought it was a very nice way for it to go, too. He was startled by the toastmaster's voice. He stood for a moment, waiting for perfect silence, fully conscious of his own appearance, tall, golden-haired, goodly to look upon; conscious, too, of the thought in his mind: "This is the first time I have ever figured on a public occasion"; conscious of the baron George Satterfield had managed to rake in, of the councillors, aldermen, and men prominent in business. He was conscious even of Miss Victoria Vernon, the famous musical comedy actress who was appearing in Manchester that week, and who, when Satterfield asked her to "grace the occasion," was quite ready to accept the publicity it offered. His voice was clear and carried to the farthest part of the room. "Bless, O God, these creatures to our use and Thy service, for Jesus Christ's sake. Amen."

Instantly the clatter broke out again and waiters, who had been standing in the wings with smoking soup plates, rushed in now that God was out of the way.

Elsie trembled when she heard Theo uttering the names of God and Jesus Christ. Only last night his arms had been around her and she herself had been swept by passion that she found well-nigh unendurable. It was a moonless night, and, invisible under a tree not far from her house, they had stood wrapped together, their faces hot with kissing, till in the extremity of her feeling she had fainted in his arms. It had been a rainy day, and there were puddles in the road. Theo had dipped his handkerchief in one and dribbled the water over her face till she recovered.

"Let me go. Let me go now," she said faintly when she could speak. "You must leave me alone, Theo. You must go away from me. I can never marry you."

She could see the white hopeless glimmer of his face as he stood there holding the sopping rag in his hand. She could feel how terribly he was oppressed. He had not recovered from the shock that struck him when George Satterfield burst out against Elsie in Daniel Dunkerley's room. He had been tempted to ask Dan what it was all about, what it was that Satterfield had hinted at; but no one knew—not even Alec, not even Mr. Burnside (he wrongly believed)—how he stood with Elsie. So he had no footing for asking that question; but for the first time he was stifled by a sense of something beyond what he knew or had guessed, a sense of disaster gathering quickly about him. He now threw away the soiled handkerchief in disgust. The high exhilaration that had carried him through thus far seemed to break within him. He let her go, and she leaned wearily against the tree. "This is all so furtive, so sordid," Theo said.

Well, she thought, in her extremity, you would have it, you wouldn't take No for an answer. And at the same time she felt resentment at his choice of words—furtive, sordid. You wait, she cried to herself, till I tell you everything, and then love me in the open air, with everyone knowing. But to him she could

only say: "I'm sorry. I feel so weak. I must go in now," and she went in on legs that tottered under her, and climbed straight up to her room lest Alec should see the blear streaked disorder of her face. By God, she thought as she lay on her bed, it *is* sordid! When a woman fainted in her lover's arms she should, according to the best models, be recovered with fragrant salts or water cupped from a crystal stream. A dirty cow-trodden puddle in the public road certainly didn't square with the books. She began to laugh hysterically, smothering her face so that Alec should not hear her, and when she had finished laughing she shivered with frustration, telling herself that all this must now end.

When she woke in the morning she felt strong and resolute. This is a new day, she said. This is the beginning of something—either of me alone, or of me and Theo. It was, whichever way it went, a day to be celebrated. Alec went to town at his customary time, saying that he would meet her at one o'clock at the hotel where the lunch was to be held. As soon as he was gone she went out and, knowing she had little time, she found a cab and had herself driven to Manchester. At the most stylish hair-dresser's she knew she gave precise orders. She had long ago determined what she would do with her hair when she was a solo violinist, and this was to be done now. The veil that had covered Bim on the snowy doorstep was shorn away, and her hair, which curled naturally, was arranged in innumerable tendrils on her head and neck. Looking at herself in the mirror, she was satisfied. Nothing of her beauty was gone, but it was pointed and given a striking significance and individuality. The sky-green eyes and white skin, framed in the dark red aureole of her hair, had a challenging intensity that startled even herself.

Another cab took her home and waited while she changed. She wore a dress of the colour of young beech-leaves—the tenderest green that can anywhere be found. She put a sash of magnolia-flower cream about her waist and a scarf of the same colour on her head. Thumbelina went up and looked into the bedroom to announce: "The cabman says to hurry up, Miss Dillworth." Elsie was just turning from the mirror, and the

child stared at her with a sagging mouth. "Lor, Miss Dillworth, you do look different," she gasped.

"Thumbs," said Elsie, using the pet name she had given the child, "there are times when you need all you've got." She patted Thumbelina's head and ran down to the cab.

She had cut it fine. The party had already assembled at the tables, and Alec, waiting for her in the lounge, was beginning to fume. But when he saw her his annoyance vanished in a wave of joy. He looked at her with surprise and delight. "Well, by God!" he said. "A ginger Medusa!" He disconcerted her by taking her hand and kissing it. "If you had asked me," he said, "I should never have allowed you to have it cut off. But you were right. It's perfect. It's You at last—the You you will always be. Van der Poorten Schootz will be delirious when he sees you tonight."

Well, thought Elsie, taking her place at the table, tonight will see the end of my affair one way or another. She looked about the room and saw Theo talking to a young woman—a child—at the top table. She was too far away to catch his eye or to be sure whether he had seen her, and at that moment the toastmaster's voice rang out. She had hardly had time to compose herself in her seat when Theo was on his feet, waiting for silence, looking beautiful, and somehow, she thought, looking as if he knew it. She had never heard Theo's voice inside a church. She had never heard it except on humdrum occasions or on occasions of desperate intimacy. Now he began to speak. "Bless, O God . . ."

It was a voice she had never heard, the voice of someone she had never known. It was Theo's voice, but it was full of inflections that were new to her, full too, she admitted of an authority she had not expected. She was acute enough to recognize that this was not just any curate conventionally "asking a blessing." Theo managed to import into his few words more than himself: the majesty of his Church and the authority of his priesthood. An artist herself, she recognized the touch that makes a trifle significant.

In that instant Elsie knew that, though she must play her hand to the end, all was lost. Her very bones seemed to shiver

when she heard the names of God and Jesus Christ on lips so familiar, lips that a few hours ago were hot upon her own and that had trembled with the words they uttered. She had thought of Theo as just that: a youth distraught with passion that he half believed to be hopeless, a youth taking his love where he could find it, in back lanes and dark by-ways. Now, suddenly, as though a fog had lifted, she saw unsuspected territories of his being, to which she had never been admitted, to which, indeed, she felt she had no competence to be admitted. This was a realm she could not share, nor could she long be happy with a man who habitually dwelt in it.

All this passed through her young mind formlessly, without precise substance, but with a very real agony that made her immediate surroundings seem chimerical. A grey old waiter was placing a plate of soup before her. Mop-headed chrysanthemums, round and curled like her own head which she had forgotten, shone before her eyes, but she hardly saw them. A side-whiskered gentleman spoke to her, and with a start she pulled herself together to answer him, realizing that this occasion must be got through somehow. And when it was through, there would be that other occasion with Theo. It would save him so much, save them both so much, if she simply told him that she would never marry him or see him again, and left it at that. But she had promised him that the choice should be his, with his eyes open. Well, she would be proud enough to let it end that way. She turned to answer her companion. "Yes. It *is* a beautiful day."

Miss Victoria Vernon, who was of an age and experience that prevented her from looking her best in the daylight, was startled when she saw Alec Dillworth lead Elsie to her place and leave her there while he went to find his own. She should long ago have taken to spectacles and going to bed at ten with a basin of groats, but she raised her lorgnette and gazed long and attentively at Elsie. She sighed, turned to Mr. Bentley who sat next to her, and said: "Who is that astonishing creature?"

A luncheon to mark the opening of Dunkerley House would have been nothing in Mr. Bentley's line if Miss Vernon

had not been present. But as a collector and purveyor of theatrical gossip, he thought her still worth a little attention. If nothing else could be wrung from her, perhaps he might be the first to announce her decision to retire from the stage. He looked where the lorgnette pointed, started, and said valiantly: "I don't know. Probably some cotton king's daughter."

His mind was in a whirl. It was undoubtedly the same girl, but what a flowering! And what was she doing here, with old Sir Robert Mardson smitten to death, evidently, as he talked to her?

Mr. Bentley remembered a street of small houses off the Oxford Road, and himself slipping away in the early hours of the morning, leaving a sovereign under the beer-bottle on the mantelpiece. And he remembered a dinner with the girl—Elsie, that was it. "Well, anyway, what's your name?" "Elsie." That was all he learned—and then a visit to the theatre, and after that a most disturbing incident indeed. He would never forget that: a brutal hand on his neck, the way he was spun into the middle of the road before the door slammed. Something fishy—something very fishy indeed—about this girl, Mr. Bentley said to himself. But he was saying nothing to this gossiping old trout—not he.

"But she's a raving beauty," said Miss Vernon.

"Ah, well," said Mr. Bentley with easy gallantry. "Manchester does produce 'em, Miss Vernon. Weren't you born here yourself?"

And Miss Vernon, whose father had been a hansom cab driver, allowed the conversation to go into other channels.

George Satterfield was thinking of the present, of the solid achievement which Dunkerley House signified and which this gathering celebrated. Later on, when most of these people were gone, a few would go on to Dunkerley House for a more intimate ceremony. Miss Vernon would be one of them. She would break a bottle of champagne against the door lintel and exclaim: "May this ship of fortune sail ever prosperously on." George had himself composed the words and conveyed them to her, together with a neat bracelet. He thought

the words rather fine and her presence cheap at the price of a bracelet.

Dan Dunkerley was not thinking of the present at all. He noticed the large number of women at the tables and wrote on the back of his menu card: "Women's Interests. 'Home and Children.' " A good title for a weekly, he thought. " 'The Englishwoman.' 'Family Affairs.' "

He wished this present affair were over. He wasn't much interested in it and had left most of the arrangements to George. Celebrating what was already done was not his idea of profitable occupation. He nodded to the toastmaster to get on with things, and the Queen's health was drunk. Almost at once Dan was on his feet, proposing "The British Press."

Alec Dillworth had written the speech, and consequently he knew just when to lead the applause or start the laughter. He fulfilled this office with sardonic satisfaction. He had his own opinion about the British Press, and especially about that part of it which Dunkerley House stood for, and therefore he felt a wicked glee as he heard the round platitudes he had prepared rolling off Dan's lips. "And therefore, my lord, ladies and gentlemen, the pride that fills my heart as I stand here today is not unmixed with other feelings. The pride I freely and frankly confess. When I see, sprung up almost overnight, this paper whose influence already is as wide as the nation itself, and see, further, this splendid building which houses not only *Hard Facts* but many a budding fancy that will, I hope, unfold itself in due season: when I see all this, how shall I not be proud? But these other feelings belong more privately to my own heart. There is the feeling of humility, proper to one who comes newly to his associations with the British Press—the finest, cleanest, and most open-minded in the world. (Cheers.) There is the feeling of responsibility towards all those thousands who week by week look to us to maintain undimmed the heritage which comes down to us through so long a line of great publicists and great publications. (Hear, hear.) Believe me, I and my co-directors and my staff are not unaware that what is reposed in us is a trusteeship, and as trustees it is our first endeavour to be loyal to the finest traditions of our call-

ing. What, after all, is the British Press but the voice of Britain herself, the honourable accent of this illustrious and beloved Empire?" (Loud applause.)

By God! Alec thought. Even that! He had wondered if it were not a bit too thick, but Dan had accepted it, he had put it across, and everybody here was accepting it too. They would accept anything, provided it were wrapped in five-pound notes. "Yes," he said to the waiter behind his chair, "fill the damned thing up—right up to the top." He seized his glass as Dan put the toast, rose to his feet, and cheered vigorously, beating the table with a spoon.

"You should remain seated, Mr. Dillworth," said the cotton merchant next to him. "We're drinking to *you.*"

"By heck!" said Alec. "So you are! What a thought! Drink deep, brother. Drink deep."

He had his glass filled again, and settled down to listen to Lord Pendleton, a considerable shareholder, proposing "Success to *Hard Facts.*"

When Theo caught sight of Elsie he was speaking to Grace Satterfield. It was only with difficulty that he finished what he was saying and, he hoped, prevented the clear-minded child from realizing his disturbance. Elsie had hung over her chair-back the scarf that had draped her head. She was the only woman in the room without a hat and she stood out like a parrot among sparrows. The sight of her head startled him. He had always loved its colour. It's new shape—all these red tendrils brushed away upwards from her white forehead, clustering about her ears and behind her neck—made her look both bewitching and dangerous.

Shine out, little head, sunning over with curls.

But he felt, with an agitation that shook him, that these were not the innocent curls that Tennyson had been thinking of. The same thought came to him that had come to Alec: she looked a Medusa. He was vaguely afraid of her; she had an abnormal air, overcharged with peril. Unable to take his eyes off her, he was troubled again by the recollection of that scene

in Dan Dunkerley's room. What had Satterfield been hinting at? Then she saw him, and smiled at him, and, far away as she was, the enticement of the smile renewed all his disturbance, made him long for nothing but to be alone with her again.

As soon as the last banalities had been uttered, he shook hands with Grace Satterfield and said he hoped they would meet again. "I'm sure we shall, Mr. Chrystal," she said in her self-possessed way; and George Satterfield, who had joined them, said: "She'll be disappointed if she doesn't—eh, Grace?" Theo was pleased with the way she cold-shouldered her father's remark and walked off. He himself went, too, turning down Satterfield's suggestion that he should come on to Dunkerley House. He felt he had had enough of Dunkerley House to last a long time. He wanted nothing now but to speak to Elsie.

This was the only wish, too, of Mr. Bentley, who had gladly surrendered Miss Vernon to George Satterfield. Mr. Bentley's feelings could best be described as optimistic. When he first caught sight of Elsie he was sober, and if now he was hardly drunk, he had at any rate permitted a good deal of wine to lubricate his imagination, so that it played about the subject of this beautiful girl with great freedom. He could not prevent his thoughts from recreating that memorable night when she added herself so unexpectedly to the company in Gert's dressing-room: a night whose climax lost nothing of its savour as now he re-lived it with his eye on the girl herself—the girl mysteriously more beautiful and appealing. It was with the expectation of something far more satisfactory than seeing Victoria Vernon waste a bottle of champagne that Mr. Bentley hurried to the cloak-room for his hat.

Elsie, with the scarf over her head, was in the lounge when she saw Mr. Bentley and Theo Chrystal coming almost side by side towards her, each unaware that the other was anything to her; and she felt a chill of the heart as these two young men approached, seeing in them the incarnation of her past and her future, one of which today must destroy the other. She did not know for a moment what to do, and then in an access

of panic she walked swiftly away. She hoped she might find an unoccupied cab at the door. To get out of Mr. Bentley's sight was what instinct urged. Theo would know that she had seen him and would think her flight strange, but she couldn't help that; she would have to put him off later with some excuse.

But Mr. Bentley was not to be eluded so easily as this. He started quickly after her, took her by the arm, and cried: "Why, Elsie! You're not going to run away, are you? Don't you remember me?"

There was nothing for it but to stop and face him, and she did so with a tragic resignation that wrung Theo's heart, as he stood a few paces off. He wondered who this young man might be, but was unwilling to thrust himself forward. Elsie neither accepted nor denied knowledge of Mr. Bentley: she stood there, looking, Theo thought, like a sacrificial victim waiting for the knife. But Mr. Bentley was in no state for sensitive perceptions. Still holding Elsie's arm, he tried to lead her towards a chair, saying: "Let's have a drink and a talk." She did not resist with any spirit, but merely opposed a dull inertia to his effort, still not speaking, hardly looking at him: and at this moment Theo stepped forward. "Miss Dillworth," he said formally, "may I call you a cab?"

She felt she was beyond anything—beyond hope and fear and caring, and the coarse realistic Dillworth humour moved her to say: "You can call me anything you like. Certainly you would be correct in calling me a public vehicle."

Now then, she thought in some last desperate recess of her mind, make what you can of that. But Theo could make nothing of it. He thought she was unwell, but she put both him and Mr. Bentley suddenly aside, ran out of the hotel, and called a cab for herself.

Mr. Bentley, on whose mind her remark had registered with unmistakable clarity, looked at Theo, more than a little surprised at the intervention of this handsome young parson. "I beg your pardon," he said. "I did not know you were with the young lady. You called her Miss Dillworth. Is she any relation to Alec?"

"His sister," Theo said, regarding Mr. Bentley with cold distaste.

Mr. Bentley whistled. "I never knew that."

"But you seemed to claim her acquaintance."

"I only knew her as Elsie. It was all rather—shall we say free and easy?"

"I see," said Theo. "Good-day to you, sir."

"Chilly sod," Mr. Bentley said to himself, and decided that he would, after all, hurry to Dunkerley House. A few more free drinks might be going there.

Mr. Bentley was not mistaken about this. Tables, provided with wines and sandwiches, had been set up in one of the rooms, and a few people were gathered there, reluctant to admit that everything was over, telling one another again and again what a great success it had been. Dan Dunkerley looked into the room, saw Alec there, heard him talking loudly, and went up, slipping a hand under his arm. He himself had drunk nothing but water, and wished Alec had done the same. The little man was too frail and excitable to be let loose at a drinking-bout.

"Alec, I thought I should mark this occasion in some special way. All the talk will be dead tomorrow. It's dead already. But I want you and the others who've been in on *Hard Facts* from the beginning to have a small memento."

They had climbed the stairs and were walking along the corridor towards Alec's room. "You've done a good job, Alec. I'm not much use at proposing votes of thanks, but I'd like you to know that I feel that."

They entered the room and sat down in a couple of easy chairs. "I know," said Dan, smiling, "that you don't in your heart think much of *Hard Facts*. I know that you put a lot of cod into that speech you wrote for me and that you must have enjoyed yourself no end listening to me mouthing it. Well, perhaps you're right. I don't want you ever to forget, Alec, that I realize that, too. I know that when you're working for me you're putting aside work that would have satisfied you more. No doubt you would have starved on it, but that's neither

here nor there. All I'm saying is that when I thank you for what you're doing here, I bear all that in mind. I'm just saying it once for all."

The drink had made Alec emotional. He felt that he had never had a finer friend than Dan Dunkerley. He got up and grasped him by the hand. Dan pushed him good-naturedly towards the table. "Well, go and unpack your little present. It's a nothing—a trifle—but it comes with my warmest thanks."

It was a thin and rather long packet. Alec untied the string with fumbling fingers. He took out a box of red morocco leather, pressed the catch, and looked down at a dagger. Gingerly he removed it from the case and turned it this way and that. It was a beautiful thing. The blade was engraved with an intricate and lovely pattern; the handle was of ivory, dull as the petals of a faded yellow rose. Alec promptly took a penny from his pocket and tossed it to Dan. "An edged present must always be paid for," he said. "You know the old superstition, Dan? Otherwise, it cuts friendship."

Dan nodded. "It won't do that between us, Alec," he said. "I found the thing in London, in an antique shop. They assure me it's early fifteenth-century work. They call it a misericord. I always understood misericord meant mercy, but that doesn't look very merciful."

"It was used in a merciful way," said Alec. "I've read about these things, but I've never seen one before. Every knight carried one, and he used it to finish off quickly a wounded enemy." He turned the dagger about in his hands, looking at it with fascination. "By God, Dan," he said. "This is a hard fact, all right. I wonder what it's seen and done in its time?"

"Well, whatever that may have been," said Dan, "it's been turned out now to end its days browsing in a paper-paddock. You can keep it on your desk to slit open your envelopes."

"But first," Alec answered, "I must take it home and show it to Elsie. Did you see her today, Dan? What's she been up to? She looked fifteenth century too. Like a beautiful fifteenth-century page-boy."

"Yes," said Dan, "she looked very striking."

"Thank you for asking her today, Dan. I'm very proud when

she's treated the way you treat her. And let me tell you this:
I did hear a hint that you had some trouble over that."

Dan said nothing, and Alec went on: "Soon, nobody will
dare to treat her except as what she is, and, by God, that's something. In the meantime, she's my business, and I shall know
how to deal with anybody who doesn't show her proper
respect."

His hand tightened on the dagger, the knuckles standing out
suddenly drained to the colour of the hilt. Dan looked at the
narrowed eyes and taut figure for a moment, thinking what an
untamable wildcat Alec could appear, then picked up the red
morocco case and handed it to him. "Better pack it away,
Alec," he said.

Theo came out of the hotel in time to see Elsie's cab turning
the corner into London Road. He followed along that drab
highway, plodding homewards in a mood of depression and
despondency. London Road . . . Downing Street . . . Ardwick Green . . . Stockport Road: it was all one bleak dispirit-
ing thoroughfare, now of warehouses, now of uninviting shops,
now of pubs and mean houses: all one length of what seemed
to him that day to be sheer misery, chopped up under various
names and having but one advantage: that if you went on long
enough you walked out of Manchester altogether and found
your feet on the road to the South. London . . . Sussex . . .
Cotter's Court.

It was by now mid-afternoon, and a thin autumnal sunshine
filtered through the invisible but ever-present pall spread over
the city by an infinity of soot-molecules held in suspension in
the air. Ardwick Green opened out once the monotony of
Downing Street was passed, but it seemed to him at best a
shabby and pathetic oasis with its carbonized shrubs and lifeless turf; and all too swiftly upon even this poor mitigation
came the slate-grey vista of the Stockport Road.

No, thought Theo, I can't stand this place. I've given it a
fair trial, and I can't stand it. I shall marry Elsie, and then we'll
get out of this altogether. But even as he thought this, even as
Elsie came to the forefront of his mind, he knew that it was

not Manchester that was depressing him: it was Elsie herself; and for the first time the idea began to take hold of him that perhaps he was fated not to marry her at all. He had never been able to clear his thought of that episode in Daniel Dunkerley's room: the vagueness of Satterfield's hints had more power to disturb him than an outspoken charge could have done. And on top of that, this fellow at the luncheon! The very apathy of Elsie's attitude suggested to Theo's oversensitive mind large tracts of undesirable experience that she could not be bothered to repudiate or explain. He had never seen her looking lovelier, but neither had he ever known her more enigmatic, more—he hated the word, but it forced its way into his mind—more dubious. He was sick and tired of a sense of the furtive that had crept into his relationship with Elsie. She had insisted that even Alec must for the time be kept in the dark. Now, he said to himself, all this had to end. He would call on Elsie tonight and square the matter up one way or the other once for all. If Alec were there, so much the better.

He felt a little more cheerful once this decision was made, and more cheerful still when he was back in his room in Hardiman Street. Here he could be himself. Here was his cell, and he had learned to fit into it as aptly as a nautilus into its whorled abode. Mrs. Hornabrook brought him tea, and urged him, as she never tired of doing: "Tak off thi boots, lad, an' rest thi feet." Like the old ladies he had stage-managed at Blackpool, Mrs. Hornabrook believed that creature-comfort spread from the feet up. "Ah've knocked thee up a bit o' parkin," she said, proudly placing the dark brown sticky cake on the table. "And 'ere's a letter coom for thee on t'afternoon post. It'll soon be comin' time for a fire in t'evenings," she added, "then Manchester'll not be so bad. Manchester's aw reight, so long as tha can pull t'curtains, warm thi toes, and not see t'damn place." She took a last look at the table. "Ay. Tha's got all tha wants."

Theo was only too willing to put on his slippers and drink a cup of tea. He took up the letter which he saw was from Lady Pinson. It was addressed from the Bishop of Chanctonbury's palace.

My dear Theo:—You see I am not writing to you from Cotter's Court, and possibly I shall never write to you from there again. You would wonder what is happening to the old place if you could see it now, with workmen clambering all over it, inside and out.

For some time I have been troubled about money. You know me well enough, I am sure, to realize that I could never be happy if I used all my privileges—which I have done little enough to deserve—merely to gratify my own whims and fancies. My father brought me up in a Spartan fashion with no temptation to waste the little money he allowed me, but when my husband died I found myself a very rich woman indeed. My father's death made me richer still. He was, you know, one of the most successful advocates of his day, and his fortune grew through clever investment and lucky speculation. His estate was much larger than anybody expected, and another thing that surprised everybody was that he left everything to me.

Forgive me, dear Theo, for telling you all this, but it will explain what I am coming to. Whenever I thought of my friend Lottie Chambers, and of other good women I know, I felt appalled at the temptation I was in to lead an utterly useless life. But I shall not need to do this. For a long time past my brother Adrian and a number of his friends at Oxford and on the bench have been anxious to found a new public school, open mainly to the sons of the clergy and other professional men who are not able easily to afford the fees charged elsewhere. A good deal of money had already been collected, but, you know, to start a thing of this sort well, more is needed than even I had dreamed.

However, I have now made a start possible. The school will be called Beckwith, which was my father's surname. Cotter's Court is being rapidly remodelled as the nucleus of the school, in which the first scholars will be housed, but of course it is an old-fashioned place, not really appropriate, but its use will be temporary. Ultimately, I suppose, it will become quarters for the staff, or something of that sort. In the meantime, my brother and I, with his long-suffering domestic chaplain and

other members of the committee, are up to the eyes in pros-
pectuses, architects' plans, builders' estimates, and all sorts of
matters which keep me occupied day and night. There will be
the delicate question of choosing the Headmaster, and he I
suppose will have to choose the staff—a small enough one to
begin with, but our ultimate ambitions are pretty large!

Forgive what is, I feel, a more excited letter than I am accustomed to write, but these are exciting days for me. However,
they do not cause me to leave you and your welfare for long out
of my mind. I hope, dear Theo, I may still expect to have news
of you. A longer time has passed since last you wrote than I
could have wished. Whatever concerns you cannot fail to interest me, and if there is anything you want to tell me about
either your work or the development of your private life, do
please remember that I am—and always shall be
Your friend and sincere well-wisher,
Adela Pinson.

The development of my private life! thought Theo. Well,
my dear Adela, we shall be able to give you some information
about that tomorrow, one way or the other. And what, he
wondered, could "the other" amount to? What alternatives
were there? He turned the letter about in his hand. "The
Palace, Chanctonbury Episcopi." An attractive address.

There was not much to do in the small house at Burnage,
but Thumbelina took delight in doing it thoroughly. As soon
as Miss Dillworth was gone she took her Bath brick, scraped
the surface till she had a saucerful of powder, and then got
out her cork and duster. She damped the end of the cork,
dipped it in the powder, and began to polish the knives and
forks. Rubbing them up with the duster, she was careful to
pass it between the tines of the forks, so that not a spot of grit
remained. Once, Mr. Dillworth had got quite a mouthful of
grit, but he didn't call her a careless little slut, which is what
she would have been called in her last place. He just said:
"Look, Miss Small, this is quite easy when you know how to
do it," and he had come out into the kitchen and polished and

wiped half a dozen forks for her. So now she never had a spot of grit on her knives or forks or spoons, because she wouldn't offend Mr. Dillworth for anything. As for Miss Dillworth, she felt she could have put up with a lot from her if she had had to, but in fact she had to put up with nothing at all. She said to herself that Miss Dillworth was a perfect lady. She had never known any one more beautiful or more considerate or more thankful for a little job done. Miss Dillworth had even told her that she could go out into the garden and pick an apple whenever she wanted to. Miss Small decided to do this now, and stood under the tree biting into the harsh russet skin with firm white teeth that were her only good feature. She was just thirteen—the same age as Miss Grace Satterfield, who even at this moment was talking in her self-possessed way to Theo Chrystal.

But Thumbelina had not an envious soul. She was well content to be where she was and doing what she was. She knew that she was better off than if she were at home with her mother, the widow Longbottom, a woman of violent tongue and deed. She might almost be in the country, she thought, biting with succulent appreciative noises and looking up at the blue sky where a few swifts were wheeling. Then she threw away the core—over the wall into the next garden, so that there should be no untidiness here—and, smitten with penitence for this dilly-dallying, went indoors, panting purposefully.

She gathered together all Mr. Dillworth's boots. What a one he was! she said to herself, clicking her tongue with mildly reproving t't, t'ts. You never knew where you'd find his shoes. Some in the bedroom, some in that untidy place he called the study, where she didn't dare lay a hand on anything, some in the kitchen. That old study! She stood in the doorway, alternately clicking and panting, itching to have what she called a good go in at it. But Mr. Dillworth had said: "Thumbs, if I ever find you over this doorstep it'll be as much as your job's worth—though God knows that's not much."

So, making sure no shoes were there, she went downstairs with the ones she had, and vibrated over their cleaning with a fury of good-tempered industry. When she had done that, she

laid the tea-things in the sitting-room in case Miss Dillworth
wanted tea when she came in.

Then there really wasn't anything else she could think of,
so she sat down and did nothing at all. In her last "place" she
had been scolded for doing this. "What will the young gentlemen think! When you've got nothing to do, make it appear as
though you have." She had told Mr. Dillworth that, and he
said: "Well, s'truth, Miss Small, when you've got nothing to do
here, just get your roots down and try an' grow a bit."

Didn't she wish she could! she thought, sitting in an old
rocking-chair that left her feet well off the ground. She'd like
to be as tall as Miss Dillworth. She'd like to be everything that
Miss Dillworth was: as beautiful and as kind and as clever.
The way she played that old fiddle! You couldn't work when
she was doing it: you had to stand there at the bottom of the
stairs with your heart in your mouth. She had such lovely
hands. There was that time Mr. Dillworth had brought her
home a picture of a dreadful old man—a real terrible-looking
old devil he was, nothing but a walking skellington, and he
was playing the fiddle, too. Miss Dillworth seemed no end
pleased, just as much as if he'd been as lovely as an angel, and
she said she'd hang him in her bedroom. She went up with a
hammer and a nail, and soon there was a howl, and when she
and Mr. Dillworth went to see what was the matter, Miss Dillworth was hopping about and sucking one of her fingers that
she'd whacked with the hammer. There was a bruise on it,
and it was bleeding. Mr. Dillworth didn't seem a bit sym-
pathetic. He was just furious. "For God's sake!" he said. "Do
you have to do that? Couldn't you have asked me?" Miss Dillworth said: "Oh, it's nothing," and he shouted: "What d'you
mean, nothing? Your hands are everything." He took hold of
her fingers and looked at the bruise, and then he said: "We'll
have to get your hands insured."

Well, did you ever hear anything like that? Insuring a bit
of someone! You could insure all of anybody; she knew that,
because out of her wages she had to give her mother the money
for the Prudential, and more than that, too; but she'd never
heard the likes of insuring a hand or a foot. Miss Dillworth

said: "Time enough for that when we know whether they're worth anything." Then he went all sentimental, and kissed the finger where the bruise was, and took her off to have it properly bound up by a chemist.

That was the only time Thumbelina felt what she called real vexed with Mr. Dillworth, because she couldn't bear to hear anybody, not even him, speak crossly to Miss Dillworth. If it hadn't been Mr. Dillworth she'd have spoken up real sharp, because no one was going to speak to Miss Dillworth like that when she was about. When they went out together, friendly once more, the pudgy mite watched them through the front window with tender approval.

This was why it seemed to Thumbelina that evening as though her world had been torn up by the roots and was rocking under her feet. First of all, Miss Dillworth came home in a cab, looking tired and sad.

"You sit down, Miss Dillworth," the child said. "Your tea's laid in the sitting-room, and I'll have the kettle boiling in a jiffy."

"Don't bother, Thumbs," Elsie said. "I'm feeling very tired. I shall just go straight up to my room and lie down. You have your own tea now, and then go for a bit of a walk. You've been stewing in here all day."

She went slowly and draggingly up the stairs, and Miss Small stood at the bottom, feeling each heavy step as though it were planted on her heart. But there was nothing she could do. There were times when Mr. Dillworth and Miss Dillworth were very near to her; she had a silly feeling that they were like an elder brother and sister of her own; but at other times they seemed miles away, wrapped up in themselves, in another world. She felt that Miss Dillworth was like that now, and when she had heard the bedroom door shut she went into the kitchen, all her palpitating energy gone from her, and sadly sat down to her tea. But go out she would not, she said firmly to herself. Not while Miss Dillworth was like that. So she washed up her tea-things and then sat rocking quietly in the quiet house. Presently the chair ceased rocking. Thum-

belina's head began to rock, and a small neat snore sounded in the kitchen.

The door-knocker's peremptory rap brought the child awake with a start. She saw that it was six o'clock. As she stood half-dazed with sleep, taking note from sounds in the sitting-room that Miss Dillworth was up and about, the knock was repeated with angry impatience, and she hastened to the door. She was surprised to find that the caller was her mother. She could not remember a time when she had been glad to see her mother, and she was not glad now. Mrs. Longbottom had but lately come to Levenshulme, having made Gorton too hot for herself. Her violent quarrelsome nature had raised such enmity that she could hardly venture into the street without risk of having her hair pulled down. Thus far, in her new surroundings she had controlled herself, but little Thumbelina, trembling within the doorway, looking up into the bloated scorbutic face, saw that one of the old explosions was about to take place.

"Get inside, you, and get your box packed," Mrs. Longbottom said, and taking Thumbelina by the shoulder she gave her a vigorous shove, so that she reeled backward and collided with the hat-stand. Faced by this mother of hers, she was no longer the little woman she tried so hard to be. She was a terrified child, but there was rebellion under her terror. The idea of never seeing her mother again, never again handing over all her small earnings, was one she secretly nurtured; and now, recovering herself, she cried: "You go on, our mother. Who're you pushin'?"

The disturbance brought Elsie out from the sitting-room, and her appearance gave Thumbelina great comfort. She was still wearing her green frock, and her hair, the child thought, looked wonderful. Oh, Miss Dillworth would soon deal with our mother! Mrs. Longbottom advanced into the passage, walked up to Elsie, and glared into her face. Elsie could smell her rancid skin and the liquor on her breath. She felt sickened and frightened, seeing that red face blotched with scurf thrust towards her own. "So you're the whore?" said Mrs. Longbottom.

Thumbelina did not know what a whore was, but she knew that this was a dreadful word. She saw Miss Dillworth go pale, and in anger she cried: "You shut your dirty mouth, our mother. Don't you come here making trouble. This is a good place, this is. An' you've got no right to talk to Miss Dillworth like that."

Mrs. Longbottom did not answer, but landed a flat-hander on the child's cheek that sent her staggering. It was so aimed that Thumbelina's stagger took her backwards, towards the still-open front door, and she would have fallen upon the threshold if a pair of strong arms had not caught her. Theo propped her upright, looked at her flaming cheek, at this un-known evil-featured woman standing with hands on hips, el-bows aggressively out-thrust, glaring into Elsie's face, at Elsie herself, wearing still the defeated apathetic air with which she had stood before that youth in the hotel lounge, and he asked: "What is all this? Is there anything I can do?"

Elsie said, as if talking from the end of the world: "Nothing whatever."

Theo shut the door behind him, and the passage darkened. He felt as though it was full of evil. In the twilight the woman's voice spoke: "You go and get your box packed, Sarah. I won't have you staying in this little bitch's house a moment longer."

Thumbelina did not move. She stood behind Theo's legs, trembling. Then Mrs. Longbottom suddenly screamed: "Look at her! Don't she *look* a whore? Look at her hair!"

She raised a hand to snatch at Elsie's hair, and Elsie stood there as though she would have suffered it to be done. But Theo grasped the woman's wrist. It was an iron clutch, and hurt her. Something of the festering resentment he had felt at Blackpool went into it. He didn't like Levenshulme old women, and in the convulsive strength of his fingers he ac-knowledged this. "What I ought to do with you," he said, "is throw you out into the street, you beer-stinking old slut. And parson though I am, for two pins I'd do it."

He was amazed to hear himself speaking like that, and Mrs. Longbottom was amazed, too. For a moment she quailed, then

recovered her brazen assurance. "All right," she cried. "Throw me out, and I'll shout all I know from one end of the street to the other. You—you a parson—didn't you ought to know better than to stop a mother from taking her innocent child out of a whore's house? Is this the place for a poor little lamb like my Sarah? I'd have worked my fingers to the bone for her rather than let her come here if I'd known then what I know now. You let go of my hand. You got no right to lay a finger on me, a mother protecting her own poor child."

Theo threw her hand from him, pushed open the door of the sitting-room, and said: "Get in there, and if you have anything to say, try and say it intelligently, not like a brawling drunkard."

Mrs. Longbottom moved into the room, but protesting: "Don't you go ordering me about. Who d'you think you are? And I haven't come here to say anything. I've come here to take my poor child home, and take her home I will."

Elsie followed them into the room and sat with her face averted, looking out of the window, as though all this did not concern her. Theo shut the door, leaving Thumbelina outside. He turned upon Mrs. Longbottom, and said: "Whether you came here to say anything or not, you've managed to say a good deal. You've made the foulest possible charge against this lady. You could go to prison for half you've said. Do you realize that?"

Mrs. Longbottom grinned at the high peremptory tone. "Ay," she said, "go to prison, where her old man is. That's another thing. I won't have my poor child in no gaol-bird's house. You let me make my Sarah pack up and get out of this. You got no right to keep me here."

She made towards the door, but Theo stood leaning against it. "I want to know——" he began; but Elsie interrupted. She got up and faced in to the room. "For God's sake," she said wearily, "end all this. You *do* know. There is nothing else for you to know."

The words released a spate from Mrs. Longbottom. "There!" she crowed. "You hear that? You poor bloody fool

of a parson. Everybody all over Levenshulme knows it except you. I was a poor innocent woman when I came into this district, and how could I know till this very day when they begin twittin' me in the Bell? And don't you call me drunken neither. A woman who works as hard as I do to make a home for her child, she's entitled I hope to keep her strength up. Well, there was I, and those women just discovering where my poor Sarah was working, and sniggering and tittering and asking whether my Sarah wasn't a bit young for it. Fair flummoxed and baffled I was, I can tell you, about what they was hinting at, till one of 'em comes right out with it and asks me didn't I know Elsie Dillworth had been on the knock? Christ! You could've pushed me over! I didn't have the strength to blow the froth off a pint I was that taken aback. And what could a mother do then, I ask you, but come an' take her lamb into safety?"

Elsie spoke again. "All right," she said. "Take her. Take her and for God's sake go."

Theo stood away from the door, and Mrs. Longbottom rushed through it, shouting: "Sarah! Come on now. Pack your box."

There was no answer. Theo and Elsie stood there, without words, listening to the brazen voice and the heavy feet. They heard her trampling through the house, upstairs and down, her cries becoming more vehement and more obscene. "Come on, you little bitch. I'll find you. You've got a taste for it yourself by now, I shouldn't wonder, but, by God, if you have I'll beat it out of you by inches."

But she couldn't find the child, who, indeed, had fled from the house as soon as her mother entered the sitting-room; and presently they heard the thud of her boots down the stairs and her voice shouting in the passage: "You two in there, I'll find her! You'll see! I'll find her! An' if I've got to come back here for her the street'll know it. You'll see!"

The door banged, and they saw her, cowled in her shawl, go by the window in the quiet evening light, and then there was nothing but the emptiness and the silence and themselves among the ruins.

While the woman was there, a certain resolution had been necessary to deal with her; but now that she was gone Theo suddenly felt sick and weak. His mind lost control, and imagination took command. He knew nothing whatever of this matter which Mrs. Longbottom had so ruthlessly thrust before him. The humdrum and deadening daily life of a prostitute in a great city was something whose detail he could not conceive, and upon his innocence there now rushed pictures charged with lubricity and excitement. Elsie's altered appearance did nothing to stay the flight of his untutored imagination. He saw her as she was now, not as he knew her to have been. He saw this head of red tendrils shining above her naked body in a scene ridiculously, but for him terribly, composed of wine-cups, red mouths, flashing limbs, and rosy breasts.

The room was darkening. He leaned backwards upon the table, clutching it with both hands behind him. He felt his palms sweating and his body shivering. Elsie stood before the window; all the light there was throwing her into relief. She was quite still, like a picture framed in the luminous oblong, with the gossamer muslin of the curtains rising from her shoulders like a wing on either side. Her green dress was of tenuous stuff, and the light shining through it blurred its edges. A priestess of evil, a lascivious Salome: such were the pictures that rose in the mind of Theo, unable to grasp the sorrowful commonplace, the drab monotonous reality.

"Oh, my love, my love! What did they do to you?" It was all he needed to say (it was all that Alec's secret heart cried daily) in order to scoop the pool of all that she had so abundantly to give. But he said nothing: he gripped the table and looked at her till his regard became a glare and the insubstantial edges of the picture framed in the window wavered as if with the pulsation of heat that may be seen dissolving the surface of the earth on a midsummer day. This was not Elsie he was looking at any more. This was Desire incarnate.

Troubled by the long silence and by the sound of his strange hard breathing, presently she stirred and said uneasily: "Theo!"

Still he did not move or speak, and she said: "Theo, why

don't you go away now? It's all over, isn't it? There's nothing to stay for any more."

She came towards him, and frightened now by the tenseness of his look, she said sharply: "Theo! Theo!" and with the flat of her hand she struck him a light smart blow on the cheek, as she might have done to awaken someone from a trance.

Then he seized her hungrily, and for a moment she imagined that love for her had overleapt the monstrous circumstances that she had thought to be too much. In that moment she slackened in his arms, expecting to hear the words that would dissolve this ice of misery that was freezing her heart. But no words came, and his grip upon her had so unloverlike a strength that she looked up into his eyes and shuddered to see their frenzied burning in his white face. She was experienced enough to know what fetters and formalities had crumbled in him, and she began to struggle: "Theo! Don't! Don't! For God's sake!" she panted. "You'll never forgive yourself!"

Still he said nothing, but the feel of that strong young supple body wriggling in his hands inflamed and in some sort exalted him. Now—now—whole tracts of life that had been supposition and surmise were clearing in his mind, giving to this carnal tussle a sweet delight that intoxicated him. After that first cry Elsie said no more, but fought him with a lithe feline strength. To get out of his grasp, to flee the room and the house, leaving him to come to his senses: that was what she wanted. She heard a crash as a small table went over and a vase splintered on the uncarpeted edge of the floor; and then with a wrench of her body and a push at his chest she was free.

She did not at once escape. The struggle had been too much for her, and she stood panting and fighting for breath. Her dress was in ribbons. She flung a rag of it across her shoulder to hide her breast. Her push had sent Theo almost sprawling. But he came up again, a tatter of green in his hand, and now in real fear and agony, for herself and for him, Elsie screamed: "Don't! Don't! For Christ's sake leave me alone!"

It was at this moment that Alec came into the room. The crashing of the vase had hidden the sound of his key in the

door, and standing in the passage, his brain's edge blurred by the liquor he had taken, he listened in amazement to the crash and the scuffle. What in God's name, he asked himself, was going on here? He had come home in a happy if hazy mood. Dan had been kind to him and had given him a present. It was a lovely dagger, a misericord, and he was itching to show it to Elsie. And here was this racket and rumpus like a football scrum. He felt at first, standing there listening, annoyed and upset; and then came Elsie's cry, full of anguish and supplication. Alec felt his hair bristle on his head. He felt his nerves stiffen and craft invade his brain. That cry would have brought him back across the world. He laid the red morocco box on the hall table, took out the dagger, clasping the ivory haft firmly in his right hand, and quietly opened the door.

At first he could see little: the darkness by now was almost complete. He stood just within the door, turned the key in the lock behind him, and put it in his pocket. Elsie and Theo, startled by this sudden soft intrusion, remained as if frozen where they were. Gradually Alec's eyes picked the scene up out of the grey twilight. He saw Chrystal, white and panting and distraught, and Elsie with the gleam of her flesh shining through her torn garments. His imaginative power encompassed in its completeness all the hot action that was now stilled there before him as though waiting for his comprehension and comment. He said nothing, but slowly he began to move towards Theo Chrystal, his right hand behind his back.

Theo was across the room from him, and Elsie stood halfway. It was not till he had passed her that she screamed. She saw what he held behind his back. "Theo! He's got a knife!"

Chrystal, who had been out of his senses since the struggle began, and who had been as still as if enchanted while Alec stole towards him, received that cry like an awakening blow to the brain. He gazed for a second, as if wondering how it came there, at the tatter of green in his hand, threw it to the ground, and shouted: "Get out, Elsie! Get out of here!" He leapt towards the door to open it for her, spinning Alec's tiny body aside with a brush of the hand. He turned the knob and pulled, but the door would not open, and he faced about, all

his brain now alert, to see that Alec, nothing but a creeping remorseless shadow in the dark room, was advancing upon him again. Elsie stood between them, and suddenly Alec yelled and rushed. Theo was aware of the upraised dagger, of the blow delivered towards his face, and of Elsie's figure suddenly flung upon his, her arms thrown out, so that he seemed to stand behind a cross. He heard her groan. There was no more sound than that.

And now Alec, too, was sober. He spoke in a whisper. "Christ, Chrystal! Look!"

One of Elsie's outflung arms, the left, had dropped to her side. The other was pinned to the solid wood that framed a panel. Alec's blow must have been delivered with a maniac's strength. Her whole sagging body seemed to be hanging from the ivory hilt. Theo lifted her up with a tenderness that remembered nothing of his frenzy. Tears were streaming down his face. Alec stood on a chair and wrenched out the dagger. He cried shrilly: "Between us we've crucified her."

He drew the curtains and lit the gas. Theo laid Elsie on a sofa, and Alec brought hot water and a clean towel. There was not much blood. They bathed the hand and bound it up, and Alec said: "Stay with her while I get a doctor."

He went at once, and Theo sat on a chair by the sofa holding the undamaged hand. Presently Elsie opened her eyes and smiled. "Well," she said, "this has been a day, hasn't it! Not much more could have happened."

She looked at her swathed hand and said: "Take all that stuff off. I want to see it."

Theo protested, but she struggled up till she was sitting and began with her left hand to fumble at the wrappings. Then he did it for her. She held out the hand and looked at it. Deep purple bruises were forming back and front and it was swelling to shapelessness. A little blood was still oozing. She tried to work her fingers and could not. "I reckon that's the end of it," she said, and it was only then that Theo remembered her music. Tears again broke from his eyes and he tried to put his arm about her to comfort her. But she would not have it. "Bind it up again," she said. When he had done that, there

was a timid knock at the front door. Theo went to see who it
was, and found Thumbelina there. She came running into the
sitting-room, crying: "I've come back, Miss Dillworth. Whatever she says or does, I'll always come back." Then, seeing the
bandaged hand, she cried in fright: "Oo! You've been hurted!"

"Sit down, Thumbs," Elsie said, patting the chair that Theo
had left. "Thank you for coming back. Yes, I'm afraid I've
been hurt."

Theo had returned, and was standing just within the room.
He was astonished by her tranquillity. "And now," she said to
him, "you'd better go. There's nothing more to wait for, is
there? Now that Thumbs is here, I shall be all right till the
doctor comes."

Still he could not believe that this was the end, but she
turned from him as though he were no longer there, and he
took his hat from the hall-stand and went, walking for hours
through the dark night before he could trust himself alone in
his room.

When he was gone, Elsie said: "Thumbs, go up and bring
my fiddle, will you?"

"Oo, Miss Dillworth," the child said, "you can't play with
a hand like that! And your lovely dress is all to bits."

"No, Thumbs, I certainly can't play with a hand like that,
and I'm afraid a great many things are all to bits. Now go and
do as I tell you."

Thumbelina went, her mind deeply puzzled by the tattered
dress, the wounded hand, and the disordered room. Vaguely
she put it all down to her mother's visit. Where her mother
went, wounds and broken furniture and clothing snatched
at and torn sooner or later followed. She took the violin downstairs.

"Open the case," Elsie said. "I can't manage it."

Thumbelina took the violin out of the case, and Elsie held
it in her left hand. She looked at its rich and lovely colour, its
skin shining like the skin of a well-groomed horse, its shape,
slim-waisted like herself. She got to her feet, and for just one
moment rested the fiddle beneath her chin, bending down her
head with the old familiar caress. Her curls all fell over side-

ways. She rubbed her chin and her cheek once or twice upon the silky wood. Thumbelina heard one sob wrench itself out of her throat and her heart as she made this farewell. Then she saw the violin swung' through the air and brought crashing down upon the marble corner of the mantelpiece. Elsie threw the remains of it inside the fender and sat down again, trembling.

After a while she said: "Thumbs, I feel very weak, but I can't stay in this room any longer. My brother's gone to fetch a doctor. Let's wait in the garden till he comes."

"It's getting cold, Miss Dillworth, and you're not properly dressed."

"Go and bring my cloak, child, and you'll have to lend me a shoulder."

They sat on the bench beneath the apple-tree, and Elsie wrapped the large cloak about the child as well as herself. She put her left arm round Thumbelina's waist, and the child sat swinging her legs that could not reach the ground. Presently Thumbelina asked timidly: "Who did it, Miss Dillworth? Was it our mother? Did she hurt you?"

"No, Thumbs. I hurt myself. No one else can do much to you, ever. You do it all to yourself."

Out in the air she felt a little better. But her hand was throbbing and shivers passed through her body. She pulled the child closer to her, for warmth and for affection. It was a still, windless night, without a moon. The sky was full of stars, and against their flashing mosaic a bat floundered through the air as senselessly as humanity, homeless amid a million homes. There was nothing else to see except the bat and the stars as they sat there pressing close to one another, waiting.

Epilogue

March 17, 1887.

Dear Miss Dillworth:

Your letter has reached me through Mr. Burnside. My dear child, I am deeply touched that you should wish to thank me for an intention which, alas! I was never able to fulfil. It would have been a great joy to me to help you, if only because I knew how deeply Theo was interested in you. Forgive me for mentioning a matter which must still, I am sure, cause you much pain. I have never pressed Theo for an explanation of his leaving you, and I have never understood all the ins and outs of the accident that had such terrible consequences for you. Mr. Burnside, I imagine, knows more than he cares to tell me. All he *does* tell me is that you have no wish to "burden" me with the matter (my dear! it would be no burden) and that, so far as Theo is concerned, this complete nervous breakdown which he has suffered should make it clear to me that the less said about the experiences of his last days in Manchester the better.

Well, I must leave it all like that and go on in the dark. But, as Theo's wife, of course I don't find it so dark as all that. He has asked me to send you his greetings and to give you some account of what has happened between last September and now. Well, you know that as soon as he was fit to be moved I had him taken to the South of France. It was a long time before he began to make the first steps back to health. He was sunk in the deepest apathy and unhappiness, sleepless for the most part, and, when he did sleep, troubled by the most terrible dreams. But slowly he came back to health, and somehow he seems now a graver and—though I should never have thought it possible!—a more lovable man. Perhaps it is just that he has *become* a man, whereas he was a boy. We were married here at Nice a month ago.

For the time being, Theo will not go back to the work of the

282

Church, though it is my hope that in due course he will do so. I am greatly interested in a school which will be opened a few months hence in what was once my home. Theo has accepted a mastership there, and I think this will be a sphere in which his talents will have full play. We leave here almost at once, and between now and the opening of the school we shall be travelling.

One thing about your note delighted me, and that was to learn that you had written it with your *right* hand. And your description of the way in which with your left hand you must carefully place the pen between the third and fourth fingers of the right shows that you keep a blessed sense of humour. It is beyond words tragic that the doctors have now abandoned hope of bringing about a further improvement. But I am sure you are one of those rare people who thank God for what they have rather than blame Him for what has been taken away.

My dear—will you give me your friendship? I have taken so much from you. Let me take that also.

Ever yours sincerely,
Adela Chrystal.